The
DAGGER

THE MADIGAN CHRONICLES
BOOK ONE

Marieke Lexmond

ACKNOWLEDGEMENTS

Writing a book is not something that I thought I would ever do, but it has given me so much joy and it would not have been possible without the help of others. I've been lucky to have had the support of some incredible friends. First of all, this book would not have been here without the dedication of Nicole Ruijgrok. Her wicked mind and fun ideas propelled this story forward. On top of that, she's a great artist and brought the tarot cards to life. Yvonne Borgogni, Annelies Meerbach-Kik and Charlotte Crocker, all contributed and gave their unwavering support and time. I feel very blessed with their belief in my abilities. Further, I want to thank my first test readers for their encouragement and honest assessments, Annette Beil, Karen Karlovich, Yvonne van den Oever, Kim Young and Theo Lexmond. A big thank you to my mom, Ria Lexmond-Wooning, who enabled me to self-publish this book; the BookBaby team for holding my hand during the publishing of my first book. And of course, the support from my brothers and sisters- in-law for always cheering me on. Last but not least, to my husband, Jeroen Hendriks. Thank you for your unwavering belief in me and for always supporting any crazy idea that I come up with. Your help, love, and support means the world to me.

Happy reading!!

Marieke

TABLE OF CONTENTS

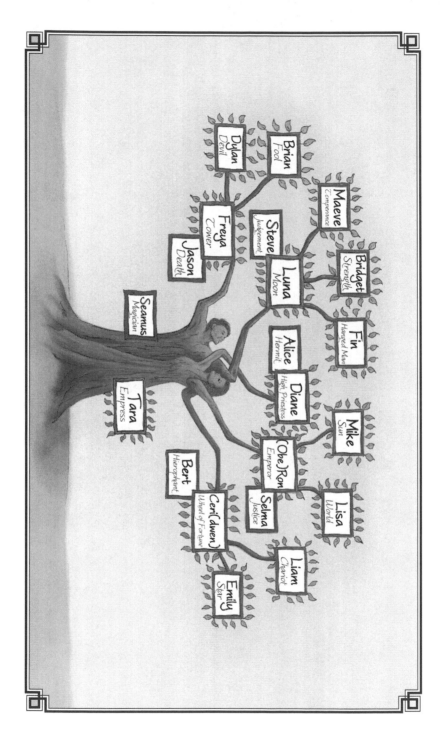

FAMILY TREE

PROLOGUE

NEW ORLEANS, GARDEN DISTRICT, 1965

The full Sturgeon moon rises above the horizon. The air feels heavy and pregnant with possibilities. A bubble is ready to burst. This is one of those nights when people don't linger at the Madigan mansion in the Garden District of New Orleans. This house has a history: the family that lives here is different. On a sunny day they look like your average neighbor, but on nights like this, parents warn their children, "Don't linger. Strange things happen there."

The Madigans arrived in the area around the 1800s and were one of the first families to build a mansion in the neighborhood. Even though they never seemed short of money, they didn't mingle with the elite and were more comfortable in the rowdy French Quarter. Quickly, superstition and their reputation for trouble grew. Whispers about them being "different" spread like wildfire, fueled by animosity against them. People started to keep their distance. They were both attracted and afraid of the Madigans' mystical and herbal healing skills.

The backdoor opens and Sarah Madigan nervously looks around before she steps out. Her black summer dress billows around her, although there is not a breath of wind. Her unruly red curls are laced with gray streaks, and her worry lines betray her age. She clutches a heavy, old manuscript to her chest. She glances at the full moon and lets the moonbeam wash over her while she whispers, "Help me, goddess of the moon. Help me make the right choice." This seems to calm her.

1

Sarah makes her way past the meticulously kept vegetable and herb gardens, over the grassy field, and towards a pretty kind of wilderness in the back. The trees and shrubs are thick like a wall. When she approaches, the trees bend and twist to create an opening for her to slip through.

Sarah steps into a clearing and looks at an overpowering stone tomb. It's elaborately decorated; a statue of a phoenix stares down at her, and a salamander chasing its own tail encircles the tomb. An image of a fierce woman is etched into the door; swirling around her are the four elements—earth, air, fire, and water—the zodiac signs, and various animals. A nervous sigh escapes her before she puts her hand on the fire symbol—a triangle pointing upwards. The door silently slides open and, without hesitation, she disappears through the opening. Immediately the door slams shut behind her. The inside doesn't match the outside; magic must be at work here. The space is a huge dome. With a snap of her fingers, the torches along the walls flare to life. Eerily life-like ceramic hands come out of the wall holding up each torch. In the middle stands an altar made of birch wood with four huge candles on each corner. After many years of rituals, the wax from the candles that dripped down to the floor has formed its own misshaped, sinister castles. The walls are covered with ivy, and although there's no sunlight, the plants seem to flourish. Ancestral tombs encircle the altar. Each tomb is unique with stone-etched lids full of flowers, animals, zodiac signs, and food. Very carefully Sarah lays the book down on the altar. Her family's Book of Shadows; it's an heirloom full of spells and occult knowledge of generations of Madigans. Reverently she opens it and aimlessly turns the pages, which are filled with old-fashioned handwriting, stories, spells, and drawings. Some pages are orderly, while others are chaotic and creative, reflecting the personality of the witch who filled them. The book is incomplete. Sarah's name is followed by her contribution, but it stops abruptly; much of her story is still unwritten. For several minutes she stares at them, wondering what she will write about tonight. Hopefully her daughters understand her wishes and all will be well. She closes the book. It's very quiet, even the dead ancestors hold their breath. Their spirits linger in the tomb and it's hard to concentrate when they give their opinion on one thing or the other.

Sarah wanders along the tombs, her left hand brushes over them until she reaches the most recent one. "You made it sound so easy. It's not. And now I have to burden one of my children with it. I was never the right person." Sarah reaches in her pocket and takes out a Wand, a long piece of elegant wood, which at the end becomes thicker like a natural handle. It feels familiar in her hand. Such a plain thing that holds so much.

The sound of the door sliding open pulls her out of her train of thought. Easy chatter reaches her before she sees her daughters, Lucy and Tara, identical twins in their mid-twenties. Tara radiates spunk in her colorful, easy-flowing clothes, while Lucy seems more uptight in her pencil skirt. Their clothes express the difference in their personalities. Lucy is ambitious, a go-getter—not many things can keep her from her goals. She's a talented witch and she easily overpowers her easygoing sister. Although Tara is just as powerful as a witch, her caring and nurturing nature indulges her twin and lets her take the lead most of the time. Sarah wonders how they can be exactly the same and still be so different. She smiles at them and gently places the Wand next to the book.

Lucy follows the gesture. "So what are we doing here tonight?"

Seamlessly, Tara adds, "The energy of the full moon is delicious; we can't let it go to waste."

"A love spell for Mrs. Flowers perhaps?" jokes Lucy.

Tara bursts out laughing, "Then we need all the help we can get for sure!"

"Or are we finally getting rid of those pesky toads in the yard?"

Sarah's face turns serious. "It's a family matter."

This gets the girls' attention. Lucy glances at the Wand. "Is it about the Wand?"

Sarah is shocked. "How do you know?"

Tara gives her a reassuring smile. "We've known about the Wand since . . . when?" She glances at Lucy, who finishes, "I think we were about fourteen. You're always different when you use this particular Wand."

"I never use it!" defends Sarah. Tara shrugs in a carefree manner.

Sarah takes a deep breath. "It's time for you to know about our family legacy." She picks up the Wand and touches the Book of Shadows while she mumbles, "Show us the secrets past, power of fire, element of action, passion, and strength—guide us." She taps the book again and it flips open. The book riffles through its pages and falls open at the beginning. A three-dimensional image folds out of the book and hovers above the page. The girls are fascinated.

Thirteen witches form a circle in the woods under another full moon. The circle contains on the east side a small tornado; on the south side a fire; on the west side a small waterfall; and on the north side a small tree in full bloom. The witches hold hands while they chant in union. Sarah explains, "In the 1780s, the Industrial Revolution started to change the world. People lost touch with the natural world and a coven of witches formed a bond with the elemental powers."

Slowly the tree, the waterfall, the fire, and the tornado start to shrink. It looks like the tree has been sucked into a Wooden Disk, the waterfall into a Cup, the fire into a Wand, and the tornado into a Dagger.

Sarah continues, "The elements gave the witches an object that contains part of them, so they could call upon them when needed and, in return, the witches promised to keep them safe."

The image starts to change. It's day and the witches are in a heated argument. Sparks fly and some of them glance around to see if they're being noticed.

"The objects were so powerful, the temptation was too much for most witches and they started to fight over ownership of the elements. Dark powers began to consume them. To prevent total disaster—"

The image changes again. This time it's a dark stormy night, the wind is fierce and four witches huddle together. Each of them holds one of the objects of power. They raise their objects and solemnly repeat an oath. To seal the deal they clink the objects together. Lightning crashes down and, even in the tomb, the thunder resonates like a loud rumble.

"Four of the strongest witches decided to hide the objects from the others. They vowed to never use them again. If all the elemental objects came together and someone would use them, then it could destroy the world."

The four witches embrace for one last time and disappear into the dark night.

"One of these witches was Mary Madigan, our ancestor, a powerful witch who started this book of shadows. Our grimoire."

The image starts to dissolve and Sarah looks at her daughters. She catches Lucy staring at the Wand. A flicker of desire crosses Lucy's face. Sarah feels a pang of disappointment.

She picks up the Wand and holds it reverently. "It's been passed on to the eldest daughter ever since. We are the guardians of the Wand of Wisdom." Both girls take a closer look. It appears rather insignificant, but the waves of power that flow from it are exceptional.

"Wow, how does that work?" Tara is curious.

"When I'm ready to pass it on, we will do a ritual to attune the Wand to you."

"Can it be attuned to two people?" Tara asks and looks at Lucy, barely hiding their excitement.

"No. So I have a dilemma. This Wand is a huge responsibility and I've always found it hard not to be able to talk to anybody about this. I hoped it will help to have your twin as support." Sarah looks from Tara to Lucy.

"I'm the oldest." Eagerly Lucy reaches for the Wand.

Sarah appears resigned. "I've decided that the burden should go to Tara."

"What?! That's not fair!"

As always, Tara tries to calm the situation. "You can have the Wand, Lucy. I don't want it."

Sarah shakes her head, "I asked guidance from the element—it's you, Tara."

"I want it!" Lucy steps forward and Sarah immediately steps back, keeping the Wand out of reach.

"You can help me. It would be for both of us." Tara insists.

Lucy turns to Tara. "You want it for yourself—all that power."

"No! I would share it . . . with you."

"You can't share it. I'm the oldest. It's mine." Lucy gathers her magic. A wind blows through the tomb. Their hair and clothes start flapping in the wind.

Sarah is alarmed, "Lucy! Control yourself!" She inches backward to create some distance between her and Lucy and Tara. Ominously, the lids rattle on the coffins.

"You're scared that I will be more powerful than you." Lucy turns toward her mother.

"Oh Lucy . . ." Sarah's heart sinks.

Lucy lashes out; she throws her open hand forward, a fireball erupts from her hand, and she hurtles it towards Sarah. The fireball hits her surprised mother in her chest.

Tara screams. "Lucy! No!"

Sarah topples backward, and while she tries to regain her balance, the Wand slips from her fingers and flips through the air. She lands hard on her back. Tara is frozen in place. Lucy doesn't falter. She grabs the Wand and without hesitation points it at Tara.

"What are you doing?" Tara is confused; she doesn't recognize her twin.

"Don't come closer." Lucy reinforces her threat with a little wave of the Wand.

Sarah tries to scramble back up. "Resist the temptation!"

Concerned, Tara steps forward. Lucy starts to breathe harder, which makes the lids fly off the tombs. They're dangling in the air. Startled, Tara looks at them. Sarah manages to get back up. The remains of the ancestors are moving! Curious, they look around.

"I can feel the power!" Lucy is ecstatic.

Sarah slowly makes her way towards her against the wind. "Please, Lucy—"

Lucy raises her hands; fire drips from the tip of the Wand. Power consumes her. She points the Wand at Sarah. Sarah puts her hand up and shouts, *"IGNIS VENI AD ME."* Fire, come back to me. The Wand is ripped from Lucy's hand and flies back into Sarah's hands. "I'm still the most powerful witch in this family," resonates Sarah's commanding voice through the tomb.

For a moment, Lucy is shocked, and then anger takes over and she starts to weave another spell. Sarah stands her ground. "Lucy, stop!"

Lucy slings another spell; Sarah mumbles a quick counter spell and waves her Wand. Lucy's spell hits her shield and slides off. "Don't! Or you'll leave me no choice."

Lucy chants another spell. Sarah shouts; her desperation is mounting. "Find the light! I beg you—"

Lucy slings her spell; it falls apart into a thousand sparkles against Sarah's shield.

Tara tries to reach her sister, but an invisible wall stops her. She bangs on it! She's sure she would get through to her twin if she could only touch her. "Lucy! Lucy!"

Lucy's face is full of hate.

"It's me, Tara."

Sarah's voice is full of anguish; "You leave me no choice." She waves her Wand, takes a deep breath, and says with a booming voice, "With the power of three, I ban thee from this family."

Tara is shocked. "Mom, no!"

"One, your name will never be uttered by us. Two, you will never be able to set foot on family property again."

Slowly awareness comes back into Lucy's face. She lowers her arms. "Mom?!"

"Three, you will not be able to use our name or heritage."

Suddenly, Lucy looks agitated. "Mom! I didn't mean it!"

The wind picks up, and Tara struggles against it to reach her sister. Lucy desperately stretches for Tara, but the wind is too strong. Tears stream down Sarah's face while she watches her girls. She never imagined this would happen.

Lucy looks terrified, and Tara doubles her efforts to reach for her twin. Their fingers touch, and with an extra push Lucy manages to lock fingers with Tara. The wind picks up Lucy, and the girls scream. The pull is too strong. Horrified, Tara feels Lucy's fingers slip through hers. "TARA!" Lucy gets slung out of the tomb and of the property. Abruptly the wind dies. The ancestors fold back into their tombs, and the lids tumble down back into place. Tara stands frozen; slowly she looks full of horror at Sarah. Silent tears still stream down her face. The book on the altar starts to riffle through the pages. It stops on the page with Lucy's name on it. A loud sizzle, and Lucy's name gets scorched out of the family chronicles.

Ace of Swords

PART 1

ACE OF SWORDS "THE SEED"

"You and only you are responsible for your life choices and decisions."

—ROBERT KIYOSAKI

NEW ORLEANS, PRESENT DAY

The sun peeks over the horizon and its golden rays fall on a ghostly white figure. Tara Madigan walks towards the family mansion. Now in her mid-seventies, her white nightgown flows freely around her as she moves through a big grassy yard. Her long gray hair cascades down her back. She seems to absorb the sun and radiate it from within. Her feet barely touch the ground. Tara's herbal healing skills are renowned in the area; people love her compassion and endless energy, as she is always willing to help her neighbors. But word goes, if she turns those crystal blue eyes on you, she looks straight into your soul and sees your deepest darkest secrets. So, people still keep their distance from the Madigans. In all those centuries, not much has changed.

It's quiet in the early morning except for the joyful chirping of the many birds in the yard. Tara stops for a moment to talk to them. They fly around her. One brave one flutters towards her and lands on her finger. It makes her smile—just for a second. Her night meditation in the tomb didn't bring her any answers, and the cheerful world is a stark contrast to her inner turmoil. Doubt and bad omens make her wary. Questions rattle around in her brain. She's running out of time to pass on the Wand, but to whom? None of her daughters seem ready. Is anybody ever ready for such a burden? She wasn't. Age aches in her bones and she knows that her days on this earth are numbered. Time to consult her tarot cards. They have been her trusted companions; maybe they can give her guidance. She reaches the backdoor and disappears.

The inside of the house is very welcoming. Candles are lit throughout the house. A giant wooden pentacle demands attention in the cheerful hallway, and there are many family pictures on the wall—happy memories. A horseshoe hangs above the door for luck. A broom is parked next to the door, and colorful spring flowers are in a vase. Everywhere you look, witchy trinkets from all over the world, collected by family members over the centuries. Noises from the kitchen let Tara know her granddaughter is awake. She's tempted to go in, but instead, she quietly moves upstairs into her bedroom.

A fireplace with a stucco hearth dominates her traditional, spacious, high-ceilinged bedroom. The playful images of angels, the sun, the moon, stars, flowers, and birds are impossible to ignore. The walls are lined with bookcases filled with books about herbal healing, witchcraft, symbolism, New Orleans, native tribes and old traditions. An altar full of witch necessities faces north. Above the altar hangs a painting of Seamus, Tara's deceased husband, a mischievous old man. His witch cape swirls around him. He stands next to an ancient stone surrounded by beautiful trees. When Tara enters, his image starts to move and he seems to grow in the frame. He smiles at her. Tara cheers up. "Hi, darling." Seamus blows her a kiss. The magical painting has been a great comfort after Seamus' passing. It's like a window into the afterlife. They're able to see each other, but not speak.

She sits down at a little desk and opens a drawer. It's full of small drawstring bags in various colors and fabrics. She lets her hand hover above them; she hesitates before grabbing one. Tara opens it, and slides out a tarot deck. She smiles at Seamus. "Let's see what this week will bring." After a practiced shuffle, she fans out the cards in front of her. Her left hand moves up and down above it before she picks the one that calls out to her. She slips it out and turns it over.

"The Ace of Swords." Tara utters.

A sword hovers upright in a blue sky with some wispy clouds, while two storks are flying by. Seamus frowns.

"A beginning, I need to make a decision. I know . . . I left it too long. But whom should I choose? You know the girls. None of them seem right. I don't want to make the mistake mother made with . . . her." Seamus' frown turns to worry. "I'll figure it out. This card is a good sign—a time to decide. The sword is double-edged, so whoever I chose, there will be some unpleasant consequences." She ponders the card for a minute before placing it on her altar.

A knock on the door startles her out of her train of thought. She walks over and opens the door. Maeve, her granddaughter, a siren beauty in her mid-twenties, can't hide her impatience as she notices her grandmother is still in her gown. It makes Tara smile. Maeve is always trying to please everybody. Getting her grandmother to work on time is not an easy task, and she battles with it daily. Tara is happy to have her around; she's the only family living with her. "I'll be ready in a couple of minutes."

Maeve frowns, "Gram, you know how Ron is when customers have to wait. You better hurry."

BOSTON

An alarm goes off. The bed is full of dogs of various breeds and sizes. It's hard to imagine that people fit in there. A hand manages to free itself from under the blankets and reaches for a cell phone. "Come on guys move," Bridget Madigan sits up. She is an unpolished version of her twin, Maeve—not identical twins, but unmistakably sisters. A little Chihuahua jumps up and starts to lick her face. "Thanks Kiki, that's not necessary."

A moan comes from under the covers, and another human form surfaces, Bridget's boyfriend, Wes. She smiles in anticipation, still amazed that he's hers. How did she get so lucky? First, his black curls pop up above the blanket, followed by two big hazel eyes. He's an aristocrat in a bad boy package, only a few years older than she is. They met at an opening of an exhibition by a local painter. His humor and insights attracted her, and they immediately hit it off. When you know, you know. So, it's only a couple of months later and he's moving in.

"Coffee?" He always seems to know what she wants.

"That would be perfect." She gives him a thorough kiss. The dogs are awake now and mill around, ready for their breakfast. Bridget extracts herself from the cozy bed and tries to find her clothes. The bedroom is messy; clothes are scattered around, and half-opened boxes are everywhere. She digs for a pair of jeans and a T-shirt before disappearing into the bathroom.

Bridget wanders into the kitchen followed by a train of dogs. She clips on her gun, her police badge, and transforms into a bad ass. The dogs impatiently try to herd her towards the kitchen counter. But she has only eyes for Wes, who's preparing her coffee, in just his sweats. He looks downright delicious.

"Here." He gives her a mug. "Stop ogling me. You don't have time for that."

She laughs and starts picking up the dog bowls. "You'll be okay unpacking by yourself? I feel guilty for leaving you with all this."

"No you don't! Hell, I wouldn't feel bad."

Bridget laughs, she never thought she would enjoy sharing her house with someone, but Wes changed her mind. "If you need to make room, don't hesitate to chuck my stuff aside."

"I'll be fine. Are you sure I can take over the spare bedroom? It will be messy. I'm far from organized when I paint."

"I love the smell of paint. My grandfather was an artist." The memory makes her smile.

"Really?!" Wes is surprised; Bridget doesn't usually mention her family. "Don't you think it's time for me to meet your family? Now we're living together and all."

Bridget's face closes down in a millisecond. "I told you I'm not in touch with my family. They're—different." She quickly fills the dog bowls. Some are drooling in anticipation. "Sit." The dogs obey, and she puts down the bowls in front of them. "Go ahead." They attack their food.

Wes doesn't give up, "What are you afraid of? That they won't like me? Which, of course, is highly unlikely. Or that I won't like them?"

"I don't want to see my mother. She's very controlling."

"Everybody's mother is controlling!" Wes rolls his eyes.

"Not like her!" Bridget stares off into the distance, thinking back in time.

Several years earlier in a homey witch kitchen Bridget argues with her mother, Luna Madigan. It's clear where the girls got their good looks from. Luna emanates power and confidence; she is someone used to getting her way. Bridget can still smell the herbs that were drying in the kitchen that night. It draws her even further into the memory. Her mother becomes rapidly irritated while she argues with Bridget. Maeve tries to mediate without much success. The girls are sixteen and not easily satisfied.

"Why can't I go?" demands Bridget.

"I'm your mother and I say so. Besides, you have to do the dishes."

Carelessly, Bridget waves her hand and mumbles a quick spell. The dishes wash themselves. "There. Done."

"You're not going. End of story." Luna's stern look would silence anybody.

Bridget ignores it, "We're like prisoners, never allowed to do anything with anybody."

"We are different." Luna almost spells out.

"So what? I'm not doing anything to stand out. I know the rules. I'm not a child anymore. You should trust me."

"Trust you? You're acting like a little kid having a tantrum. Maybe you should go to bed instead."

Bridget decides to change tactics. "Please mom. This once."

But Luna doesn't budge. "No."

Maeve tries to distract her sister. "Come B, we can catch a movie or something."

"I'm going to that concert with Josh. You can't stop me!" Bridget turns and strides toward the door. Luna starts to get angry. "You're not going."

"Watch me." Bridget grabs the door handle when Luna's commanding voice resonates in the kitchen, "STOP!"

Bridget freezes in place with the door half open. She's unable to move, and panic overtakes her. Desperately, she tries to move. Nothing is hers anymore, not even her face muscles. Her eyes shoot daggers at her mother. Maeve realizes something is very wrong. As a witch you should never use your powers on another witch. Never. "Mom? What are you doing?"

It doesn't stop Luna. "GO TO YOUR ROOM AND GO TO SLEEP!"

Bridget tries to resist with all her might. But her body betrays her, moving out of the kitchen and up to her room, while tears of frustration stream down her face, unable to stop herself. She never dreamed that her mother would do such a thing to her—betray her like this. Luna is powerful, but Bridget never realized that her mother has such a dark gift. Bridget goes through all the spells in her mind, but it's no use; she goes into her room, not bothering to undress, gets into bed, and promptly falls asleep.

In the present, Wes frantically waves his hand in front of Bridget's face. "Hello. HELLO! Earth to Bridget." The dogs bark, fueled by Wes' concern. At last, Bridget snaps out of her trance.

"Are you okay?" Wes, concerned, pulls her into an embrace.

Bridget shudders from the strong memory of a night she had tried so hard to forget. She had left that life behind, nothing to concern Wes with. "Yes. Yes, I'm fine." She gently frees herself.

By the look on Bridget's face, there is a whole lot more to this story. However, he knows her long enough to know that this is not the time to push for answers. Wes wisely says, "I get it—don't mention the family."

"I would appreciate that." They finish their coffee in silence. Bridget says goodbye to each dog and finally turns to Wes. "You're sure?" Wes nods. "Well, good luck then with this mess." Thoughtfully, Wes stares after her when the door closes behind her.

Bridget jogs up the steps into the police station. Her friend, Carla, is manning the front desk. "Any messages?"

"None." Carla glances at the clock. "You're late."

"Wes—what can I say." Bridget and Carla laugh simultaneously. Bridget gets in the elevator to the 3rd floor. When she steps out, she immediately spots Tom Walsh, her partner, for several years. In his fifties, he's a "been there, done that" cop, reliable like an older brother. He's not known for his patience and bellows, "Madigan, you're late!"

"Yes. Yes. Wes is moving in and—"

"I don't want to hear your stories. Suit up," Tom interrupts her. "We got a lead on Sanchez, and we are meeting SWAT in half an hour for the briefing."

NEW ORLEANS

Tara and Maeve weave their way through the crowds on the street in the French Quarter. The heavy heat doesn't hinder the millions of people every year from visiting this mysterious city. The famous Bourbon Street with its bars overflowing with music and curious characters. Who doesn't want to visit a voodoo priest or bump into a vampire at night? Everything is possible in New Orleans.

The Madigans have been calling it home for hundreds of years. It's the ultimate city to blend into. They can hide in plain sight while making money with their gifts without raising any questions or being judged.

They finally reach Under the Witches Hat, a not-so-average bar. A big black pointy hat hangs above the door and two wooden dragons twist and turn to form an otherworldly doorway. Easy New Age music drifts outside. The eclectic witchy storefront is dominated by signs: 'EVERYTHING FROM TEAS,

ELIXIRS, POTIONS AND COCKTAILS', 'TAROT READINGS, ASTROLOGY, DIVINATIONS'. They disappear inside.

A soft slightly tinted light illuminates the bar. It emanates from round orbs that float around. Slowly they change color, blue to orange to yellow to white, very peaceful. The walls are decorated with witchy images—witches flying on brooms, witches around a cauldron, you name it—it's stereotyping galore. There is already a nice morning crowd. Almost every table is filled. On the corner of the bar stands an enormous crystal ball, a sign invites you to gaze into it. Tara and Maeve move past the bar. The bartender, Ron Madigan, in his early forties, is Tara's only son. She's always struck by his resemblance to his father. Although he's as charismatic as his dad, he is far more serious and there's no joking about him running the shop. He's dressed in black with a large pentacle dangling around his neck. With an easy charm, he chats up two older ladies at the bar. They stare at him in admiration while he fixes some cocktails. He finishes one bright pink cocktail and sticks in a little umbrella, making it spin with a spell while he touches it lightly with his finger. The lady is delighted and takes a sip. Ron glances at Tara and Maeve and points at the clock. Tara ignores it, but Maeve blows him a magical kiss; blood-red lips flutter through the air and land with a loud smack on Ron's cheek. The ladies can't believe what just happened and burst out laughing. Ron rubs off the lipstick and wants to say something, but Tara and Maeve have already disappeared into the back room.

The back room is surprisingly big. As many New Orleans houses in the French Quarter, the front doesn't always match the rest of the house. On the right wall, there are smallish private areas, separated by bright curtains creating privacy. People don't have to worry that their neighbor will hear their fortunes being told. They're infused with privacy spells.

On the left-hand side, the wall is covered with shelves full of witch paraphernalia. All you need if you're making potions, spells, and whatever else your heart desires. Diana Madigan floats around the room. Tara's third daughter has never fitted in. Her otherworldly features make her stand out and scream "witch," even if you don't believe in such things. Her faraway look is turned inside, very Zen, or some might call it creepy.

Luna is bent over a cauldron and is focused on her spell. The years have been kind to her. Her confidence is touching on arrogance these days. Her ego takes up a lot of space. Or as the witches like to say—her aura is spreading wide. Luna adds three last drops from a tiny bottle and twirls her finger to stir the potion.

Diana notices Tara and Maeve and plops back on the floor. "You're here." She gives them both a kiss on the cheek before turning to Luna. "How long?"

"Leave it for an hour, then give it a good stir, add the last of the hazel flakes, and it should be done after another hour." Luna gives it a final sniff.

"You're the best. I owe you one."

Only now does Luna acknowledge Maeve and she gives her a quick motherly kiss. Her mother, on the other hand, gets a formal, "Mom."

Tara, in stark contrast, radiates warmth. "It's good to see you dear."

Luna, in no mood to chitchat, hurries out the backdoor, "I'd better move before **Ron** spots me and puts me to work."

Tara turns her attention to Diana. "Any news?"

"You know, nobody ever tells me anything." Diana smells Luna's potion to avoid looking at her mother.

"That's not what I mean." Tara gently pushes.

Diana knows exactly what Tara meant. Her special gift is foresight. It's near impossible to get a clear prediction; with every choice someone makes, the future is changing. When she was a child, she tried influencing the future with devastating consequences. These days, she mostly tries to ignore them. Generally, they don't ask her and she sure as hell doesn't share anything she sees. "I don't want to talk about it."

"It might be important. Even we can feel a storm brewing. You must see something." Tara insists.

"What do you want to hear? That I can see the end of the world? That I see my family getting hurt? It's always changing. It's too much. It's not helpful to anybody, so stop bugging me. Do your own divination if you really want to know." Diana storms out of the backdoor. Maeve wants to follow her, but Tara grabs her arm. "Give her some space. She has a difficult gift. It's hard to imagine what it is like to constantly have your world flooded with images of the ever-changing future and trying to make sense of it."

"Why did you pressure her then?" Maeve is puzzled.

"Because she is a great seer, and you must feel it too: there's something coming."

Ron walks in with two clients, which abruptly ends the conversation.

Tara disappears with a young woman behind one curtain, and Maeve takes the other one behind the next.

A couple of hours later, Maeve is chatting with Diana when Tara opens her curtain and an older man pushes past them to hurry out the backdoor. Diana looks at her mother. "You scared that poor man."

"I would never do that," says Tara with a twinkle in her eye. They all laugh. "He'll be back, don't worry."

"Gram, we're heading out for lunch. Are you coming?"

Tara has other plans. Using her old age as an excuse, she says, "Just bring me something small. I'll take a nap."

"Are you okay?" asks Maeve, concerned.

"Stop worrying. Go!" Tara ushers them out.

Once they're gone, Tara goes back into her little cocoon behind the curtain. It's cozy with a round table and two chairs. Along the wall is a small altar; two candles are lit, and a little bunch of daffodils represents the first sign of spring. On the wall are pictures of fortunetellers, some good luck charms and a witch's broom. Tara sits down and lets out a big sigh. For a minute she savors the solitude. Closing her eyes, she gently breathes in and out. More centered, she pulls a small bag out of her purse and opens it. A different-looking tarot deck slides out; it seems handcrafted and has only 22 cards. When she leafs through the individual cards, they're filled with familiar faces; Luna, Bridget, Maeve, Seamus, Diana, Ron, and Tara herself. On the rest of the cards are the remaining members of her family, even her grandchildren. The images are so real. Tara stops at several images and smiles fondly at them. Finally, she pulls Seamus' card. "Okay

Seamus, time to put your deck to good use." She gives the card a quick kiss. Seamus' image on the card comes to life—growing slightly three-dimensional. Seamus' face bulges outward while kissing Tara back. She giggles and Seamus grins mischievously. Tara puts her hand quickly over the card, changing it back to normal, and puts him back in the deck.

Another deep breath focuses her attention back on the problem at hand. She fans the cards face down in front of her. She gets up and grabs four candles from the shelf, putting them in the four wind directions. With a snap of her fingers, the candles flare to life. She lights an incense stick on her altar and picks up a small dagger, also known as a witch's athame. Satisfied, she positions herself in front of the cards. "Elemental power of Fire, as your guardian, I ask for your help to show me 'the' one who will be fit to carry on our family's responsibilities. To honor you and guide the family in these changing times." She unsheathes the athame. "Open my eyes. Open my heart. Guide my hand." Carefully, she makes a tiny prick in her forefinger. A drop of blood wells up. She slowly moves her hand above the cards from left to right while turning her finger. The drop grows and stretches, almost letting go. Her hand keeps steadily moving back and forth when at last, the small drop of blood falls down—landing on one of the cards. Tara pulls the card out and turns it over. "Hmmm, this is going to be interesting." Not one of her daughters, who would have thought? Fire chose her stubborn granddaughter.

It's STRENGTH; Bridget stands proud in a green hunting tunic. She looks like a hunter from many centuries ago. A bow and arrow are strapped to her back. Her hand rests on the head of a lion, which sits calmly next to her.

The card wants to come alive. Tara taps the card. "Not now. Stay in." Gently she strokes Bridget's figure on the card. "Come home, we need you."

BOSTON

This makes Bridget shiver and sway for a moment. Tom eyes her. "Are you okay?"

Bridget snaps out of it. She reaffirms her grip on her gun to ground herself while leaning against the wall in the hallway. Bridget, Tom, and SWAT are ready to raid an apartment.

Who the hell just gave her a mental call? This is a bad time to get caught up in something magical. She's the last in line behind Tom, and whispers, "Let's do it."

Tom signals the SWAT commander. No time is wasted, one of the team slams down the door. Bridget is having a hard time focusing and gives herself a mental slap. Inside her head she imagines a brick wall. Hopefully, keeping out whoever tried to reach her. She wonders if it's a coincidence or that she called it upon herself because she talked about her family this morning.

Shouts from the apartment draw her back to reality. Tom and the SWAT team have already disappeared inside. Bridget has to hurry to catch up and look engaged. Shots are fired! One of the SWAT guys pushes her against the wall. She walked in without paying attention. His angry stare tells her how stupid she was; easy to get killed that way. More shouts and shots in the apartment. Bridget is eager to get in, but the SWAT guy doesn't take any more chances with her and holds her in place. Angrily waving her arms, she tries to persuade him to let her go and get inside. He doesn't budge. She lets out a sigh of relief when finally the sound of voices shouting, "Clear!" "Clear!" reaches her.

A heavy bark is quickly followed by Tom's scared, "Help!"

This time, she pushes past her SWAT teammate, who tries to go in first. "We're coming!" With more caution and focus, she swiftly moves toward Tom's voice. Her SWAT teammate is glued to her side. In the living room is one man down and another is being cuffed by SWAT. When they enter the bedroom, Tom and his teammate face a big Rottweiler. His back hair standing straight up, saliva drips down on the floor and his snarl shows his impressive teeth. His anxiety level peaks when more people enter the room.

"Do something!" urges Tom. Without hesitation, Bridget's teammate points his gun. She quickly puts her hand on the barrel and pushes it down. "Hey! What are you doing? Stand still. Let me deal with him." She has only eyes for the dog.

"Get out of the way!" shouts SWAT, but Bridget ignores him, making sure to block his shot.

"Take your time." Tom tries to sound sarcastic, but the timber in his voice betrays him.

"Wimp," she jokes, before turning her full attention to the dog. Her voice changes tone, "Calm down buddy. Here." She put out her hand, and the dog snarls. "It's okay, I'm a friend."

Slowly, he calms down and sniffs her hand. "Good boy. It's okay, come here."

Gradually, he inches closer. She gently tries to pet him. When he relaxes, she runs her hands over his body. She can feel his ribs and he's full of cuts and bruises. The poor dog had it rough; this irritates her no end.

"I'll call animal services." One of the SWAT team grabs his cell phone, but before he gets a chance to dial, Bridget cuts him off. "I'll take him."

Tom bursts out laughing. "How many dogs do you have now?"

"He's been abused, he needs a good home." Bridget shoots him an angry look.

"Sure. Wes will be so thrilled."

"He loves dogs!" In the meantime, she waves her hands over the dog, and nobody notices that his cuts and bruises disappear.

"It's a miracle you found anybody to live with you." Tom is feeling instantly better now that the dog has chilled out. The dog barks. Tom smiles at him. "You're a lucky boy," he says, reaching out to him—the dog growls. "Jesus," he curses, quickly snatching his hand back.

"Give him a break. He's had a hard time." Bridget has no problem snuggling with the dog.

NEW ORLEANS

It's later in the evening when Tara and Maeve enjoy a well-deserved cocktail at a table in the bar of 'Under the Witches Hat'. The bar buzzes with excitement.

Even on a weekday there's quite the crowd. Luna works behind the bar. She looks fabulous in a sexy witch dress and whips up cocktails and elixirs at an uncanny speed. It all seems to flow; it's a miracle she can manage by herself. Only her own kin can recognize her talents. It's old magic at work. Her cocktails are the best. It lifts up the crowd, and the atmosphere in the bar is one of happiness and joy.

Tara looks at the crowd with satisfaction, while she drinks in the emotions. Magical globes float around people's heads and give off a mysterious light. Some heated conversations give off sparkles which make people slightly uncomfortable and create nervous laughter.

Tara twirls her finger and a little sparkle forms at her fingertip. She whispers to it and it slowly dances through the air towards Luna. Maeve follows the spell with interest. The sparkle reaches Luna and attaches herself to her ear like an earring. Luna's head whips in the direction of Tara. Tara gives her a small smile. Luna doesn't look pleased at all. Maeve puts her hand on her grandma's arm. "What's up, Gram?"

"Don't worry dear, I need to ask your mother something." Tara gives her a reassuring smile.

"Here?" Maeve's doubts show through.

"Sometimes, that's best."

"Oh Grandma, she's not going to like it, is she?"

Luna's hackles are already up while she motions Ron to take her place; he's at the end of the bar talking to two young women. Luna elegantly weaves her way toward the table. People seem to make just enough room for her to pass without effort. Tara watches her while she wonders why it's never easy with Luna; she's the most powerful of her daughters in spirit and magic. There's always been an undercurrent of tension in their relationship, even when she was very young. This will be uncomfortable, but that's how life is sometimes. The Ace of Swords told her this morning she needs to cut through the crap and deal with it. This is one of those things. Tara feels Maeve's anxiety build next to her. Luna reaches their table and doesn't waste any time while she slides in the chair opposite Tara. "You summoned me?"

Here we go, thinks Tara; however, she mildly says, "You of all people should know that this is just a little nudge."

"I don't have much time." She glances at Ron, struggling to keep up with the orders.

Tara waves her hand and mumbles a quick spell. All of a sudden, the sound around them is muffled. "Some privacy."

"Come on Ma, enough with the suspense." Luna's patience is running thin.

"Mom!" Maeve is worried, trying to mellow her out. She slides her cocktail over to her mother. "Want a taste?"

Luna shakes her head. Tara takes a deep breath. "I need a favor."

Maeve takes a sip from her cocktail as Tara continues, "I need you to patch things up with your daughter." Maeve spits out the cocktail all over the table. Luna is unmoved.

Maeve shouts in disbelief, "Bridget?!"

Tara and Luna both ignore Maeve.

"How can you ask me that? You know she never wants to see me again. Which part of NEVER don't you understand?" Luna's angry reply hides her true feelings about this.

Tara keeps her calm, she was expecting this. Bridget's leaving had cut a deep wound into Luna's heart. For years she had tried to patch things up, but to no avail. "I wouldn't ask you if it wasn't very important."

"What on earth is so important?" Luna sounds exasperated

"I can't tell you—" replies Tara stone-faced.

Luna icily interrupts her. "What? You want me to take your word for it?"

"Yes. I'm asking you as your mother and as your high priestess."

"I tried everything. I'm not going through that again, not even for you." Luna pushes back on her chair, signaling that this conversation is over.

Tara feels for Luna as she watches the pain cross her face. However, they need Bridget and she can't afford to feel sorry for her daughter. Tara glances at Maeve, who has recovered from her initial shock and is following the conversation with interest. Nobody mentions Bridget anymore these days, and Maeve's feelings towards her twin are complicated too. They're not all that friendly, but nevertheless, she would welcome seeing her again. Maeve is always trying to find a middle ground; it's one of her gifts to mediate and make everybody happy. Deciding to give her grandmother a helping hand, she tries, "It's been a long time. I'm sure B has mellowed by now. It's hard on everybody, and I'm sure Gram has a good reason to ask."

Luna looks at her daughter and she softens a bit.

Tara weighs in, "Will you at least think about it?"

Luna's full attention is back on her mother. "You have to give me something more if it's THAT important."

"I have bad dreams; Diana doesn't want to talk about her visions. You know that means it's bad. You have to trust me. I know the family needs to be whole." Worries shine through Tara's words.

Witches are attuned to emotions. Luna knows her mother is holding back and gets up. "Not good enough. We're not little children anymore, mother, and you might think about telling us what's really going on."

"It's the truth," Tara counters.

"HA! We're all witches and we can smell a lie—"

"It's not a lie!" Tara realizes she's losing the argument.

"Even a half-truth," Luna leans forward towards her mother—their faces almost touching. "We can see you're pregnant with secrets. Maybe it's time for you to trust someone." Luna pivots and leaves a startled Tara and Maeve behind.

BOSTON

At the same time on a hilltop, two witches are witching it out. Lucy Lockwood, Tara's identical twin, might look the same, but there's nothing the same about her. Lucy's hard features, her dark and stark clothes show nothing of Tara's warmth. She's an evil witch personified, challenging Alana Jansson, a modern witch half her age.

A fierce cold wind blows, snow and icy rain batter down on the women. A mere distraction, it doesn't seem to affect them in any way. Alana has to work hard to keep Lucy at bay. Lucy taunts her, "You're no match for me. Give it to me."

"Never!" Unconsciously, Alana touches the Dagger on her back. It's stuck in her belt, The Dagger of Consciousness, one of the four elemental objects of power. It governs the power of Air. She's only been its keeper for a short number of years. Her mother stressed the importance of never using it and making sure it would never fall into somebody else's hands. In all the years it has been in her family, nothing like this ever happened. She should have hidden it somewhere instead of taking it with her tonight. But there's no way back now. Who is this witch? How does she know so much about the object? Questions she tries to push to the back of her mind. This woman is powerful, and she needs to focus if she wants to overpower her. Again she quickly touches the Dagger. Maybe she can draw a little of the Dagger's power; after all, it's to defend it.

Lucy shouts above the winds, "This is your last chance!" and points a wand at Alana.

"Where do you get your line? Witches-R-Us?" Alana circles her index finger and chants a spell. All of a sudden, Lucy has trouble breathing. Alana smiles. Lucy tries to draw a breath, but instead, the air seems to be drawn out of her lungs. She clutches her throat.

Lucy slowly sags to the ground, but manages to gurgle a spell and a small fireball hits Alana full in the chest. She staggers backward, losing control over her spell. Lucy can breathe again, drawing in full jagged breaths. Color returns to her face and she scrambles back up. She immediately shields, and when Alana regains control, her spell slides off Lucy's shield. With a wicked smile and a flick of her finger, she hurls another fireball. Alana puts her hand up and the fireball bounces off. She waves her hands in front of her and the wind builds up to a gale force. Lucy leans into the heavy wind and puts her finger to the ground, ice starts to form around her finger, and an ice crackle shoots toward Alana. Lucy has to struggle to keep her finger on the ground. The ice tries to find Alana, who hops around to evade it, but doesn't want to lose her focus on Lucy. Alana's wind forms a funnel, sucking up Lucy.

Lucy stares at Alana, unimpressed. The ice still grows on the ground. Alana concentrates fully on the spell to keep Lucy contained. She doesn't notice the ice reaching her and quickly encapsulating her legs. It inches upwards. The tornado spins faster and faster, while the ice reaches above Alana's waist.

NEW ORLEANS

In the meantime, Tara watches Luna back at work. "She's good."

Maeve looks from her grandma to her mother. "Bridget wants to be normal, Gram. We don't need her. I can help you. Why don't you trust me?"

Tara smiles fondly at her. "I trust you sweetheart, it's just that we all have our gifts."

"I'm good with everybody." Maeve can't keep the hurt out of her voice.

"That's not the—" Tara clutches her throat and can't seem to breathe.

"Grandma?"

Tara claws at her throat and pulls away her shawl. Maeve jumps up and starts to pound on Tara's back. Tara shakes her head, it doesn't help. Maeve mumbles a spell. Blotches of darkness cloud Tara's vision and she starts to turn blue. She's not choking, this is magical. She tries to look around to see where the threat is coming from. People are in the way, and Maeve is not helping. Maeve frantically tries to get Luna's attention. Customers around them start to notice something is wrong, and a doctor offers his help. Tara swats his hands away while she struggles to remain conscious.

Luna rushes over to Tara and Maeve, pushing away people crowding them. Tara is on the edge of losing consciousness. Luna mumbles a spell when all windows and doors bang open. A gale-force wind rages through the Hat. Customers are ducking and searching for cover from the flying debris. Luna and Maeve scan around, trying to pinpoint where this is coming from. Tara sits up and gulps in deep breaths, regaining her ability to breathe before she falls backward and faints. Luna manages to break her fall. The wind stops abruptly, followed by a deadly silence.

After several seconds, the crowd panics—screaming and shouting while they rush to the door. Luna motions Maeve to take care of Tara, while she and Ron work spells to calm the customers. Maeve pulls her grandmother to the side, preventing her from being trampled by the mass exodus from the bar.

BOSTON

Cal Lockwood leans against a gleaming black Bentley, while he browses the Internet on his phone, ignoring the occasional light flashes and weird weather on the hilltop. He's in his early twenties and dressed in sleazy gothic black. His outfit definitely doesn't fit the fancy car. He's bored and has been left behind once again by his grandmother to wait by the car. She doesn't value his opinion and treats him like shit. He understands why his dad left, but why didn't he take him with him? His grandmother is downright scary and doesn't tolerate any opposition.

A loud bang startles him, and to his surprise, he sees Lucy hurtling up into the air and then coming down fast. He fumbles with his phone and can't seem to find his pockets. Frustrated, he throws it aside and starts to weave his hands in front of him while he chants, "Oxicodendron radicans, grow, hang, obey. Oxicodendron radicans, grow, hang, obey." Poison ivy starts to grow at a rapid rate from the ground, it forms a net about six feet above the ground. He glances up and his grandmother falls fast. Now he shouts, "OXICODENDRON RADICANS. GROW. HANG. OBEY!" The last strands tangle together when Lucy hits the poison ivy. For a moment, she just lays there. Concerned, he rushes over. "Grandma, GRANDMA, are you okay? What happened? Jesus, that was a long way down."

"Help me up." Lucy roles to the side of the net, suddenly showing her age; this definitely hurt. Cal helps her down. "Grandma, are you—" He doesn't get a chance to finish. His concern is met with disappointment.

"Poison ivy? You moron." Lucy's face and uncovered arms are turning red with irritation.

Cal's face falls. Another missed opportunity to please Lucy. He half helps-half herds Lucy to the car. She slides in the back, touching her irritated face.

"Do you want me to do something about that?" Concerned, Cal bends forward.

Lucy slams the door in his face.

"I guess not." He quickly makes his way around the car, hops in and drives off. He keeps his eyes fixed on the road, feeling the angry stare of Lucy on his back. Uncomfortably, he twitches his shoulder.

"Get me home as soon as possible." Her clipped command comes from the backseat.

"Yes, ma'am." He picks up speed.

Lucy moves her hands over her arms and face. Slowly the red irritated skin returns to normal. Carefully, she pulls the Dagger from her pocket. Her eyes shine with desire, gently stroking it. "Justice, finally."

"What?" Cal looks in the rear-view mirror. "What is that?"

"Watch the road. Get me home. I have work to do." Lucy covers the Dagger.

"But—" Lucy silences him with an angry stare. He shrinks two sizes and drives as fast as he dares.

NEW ORLEANS

It's in the wee hours of the night. Luna and Maeve have taken turns watching Tara. She hasn't woken yet, and they are concerned. This is clearly something magical. Luna can hear Maeve coming up the stairs, while she watches her mother's chest rise and fall. She wonders when Tara became so fragile. She's always been so strong and had such drive. Even when Seamus died, she carried on and managed the family. How she loves to meddle in everybody's affairs. Maybe she shouldn't have been so harsh on her earlier tonight. Then again . . . Tara's secrets always drive her crazy. The door opens and Maeve comes in. For the tenth time, Luna lets her hand move back and forth above her mother—still nothing. She can't sense a residue from a spell. Tara's hand snaps up, grabbing Luna's hand. Luna jumps up. "Mom?"

Tara coughs and slowly opens her eyes.

Luna touches her face, "You scared us."

Maeve moves in next to Luna. "How are you feeling? Can I get you anything?"

Tara coughs again and rasps, "Water."

"Of course," Maeve hands her a glass of water.

Tara has trouble getting up.

Luna supports her, while she gulps it down. "Slowly, don't drink too fast."

Panicked, Tara looks around. "The Dagger."

"What? Mom. Focus. You make no sense." Luna takes the glass from her hand.

"Something terrible has happened." Tara insists.

Luna coaxes her to lay down, "You were out for at least three hours. Take it easy."

"There is no time." Tara tries to sit back up.

"Why don't you tell us?" Luna suggests, "We know it's some sort of magical attack, but we couldn't find anything wrong or find any spells."

Tara takes a minute to regain her calm. Seemingly, more like herself, she replies, "It's complicated."

Luna rolls her eyes as if to say 'here we go again'. "We're not stupid, mom. I'm sure we can follow you."

Tara ignores Luna. "We need to get the family together."

Luna's irritation is mounting, she hates a family pow-wow. "There's no need to get everybody together. That's an impossible task. You know there's always something."

"We need to discuss this as a family, and I mean everybody." There's no doubt what Tara means with that statement.

Poof—there goes the last of Luna's sympathy. Her mother always has a reason. Always. It would be a stupid mistake to presume she's old and fragile. "Nice try, mom, it's not going to happen."

Tara turns to Maeve. "Can you try? She'll listen to you."

Maeve feels sandwiched between an irritated mother and a begging grandmother. "I have no contact with her either. We can take care of you, Grandma, we don't need her."

"Please, Maeve," the silence stretches, "you're my only hope."

Maeve caves, "I don't think it will work. I've tried and never heard anything back. But I will try again, for you."

Tara gives her an encouraging smile. "You're a good girl."

"Come on Ma, she's not twelve," Luna speaks up for her daughter.

Maeve leaves the room and finds her way to the balcony. She breathes in the midnight air, the smell of jasmine that covers this side of the house is intoxicating. The moon is out, lighting up the garden. She soaks up some moon energy before she gets her cellphone out.

BOSTON

That same moon is shining through the bedroom window onto the pile of humans and dogs in Bridget's bed. They're snoring away until Bridget's cellphone rings. A big dog raises his head, while the little Chihuahua starts to dart around on the bed. Bridget wiggles up and grabs her phone. She takes a peek at the caller ID. "Hmm this is going to be interesting."

Wes is awake, too, and watches Bridget. "Hello?"

"Hi, Bridget." Bridget feels a pang of regret when she hears her twin's voice.

"Maeve, is that you?" She stalls, wondering why Maeve would reach out to her. Did she make that mental call earlier today?

"Yes. It's been a while—"

Bridget doesn't let her finish; she wants to keep this as short as possible. "What do you want?"

"We have a problem." She can almost taste Maeve's uncertainty about how this is going to be received.

Bridget had resisted her family all this time, not planning to stop now, "We? I don't think so."

Wes is getting more interested in the conversation and scoots upright.

"Gram collapsed. Something is wrong." Maeve sounds genuinely worried.

"Call a doctor," is Bridget's snappy reply.

Maeve's disappointment is palpable when she says, "She's asking you to come home."

"So she orders you to call me, and good old Maeve—"

"Stop it! You have no right to judge me."

Bridget can't hide her surprise. Did Maeve just snap? "Maeve?"

But she's done with Bridget and is on a roll now. "Stay where you are, I'm glad that you're gone. Always high and mighty and so selfish." Maeve hangs up.

Bridget is shocked. Maeve has always been so compliant. What is going on? She feels Wes' eyes on her, slowly she looks at him, daring him to say something. The little Chihuahua, Kiki, feels the tension and starts to lick Bridget's face. This slightly relaxes her. Wes touches her cheek and draws her in for a kiss.

NEW ORLEANS

Maeve doesn't get that kind of comfort. Her cheeks are bright red and she breathes heavily. It feels good to finally tell her sister what she thinks. Why didn't she stay in touch with her? Twins should have a special bond. What did she ever do? That will teach her. Then it dawns on her that she has to tell her grandmother that she failed. She will understand, but she will feel the underlying disappointment. Shit. Well, it's too late now.

BOSTON

The next morning, Bridget arrives late at a crime scene. She drinks the last of her coffee before stepping out of her car which is parked in the exact same spot as Cal's last night. Looking around, she wonders where the crime scene is. There are plenty of police cars, an ambulance and unmarked cars, but there are no people. She takes a deep breath and coughs. That's weird, it feels like there's not enough air. She shakes it off and walks towards the familiar yellow tape. A young police officer rushes forward to stop her. Irritated, she waves her badge, "Where is it?"

"It's up the hill," he motions to the top, while holding the tape up.

Bridget ducks under it and makes her way up the hill. In no time, she starts breathing hard even though she's in good shape. She looks around—what's going on? There is something terribly wrong here. She stops dead at the top of the hill, taking in the devastation. The tornado has wreaked havoc, toppled trees and debris are everywhere. In the center of it all she spots Tom next to a dead body. Careful not to disturb any evidence she makes her way to him.

Without looking up, he says, "That boyfriend is keeping you busy."

"I'm here, aren't I? What have we got?" Bridget turns her full attention to the blond woman at her feet.

"Meet Alana Jansson, thirty-six years old. She still has her wallet and ID on her. No sign of a robbery. The Medical Examiner estimates Time of Death around 11pm." Tom rattles off the specifics.

Bridget bends a little closer. "Okay, I don't see any visible wounds. What's her cause of death?"

"That's where it gets interesting." This gets her attention as not many things surprise Tom anymore. "She froze to death. Instantly."

"What?" She looks around and takes in the surroundings with new interest, "Was this a freak tornado or something?"

"Your guess is as good as mine. Nothing out of the ordinary reported in the area. Hell, I thought it was downright balmy, like the 60s, last night," Tom shrugs.

"This doesn't feel right. The air feels thin, like it's hard to breathe, but we're only up, what? 300 feet? Makes no sense."

"None of this makes sense," replies Tom frustrated.

Bridget puts on her latex gloves and kneels next to Alana's body. Very gently, she picks up her hand, and in a second, is back on the hilltop last night, in the middle of the fight between Alana and Lucy. Although Bridget sits right between the two witches, neither of them react to her presence. Bridget looks up just in time to see a fireball hurdled at her. Automatically, she throws herself backward.

Back in real time, she falls backward. Tom jumps up and is ready to help her up. "Jesus, Madigan? Are you okay?"

"Yeah. Yes. I'm fine." She ignores his hand and gets back up herself. "I lost my balance."

"I can't leave you alone for a minute!" Tom jokes.

"Piss off." Bridget is relieved he didn't make anything of it.

He walks away laughing.

Shit, this hasn't happened this bad in ages. She can't completely deny that she has this tiny advantage, sometimes she gets flashbacks upon touching a dead person. It's not really using her magic, right? She can't help it. She's been down this narrative path a thousand times. As she can't switch it off, she might as well use it.

It looks like her past is coming back to haunt her. Maeve's call, and now this woman is a witch. That's too many coincidences.

Bridget looks around. Tom is talking to the coroner and others are busy. Nobody pays attention to her. Once, just this once, she's going to use her magic to see what went on here. She gets up and walks around the body as if she's studying it from different angles. When she passes North, she starts an incantation and walks a circle around the body, invoking every wind direction and asking them to guard her circle. When the circle is closed, she kneels down next to Alana's body. Tom glances her way and she gives him a reassuring smile. When he has his attention on the coroner again, she leans forward as if she's studying something on Alana's torso, and she slowly but surely puts her hand on Alana's chest.

Instantly, she's back at the hilltop. This time she's better prepared and takes in the wild tornado with one of the witches locked in it. The crazy wind makes it impossible to see who that is. She gets up and turns around. She's invisible to the other witches and can move around without being affected by what's going on. She stands close to Alana while she watches the ice climb up her body. Alana panics and screams. Too late. She tries to move her arm, but the ice grows quicker and quicker. Bridget feels frustrated not to be able to do something. Helpless, she watches Alana's last desperate moments. When Alana is fully covered in ice, the tornado abruptly stops and drops the other witch unceremoniously on the ground. Bridget wants to touch Alana but thinks the better of it, a small tear makes its way down her cheek. There's no time to linger. She turns and is shocked—an involuntary gasp escapes her as Lucy passes her. Grandma? This can't be happening. Tara is a powerful witch, but Bridget never thought she was evil. She would have known, right? Lucy walks around Alana, laying a hand on her back, while she commands, "Power of the East, wind, show me your presence." The ice melts and Lucy's eyes start to glow. Quickly she grabs the Dagger, but the power doesn't want to leave her guardian that easily. There's a loud bang when all the ice shatters, and wind emanates from Alana. Lucy gets hurtled into the air and flung down the mountain.

Bridget is back in her body and breathes heavily. *No, no, no, no, no! This is crazy.* Her own grandmother? Frantically, she looks around, gets up and walks the circle backward, trying to put some distance between her and what she has just learned. She jumps in the air when she feels a hand on her shoulder. Quickly she turns around, ready to—oh, it's Tom. Air leaves her lungs in a long ragged breath. "You're giving me a heart attack!"

Tom raises a skeptical brow.

"It's crazy. This. It makes no sense." Her mind is racing.

"Thank you, Sherlock. You're late, you're not focused and you're jumpy. What's going on?" Panic returns. What can she say? My own grandmother did this. She must have seen it wrong. "I can't breathe up here." She pushes past Tom and is a couple of steps downhill before Tom catches up with her.

"What the hell was that all about?" Tom demands to know. Bridget keeps walking. Tom grabs her arm and spins her around. "Stop. Look at me." Reluctantly, Bridget looks at Tom. He notices something has put her off balance. "What rattles you about this case? Is it the woman?" Frantically, Bridget tries to gather her thoughts. "No. Yes. She looks familiar."

Tom pauses, for a moment Bridget is worried he doesn't buy it. His eyes soften, "We'll find who did this." Bridget nods in acknowledgment. Tom finally lets go of her arm, and they make their way downhill. "Come on. We need to tell her family."

Bridget looks around, no way to escape. "Could you . . . "

"Do you know them?" When she doesn't respond, he offers, "I can take Jordan."

"Thanks." Bridget is clearly shaken.

Tom looks worried. This is not her normal steadfast behavior. "You're sure you're okay?"

"Don't worry. I'll see you at the station." Tom turns away and Bridget can't get into her car fast enough. There she lets the tension go and starts to tremble uncontrollably. She breathes in and out and tries to calm herself. Her inner voice keeps rambling. Stop it. It's just another case, don't be ridiculous. You can do it. In out in out. Slow down. Think.

NEW ORLEANS

In the meantime, the witches are waking up in the mansion in New Orleans. Maeve buzzes around the kitchen. In her element, she put the kettle on and hums as she mixes together a selection of herbs. When she's satisfied, she pours boiling water over her herb mix. Luna enters the kitchen in her PJs. Never an early riser, Maeve is surprised she's already up. Without a word, they kiss each other on the cheek. Luna walks to the potion and takes a long sniff. "Excellent. This will help Tara heal and support her through the day. Whatever it is that's going on with her, she should tell us."

Maeve doesn't want to get into that again, "Gram wants to go to the Hat today. I don't think that's a good idea. Why do you think she wants Bridget to come home?"

"Who knows? Who cares?" Luna shrugs, while she obviously does care.

"Gram said you were very talented," Maeve gently pushes.

Luna gives a startled laugh, "I'm not doing it. You should know better than to try to manipulate me."

"I'm not. I'm just worried about, Gram."

"Stop being so freaking reasonable! It's boring." Luna walks out and slams the door behind her. She might as well have slapped Maeve in the face. Maeve is speechless, it looks like she's losing her touch.

Tara watches the news from her bed on an ancient television. A news reporter stands in the middle of a town ravaged by a tornado. "Pine Bluff, Arkansas, got hit today by a series of brutal tornadoes. Two confirmed deaths, and it's unclear how many more are injured."

Tara turns to Seamus' portrait, who also watched the news. "I told you. Something is wrong with Air." Seamus shrugs.

"The town is totally destroyed!" The reporter continues, "the tornados came out of nowhere. There was no indication or even a weather pattern that suggested its coming. Like a freak storm—"

"See! I have to try to find the other guardians. Maybe they need help. I can't just sit and wait." Tara slings her legs out of bed. Seamus is concerned. His portrait bulges and his hand reaches out, trying to touch Tara. She's hurrying around the room looking for some clothes when her cell phone rings. "Voicemail can take it." And she focuses on gathering a wand, some incense and her spellbook. When she has everything, she picks up her phone and checks her missed call. "Oh, that was Bridget." Seamus perks up. "She didn't leave a message."

BOSTON

Bridget is still in her car at the crime scene. Tara didn't pick up, that's not a good sign. She puts her phone down and grabs the key, flashing back to Tara's face on the hilltop. Maybe she should try again. She picks up her phone and dials. This time, Tara picks up on the second ring.

"Bridget? Are you on your way home? When can we expect you? Do you need to be picked up from the airport?" Tara's familiar voice floods through the phone. These questions are confirming that she had been on the other end of the mental call yesterday.

Bridget ignores that, focusing on the more troubling problem. Her grandmother is a murder suspect, and this sobering thought helps her to put her feelings aside and snap into cop mode. "You don't sound sick."

This stops Tara's stream of questions

"Feeling better? Are you in Boston by any chance?" Bridget continues.

Tara hesitates only for a second, "You called me at home, dear."

"It's your cell, you could be anywhere," counters Bridget.

"I don't fly that far anymore." Tara sounds genuine.

Doubt creeps in, "You could take a plane."

"You're kidding me, right?" Now, Tara sounds amused.

Her grandmother had probably never even been on a plane. Bridget rakes her fingers through her hair, but doesn't respond.

"What is this all about? What's with the interrogation? That's no way to talk to your grandmother. I fainted in the Hat last night. I asked Maeve to contact you. That's it." The impatience is palpable, it seems she did get through to Tara after all.

"I'm at a crime scene."

"I'm sorry, dear," Tara sounds sincere, and adds matter of factly, "Something is wrong."

"You don't need to be a witch for that. I'm calling you." Bridget has a hard time hiding her frustration.

"You're the police officer, dear," responds Tara mildly.

"Witchcraft was involved." There's a slight threat in Bridget's voice now.

"And then you call me? Do you need advice?" Tara sounds puzzled.

"I don't need advice."

"Bridget. Bridget. These cryptic short sentences make no sense. Do you think we have something to do with it? That's ridiculous." Tara sounds offended. "There are plenty of talented witches where you live. If you wouldn't have behaved so stupid and mingled with other witches, you might actually have known a couple that would be able to help you. And, by the way, we do no harm."

Bridget becomes angry "Whoever did this meant harm."

"Not all witchcraft is our fault." Tara is becoming fed up.

"I have reason to believe—"

Tara cuts her off. "I need you to come home as soon as possible. Your family needs you."

"I'll get to the truth, Gram." Bridget doesn't give up.

"I'm counting on that, dear," Tara responds mildly.

"Are you sure?" This doesn't get Bridget anywhere. Her grandma seems to have an alibi, and still . . . she's absolutely sure what she saw.

"The truth is always best."

That is not a straight answer. So, Bridget pushes, "Do you want to share some truths now?"

"I have nothing to hide." Tara is losing her patience again.

"That's not really an answer, is it?" Bridget prods.

Tara sighs, "I was in the Hat. It was around 11 pm when I fainted. I couldn't breathe. There are plenty of witnesses if you don't believe me." Clearly done with this. But she changes her tone before adding, "I've missed you. Please . . . I need you."

Reluctantly, Bridget admits, "I've missed you too."

"Come home." Click. Tara ends the call.

"Grandma! Damn it." This didn't explain anything. Maybe Tara made a shadow self, a familiar. Hell, she doesn't know enough about this stuff, time to do some research. She shakes it off, starts the car, heading to the police station.

Bridget stares at her computer screen, multiple windows are open. Witch familiars and how they work, astral projection, out-of-body experience. None of them has any real information, and she highly doubts if there was even a real witch involved in these articles. She would love to be able to look in the family grimoire now. Obviously, the web is not a reliable resource for witchcraft. She could try Maeve . . . Probably not—after last night. It was so good to hear her voice, Bridget hadn't realized that she missed her sister. This is not the time to become sentimental, better to approach this as a police officer. Where to begin? Let's run Tara's info through some databases.

NEW ORLEANS

Tara is not hanging around. Her window is open and her curtains billow in the wind. It's already warm, but thankfully it's too early in the season for the humidity to have kicked in. Tara distracts herself by watching some Blue Jays building a nest in the tree close to her window. Spring is her favorite season; it's so full of life and hope. Today, she needs all the hope she can get. There are still moments she's so anxious about the future that she can hardly breathe. She puts out her hand and sends a whisper out into the wind; very soon a Monarch butterfly flutters by. Tara smiles while the Monarch lands on her finger. She bends down and whispers something in her ear. The butterfly rises into the air. Tara follows her until she disappears. Luna is right to question her. How much can she tell her children? Too many secrets for far too long. Maybe her sister can help her sort some things out. She did stay in touch with Lucy. It's the only time she ever did something against her mother's wishes. How could she not? They don't understand the bond between identical twins. Lucy didn't mean it, and she was banned from the family forever. Although over the years, they saw each other less and less, Tara can still feel her twin. It's not like the old days when they could finish each other thoughts. Now it's more like a feeling that you miss something, or something is just out of reach. Well, Lucy is one thing she will absolutely not tell her children about.

BOSTON

Lucy, at that moment, is totally engrossed in trying to attune herself to the Dagger. She's working in her occult dungeon. The room is dark; the windows are blacked out, except for some tiny sunbeams that manage to shine through the cracks. Candles burn around the room. The walls are lined with shelves and every possible piece of bad-witch paraphernalia imaginable; skulls, rat-tails, chicken legs, voodoo dolls, you name it. In the middle of the room stands a big old wooden table. The legs are elaborately carved, naked people in agony swirl up. It's very disturbing. Candle wax drips down to the floor. An old manuscript lies open on the table. Lucy is bent over it, she tries to make sense of the spell. With a smile, she turns to the Dagger on the table. Gently she pets it, the Dagger makes a purring sound. Encouraged, she picks it up. "AGH!" she opens her hand and the Dagger clatters to the floor. Blood forms from a gash on her hand. "You bit me! That's not nice."

The monarch butterfly peeks through one of the tiny openings. She flutters against the window, trying to draw Lucy's attention.

Irritated, Lucy looks her way. "Not now." The butterfly is persistent. Lucy waves her hand carelessly and the monarch combusts Lucy's attention is already back on the book. "It must be somewhere in here. One of them must have written down how to attune to the elemental objects." Without touching it, she lifts the Dagger and puts it next to the book.

Bridget forgets about the time as she digs deeper and deeper into Tara's life. No strange things so far, and definitely no signs of Tara making it to Boston. She's not crazy, she knows what she saw. She's looking through Tara's bank statements when Tom startles her. He stands next to her desk. Quickly Bridget minimizes the screen. "Back already?"

"It's three o'clock. Did you find anything?" He bends forward, but the only thing on the screen is Tara's driver's license.

"Not yet. How was the family?" Bridget says, trying to distract him.

"I wish you would have come. They're your kin." Tom says wistfully.

"What the hell does that mean?" She gets up and tries physically to create a bit of room between Tom and her screen.

"You know, a little spooky," he jokes.

She punches him playfully on his arm.

"Her sister is on her way to identify the body. Why don't you handle that one?"

A little later, Bridget stands opposite Gwen. You wouldn't take her for a witch in her white T-shirt and skinny jeans, but it's clear that she's Alana's sibling. She has the same nose and sturdy chin. Quietly, Bridget nods to the medical examiner, and he slowly pulls back the sheet. A sob escapes from Gwen, tears start to stream down her face.

"Take your time." Everybody dreads this part of the job. It's always heartbreaking to show the family.

"It's her. Knowing is different than—" Overtaken by grief, she can't finish.

Bridget waits patiently. Gwen draws a deep breath, gathering herself. Slowly she reaches for her sister. Before Bridget can stop her, Gwen touches her cheek and whispers, "Be at peace, dear sister." The body sighs.

The ME jumps up. "She's still alive?" he squeaks in disbelief, feeling for a pulse.

But Bridget and Gwen pay no attention to him as they watch Alana's spirit rise from her body. A ghostly face turns towards Gwen and smiles before she dissolves into a million twinkling stars, which slowly dim.

Now, Bridget turns to the ME. "She's gone."

"I know how to do my job," he answers snappily to hide his discomfort.

"Of course. It was just a fluke." She tries to calm him down. The medical examiner sputters some more, but Bridget gets distracted by a voice in her head.

"So, you're a witch," states Gwen with her voiceless witch communication.

Bridget looks Gwen in the eye and confirms Gwen's statement. It's been a while someone reached out to her like this. Gwen's voice in her head continues. "Did you say your name was Madigan?" Bridget only gives her a small nod, unwilling to say anything. Gwen looks away and Bridget can feel her anxiety building.

"What's wrong?" asks Bridget out loud.

"Where are her clothes?" demands Gwen.

The ME snaps back into duty. "They're bagged for evidence."

"I need to see them," she insists.

"We will return them if you want, after the investigation." The ME dismisses it.

Gwen becomes agitated. "I need to see them. NOW!"

"Calm down, what's so important? Maybe we can tell you if it is there?" offers Bridget.

"She was carrying the family heirloom. It's extremely valuable to our family."

The ME reads from a list, "She wore a five pointed star and that was it. No other jewelry."

"No dagger?!" Gwen sounds alarmed.

"No. The star was the only thing." The ME scans the list again.

Bridget sighs, giving in to her witch side, adding in their quiet communication, "There was no magical object."

Gwen looks at Bridget again and asks aloud, "Are you sure?"

"Yes. What's so important about that dagger?" Bridget wants to know. This seems a bit over-the-top reaction, even for a family heirloom.

"Ask your grandma. We're doomed." Gwen sags to the ground and starts to cry. Heavy sobs make her whole body shake.

Her grandmother again! Bridget struggles to keep her face blank, aware the ME is staring at them. Bridget tries to console Gwen, never her strong point, while questions race through her own mind. This makes no sense. Does she know about her grandmother? She helps her up, but Gwen pushes her away, and before Bridget can try to pry more out of her, she runs out of the room, leaving Bridget with more questions than answers.

Frustrated, she walks back to her desk, but gets an unpleasant surprise when she sees Tom browsing her computer. She's not in the mood. "What are you doing?"

"Interesting stuff you've been looking at," Tom smiles mildly.

"It's private." She cuts him off.

Tom glances at the ID: TARA MADIGAN. "Any relation?"

"It's my grandmother."

"Is this what's been keeping you occupied? I thought it was the case. Side project?" Tom doesn't give up.

Bridget decides to ignore his questions. "Gwen, the murder victim's sister, was very worried about some dagger, a family heirloom. Did she mention that before?"

"No, she didn't." Tom taps on the screen.

Again, Bridget ignores it. "I know what you mean by that—she's a little different. I think she's one of those new age witches or something."

"Or something, alright," laughs Tom. "You two freaked out the ME! He called me."

"Oh that. He spooks easily." Bridget rolls her eyes.

"That nothing cost me a half an hour, listening to his rambling."

Bridget shrugs, "It was something spiritual."

"Spiritual? So I was right? It is your kin." Tom lightens the mood.

Bridget laughs, time to get out of here now that he's on a positive note. "I'm going to see if my apartment is still in one piece. Wes and the dogs, dangerous combination."

"So . . . " Tom nods towards the computer again. "I'm a pretty good detective."

"Okay." Bridget takes a deep breath, he's not letting her off the hook. "My sister called to say grandma is sick."

"So you check her records?" says Tom in disbelief.

"We have a strange relationship, what can I say?" She grabs her coat.

Tom is clearly dissatisfied with this answer, but decides to let it go. "Spooky alright." They both laugh and make their way out.

NEW ORLEANS

It's night and Luna walks around in her bedroom. The room is an elegant combination of modern and more classic furniture, with subtle signs of witchcraft. Luna slips into something more comfortable, a short wide shirt. Her long hair is brushed and hangs freely down her back. She blows out the candles around the room, until she stops in front of a picture of her with Maeve and Bridget. The girls must have been around fourteen. They are all smiling at the camera, and the famous Yosemite dome rises behind them. Steve, her husband, had taken that picture on their summer vacation, in happier days. Hesitantly, she touches Bridget's face. Why didn't she understand? She did it for her. Luna opens one of the drawers and takes out her wand. She starts a sweeping move and halts. No. She can't go through the pain of being rejected. Not again.

What she hadn't told Tara or Maeve is that every year she still tries to reach Bridget on her birthday. "It's been seven years. If she hasn't forgiven me now . . ." She mumbles to herself, puts her wand back and slaps the picture face down on the dresser. Without looking back, she slides between the fresh sheets, time to get some sleep.

BOSTON

At the same time, Bridget sits at her living room table with a sketchpad. There's no sign of witchcraft in her house. It's a normal everyday home. It's quiet, except for the snoring of a couple of dogs sleeping on the couch. Only the light of the table lamp illuminates her work. It's a pretty accurate drawing of the Dagger. She looks at it, closes her eyes and adds some little details. Pretty perfect.

Satisfied, she leans back. She hears bare feet coming closer and watches full of anticipation when Wes rounds the corner. He looks delicious, even just after waking up. He smiles at her and walks over to take a peek at what she's doing. He turns it more towards him. "Your grandpa is not the only artist, I see. You've been holding out, babe."

Bridget shrugs, "This needed to come out."

"Are you coming to bed? It's late." He rubs her back.

"Go to bed, I'll be there soon."

Wes kisses her, she melts into it, and he kisses her more thoroughly. Finally, she pushes him away. "I promise." With a knowing smile, he walks away. Bridget lets out a deep breath; she can't resist him at all. Right now, she wants to run to bed, but the Dagger needs her attention. She glances at the trunk in the corner of the room, buried under a bunch of stuff. Shaking her head, she grabs her laptop instead. She searches and searches but nothing comes close. Finally, she gets up, snaps her laptop close, and moves in the direction of the bedroom. Stops. Damn, she has to check it. She would never forgive herself if it was in there, and she just didn't check it because it interfered with her no-witchcraft rule. Now that she has decided, she resolutely uncovers the trunk and opens it. It's full of her personal witchcraft stuff. Books, a wand, a crystal ball, incense, candles, and when she digs deep enough, her own spellbook.

Bridget takes it back to the table and starts to browse through it. It's filled with drawings, spells, stories, and dried herbs, you name it. But she can't find anything about a dagger in there. She's tired and frustrated; time to go to bed. She closes the book, but leaves everything on the table when she finally joins Wes in bed.

NEW ORLEANS

In the darkest hours of the night, Tara makes her way to the tomb. A light globe above her hand leads the way, although she can probably make this trek with her eyes closed. At the tomb, she puts her hand on the fire symbol and barely waits till the door opens wide enough to disappear inside.

She snaps her fingers and the torches along the walls flare to life. For a moment, she touches the most recent tomb. She always takes a moment to say hi to her mother—a small, private ritual. Now she needs all the help she can get. Tara feels the pressure of bad things coming. It feels like a freight train coming towards you and you're frozen on the track. These days she doesn't sit and wait, hoping things will get better. She learned the hard way that it's better to do something than to do nothing. Some might question her sanity, though, to go and search the astral plane for answers. Stop stalling; she gives herself a mental shake and gets to work.

With another snap of her fingers, she lights the candles on the altar while rearranging some of the objects on it. Quickly and with confidence, she grabs a cup with salt and sprinkles salt on the ground while she walks in a circle. Starting in the north, she moves east, invoking the elements, "Guardians of the East, protect my circle. Guardians of the South, protect my circle. Guardians of the West, protect my circle. Guardians of the North, protect my circle." When the circle is complete, she sits down in the middle, while she takes the Wand out of her tunic. She holds it upright between her two hands and recites, "Covenant sisters, come to my aid. Covenant sisters, we cannot wait. Covenant sisters—"

Suddenly, she finds herself standing in a forest. The sun peeks through the leaves and her clothes have changed; she is now wearing a red cape that flaps in the strong wind. She has entered the astral plane—a sort of dream state, a doorway of sorts. Although her body is still in the tomb in the real world, what happens to you in the astral plane happens to your actual body as well. As strange and dangerous creatures inhabit the planes, it can be perilous. It can give you the advantage of fast travel between two points, or you can search for things that are lost. Tara still holds the Wand. She quickly scans her surroundings—all good so far. She touches the Wand to her forehead and whispers, "Please help me find the Dagger, your sister of Air. Find it now, find it quick. Things are afoot." Like a divining rod, the Wand starts to quiver and points her in a direction. Without hesitation she walks that way, all the while glancing around her. The Wand leads her deeper and deeper into the woods. The wind rustles the leaves and Tara glances nervously behind her. It's like the color is leaving the world; and leaves are starting to fall around her. A piercing cry makes her jump. She's getting too old for this. *Calm down, calm down,* she tries to assure herself. A gust of wind rains leaves on her and she picks up the pace again. *Better get this over with.* The wind is picking up and it gets harder and harder to make her way forward. Something brushes her shoulder; she freezes and slowly turns around. A big goat-like figure looms over her, showing his big, jagged teeth in a demonic smile. Drool escapes from the side of his mouth. She swallows a scream. Two claws are about to touch her. Without thinking, she touches the point of her Wand to its middle mass, *'et in ruina ardeat.'* Crash and burn. The demon explodes into a million pieces. Cries are erupting everywhere around her. She swears like an old sailor. Everything seems to press into her. She mumbles another spell.

In an instant, she's back in her protective circle. Her eyes snap open, and in her shaking hands she still holds the Wand. Too old, she's getting too old for sure. Damn, that was close. The candles have almost burned down. Tara's been in the same position for a long time, and she can't really get up. She lets herself slide to the side, then rolls on her back and just lays there for some time. Finally, feeling comes back to her legs and she scrambles up. She still hobbles while she unwinds the circle. What is she going to do now? Something happened to the element Air and now the astral plane is even more dangerous than normal. Generally, she keeps the Wand in the drawer in her bedroom, but with her mounting feeling of trouble, she feels it is better to make sure it stays safe. She looks at the tombs, walks over, and slowly moves from one to the other, letting her senses touch her ancestors. The tomb of her great grandmother gives her that little shiver up the spine. That's the one. She waves her hands over the lid and it moves aside, revealing a skeleton with some remnants of clothing attached from an era long gone. The skeleton head moves to face her, and the empty sockets stare into her eyes. "Hello, Great Grandma. I need to ask you a favor. Would you mind holding on to the Wand for me for a little while?"

The skeleton mouth moves, although no sounds come out. Tara understands perfectly. "I know it's my responsibility. There's trouble, something happened to Air. The paths of the astral plane are guarded by dark creatures. I fear for the family. Please. For a little while till I know what's going on. I need to know it's safe."

Great Grandma sticks out her boney hand.

"Thank you." Tara gently places the Wand in it.

Great Grandma takes it and the lid slides back into place.

Back in her room, she can't sleep and paces around. Seamus follows her every move. "It was bad out there, I know it's been a while, but bad things are out. More than usual. I had to flee." Tara feels so agitated it's hard to think straight. She needs to calm down, but the pressure on her chest makes it hard to breathe. Throwing the window open, the night air blows in, and with it the spring scents and quiet noises of the night. Deep breaths in and deep breaths out—it calms her down a bit. The cards—she needs to consult the cards. Pulling open her desk, she lets her left hand glide over the bags full of tarot decks, and picks one. Tara slides the cards out, shuffles them, and thinks about her question. What does she really want to know? Is it what happened? Or what she needs to do? It's important to ask the right question.

"What do I need to know about the situation and what can I do about it?" That should do it. She cuts the deck and pulls four cards.

The first one is STRENGTH: A woman and a lion.

FIVE OF SWORDS: A battlefield with people walking around defeated while one guy collects his winnings.

KNIGHT OF WANDS: A knight on a horse charging forward with a wand pointed forward in his hand.

THREE OF SWORDS: Three swords piercing a bleeding heart.

For a minute, she touches the cards and thinks. Bridget is again at the center of it all; she will charge into a situation that will bring her tremendous heartache. And somebody will take something from that situation.

How can she warn her? It's clear she doesn't respond to the normal ways of contacting her. Would she dare to use Seamus' deck? Conflicted, Tara decides to go to bed and make a decision in the morning.

BOSTON

The next morning, Wes wakes up early and Bridget is still fast asleep. Some of the dogs wake up when they feel him stir, but as he's clearly not the person who feeds them, they settle back down while Wes quietly slips out of bed. He pads through the living room in his bare feet and sweatpants. His eyes are drawn to Bridget's spellbook. He reads the cover, *Bridget's Book of Shadows.* Now that sounds interesting. He glances around but the rest of the house is still quiet. He leafs through the book and can't hide a smile. The beginning is clearly written by a child; it's adorable. His last feelings of remorse melt away; Bridget is always so closed off about her past, and this is a chance to get a glimpse of it. He touches some of the writing or drawings and reads out loud, "I will the flowers to up and bloom, pop open, and smell the perfume." A laugh escapes him—this is too cute! "A true love, handsome and free, bring him here for all to see. Kind and fun, a true love is when my story begun. So mote it be." Bridget, a romantic—that's unexpected. He quickly glances in the window and at his dim reflection. Handsome and free, all right. With a smile, he flips another couple of pages. Hmm, this looks like another language. Wes uses his best sorcerer's voice, *"Crecer, ramas crecen, sobre premido amplo. Mentres me gustaría que así, non deixar ir."* A loud crack follows. Startled, he looks around. Floorboards start to pop loose and branches sprout from the floor. He backpedals, but the first branches have found him and start to wrap around his legs; the more he struggles, the tighter they get. He shouts, "Help! HEEEEEELP!"

Bridget runs in with her gun drawn, followed by her dog posse. She freezes when she sees Wes, now covered in branches barely able to open his mouth. A sad, "Help," comes out.

"Oh shit." Bridget quickly stuffs her gun behind her back and pulls at the branches. The dogs bark and attack but that only makes it worse. "Stop. Stop it!"

The dogs growl but stop their attack. A sad sound comes from Wes. Bridget finally spots her spellbook open. "You didn't . . ."

Only one of Wes' eyes is still visible. Wes is pleading for help, spurring her into action. She rushes to the trunk and throws stuff out till she jumps up triumphantly with her wand. She positions herself in front of Wes and says, *"Deixar ir, eu non quería dicir iso así, liberalo lo como é para min."* Let go! Reverse the spell, he's mine. It does absolutely nothing. It's getting harder and harder to see Wes, and he seems to be screaming with his mouth closed. Bridget tries again "Oh Goddess, hear me, help me set him free." Nothing.

"Shit, I'm rusty." She rushes to her book and leafs through it. "Don't worry, honey, I got this." Only the creaking of branches this time. She glances and Wes is completely covered.

"Shit, shit, shit." Frantically, she tries to find a spell. "That's it." She stands in front of the branches, centers herself, raises her wand and says, "With the power in me, I set you free."

The branches quiver. "Reverse this spell and all is well. I command earth spirit, let it be." She touches the branches with her wand. For a couple of seconds, which feels like an eternity, nothing happens. But then the branches recede. Slowly, they unwind and the shocked face of Wes emerges. The dogs chase the branches until they're all gone. Wes and Bridget just stare at each other.

Wes starts to shake violently, "What the fuck?!"

Bridget steps closer to embrace him, but he steps back and puts his shaky hands up. "What are you?!"

Bridget's face falls; this is what she had always feared if he knew who she was. Dear Goddess, why did he need to find out like this. This is worse than she ever imagined.

"What the hell was that?" He hugs his arms around himself to try to stop the shaking.

"You conjured up an earth spirit and it bound you," she softly whispers.

Wes tries to process this. "And you're a witch, sorcerer, magician, crazy person . . . ?"

"I come from a long line of witches," she says, as if that explains everything.

Wes rubs his arms where some bruises start to appear. "Great, crazy person."

"No, for real. Witches do exist." Bridget can almost taste Wes' disbelief.

"I just never told you because . . . " She plows on. "Because . . . my mother . . . well, my mother—it's a long story. Short version, I didn't want that life, so I broke with my family and became a police officer."

Wes looks skeptical; it breaks her heart. "Apparently it's not something you can switch off."

"I realize that now." She closes her book of shadows. "I should have never left this lying around. I'm sorry."

"Sorry?!" Wes' hands gently feel his face, remembering the suffocation. "Jesus! You almost got me killed!"

Bridget doesn't know how to make this right. She has never been very good at comforting someone. "It's still me. Nothing's changed."

"Nothing's changed?! Everything's changed! You're a freaking witch and a sorry one at that."

Somehow this pushes the wrong button with Bridget. She's actually a very strong witch. She's only a bit rusty. "I never wanted to use magic again."

"How is that working out for you?" Wes lashes out.

A tear wells up in her eye and rolls down her cheek.

"Don't you dare cry. You left that bomb lying around." He gestures to the book.

"I didn't know spells could work for normal people." It feels like a lame excuse, even to her.

"Now you know. What kind of stupid witch are you?" Wes is clearly not ready to accept what happened. Of course he's upset, but he could cut her some slack.

"I'm actually a pretty powerful witch, just rusty." And with a small voice, she adds. "Nobody got hurt."

Wes raises his eyebrow. "You lied to me."

"I didn't lie; I only neglected to tell you about it. That life is behind me. You probably wouldn't have believed me anyway if I told you. I dug my spell book up because of this case," Bridget says, sounding more like herself.

Wes looks at her and can't hide the feeling she has let him down. It pierces through her heart. She's losing him. She doesn't know how to stop it. "I'm sorry."

Wes motions her to go, she steps forward but again he puts up his hands. "Please. I need to . . ." He looks so bewildered; it hurts more than she ever imagined. Slowly, she walks backward while she looks in his eyes. He's hurt, really hurt. Confusion and disappointment come off him in waves. When she's at the door, she turns, and looks back at him one last time. He'll be gone when she comes home. She's sure of it. Another life she messed up. He's right; she is a failure.

In the bedroom, she collapses on the bed and pulls Bouncer, a big black lab, close. He licks her face and knows how to calm her down and bring her back out of her downward spiral. Her phone beeps. She has five messages; they're increasingly annoyed.

Tom: "Where are you? Better come out now. Will wait one more minute."

Shit, she forgot. She gets up—dresses, and is out the door within a minute.

Bridget jumps in the car with Tom. He opens his mouth to say something, his irritation evident. She doesn't give him a chance to start, "Take a number."

"That kind of day, huh? You look like shit."

Bridget doesn't want to talk about it; it's better to focus on the case. "Don't get me started. We need to go to the Boston Public Library."

"Because?" Tom might cut her some slack. However, he's not taking orders from her.

"I've been digging into that Dagger, the family heirloom. Here." She hands him her drawing. "When did she give that to you?" As she can't tell him she has visions, she chooses to ignore the question. "I searched online but couldn't find any information on it. Let's check out the library. They have a great selection on the occult."

Bridget is not the only one with a bad start to her day. Elsewhere in the Boston area, Lucy still struggles to attune herself to the Dagger. She places the Dagger on her altar. Four candles are lit for the four wind directions. While chanting, she raises both hands to the sky. Small storm clouds form above the altar, and a flicker of victory passes over Lucy's face. She intensifies her chant. The clouds swirl into a small tornado reaching for the Dagger. She smiles and chants louder and louder. A lightning bolt shoots from the clouds and hits Lucy in the face. She screams and topples backward. Her eyebrows are badly scorched and her hair still sizzles. The bad smell of burnt hair fills the room.

Cal runs into the room and sees Lucy's red, scorched face. "Are you okay?"

Lucy doesn't immediately answer.

"Grandma? GRANDMA?"

"Don't shout. Help me up." Cal helps Lucy up and quickly pulls a chair close.

Lucy plops down and breathes hard. "Damn. This should have worked. I tried every connection spell I could find."

"Can I help?" Cal asks, hopeful to be of use. Maybe this time she will let him in.

"You?!" That one word says enough.

Cal flinches.

"Get the car. I need to do more research," Lucy orders him.

NEW ORLEANS

In the meantime, Tara sits in her bedroom and stares at the Magical Tarot Deck in front of her. Seamus paces up and down in his portrait. "Stop it. I know what I'm doing."

He raises an eyebrow, which clearly says, 'I highly doubt that.'

With a snap of her fingers, the candles on the table are lit, and she picks up the deck and searches for Bridget's card. Seamus leans forward, as far as his portrait allows. Tara states her intention "She needs protection." Tara intentionally stares at Bridget's card, Strength. Slowly the image of Bridget in the card begins to stir. "Oh Seamus, something is happening." Seamus's worries have now turned to curiosity.

BOSTON

Bridget moves uncomfortably back and forth in her seat, while Tom steers the car expertly through the morning rush hour. "What's up with you? Come on. You can tell me."

She feels her chest and her head. "I don't know, I feel a bit queasy."

"Are you pregnant?"

"What? Hell no." But something is seriously wrong, for the lack of a better word. She feels thin, and not in the skinny sense of the word. She needs to get out. Frantically, she taps Tom on the shoulder. "Stop the car. Stop the car!"

Tom doesn't hesitate and stops the car at the curb. He looks at Bridget and it almost seems like he can see through her. "Bridget?"

"Tom! Help!" Bridget dissolves before his eyes. Frantically, he jumps out, searching around the car.

NEW ORLEANS

The image of Bridget stretches and bulges out of the card. Tara quickly puts it down on the ground as the image is growing and growing. She steps backward. Seamus can't hide his excitement. The cards really work! This exceeds even his wildest expectations. The image becomes life-size and then comes to life. Bridget is standing in her grandma's room, dressed in the tunic from the card. The unexpected by-product, a giant lion stands next to her. The animal leans into her and gives a powerful roar. Seamus' eyes are as big as saucers before he puts his hands to cover his face, and Tara jumps even further back. Bridget looks totally disoriented. The lion starts to rub his head on her thigh and she absent-mindedly pets him. It's like with the dogs, the lion pulls her into the reality of things. She takes in her clothes, touching her arm to see if she's real. She's real all right, this is too fucking weird. Only then she looks around and sees Tara. "What have you done?"

Tara replies, "I can explain—"

The lion roars again cutting off whatever Tara was saying as he feels Bridget's frustration.

"It's still you. I called you through Seamus's Magical Tarot Deck." Prides shines through Tara's words.

"His what?!" Bridget is confused.

"Magical Tarot Deck." As if that explains everything.

She should have known only her grandfather could come up with something crazy like that. "What happened to the real me?" Bridget flashes back to a confused Tom.

"You are the real you." Tara is sharing Seamus' excitement.

Bridget's eyes shoot daggers. Focusing Tara on the problem at hand. "Uhhh, I mean . . . I'm not sure."

"Not SURE!" the lion shows his teeth this time.

"It's the first time we've used it. We didn't get a chance to try it before Seamus died." Tara explains, while Seamus smiles at her apologetically.

Bridget looks at the portrait. "Gee, thanks, Grandpa. You have to send me back. I was in a car with Tom."

Seamus wildly gestures.

"You can't send me back?!" Tara and Seamus's faces say it all. They have no clue what they're doing. How did she end up in this mess?

Tara recovers, "It doesn't work that way."

"How would you know? You never used it before!" Bridget's anger bubbles to the surface.

Tara shrugs. "You were with a normal?"

"YES! Heaven knows what is happening. I'm a police officer for God's sake. If he rallies the troops—I can't think of that right now. We need to do something. I need to go back!" Bridget is furious, and adds, "right now!"

Tara focuses on the reason she started this—her message—"Something terrible has happened. Somehow you're involved. I read the cards—something is going to happen to you."

"Are you even listening?! Yes, something happened. You did this." Bridget is steaming.

"You know that's not what I mean." Tara starts to lose her patience as well. "I know you know. You need to focus, and I'm sure if we square this away, you will be able to return."

Of course, Bridget knows. She's aware something is terribly wrong, although she will never admit it. This whole case, all the signs. Okay, if it will help her get back, she'll cooperate. "Okay, tell me."

"If I knew what exactly is wrong, I would tell you, but it's a feeling."

Bridget sighs impatiently.

"Take this." Tara hands her a talisman. "Wear it on your body. It will give you some protection." Bridget stares at it, and then puts it over her head. "You have some serious—" before Bridget can finish, she starts to dissolve. Tara groans in frustration, she needed more time.

BOSTON

Bridget is reappearing in the car, freaking Tom out! He draws his weapon and points it at a slowly solid growing Bridget. "Tom. TOM! It's me. Bridget." His gun wavers. It's even worse than she imagined. What is she going to do? "Put it down, please."

Very slowly he lowers the gun. Bridget lets out a sigh of relief.

"You . . . you disappeared," Tom stutters.

Bridget's mind races; she makes a snap decision. "What are you talking about?"

"You were gone." There is confusion in his voice.

"Tom. Don't you remember? We stopped because you felt faint. Then you sort of zoned out. It was scary, I shook you but you didn't respond. I was about to call an ambulance and then you popped up and pulled the gun on me." Bridget makes up a story that could explain this.

"You were gone. You . . . dissolved . . . " he insists.

"I'm taking you to the hospital. I was here the whole time," she lies.

"You were gone." He sounds a little less convinced this time.

"Here, feel me." She holds her arm in front of his face and pinches it. "How is that even possible?! You must have had some sort of hallucination or something. You freaked me out."

Tom is starting to doubt himself. Bridget takes advantage of this. "Come, let me drive. We need to have you checked out."

"No. No hospital. I think I'm fine . . . now," he says, shaking his head.

Still she gets out and walks to the other side and holds the door open. "Let me drive."

Tom is clearly confused but lets her take control. They drive on in silence, and Bridget is relieved when they reach the Boston Public Library. She parks in a no-parking zone but decides not to care today. They both get out of the car. Tom has a hard time snapping back into normal mode. He looks like an old man the way he climbs out of the car. Normally they would have some banter over that, but Bridget lets it go.

Instead, she admires the stone building. It's beautiful and impressive. Tom stands next to her. "You know what we're looking for?"

She waves the drawing and walks up the steps. Inside a cheerful middle-aged librarian greets them. "Welcome to the library. Is there something I can help you with?"

"Yes. I'm detective Madigan and this is detective Walsh, we're looking for more information on a dagger." She shows her the picture. "If you could point us in the right direction."

"Up the stairs to your left, the rare book room. That's probably your best bet. It looks pretty old. There will be a librarian there as some of the books are very delicate and can only be handled by a professional." The lady waves them on.

"Of course. Thank you." Bridget smiles.

While they make their way to the stairs, she glances at Tom. "You sure you're okay? Why don't you go and have a glass of water, cup of coffee or something."

"I don't know, what's wrong with me. I never—maybe some food will help. I'll catch up with you." He motions to the sign pointing in the direction of the cafeteria.

Bridget doesn't hesitate and moves on upstairs. She feels bad she did this to Tom, but this will also give her the opportunity to move around a bit more freely. After all, it's about magic and look what it did to him. You can't miss the rare book room; it's a feast for the eyes, if you like old books, that is. She would have loved to spend time browsing the shelves. Tom will follow soon, so she'd better get started. The librarian directs her up a short flight of stairs to a row of books, and Bridget is soon engrossed in her search.

In the meantime, Tom leans against a pillar in the cafeteria where he drinks a coffee and nibbles on a sandwich. He's actually starting to feel better. His thoughts race through his head and don't make any sense. He watches the people getting food and drinks. It calms him a bit. After a while he feels human again and pushes away from the pillar and makes his way to the rare book room.

At the same time, Cal pulls up in front of the library and jumps out, rushes around the car and opens the door for Lucy. She has managed to tame her scorched hair and eyebrows and looks like a dignified old lady. Cal offers his arm but she waves him away. "I'll let you know when I'm done and you can pick me up here again."

Cal is dismissed, "I'll be right here if you need me."

Lucy has already walked away.

Bridget found a promising book and takes it down to the reading table in the middle of the room. It's an old grimoire and packed with old knowledge and drawings, texts, and symbols. She should come here more often; the things she could learn from this. For a moment, she totally forgets she swore off magic. This is too exciting! Then she turns the page and sees the Dagger. This is it! She compares her drawing. Wow, it really is. She bends forward to try to decipher the text next to it when she hears a small cough and glances up. An old lady enters the room. She is back to her drawing when the realization of whom she just saw sets in. Her head snaps up and she meets Lucy's eyes. Lucy smiles knowingly, the family resemblance is not lost on her. Bridget is baffled, is this her grandmother? She looks different, she feels different. "Grandma?"

Lucy doesn't hesitate. Her hand shoots forward and she says a quick spell. Bridget is too late, but in a flash, Tom shields her from whatever comes her way. It hits him square in the chest and he falls to the floor. Lucy already has another spell on the way. This time Bridget stands protectively over Tom's body, like the lion in her tarot card. The talisman around her neck lights up and the spell slides off her protective shield. Who is this woman? It's not her grandmother, that's for sure. Lucy turns around. Bridget wants to run after her but remembers Tom. She can't leave him. Lucy glances back one last time before she disappears out of sight and smiles a wicked smile. Jesus. It's like Grandma's evil twin—this is too weird. She kneels next to Tom and starts to examine him. She looks around for the librarian who is frozen in place. "Call 911. Yes you! Call 911, quick!" The librarian snaps out of it and is on the phone. Tom has no visible injuries and he starts to snore. Bridget shakes him in the hope of waking him up. "Tom. Tom! TOM!"

Seven of Pentacles

PART 2

SEVEN OF PENTACLES "CONSEQUENCES"

"Sooner or later, everyone sits down to a banquet of consequences."
—ROBERT LOUIS STEVENSON

NEW ORLEANS

The sun sets and a last ray of sunshine hits Tara, who's working in her herb garden. She's not in her traditional colorful dress, but in black linen, which flows around her while she weeds and picks some herbs. The smell of tansy is strong in the air. Their bright yellow flowers light up in the last sunshine of the day. A wicked smile crosses Tara's face and on closer look, all the herbs in this garden are toxic. Her gloved hands carefully touch the plants to determine if they're ready for harvest. The night is falling and there's the feel of dark magic in the air. Tara gets startled when Bridget seems to appear out of nowhere. Her face darkens and she weaves her hand quickly through the air. Bridget tries to enter the garden through the gate but she seems to hit an invisible wall. The gate won't open—she pushes and pulls. She starts to yell at Tara, but she's back to her weeding and has turned her back on Bridget. Bridget starts to move around the garden with her hands flowing over the invisible force field in the

63

hope of finding a weak spot. This annoys Tara, but she pretends to work. She follows Bridget out the corner of her eyes. Bridget starts to chant; Tara turns on her and points her wand at Bridget. The invisible wall disappears and Bridget loses her balance, falling forward straight into the leadwort. Tara doesn't hesitate and slings a spell at Bridget. Bridget screams! Her screams are drowned out by loud music and the image morphs into the homey Madigan's kitchen.

Maeve is handing out cookies. Their enchanting smell fills the air. Her food is downright irresistible. Luna sits at the kitchen table and has a discussion with her older sister Freya, a sour-looking witch. Maeve sighs as they never seem to agree on anything and she hands them a cookie. Even Freya can't help but smile when she bites into the cookie. She closes her eyes to take in the still slightly warm chocolate and the hint of sea salt. When she opens her eyes again, the kitchen is full. It looks like the whole family is gathered in the kitchen and they're all shouting. Maeve moves around trying to calm everybody down. Sparks fly in the air—the sign of witches in heated argument. Freya is sweating. "Isn't it hot in here?"

Maeve opens the windows and air gets sucked in. A strange noise seems to come from upstairs. The room falls silent.

At the end of the hallway, smoke appears under Seamus' old atelier. The door bangs open and the room is in flames. On his worktable is a drawing, held down by his wand and his reading glasses. The figures in the paintings, stacked along the wall, move. Desperately, they try to escape the canvas while tongues of fire lick at the edges of the painting. The whole room seems to scream.

The Madigans are all outside on the lawn and watch powerless while their family home goes up in flames. The orange glow flickers on their tear-stained faces.

Diane gasps and shoots straight up. Sweat pours down her face and she breaths hard. The vision is still playing in her mind, and she can even smell the smoke. Never ever does it seem to get easier. She hates her gift. What does it all mean? She puts her head in her hands and sobs. Next to her, her wife, Alice, stirs. A fellow witch, she has been Diane's rock for the last fifteen years. Diane tries to stifle her sobs, but Alice turns towards her. "A vision?"

Diane just nods; she can't find the words yet. Alice opens her arms and Diane doesn't hesitate to find refuge in her lover's arms. Alice makes soothing noises and caresses Diane's back. Slowly Diane calms down. "Do you want to talk about it?" whispers Alice.

"You would think that after my whole life full of this shit, I would understand it better. It made no sense. Mom did something utterly evil. Our family home burned down." Diane gasps. "All Seamus' work went up in flames. We were powerless." She starts crying and Alice just hugs her. "And Bridget was there. Something is going on with her."

"Oh honey," Alice draws her in for a kiss. She always seems to be attuned to Diane's needs.

Diane doesn't want to talk about it. It was too crazy. But should she try to do something about it this time? That generally has mixed results. The future doesn't like to be meddled with. Sometimes by solving one problem, you create another. After all, there is a balance of things. Who is she to judge what's right or wrong? And then again, why would she have this gift? Alice's hand travels down the curves of her belly. For now, she lets herself be distracted and all the questions and doubts are silenced with love.

BOSTON

Bridget leans against the wall in the hospital, checking her phone for the umpteenth time. Still nothing from Wes. How she hates the smell of disinfectants and the feeling of people dying. She usually avoids hospitals like the plague—it's not all fun being a witch, and there are some things you just can't turn off. But she doesn't care about any of that right now, she's so worried about Tom. *Please, Goddess, let him be okay.* She keeps replaying the moment of that 'Grandma-like woman' slinging a spell and the feeling of inevitability, and then . . . Tom was there, getting hit in the chest, tumbling to the ground, which seems to happen in slow motion. It was the worst moment of her life. He saved her. Her inability to jump into action makes her feel totally and utterly disgusted with herself. She should have gone after that woman. She should tell somebody she looks like her grandmother. Hell! For all she knows, her grandmother has gone rogue.

Talking of which, it's time to get some answers. She pushes herself off the wall and turns her back to the waiting room.

She can feel the glances and unasked questions of her friends. They know she was inadequate; Tom is a well-loved cop, and his friends and colleagues rushed to the hospital to show their support. Nobody, however, seems to want to talk to her; she could actually really use a hug right now. News had spread fast through the department of the strange circumstances in the library. Cops might not be witches, but they do have a sixth sense when it comes to trouble, and Bridget, right now, is trouble with a capital T.

She dials her grandma, who picks up on the second ring. "Bridget! Are you okay?!"

"Yes, yes," she mumbles.

Relief floods through the phone. "Thank Goddess for that."

"You have some explaining to do, Grandma. My partner is in some sort of coma. He got hit . . . " Bridget lowers her voice even more. "By a spell, from your . . . your—"

A doctor walks into the waiting room. All the cops around her get up, eager for news.

"Shit. I have to call you back." She quickly ends the call.

The doctor looks young and a little overwhelmed by the overpowering presence of the police force. She clears her throat and asks, "Is Mrs. Walsh here?"

Bridget moves forward, and says, "He's not married, and his children don't live in Boston. I'm his partner." The doctor looks uncertain.

"Please. What's wrong with him?" Bridget gently pushes her.

"Nothing." The cops start asking questions all at the same time.

Bridget makes eye contact with the doctor and waves the rest of her colleagues down. "What do you mean nothing? Is he awake?"

The doctor is uncomfortable. "We ran a lot of tests and Mr. Walsh is in excellent shape for his age."

"So why doesn't he wake up?" Bridget asks the obvious question.

The doctor actually looks embarrassed. "We don't know. We can't explain it. For now. We will run some more tests in the morning. I'm sorry."

"Can I see him?"

Now that the doctors can't find anything, an ominous feeling is growing inside her.

The doctor looks around as if she's looking for some form of permission.

"Just for a minute."

The doctor nods, and Bridget follows her out, escaping the buzzing noise of the other cops. No doubt they're speculating about what is wrong and what really happened. When the hallway door closes behind her, Bridget feels the tension leave her shoulders. Down the hallway, the doctor opens a door. "Keep it short. As long as we don't know exactly what is wrong, he needs to rest."

Bridget nods and goes in. Tom seems so small in the big hospital bed. Even though nothing is wrong, they've hooked him up to a lot of equipment. To **monitor** him, she guesses. Slowly, she moves closer and touches his hand. Nothing happens; he looks pale. "Hey, buddy. How are you doing?" What a stupid question! Tom is in the hospital because of her. That Grandma lookalike's slinging spells had shaken her. Deep down she knows why they can't find anything wrong with him. It's not a medical problem. For at least a minute, she stares at him and listens to his quiet breathing. Peaceful breathing? Sleep! Bridget snaps into action; how could she be so dense?! Slowly, she moves her hands about six inches above his body. With her eyes closed, she opens herself to her witch's sixth sense—*there it is!* A spell clings to his chest. It feels complex, not familiar, undoubtedly made by an accomplished witch. She needs to pick up her wand and her spellbook. It helped her with Wes, so it might be able to help her out this time as well. She sneaks out the back and quickly goes home.

Bridget parks across the street from her house. It's dark, and now that she's home, she doesn't want to go in. Wes didn't respond at all to the message she left him about Tom—it's not like him. He's always very considerate. Maybe he already went . . . The lights are still on in the house though. The front door opens and Wes struggles to get out with six dogs on leashes—he's like a spider with uncontrollable legs. They twist and turn around him and mummify his legs in no time. It takes him several minutes to organize them and walk down the street. Despite everything, this makes her smile. Hiding feels like a cowardly act, but she can't bear to see his disappointment again. Tears well up in her eyes while she waits for him to disappear around the corner. It takes her less than a minute to go inside and grab her wand and spellbook. She opens the door, and the dogs are all over her. They lick her hands and her face; she crouches down and snuggles them.

"You thought you could sneak in and out without us noticing?'

Bridget stands up and finally looks at Wes. "I thought you never wanted to see me again."

"Who said that?" He sounds irritated.

"You never responded to any of my messages." Bridget tries to hide her wand and spellbook behind her back.

"How is Tom? What's wrong with him?" he asks, at last worried.

This is not the way she wanted the conversation to go. Here we go again. She takes a deep breath. "He's in an enchanted sleep."

"He's what?!" Unconsciously, Wes takes a step backward. "Did you do that?"

"Of course not!" She tries to hide her irritation but fails terribly. "It was my . . . uhm . . . another witch."

Wes sizes her up. "So now you'r—" he's struggling to find the right words. He's still not sure what really happened to him this morning. It's not every day that you find out that your girlfriend is a witch. And accepting that is a whole different story. "Un-spell him, or something?"

"Or something. Right." Bridget clutches her spellbook and wand now against her chest.

"Are you coming home when you're done?" He eyes her.

Bridget doesn't dare to hope. "Do you want me to?"

"Bridget, I just found out you're different. Even more different than I thought. That doesn't mean I've stopped loving you. I need some time to . . . process this. We need to talk."

Bridget doesn't hide her relief. She quickly hugs him and gives him a kiss. "I'll be back as soon as I can."

At the hospital, she doesn't hesitate and takes the back door. It's getting late, so there are definitely less personnel around. A nurse hurries past her and only quickly glances at her badge; being a cop sure has its advantages sometimes. When she approaches Tom's door, she looks around; it's quiet as she sneaks inside. The beeping and the glow of the monitors make it a bit creepy. Again she looks around and listens; there's absolutely nobody. No more stalling, she plops the book on the end of the bed near Tom's feet and starts to leaf through it.

Here, this is to break a spell: *"Et suscitabuntur lacerantes te tantibus de pop consurgant."* Nothing happens, she shakes Tom. Nope. Maybe her Latin is a bit rusty. She tries again *"et suscitabuntur lacerantes te tantibus de pop consurgant."* Hmmm, let's try another one. She leafs through the book again and comes upon an old language spell. It says life, but she doesn't know what the words mean. Ah well, no time to be a chicken. *"Lavi, M'ap di lavi, lavi etensèl."* Still nothing. She stands up straight points her wands and really exerts her will and says, *"LAVI, M'AP DI LAVI, LAVI ETENSEL!"* Sparks fly from the electric sockets; Bridget jumps back and smudges the circle. The light flickers and dies out. The monitor beeps loudly. She shakes herself and walks up to Tom. By the flickering light of the candle she tries to see if he's awake. "Tom. Tom? Are you awake?" He's still snoring away, and there are running footsteps in the hallway. She quickly blows out the candle, gathers her stuff and hides behind the door. Nurses run in and start to work the machines, but the power in the room is fried. Bridget quietly sneaks out the door while the nurses discuss how to move Tom.

In her car, she finally takes a deep breath. Such a fuckup. She's no use as a witch, what was she thinking? She's totally out of practice. What is she going to do now? She could try to employ a local witch. Or better, she should nail that Grandma lookalike. It seems like all the answers are in New Orleans. She can grill her grandmother, and her family could help her create a spell to wake up Tom for sure. Damn. It's the last place on earth she wants to go to. To see everybody again will be . . . painful. No, there must be another way. She leans back in her car seat, closes her eyes and thinks. But all roads lead to New Orleans; she needs to go. She owes Tom.

NEW ORLEANS

Tara sits on her bench on the windowsill, staring over the garden while the sky slowly brightens. Dawn is her favorite time of day—the light, the smells, the promise of a new day. But today doesn't fill her with hope, instead it fills her with dread. What is she going to tell the kids? How much is wise? It sucks getting old, she used to be able to sit like this for a long time, now her legs ache and her body complains, forcing her to constantly shift her position. She's also still a bit off from last night. What the hell caused such a disturbance in the balance of the elements. She tries to shake off the feeling of foreboding and as she slowly gets up from her seat, she moans. Seamus stirs in his portrait. "Yes, yes, I know. I'm old and slow." Seamus gives her an encouraging smile and blows her a kiss. "I miss you, sweetie. To see you every day is great, but I miss your advice, your guidance. You had such a calming presence. Ah well, it is what the Goddess gives us, right?!" Seamus shrugs. Tara walks over to her desk and gets out her regular tarot deck. She grabs the Ace of Swords from her altar and shuffles the cards while she thinks about today. She draws a card. The Seven of Pentacles—a laugh escapes her. You reap what you sow. The fruits of your labor. Bees are busy on a honeycomb; the seven pentacles show their hard work. The excess honey drips down. Consequences, karma, well, let's see what her choices will bring her today. Good or bad?

BOSTON

Bridget waits for the cab driver to get her bag out of the car. This day is not off to a good start. When she woke up, Wes and the dogs were not home, and she couldn't wait for him to come back and say goodbye. They had a talk last night when she got back, but they didn't get far. She needed to book her flight and had fallen asleep. Too tired after a stressful day. Poor Wes, it must be so confusing. Finally, the driver pulls her suitcase out of the trunk; she tips him and barely steps on the sidewalk when a minivan comes to a screeching halt in front of her. "Hey! What are you thinking?!"

The door sweeps open—Wes, together with all her dogs, tumbles out.

"What are you doing here?" Bridget asks wearily.

Wes kisses her on the cheek. "Hi honey, can you hold the dogs please?" He hands her the leashes, grabs his duffle bag out of the car, pays the driver, and smiles brightly at her.

"What do you think you're doing?" This can't be happening. No way can they come along.

"We're coming with you." He waves a bunch of health certificates for the dogs in front of her face. "You're going to see your family. You didn't think I would let you face your evil witch mother alone."

"My mother is not evil. We just don't get along," Bridget automatically answers before she adds, "and no! You're not coming."

"I can't wait. A family of witches—how cool is that?" Wes is apparently over his shock from yesterday.

"Not cool at all. You can't come," Bridget insists.

"Well, we're booked, so we'll see you on the plane then." He snatches the dogs' leashes from her hand and marches into the airport. Bridget takes a deep breath and follows him. This is a disaster. "Wait!"

NEW ORLEANS

The cab moves slowly forward through the narrow streets of the French Quarter in New Orleans. Wes looks around enjoying the sights, the different houses, the colors, and the lively atmosphere. Every facade is different, and during the warm days, most shutters are kept shut. The hot, humid weather is like a heavy blanket, and it adds to the mystery. You can imagine vampires living here, voodoo priestesses, and maybe even werewolves. The dogs are piled up in the back, panting as it's so much hotter here. Bridget has grown more and more quiet. Even Wes picks up on her mounting anxiety level. "Are you nervous, sweetie?"

"It's been so long. I'm not sure what to expect. I know some of my family will not be thrilled to see me." Bridget confirms her discomfort.

"Does your grandmother live here?" Wes tries to distract her.

"No. I want to see my uncle first; he runs the family business. He's cool. I was hoping he could bring me up to speed." She's not sounding convinced.

The cab stops in front of Under the Witches Hat. "A witch bar! That's even better than I imagined." Wes laughs and gets out, hiding his own uncertainty. He hasn't forgotten what happened yesterday—coming along seemed like the perfect opportunity to get to the bottom of what is going on. Apparently, this witch delusion runs in the family. It might be a bit crazier than he hoped. He takes in the entrance and can't help but be excited though. He's a free spirit and this is different.

Bridget pays the cab driver and joins him. She takes in the outside, it's the same as she remembers. This used to be her favorite place when she grew up. Stealing sips from a cocktail, experimenting with spells and fooling customers with stupid teenage witch jokes. The happy memories make her smile, sadly those days are over, and she alienated her family. This might not be the refuge it once was. Wes can't hide his enthusiasm for going in. No reason to stall any longer. She says out loud, "Let's do it."

Bridget opens the door. A familiar smell of incense, liquor, and herbs drifts her way. Something deep inside her unfurls. Home—it feels like home. It's not something she would admit, but it feels good to come home. That feeling quickly disappears when she hears a familiar voice. Things are not going as planned.

"No dogs allowed." Luna waltzes towards them from behind the bar. That voice resonates with an anger deep inside Bridget. She straightens and braces herself for what is to come. Luna comes to a grinding halt when she recognizes Bridget.

"Hi Luna," says Bridget. Wes follows the icy exchange with interest. He could swear he sees snow flurries falling down on Luna. Luna is stuck in that awkward moment—wanting to give a hug that is obviously not welcome. The silence stretches and the uncomfortable greeting is becoming painful; neither woman willing to make the next move.

Wes steps forward and offers his hand to Luna. "Hi! I'm Wes, her boyfriend."

Luna snaps out of it and manages a warm smile. "Pleased to meet you. I'm Luna."

"You don't look like a wicked witch at all," he says surprised.

Laughter roars through the Hat, customers turn their heads as Ron makes his entrance. "Be careful, young man, looks can be deceiving. She's different." He winks and at the same time envelops Bridget in a bearhug. "The black sheep returns home."

Luna visibly relaxes further.

"Hi Uncle Ron, it's good to see you too." This time Bridget's voice is full of warmth.

"You have changed." He puts her down and takes a step back. "What do you say, Luna? She's a grown woman now. What have you been up to all those years?"

"I'm a detective; I work for the Boston Police Department."

A full belly laugh again. "Do they know you're a witch?"

"Bridget tried to be a normal person," says Wes, before Bridget has a chance to answer.

Both Ron and Luna stare in disbelief. Bridget's eyes darken.

"He's kidding, right?" Ron looks worried now.

Luna can't help but say, "That never ends well honey. You should know better. You should have never left. Denying your magic . . . I taught you better than that."

Bridget turns bright red and manages to squeeze out, "Thanks for the lecture, Ma." The dogs start to move around restlessly picking up on Bridget's discomfort.

Ron tries to diffuse the situation. "How many dogs do you have? Come, have a drink. You can tell us how you've been doing."

"Where is Grandma?" Bridget looks toward the back.

"She's home, she had a—episode," replies Luna.

"Episode?" That sounds vague.

"She fainted here a couple of nights ago. Something shifted in the balance, and it hit her hard. We're sure it's magical, but as always, she refuses to share her thoughts." Luna sighs.

"That sounds familiar," Bridget pulls at the leashes and turns to Wes. "We'll catch up later okay." She turns and practically drags Wes and the dogs out.

Ron throws his arm around his older sister. "That went better than expected."

Luna stares after Bridget and watches the door fall shut. "We'll see."

"At least she's home, and she can't avoid you anymore. It will be good for you two to sort this out." He encourages her.

"Thanks, Dr. Ron." Luna rolls her eyes at him.

Outside Bridget turns on Wes. "Don't ever give my family information about me."

"They're your family!" He doesn't understand.

"Exactly and knowledge is power. Power over you." She glares angrily in the direction of the bar.

"A little tense aren't we." He kisses her on the cheek. "Chill out, kitten, I'm an aristocrat, I can handle family politics."

This makes her smile. "I hope so."

BOSTON

In the meantime, Lucy is poring through piles of old grimoires, historical books on the occult, and anything remotely related to magic. Her living room is in chaos—books everywhere—and Lucy looks like she hasn't slept in days. She knows there is one book that holds the answer—*The Madigans' Book of Shadows.*

If she could only get her hands on it. The stupid curse! After she first got banned from her family, she tried to go back to their house in the Garden District. It was like hitting an invisible wall. Even if she took a cab, she would somehow disappear from the back seat and materialize at the edge of the Garden District. She also tried to go to their family bar in the French Quarter, she could get closer to that, maybe a block away, but still she couldn't come close to any family property. Frustrated, she hurtles a book across the room, and barely misses Cal's head as he just steps into the living room.

"Wow, grandma!" He bends down and picks up the book and gently lays it on the coffee table. "Can I help you with anything?"

Lucy snorts, she doesn't understand why he keeps trying to please her. Such a weakling—that he's her grandson is a disgrace. Then it hits her; she jumps up. Her grandson is not cursed, or is he? It's worth a try and without any inconvenience to her. He wants to help; he can be a guinea pig. Lucy turns to Cal and smiles. Cal takes a step back. His Grandma never smiles—better be prepared for anything.

"Cal, you're going on a trip."

"A trip?" He's confused.

"Yes, are you deaf or something?!" She lost patience with him a long time ago.

"No, Ma'am. Where am I going and what do you want me to do?" Cal is getting excited. Finally, his grandmother is trusting him with a mission.

"New Orleans, to find out what my sister is up to," Lucy explains.

"You have a sister?" He can't hide his curiosity.

"A twin sister, to be exact, and I want to know how she is. We don't get along well, so it's important they don't see you. Can you manage that?"

"Of course, I can." Cal is surprised—this actually sounds like fun, and he loves New Orleans.

"Here's the address, I want you to call me every day," Lucy instructs him.

"Yes, Ma'am."

"If you hurry, you can still catch a flight." Lucy waves him away, and Cal leaves immediately. She can't believe she didn't think of this before. She can't wait to find out if this works!

NEW ORLEANS

Tara stands in front of her altar and holds her athame—a ritual knife. For a moment she hesitates. She got a text from Ron that Bridget is on her way and she would rather not tell this story multiple times. The Wand needs to be protected at all costs. In the wrong hands, it can have devastating consequences. Her family has taken an oath to protect it. She can't let anything happen to it on her watch, and she has a feeling that she will not be able to see this through to the end. It's time they all know. So this might freak them out a bit, but they will have to get used to it. It's the first time she's tried to call them all home. Let's see if it works. She extends her arms wide and looks up. "Goddess, mother of all, I'm calling all my children and grandchildren home." Gradually, Tara lowers her arms. She brings the tip of the athame to her left index finger, slowly she pushes, her skin breaks, and a small drop of blood appears. She holds it above a cup with a little water in it. The drop falls into the cup. She stirs the blood through the water while she recites. "Children far and away, hear the call of blood and come home straightaway."

She rings a bell, and the sound seems to echo through the house. She downs the cup and blows out the candles. "Hurry."

From his spot on the wall, Seamus curiously looks on.

Tara turns to him. "Let's see if it works."

BANG, the door is pushed open and Maeve rushes in. "Gran, are you okay?"

Tara smiles at Seamus. "I'm fine dear, I'm fine. Everybody is coming home, why don't you put the kettle on." Maeve looks puzzled. "I have something important to share with all of you and I wanted to make sure they're all coming. So I called the bloodline."

Maeve knows better than to pry for more information, her Granny is the most secretive person she knows. Not everybody will be pleased to be summoned home. This is going to be interesting. "I'm on it." She turns around and heads down the stairs.

A sharp knock on the door is followed by the sound of dogs barking. Who the hell is that? Nobody in the family has dogs. Maeve walks to the heavy wooden front door. The door might be old but it is well-maintained, and she slowly opens it. A Chihuahua rushes past her, followed by several different-sized dogs "Hey, where do you think you're going?"

The door is pulled further open from the other side, and Maeve stands face to face with her twin. Bridget can't help but smile on seeing the surprised face of her sister. "Maeve, I've missed you."

For a moment, Maeve forgets she's angry and hugs Bridget tight. "Welcome home."

The dogs jump up on them and they let each other go. Maeve looks around. "How many?"

"Six, Wes insisted we take them." Bridget steps aside, revealing Wes. "This is Wes, my boyfriend. We live together."

Wes offers his hand, "Now I understand why Bridget never told me about her family. You are breathtaking." Wes brings her hand up, and kisses the top like an old gentleman. *"Enchanté."* Maeve blushes and is tongue-tied.

Bridget laughs, "That will do. Where is Gran, I heard a blood call. She doesn't want to face me alone, does she? GRANDMA!!! I'M HOME!"

Tara's bedroom door opens and she appears at the top of the stairs. Three of the dogs race up and say hello to her. "Well, hello dear, perfect timing. Look at you, you brought your family. I'm so happy you're home."

Bridget tries to hide her shock as her Grandma has aged quite a bit since she'd seen her last. "We'll see about that. I'm here on official police business."

Tara waves it away with her hand. "Get settled, the rest will be here soon. You can use any of the bedrooms upstairs."

"I think we should talk in private," Bridget mildly suggests.

"Well, I don't." Briskly, Tara turns away, and the door falls shut behind her.

Maeve winces, and says, "She's been acting strange the last couple of days. What are you doing home? I thought you didn't care about us." The old hurt comes creeping back in.

"Gran has something to do with a case I'm working on, and it's not something I wanted to talk about on the phone," Bridget explains.

"So you hop on a plane and take your boyfriend and six dogs along?" Maeve clearly finds that ridiculous.

"It's complicated," Bridget evades, finding that it's over the top herself.

Maeve folds her arms and waits.

"You have to work on your stare." Bridget walks past her and heads for the kitchen. "I'm hungry, and the dogs need water."

Wes looks apologetically at Maeve. Resigned, they follow her.

Bridget glances up the stairs; for a moment, she contemplates going up and confronting her Grandma, but she knows Tara well enough that she will not budge until everybody is here. She probably had put wards on the door. The blood call is intriguing; she's never done that before. What is so important? It will put them all on edge—that's for sure.

The kitchen hadn't changed one bit—the sweet smell of freshly baked muffins, the kettle on the stove, the scent of nettle, chamomile, and peppermint hanging to dry in bunches from the ceiling. Bridget's stomach grumbles and she grabs one of the muffins on the table, her teeth sink into the soft cake, and the still warm blackberries give little taste explosions in her mouth. Nobody can bake like Maeve; her siren song goes through the stomach.

The kitchen door bangs open and her aunt Freya strides in flanked by her two sons. The dogs bark and Bridget silences them with her inner voice. Waves of anger emanate from Freya—well, that hadn't changed. Bridget has never been a fan of her oldest aunt. It's the one thing she and her mother probably agree on. What has changed are Dylan and Brian, now well into their twenties, and they've become some fine-looking gentlemen. Brian's red hair and wicked smile immediately makes her think of her uncle Jason. "Hello, Brian."

He rewards her with a broad smile. Dylan represents his mother with dark features and a more brooding presence. He just nods to acknowledge her return.

"Who is this?" Freya points her finger at Wes.

He's like a deer in headlights. Aunt Freya is a force and if you're not prepared, she will waltz over you. Bridget slowly steps between Wes and her aunt. "Hello, Aunt Freya, it's been a while."

"You put her up to this, didn't you?" Now Freya's displeasure is at least focused on her.

Maeve dries her hands on a towel and comes to stand next to Bridget. "Now, come Aunt Freya, Bridget only just arrived. Have a cup of tea and let's wait for what Granny has to say. It might have nothing to do with Bridget."

"Sure . . . " adds Dylan, with a voice dripping of sarcasm, "she just conveniently comes home at the right time."

"I'm glad you're back." Brian diffuses the situation by giving Bridget a hug, which right away relaxes her and she turns to Wes. "This is Wes, my boyfriend. Wes, this is Brian."

He offers Wes his hand. "That's my mom, Freya, and my younger brother Dylan."

Wes gives them his best smile. Brian and Wes start chatting, and that leaves Bridget with Freya and Dylan. Luckily, she doesn't have to come up with conversation as somebody comes to a sliding stop on a broom just outside the kitchen's French doors. Freya immediately turns her attention to the new arrival. "You've got to be kidding me! How old is she?!" Freya throws her arms in the air. Bridget can't help but smile when her Aunt Ceri comes in through the doors. Her wild curls and ready smile make her loveable straightaway. As the youngest of Tara's children, she has a carefree attitude and a perfect gift for pushing her older siblings' buttons.

Wes is closest to her. "That was impressive."

"Thank you, young man. I'm Ceri." Her easy manner is in stark contrast to her older sister's moody behavior.

"Wes, the boyfriend," he says, pointing at Bridget.

"Oh Bridget." Ceri darts over and hugs her tight. "Where have you been? We have missed you, and your mother has been so miserable. It will be great to have you here, so she can forget about micromanaging our lives."

"I'm not staying that long, Auntie," is Bridget's instant reply.

Ceri laughs. "We'll see about that." Her eyes twinkle knowingly, as if she's in on some secret. She walks over to Maeve, kisses her on the cheek, and stuffs a muffin in her mouth. Then she moves over to Freya and snatches the tea she just poured. She quickly kisses her older sister on the cheek as well. "I thought that was you in the car."

Freya grumbles but doesn't take the bait. They all watch Ceri fluttering around the room—a welcome distraction. The dogs mill around the kitchen making friends and Wes hugs Bridget from behind. For a moment, she lets herself sink into him. It's hard for her to see her family again. Apparently, not everybody is happy to see her.

"Interesting bunch," whispers Wes in her ear. She smiles. The door opens again, and this time it's Fin, her younger brother. "Get your hands off my sister!"

Wes freezes and Bridget laughs.

Fin rushes over and hugs her tight. "Thank goodness, you're back. That took you long enough." Fin is in his early twenties and looks so much like his Dad that Bridget immediately feels a pang of guilt. All this time, she has been thinking what it would be like to see her mother and her sister again. What about her father and her brother? She tries to hide her embarrassment by asking, "How are you?" And looks around. "Where's Dad?"

Fin quickly exchanges a glance with Maeve before he answers, "Probably teaching somewhere. You know how it goes—I can't keep up with his schedule."

Gosh, it seems like she's off the hook with that one, quickly hiding her discomfort about her lack of interest in her father.

"Who's this?" Luckily Fin's attention has shifted to Wes.

"Wes, the boyfriend." Wes happily shakes Fin's hand.

"Make sure she treats you right, B can be a little—feisty," Fin jokes.

Wes smiles, "That's actually one of the things I love about her."

"Lucky you." Fin puts his arm around Bridget's shoulders, and whispers in her ear, "You're not getting off so easy, we need to talk."

Then Luna, Ron, and Diane arrive. Diane freezes in place when she sees Bridget and all the color drains from her face. "You're here." Everybody falls quiet and looks from Diane to Bridget. Bridget feels the weight of everybody's stare, as if the ceiling is pressing down on her. You never want to be the focus of a room full of witches. And you certainly don't want to be pointed out by your seer aunt. That is not a good sign, she evidently had seen something . . . not good.

Maeve, as always, is the mediator. "Aunt Diane, are you okay? Here a have a cup of chamomile tea." She ushers her aunt over to a chair and hands her a cup of tea. It's like a spell is broken and everybody starts to talk at once.

Bridget tries to blend in and slowly makes her way to the edge of the room. Ron catches up with her though. He bends down and whispers discreetly in her ear. "It's family only." Bridget glances at Wes, who's having a ball mingling with her family. Bridget's first impulse is to be irritated, but Ron is right. "I know."

"Selma and Alice are holding the fort at the Hat; why doesn't he go and wait there with the dogs?"

"Okay," Bridget agrees.

"He can take my car," offers Ron.

Bridget takes in her family. Such mixed feelings are bubbling up, but she firmly shuts them down. She's here with a mission and it's better to get it over with as soon as possible. Wes looks at her and she gives him a little nod with her head, to meet her in the hallway. She disappears. Soon Wes comes to the door. She hugs him tight, so happy to have his solid presence.

"Everything okay, honey?" Wes takes her head between his hands and gazes into her eyes.

She shrugs. He gently kisses her. Bridget sighs and stands up straight. No time to show any weakness. "This thing is family only. Do you mind waiting at

Under the Witches Hat? My aunt Selma, Ron's wife, and aunt Alice, Diane's wife, are there. We'll come as soon as we're done here."

"You're sure? I can wait upstairs if you want." Wes is concerned.

"You're so sweet. I'm going to be okay. Can you take the dogs? I'll keep Moon. You never know." Her weariness is palpable.

"Take care, sweetie. I can't believe you kept this a secret all this time. This witch thing is growing on me." That makes Bridget shudder. He quickly kisses her, grabs the car keys from her hands, and whistles for the dogs. Wes smiles one of his heart-stopping smiles before he closes the door.

The second the door is shut, Tara appears at the top of the stairs. Bridget and Tara's eyes meet. Nothing is said, but a lot is communicated. For a moment, the Strength card seems to materialize around Bridget, but it quickly fades. She feels the pressure of expectation and hope. To be a witch is not always easy but it has its advantages. Bridget feels her grandmother's uncertainty. She's always been such a rock; to see her Granny so in doubt makes her heart ache. Then the dead body of Alana flashes before her eyes. Tara knows things, and she should tell them. This is not the time to show mercy. What if it all could have been prevented? What is so important that she has called the whole family? Some psychic self-defense is necessary if she doesn't want to be sucked in by all the emotions. Better safe than sorry.

Tara winces when she feels Bridget's shield slam into place. With a sigh, she comes down the stairs.

"You look tired Grandma—guilty conscience?" Bridget needles her a bit.

"Old age. You've become a grown woman." Tara smiles "Happy you're home."

"I'm not staying."

"As you were saying." Tara is clearly indulging her. "Lead the way." She motions for her granddaughter to open the door. Bridget hesitates, which is not like her. She shakes it off and pushes the door open. A wave of high energy washes over them. It flows around Bridget's shield and hits Tara, who seems to take it all in. For a moment, Bridget wonders about the benefits of shielding against absorbing it all, but then the room falls totally quiet. All witch eyes are focused on Tara—she smiles a warm smile. "So good you're all here! It warms an old woman's heart. It's been too long."

The room erupts in a million questions directed at Tara. Sparks start to fly through the air. Diane, the only one who is quiet, watches with trepidation and takes a seat at the far end of the table. Bridget circles around to put some distance between herself and her grandmother. Tara takes a seat at the head of the table and Maeve hands her a cup of tea.

"Thank you, my dear." She's ignoring all the questions while raising her hand and slowly, one by one, they all fall quiet and the energy in the room goes back to normal. "Why don't you all sit down? This is going to take a while." Magically, there is exactly enough room at the table for everybody. Luna, however, doesn't take her seat and leans against the kitchen cabinet.

Freya can't contain herself any longer. "What the hell is going on?" Freya sits down on the left-hand side of her mother. Tara puts a hand on Freya's hand.

Freya immediately pulls her hand back. "We deserve an explanation."

"Deserve is such an interesting word," Tara muses.

"Come on, Ma!" Luna pushes herself off and walks to the only empty chair. "This might be the first time ever Freya and I agree on something. A blood call? That's going too far."

Bridget leans back and quietly observes the dynamics. Not much has changed by the look of it. "Let's hear Gran out first before we jump to any conclusions," adds Maeve, ever the peacemaker.

"She just always thinks we should be at her back and call. We're adults, she has no right to push us around." Luna's patience is running thin, and little sparkles form at the end of her fingers.

"Maeve is right. There must be a reason. Mom?" Ron uses his regal authority to silence his older sister and put the focus back on Tara.

Tara shuffles in her chair and tries to sit up straight. How she wished she had still that natural leadership. Getting older sucks, she's more fragile, and somehow, that gives others the feeling she's incapable. She's still a strong witch. It's so humiliating to have to face her own children. No escaping it now though, so she takes a deep breath and begins. "I called you all to tell you a family secret. Something that has been passed on for generations to the eldest daughter and that has been on a need-to-know basis. And so far, nobody needed to know. My own mother always stressed the importance of keeping this secret. Now, Bridget came here with questions," she nods to Bridget in acknowledgement. "I hope this will answer the questions that brought you here." Tara looks around, and now everybody is silent, she can feel their focus. "Many, many moons ago, a coven of witches made an alliance with the elements. It was the rise of the Industrial Age and people were starting to lose touch with the natural world. The elements agreed to put part of their powers in an object. A Wand, a Dagger, a Cup and a Wooden Disk, your basic witch tools. But the power of the objects consumed the witches. Some of them wanted to use the objects to rule the world. That's not the witches' way, so the four strongest witches decided to take the elemental objects and separate them before they were discovered. The power of the four objects together is just too strong. It could destroy the world." Tara takes a sip of her tea, and the calming effect of the chamomile settles in her stomach. "The Madigans have been the guardians of the Wand of Wisdom ever since. It has been passed on from mother to the oldest daughter." Freya eagerly sits up. As the oldest, she feels ready. "So are we here so you can pass it on to me?"

For the first time, Bridget can remember she sees her aunt radiate, she actually smiles. She didn't think that was possible.

Tara only takes Freya's hand and squeezes it gently. "We're here because I have seen bad omens and I'm convinced something harmful has happened to the Dagger of Consciousness, one of the other elemental objects. Now I'm worried the Wand might be in danger too."

The room explodes with questions, everybody talks at the same time, except for Bridget and Diane. The look on Diane's face is one of dread. When Diane feels Bridget's eyes on her, she quickly hides her emotions. Sparkles are now in the air. Tara gets up slowly and waves her hand in a small but effective spell. "QUIET!" Tara sways and sits again, definitely like an old lady.

"You're getting older, Ma. You should pass that burden on to me." Freya's eyes sparkle.

"I actually haven't decided yet whom I will pass the Wand to." This gets everybody's attention.

"But you said it passed on to the eldest daughter." Freya's irritation is back.

Tara looks uncomfortable and debates for a minute on how to say this. "I know, but it needs to be the right person."

"You don't trust me?!" Freya jumps up. "It's my right."

Tara winces—she has been afraid this would happen.

"All my life you favored others over me, and now you don't even grant me this!" Freya feels as if she's been stabbed in the heart.

"That's not true, sweetheart, I love you all equally." Her mother tries to lessen the sting.

"You're going to give it to your precious Luna!" Freya is shouting now.

"No, I won't."

Freya doesn't even hear that; she storms out of the room. Surprisingly, it's Ceri, who heads after her. "Well done, Ma. Very subtle, you know how she is." And Ceri disappears as well.

The rest sit in stunned silence. Tara actually looks embarrassed. How was she supposed to tell Freya that? There was no good outcome.

"I feel a lot is missing from this story." All heads snap towards Bridget.

"It's a long story. I obviously told only the important parts." Tara easily evades her.

"Right. You're sure you don't want to add something? Although I totally enjoyed this revelation, this is not why I'm here," Bridget casually replies.

"I thought you were here about the Dagger." Tara looks puzzled.

It's time for Bridget to drop her bomb. "Why don't you tell us who that evil twin is, that's running around bespelling people?"

"Who?" Slowly it starts to dawn on Tara.

"My partner got bespelled by an older woman, who looks exactly like you! First, I thought it was you, but it wasn't. She was like an evil twin." The truth barrels literally towards Tara, and when it hits her, she's thrown backward. She slams against the wall and loses consciousness.

"What the hell are you doing?!" yells Ron to Bridget.

Luna and Maeve are at Tara's side, making her comfortable on the floor.

"I didn't do this." Bridget defends herself, while not entirely sure what did happen.

"She's an old lady!" Ron points his finger at her, and a little beam shoots towards Bridget, she barely dodges it, and it scorches the wall.

"STOP!" Diane stands up and sways. "STOP IT!"

"She slung Mother into a wall!" He's so angry.

"No, she didn't, the truth did." This seems to penetrate Ron's anger. Diane urges everybody,

"We all need to stay calm and work this through. I had a vision, and if we don't stop now and be reasonable, we burn down the house."

"Nonsense, Aunt Diane, we would never do that." This is from Fin, whose face has lost all color—he doesn't know whom to believe.

"We have to believe Diane, she knows," comes a very weak voice from the floor. Tara is awake. She wished she'd stayed blissfully unconscious, but no such luck. This is far, far worse than she imagined. Lucy had stolen the Dagger. "Help me up."

The commotion had brought Freya and Ceri back, but they are still not very happy by the looks of it. Luna and Maeve help Tara back up on the chair. Maeve produces a fresh tea, and slowly, the energy level in the room goes down.

"This is far worse than I imagined. This must have been quite a shock for you, Bridget." Tara confirms her guess was right.

"At first, I thought it was you. I got a visual of what happened at the crime scene. But it's hard to swallow that your grandmother is a murderer. When I met her—when she bespelled my partner, I came face to face with her, and I knew it was somebody else. I decided that I needed more information." Revealing why she came home.

"I'm sorry." Tara stares at her hands.

"Don't be sorry. Explain! I think we all want to know." The others look shocked.

Tara looks up and sees the doubt in her children's eyes. It hurts, it hurts a lot. "Her name is Lucy, and she's my twin. You're right, I didn't tell the whole story."

"Her name is not in the family history," Luna says with conviction.

"Not in the book?" asks Ceri.

"No, she's not in our *Book of Shadows*," Tara looks uncomfortable. "When it was time for my mother to pass on the Wand, she called both Lucy and me to the tomb. She explained like I did, she wanted us both to know, as she hoped that our twin bond would make the burden easier to carry. Still, you can pass it only to one person. Lucy was technically the oldest, but my mother had always known there was a seed of darkness in her and she decided to pass the Wand to me." Tara shudders from the memories of that night. "Lucy didn't take that well and attacked my mother. She had to defend herself, and when she saw no other option, she banned Lucy from the family. She can't set foot on family property or use our name. We never talked about her again. It was horrible. I still miss my twin. And Mother—she died of a broken heart."

Maeve gets up and gives Tara a big hug. "That must have been so awful."

Bridget doesn't feel so sorry for her grandma. If they had known, they could have been prepared. "Well, she's back. She killed a fellow witch. Stole . . . " she motions with her hand towards Tara, "the Dagger, and she bespelled my partner."

"I'm so sorry," Tara mumbles.

"Stop saying 'sorry,' Grandma, we need to talk about what we can do about it. How do we find her? How strong is she? What has she been doing all these years? How can I help my partner?"

"Bridget is right Ma. The more information we have, the better we can prepare ourselves." Ron looks around at everybody, and most of them nod in agreement.

"Lucy is as least as gifted as we are. Who knows how much she has grown over the years. It worries me that she has tapped into the dark arts, that might give her an edge." Tara doesn't seem to know either.

"Light always wins over the dark," says Ceri with confidence.

"That's all very well, but so far it's Dark Team: 2 and the Light Team: 0," adds Bridget, with a healthy dose of sarcasm. Luna shoots her an angry look. "You're not helping."

Bridget ignores her. "Did you ever see her again after . . . ?"

"I don't know where she is." Tara expertly dodges the questions, which doesn't escape Bridget, but she lets it go for now. "You do remember I'm a police officer, right?"

Dylan gives a quick laugh, "You have no jurisdiction here."

Moon gives a sharp bark and bares his teeth. Bridget puts a hand on his head, and he instantly calms down. Dylan moves away from the big dog, as far as his chair can scoot over. Fin pushes him back. "She won't let the dog bite you. Don't be a wimp."

Tara looks pale and is clearly affected by this news. She leans back in her chair and closes her eyes for a minute. The day that her twin got banned is burned in her memory forever. She can still recall that desperate feeling of trying to reach Lucy. Their hands nearly touching. The realization on Lucy's face when she saw what was happening. A tear escapes her.

"Grandma!" Bridget's voice pierces her memory. "Please, is there anything else you can tell us about her?"

Tara snaps out of it. "Not really, I don't know where she lives or anything."

Luna tries to take charge, "So where is that Wand and what do we need to know about it?"

Freya jumps up. "You see! She wants it." Immediately Luna and Freya turn on each other. The first sparks erupt.

Tara puts her face in her hands. Sad that her daughters confirm her suspicion, Tara feels she was right to keep this all a secret.

"I am the strongest witch in this family," says Luna. She was never particularly modest.

"It's the right of the oldest. It has nothing to do with you!" Electricity discharges in the air between Freya and Luna. Diane turns pale, and Tara tries to intervene. "Girls, I haven't decided—"

"I am your best choice," Luna states with confidence.

"You always favored her. It's disgusting," Freya counters and Dylan takes position next to his Mom.

"You've always been jealous, instead of improving yourself, you wallow in your feeling of injustice." Luna puts her hand up towards Freya. Now the whole room erupts, and the cacophony of voices charges the room. The flames on the candles are growing, and the sparks are out of control.

Bridget distances herself and keeps an eye on her Grandma, who's slumped down in her chair and has put her head in her hands.

Diane jumps up and frantically tries to lower the tension in the room, but she doesn't seem to be able to raise her voice enough. A towel in the corner catches fire. She doubles her attempts, but nobody is listening. She sees Bridget taking it all in and rushes over to her. She grabs Bridget's arms and shouts in her ear. Bridget follows the frantic pointing of her aunt and immediately takes action. She takes a moment to center herself, mumbles a small spell that pops up from distant memory and shouts, "STOP!" The room falls immediately silent.

Tara looks up and looks full of hope at Bridget. The silence lasts only for a minute, and everybody starts back up. Bridget calls again, "STOP!" This time the tension in the room calms down. She points at Maeve. "Can you put that fire out?" Maeve turns, and the rest of the eyes in the room follow. The whole corner of the kitchen is in flames. Maeve doesn't hesitate, and a spell flows smoothly from her lips. The fire seems to be deprived of oxygen and become smaller and smaller.

"Sit down, everybody," commands Bridget. She gently pushes Diane forward. "Aunt Diane wants us all to take it down a notch."

Diane's voice is barely a whisper, and it forces everybody to listen. "I had a vision that we would burn down the house, so please, don't fight. We can't fight right now. Dark things are coming. We need each other."

Tara takes this moment to stand up. "Please darlings, I know it's a lot. Think about it, let it sink in. We'll talk soon. The Wand is safe for now, and I will meditate on who the right person is to pass it onto. So please don't fight among yourselves. Diane is right; we need each other. The Goddess only knows what Lucy is up to. And I'm the only one who can decide and pass the Wand onto the next generation."

Freya gets up. "Fine. Come Dylan, Brian. Let's go home." The boys get up, and without a word of goodbye, they leave.

Ever since Cal entered the Garden District, he has this strange feeling. It's like little insects running around on his back, and as if the hot humid air is so thick, he has to wade through it. Usually, the heat doesn't affect him—it's weird. But what's a little discomfort; anything is better than Lucy's reaction when you disappoint her. He glances at his phone again to double-check the address. Yes, this is it. Wow, witches must be living here. The house lights up with energy. Something must be going on; the energy level is off the charts. The few normals who pass the house glance at it without stopping. Even they feel it. Cal takes a moment to take it all in. The grand old New Orleans mansion, the flowers in the garden, the overpowering smells of jasmine and lavender. The garden is full of insects and birds; he even spots a little mouse scurrying around. The front door opens. Quickly, he disappears further into the shade of the big tree that hangs over the road. A sour-looking woman and two men are coming out. They don't look happy and are way too preoccupied to notice a stranger. He snaps a picture and texts it to Lucy. She will be glad to know he's following orders.

Ping. "Don't let them see you."

Great! Not even a thank you. Sometimes he wonders why he doesn't leave. He gets it that his father disappeared, but he could have taken Cal with him. Bastard. The witches drive off, and Cal decides to stay a bit longer.

Maeve lets out a breath of relief. "That was close."

At which Tara turns to Diane. "What were you thinking to interfere? Have you forgotten the consequences?"

"No but . . . I couldn't let our home go up in flames," Diane says meekly.

"Remember Tweetie . . . " says Ceri.

As Tara, Ceri, Diane, Luna, and Ron simultaneously remember the event, they manifest a replay. A hazy cloud appears above the table. An image of a young Diane talks to Ceri very sternly.

"You told me Tweetie would fly away if we didn't close his cage," says a pensive Ceri.

"And I did. The next day, he was dead." The image changes into Tweetie lying on his back at the bottom of the cage. Little Ceri is in tears, and Diane looks horrified. "He died because of the paint fumes—nobody realized that the house was painted that afternoon. Poor Tweetie, he might have flown away, but still lived." Abruptly the image disappears.

Diane slumps in her seat. "I just couldn't let it happen. All Dad's artwork . . . The memories . . ."

She starts to cry. Ceri walks over to her and hugs her. "Come, we'll see what happens. Let's get you home." The rest stay eerily silent as they watch them get up and leave. When the door falls shut behind them, Maeve sighs "It can't be that bad. Can it?"

"Generally, something worse happens," says Tara with a morbid frown.

"What can be worse than our house burning down?" Maeve wonders.

"Let's hope we won't have to find out." Tara doesn't sound convinced.

All is quiet at the house. Bridget wanders through the garden with Moon. It's been an exhausting day with all her family, she's not one bit closer to what happened or the truth. Tara couldn't frustrate her more. Why didn't she mention the Tarot Deck? And Bridget is confident there is a lot more to the story of her and Lucy. Tara feigning she doesn't know anything, has bullshit written all over it. Maybe she should head back to Boston and do some real police work. But what if she finds Lucy? If she's truly so much stronger, how could Bridget fight her? Gosh, she can't ignore it any longer, it has become urgent to brush up on her magic. But who can she ask? Moon gives a sharp bark. Bridget snaps out of her reverie and sees a car pulling up in the driveway. All the dogs rush out and happily bark at her. Wes looks a little too happy. He dashes over to her and swoops her up. Definitely delighted.

"What have you been drinking?" He smothers any further comments with kisses that taste of raspberry and elderflower, taking away any doubt he sampled some of the Under the Witches Hat's famous cocktails. The dogs jump up to her and mill around their legs.

"I can't believe you've been hiding this from me," Wes chastises her.

"How many cocktails did you have?" Arguing is fruitless.

"Everybody has been so friendly. That place—wow, my imagination—I'm getting so many ideas. I need to paint."

Bridget's earlier irritation is washed away by Wes' contagious enthusiasm. "Come let's go inside, I'm tired." She gives him her best smile.

He suggestively rubs her back and pulls her back in a hug.

The last sunrays hit Lucy in her toxic herb garden. She wears gloves and touches some herbs to see if they're ready for harvesting. It will be a full moon soon, and harvesting by the full moon is a definite plus. It gives the plants an extra boost and will almost double the magical power. She smiles endearingly at the blue flowers of her Wolf's Bane. They're doing really well this year. A rush of air and a sudden bang on her wards alerts her to an intruder. Without hesitation, she swings around, and her wand is in her hand. Bridget is on the other side of her fence unable to find a way in. She frantically tries to find a weak point in Lucy's defense. Lucy laughs. That stupid girl, she should know by now there is none. Lucy slings a spell at her and Bridget manages to dodge it. But there is no cover around the garden and Lucy has another spell ready in an instant; it hurtles through the air and hits Bridget full in her chest. An agonizing cry escapes her.

The image dissolves into a pile of compost. It's a hot summer day and Mike, Ron's 10-year-old son, plays with a pair of glasses. They're Seamus' old reading glasses. Fascinated, he lets the sunbeams shine through them, they're focused on a certain point. He's moving them further, and closer, trying to find the perfect spot. Once he has that, a little plume of smoke rises from the compost. Mike is excited and tries again. This time the pile actually catches fire and small flames burst to life. A wind blows, and the flames grow in size. Mike is startled, drops the glasses and heads back. He's frozen in place and doesn't do anything while the wind feeds the flames. Very soon, the pile is a full-blown fire. The flames lick at the fence of the extensive Madigan's herb garden. Not only the witches' pride and joy but their livelihood. The center of their craft. It took many years to find and grow all these herbs, some are rare. Tara and Seamus traveled the world for them and even smuggled some back. The fence is on fire, and the first plants catch fire. Mike turns and runs for the house. The wind happily feeds the flames, and within minutes, the whole garden is engulfed. It's like a laugh is traveling on the wind, while the plants cry out in pain. The image of the garden in flames morphs into a flame of a candle in the Madigan's homey kitchen. Candles burn everywhere; a pot of tea stands on the table. Tara, or could it be Lucy, sit behind the kitchen table with a pile of drawings from Seamus. She leafs through them and stops when she comes to what looks like a large Tarot Deck. Quickly, she picks it up and takes a closer look. Freya tumbles out of a tower, which is struck by lightning. Ceri holds up a wheel of Fortune, and the wheel actually seems to spin. The images are so lively; they almost seem like photographs. Diane sits against an ancient tree in a forest. The back of her hands rest on her knees and are opened toward the sky. The image of Diane comes to life. Leans forward, her face now consumes everything. It's distraught and shouts something.

Diane screams snap her out of the vision. Hysterically, she looks around and screams again in agony. She's in her living room, all alone, usually a quiet place. Dominated by the fireplace, which is now empty, as the sweltering heat makes a fire unnecessary. Oh my God, what has she done? She crumbles to the floor, too exhausted to get up, and rolls on her side and falls into a deep sleep. That is how Alice finds her when she wakes up during the night and realizes that Diane is not in their bed. Gently, she tries to shake her awake. It must have been a horrible vision if she's not even stirring. Carefully she lifts her head and puts a pillow under it. She gets a blanket from the couch and lowers herself to the ground, spooning her—protecting her back. Alice pulls the sheet over them while snuggling as close as possible. A slow murmur indicates Diane's still there.

The next morning, Bridget knocks on Tara's bedroom door. Her grandmother hadn't come down for breakfast, and she's out of patience. It's time to get some real answers.

"Come in," sounds Tara's voice, clearly awake.

Bridget opens the door, walking over to Tara sitting on her window bench.

"We need to talk," she says, while putting an arm around her shoulder and kissing her cheek.

Tara points at Diane, who's cleaning up the compost heap. "She's been at it since daybreak. It's no use you know. Something bad is going to happen whatever she does. That's how the universe works. It doesn't like to be meddled with."

"If it doesn't like that, why did it give her that gift?"

"Seamus always said the Universe has a wicked sense of humor." Tara turns to Seamus' portrait. Seamus waves enthusiastically at Bridget. They had a special connection, he seemed to understand her. "Hi, Grandpa." He blows her a kiss, which makes her smile. Tara saunters back to her bed, again it strikes Bridget how old her grandmother had become. She lays down and pats the spot next to her.

"Why didn't you tell the others about the Tarot Deck?" Bridget decides to come straight to the point.

"I need to know more about it. Let's not freak everybody out. I'll be careful." Tara and Seamus glance at each other.

"Careful, like when you used it on me?" Bridget can't hide her sarcasm.

"That was the first time, how could I know?" Tara dismisses her concern.

"And that from someone who always lectured me on the careless use of magic." Bridget lays on her side facing her grandma, she puts her arm under her head, taking a closer look at Tara. Deep lines, and age spots showing on her face. In her memory, her grandmother is more vibrant. When did this happen? She hadn't been gone that long. The silence stretches. Obviously, Tara is not going to volunteer any information. Bridget sighs. "Lucy murdered somebody. She bespelled a detective. I need to do something. I need to know where she is."

Tara stares at the ceiling, not responding.

"I don't think you told us everything. Did you see Lucy after . . . you know, her banishing?" Bridget prods.

"I swear I don't know where she is. I would tell you. You know how it is—a twin bond. It was like I was amputated. For the longest time, I could still feel her. But like with everything, time took even that away from me," Tara sounds depressed.

Bridget moves uncomfortably, and says, "We're not identical twins."

As on cue, Maeve and Wes pass the door, cheerfully chatting. Maeve's musical voice pierces Bridget's heart. She had missed her sister a lot, but she's never been good at expressing her feelings, and she doesn't plan on starting now. She knows Maeve is angry with her—that's the price she paid for leaving.

"I told Maeve she could show Wes Seamus' atelier. He's welcome to use it," Tara offers.

"We're not staying," Bridget automatically answers.

"As you were saying." Her disbelieve shining through.

"I mean it. The police will keep on searching, and they will find clues that lead them to Lucy," says Bridget full of confidence, pushing the conversation back to the problem at hand.

"Lucy is not only powerful, but she's also brilliant. I'm sure she's aware."

"We'll see, but I can't leave Tom in an enchanted sleep, and I can't let them face Lucy on their own." Bridget shrugs it off.

"And what are you going to do? Your magic is rusty at best. She'll kill you," counters Tara, not sugarcoating it.

"Gee, Grandma, thanks for rubbing it in. That's why you should be honest with me." Irritated, she gets up and looms over Tara.

"You need to practice," adds Tara, unaffected by the waves of annoyance coming from Bridget. "Thanks, as if I hadn't figured that out yet." Of course, she knows she's outmatched. Tara is infuriating. She's not giving her anything. "I need help with the spell on Tom."

"Your mother should go with you, she's a very gifted spell maker."

"Hell, no!" Bridget loses her temper, and tries to find the right words. But they don't seem to want to form in her head. Instead she storms out of the room. The door bangs shut behind her. Tara looks at Seamus. "She'll come around."

Bridget charges into the kitchen, but comes to a grinding halt when she sees Maeve and Wes enjoying each other's company. Great. Just what she needs, her sister stealing her boyfriend. She doesn't stand a chance; Maeve is like a siren. Men always have preferred her over Bridget. The soft touch, the melodic voice, she's toast.

"B!" Wes gives her a full-on smile. But Bridget is unable to deal with it now, the pressure of Tom, the investigation, her grandmother, she needs to get some air. Without a word, she turns around, the dogs already by her side. "I'm taking the dogs out."

"I already did that," says Wes. "Why don't you join us?"

Maeve put a hand on his arm. "Bridget needs a minute alone."

Bridget glances over her shoulder while she leaves and zeros in on Maeve's hand. Maeve snatches it back.

Cal stands in the clearing in the back and stares at the beautifully carved door to the tomb. His wand is casually stuck in his back pocket, and he looks again at his phone with Lucy's explicit instructions. Yes, this is it. He should look for the fire sign, get in, and steal a book. His nausea is back. He felt better in his hotel in the French Quarter, but his upset stomach makes it hard to concentrate. Slowly, he approaches the door. If it's that important, there must be some sort of protection set up. He freezes, did he hear anything? He scans the trees around him, but there's nothing. If his Grandma saw him now, he would get a tongue lashing for stalling. He inches forward, some tingling travels up his leg. Here it is. He feels the air, no, it's not an invisible wall or force field. He sniffs, nothing that seems out of the ordinary, the fragrances are always overpowering in New Orleans. He grabs the wand out of his pocket, points it ahead of him and whispers out loud, *"Palam animun dulcedine, quam mihi, volo ut videam quid hic."* Show the spell, show me how. I want to see what's here.

"What do you think you're doing!" Bridget's voice rings through the clearing. Without hesitation, he spins around and slings a knockback spell. Bridget goes flying and lands 10 feet further down on her back. The dogs charge at Cal. He turns around and runs as fast as he can, but Moon is on him within seconds. Bridget scrambles up and heads straight for him. Cal holds the tip of the wand against the chest of Moon, who has pinned him to the ground. He starts to mumble a spell.

Bridget shouts, "Moon, here!" Immediately the dog lets go and moves toward her.

Cal gets to his feet, his eyes fixed on Bridget and Moon. For a short moment nobody moves, then Cal sets off again. Bridget follows with the dogs, but his long legs and fear are spurring him forward, he clears the fence in no time and runs down the street. Bridget and the dogs can only watch him disappear around the corner.

Diane seems to materialize next to Bridget. "Who's that?"

"An intruder," Bridget grimly replies.

"Shit." Diane frowns.

"Yes, let's inform the others." Bridget looks at Diane—she looks exhausted. "Are you okay?"

"Not really, I'm afraid we'll all have to live with the consequences of what I have done." Diane sounds resigned.

Bridget has no comfort to offer, she's full of doubts herself. She has trouble enough facing her own problems. This is all very unsettling.

At the edge of the garden district, Cal finally stops running. Damn it. Lucy will be pissed. His phone rings. Lucy. He hesitates, but he knows she won't give up. He pushes answer.

"You messed it up didn't you?!" A wave of anger comes from the phone.

"They saw me." He whispers.

She doesn't need to say anything, it's like the phone is dripping with contempt. "Come home." Click. He looks at the sky. Why, oh why can he never catch a break?

Bridget runs to the house and bursts through the door. "Gran! Gran!"

Tara emerges from the kitchen on her heels followed by Maeve.

"A man was trying to get into the tomb."

"What?!" Tara is shocked, "Somebody was on our property?"

"Yes. He surprised me and used a knockback spell," Bridget explains.

Tara's critical looks say it all.

"Yes, I know." She's giving Tara no chance to respond.

"Let's check the wards." Tara signals the girls to follow her.

Tara feels the door of the tomb, she closes her eyes and mumbles under her breath. Maeve and Bridget wait in silence. Finally, Tara turns around. "I don't think he got in."

"That's what I said. He didn't get that far. We should improve the security," Bridget's urges.

"I just had some basic wards set, I never dreamed somebody would try to get in."

Bridget can't conceal her irritation. "Times are changing, Grandma. we need to do something about it."

"Right, but you're not much help with that. So why don't you go to the house, Maeve and I will take care of this." It is as if Tara slapped Bridget in the face. Maeve reaches out automatically, trying to smooth things over, but Bridget backs away and stalks off. "Oh Gran, that was not very subtle."

"She said it herself, times are changing and we don't have time for niceties anymore." Tara shrugs it off.

Maeve sighs "Where do we start?"

"Let's go in and see what the book can offer." The women disappear into the tomb.

Bridget makes her way through the trees, slowly calming down, more upset with herself then Tara. Grandma is right; she is of no use. What was she thinking? By ignoring her magic, she's in deep shit now. Tom is in a coma! She could have prevented that, and that man would never have gotten away. She needs to brush up her skills and fast, but whom can she ask? Her family passes before her eyes, nobody seems even remotely workable. Hold on, she flips the images back in her head, and one face remains—Ceri. This makes her smile, definitely not your obvious choice, but . . . it could work. Her cell phone rings. It's the Captain.

"Madigan." Her heart beats faster. "Is Tom awake?"

"No, I'm sorry. Still no change." His concern is obvious. "We have a lead. We did find a fingerprint on the belt of the victim."

"Did you get a hit?" Bridget has mixed feelings—if it's Lucy, she needs to head back asap. It would be good and bad.

"We did, her name is Lucy Lockwood, she was arrested once in 1963," the captain continues.

"'63? How old is she?" Bridget asks with trepidation. This must be gran's twin.

"Seventy-five. That's the only thing that doesn't make sense, but it's the only lead we have."

That's it. It's her! "I'm coming back," she says without hesitation.

"Don't worry, Hayes and Connor will go and see her," he dismisses that idea.

"Can they wait for me?" asks Bridget desperately.

"You're not on the case, I just called you because I know you're worried. Stay in New Orleans, I'll call you when I know more." He hangs up—the Captain has never been one for goodbyes. Damn, she better get going.

Bridget finds Wes in Seamus' atelier. He doesn't hear her come in, as he is sketching away on a big piece of paper. The inspiration is showing. For a little while she admires him working. It helps her focus. "You seem fired up."

His hand stops, he turns and gives Bridget his lovely smile. She loves how this makes her warm and fuzzy. "It's such a wonderful space. I don't know, it feels like things are flowing here." He says enthusiastically.

Feeling nostalgic, she takes another look around, "Seamus was a special person; you would have loved him. I'm sorry to disturb you, but I need to head back to Boston."

Wes' face falls. "Really?"

"Yes, they found a clue, and I want to be there when they're confronting Lucy. With the magic—it's too dangerous." She doesn't need to explain anything more.

Wes looks around the room. "Will you be back here?"

"No doubt, I didn't get very far with Grandma." She's clearly unhappy about that.

"Would you—would you mind if I stay?" Wes stumbles.

"What?!" She must have misunderstood. Stay! This must be Maeve's doing. Anger boils up in her and before it erupts, she manages to squash it down again. She gives Wes a wry smile.

Wes moves uncomfortably. "I was in a bit of a slump. I admit. But look at this." He points at the painting he started, "I don't know, but I haven't been so motivated. It flows out of me right now. I know it's important that you go back, but this is important to me."

Bridget can't deny this is the best she had ever seen of his work.

"I would like to ride the flow," he stresses.

Bridget shakes it off. She wants the best for him, she should say she understands. But it costs her an enormous amount of effort to say, "Of course, sweetie, I'm sure Tara and Maeve will be happy to have you around. I promise to be back soon." She looks around at all the dogs. "Would you mind keeping the dogs? I will take Kiki, as she can be in my hand luggage."

Wes's face lights up, and undoubtedly relieved, he hugs Bridget. "You know I love the dogs. Hurry back, okay. Are you leaving now?"

"I will take the first available flight," she confirms.

Tara and Maeve finally arrive back at the house. They're satisfied with the new wards. *The Book of Shadows* had some excellent suggestions. They also decided to work on the property's wards, better safe than sorry. Maeve is dripping with sweat; spellwork is intense. She points at Bridget's bags, and says, "She's leaving."

"That was to be expected." Tara follows Maeve into the kitchen.

Bridget is on her laptop booking a flight. "Did it work?"

"Much better now." Tara lowers herself in a chair, and Maeve immediately puts a pitcher of water out.

"Good. I'm heading back in a couple of hours. There has been a development." Bridget explains, "You must be extra careful. Do you mind if Wes stays? He loves it here, and it helps his art."

"Of course, darling. He's always welcome. Did you let Luna know? You're giving her very little notice," Tara casually replies.

Bridget's head snaps up and her icy stare would make any normal person uncomfortable.

Tara stiffly gets up and walks over. She grabs her granddaughter's shoulders and turns Bridget toward her, forcing Bridget to look her in the eye. Tara gently brushes some strands of hair out of her face. She grabs Bridget's face in between both her hands and says quietly, "Don't let your pride get the better of you. Use your brain and not always your heart. What do you prefer? Tom in a coma? Or spend a couple of maybe not so fun days with your Mom. Luna is the best, if you want a chance at waking him, she's it. Grow up." Tara gently places a kiss on both her cheeks. "Safe journey, sweetheart. Come back soon. We'll take care of your boyfriend." She leaves the kitchen and Maeve pretends to be busy. Bridget lets it sink in for a minute. Is she too proud? She wants nothing more than to wake up Tom. So, if that means she has to suck it up and spend some time with her Mom, so be it. It will be worth it.

Meanwhile, Diane is lying down on her couch. The curtains are drawn, and she's tired. She wishes she could turn off the visions, the feelings. Sleeping pills, drugs—nothing helps. The scar tissue on her wrist even reminds her of her botched suicide attempt. If it wasn't for Alice, she would try again. It's so hard. Why did the Goddess put this burden on her? Her mind starts to drift. No. She pinches herself and tries to stay awake. *Don't go to sleep. Don't go to sleep*, she repeats to herself. You can try to resist the vision, but in the end, it will come, whether you want it to or not. Unable to fight it any longer, she slips into—

People are running and screaming through the streets of a small village, while trucks, cars, and houses are getting sucked into the vortex of a tornado. They are powerless against its destructive path. It ravages through town while they run for their lives. On the hilltop, Lucy holds the Dagger of Consciousness. An exhilarating smile on her lips, power flows around her and when she points the Dagger again, a new tornado sprouts from the ground. People scamper and run in yet another direction. A roof flies off an old mansion, which morphs into the Madigans' house.

Tara or maybe it's Lucy is sitting at the kitchen table, and Seamus' art is scattered all over it. His lively images seem to move, and the vibrant colors jump off the work. Hands sort through the images of the family and stop when they reach Bridget—the old hand caresses the picture.

Again, the vison changes, it morphs to Bridget walking in Boston. She shudders and looks behind her. Nothing. Quickly, she resumes her course when again she feels something. She whips around this time, still nothing. She fingers the amulet Tara had given her. Would it still work?

Back in the kitchen, the hand circles her index finger, a little funnel seems to disappear into the card.

A small tornado on its side reaches for Bridget. She turns and sees it; she tries to run, but the funnel sucks her in. She is lifted from the ground and slung into traffic. Cars come to a screeching halt.

Tara makes her way through the house. Little Lisa, Ron's daughter, who is only five, plays in the living room. Tara walks over and gives her a wand. It's Seamus' special wand, not only made from birch wood but it has blue crystals woven through the wood. Lisa is thrilled, and Tara whispers something in her ear, making Lisa giggle. With a snap of Tara's fingers, sparks come from the tip of the wand. Lisa is enthralled, dancing around the room waving the wand, some sparks hit the curtains and instantly catch fire. Satisfied, Tara walks away while her face turns into Lucy's. The subtle changes from sweet Grandma to wicked witch. Lisa's giggles turn into screams. Maeve runs into the room; it's ablaze. She can barely grab Lisa and make it out. The flames spread so quickly, not even magic can save the house. The whole house goes up in flames!

Diane gasps for air while she snaps out of her vision. Horror and shock cross her face. And then, she starts to shake uncontrollably.

Seven of Wands

PART 3

SEVEN OF WANDS "STRUGGLE"

"If there is no struggle, there is no progress."

—FREDERICK DOUGLASS

NEW ORLEANS

Bridget's T-shirt sticks to her back. She had forgotten about the warm and humid weather, and the constant sweating. Kiki hangs comfortably from a tote around Bridget's shoulder while they stand in front of a cheerful pink door. It has a friendly and inviting feel to it; flower baskets hang next to the door, the porch swing moves gently in the breeze. Bridget still can't get herself to knock on the door. For the hundredth time, she goes through all the options in her head; this really seems the only reasonable choice. She must get a move on; her flight leaves in two hours. She's cutting it short as it is. Self-doubt is not typical behavior for her.

The door swings open and Ceri smiles at Bridget. "Come in! You have been standing there now long enough." Bridget follows her aunt inside. The hallway opens up into a bright, cozy kitchen with all the modern comforts. You instantly know a witch lives here. Although, it's not as prominent as the family home.

No doubt Ceri has lots of normal friends with her fun personality. It's not always wise to flaunt your knowledge.

Bridget glances around. "Where are the kids?"

"Teenagers are so busy these days." Ceri rolls her eyes. "Liam has a soccer game today, and Emily is spending the night at a friend's house."

"I can't believe they're all grown up already!"

"Time goes too fast. But I doubt you stopped by to see the kids. What's up?" Ceri answers, attuned to the uncomfortable vibes coming off Bridget.

She puts her bag down and busies herself with Kiki, avoiding the question.

Ceri lets the silence stretch deliberately, until Bridget blurts, "I need help."

A compassionate smile forms on Ceri's face. "It's hard admitting you need help, isn't it?"

"I'm not good at this. My magic sucks and I need some sort of crash course. Could you help me?" Now it's out in the open, it's easier for Bridget to come to the point.

"Why not Luna? Or Maeve?" Her aunt's mild town is deceptive.

"Really?! I might as well ask Aunt Freya!" Bridget snaps back.

"I see, I'm your only choice, that's not very flattering."

Bridget moves uncomfortably. "That's not what I meant."

"I bet you didn't. What makes you think I'm any good at magic? I'm generally not highly regarded in the family." A hint of disappointment crosses Ceri's face, but she hides it quickly under her ever-sunny smile.

"Are you kidding? You're lit. The only family member to make the papers. Racing a motorcycle on your broom. It's fabulous." Admiration shines through her words.

"Ha! You're probably the only who thinks that." Ceri holds her hand up and feels the air around Bridget, she moves up and down about twelve inches from her body. "You have plenty of magic, which is no surprise as you're Luna's daughter. Your aura doesn't feel very healthy though. I guess that's because you've been denying your magic."

"So, will you do it?" Bridget is desperate.

"Why don't you sit down for a minute?" Ceri offers her a chair and a bottle of water. "I'll do it." Bridget sighs in relief. "Thank you!"

"Don't thank me yet. I'm a big believer in the trial and error approach." With a big smile, Ceri plops in the chair opposite Bridget and drinks from her water bottle.

Bridget starts to scoot in her chair. It feels like a wet spot begins to grow on her back.

"You need to improve your senses." Her aunt goes on.

"They're pretty good, I'm a fine detective." Bridget is quick to reply.

"All your senses. Your magic needs to become an automatic response. You're always too late if you have to think about it. That's why Freya always has such trouble. She's not really in touch with her feelings," Ceri muses.

Bridget is now positive that the spot on her back is growing, she reaches on her back, touching something slimy. She jumps up and turns around. "Do I have something on my back?"

"Yes, and it's growing. What are you going to do about it?" A twinkle in Ceri's eye betrays she's enjoying this.

"What do you mean?! What is it?" Alarmed, she tries to reach it with her hands.

"Lesson number one." Ceri leans back in her chair.

Bridget becomes irritated. "Stop it!" The spot quickly grows and all but covers her back, it slowly makes its way over her shoulders.

"I would stop whining and feel what kind of spell this is." Her aunt suggests mildly.

Bridget tries to fight through her anger and frustration—this is apparently what she asked for. What the hell is she going to learn from this?! She desperately tries to quiet her mind. The spot in the meantime covers her torso and drips down to her legs and starts to inch up.

"It's pretty harmless, but a bit disgusting if it covers your face. No pressure," says Ceri while she tries her best to suppress a smile.

Bridget could strangle that serene face, but instead, she tries to feel the spell. It's almost at her mouth and another wave of panic hits her. Stop it! She needs to focus; where is the spell? What is its origin? With her witch eye, she spots a tiny flower stuck on her back. With a flash, she remembers Ceri touching her back when she urges her to sit down. The slime now almost covers her head. Somehow it doesn't smother her, but it sure is disgusting. She focuses on the flower and tunes everything out; she can actually see some sort of structure. Ceri leans forward as she sees Bridget is finally latching on to the spell. Bridget wedges an imaginary finger between the knot that binds the spell together and gives it a good tug. Nothing happens.

"It would be nice if it was that easy. Can you hurry up? You're messing up my kitchen."

Bridget tries again, this time she doesn't try to think, but let the words flow naturally.

"Unbind, unwind, set me free." SNAP! The spell is broken.

"That took you long enough. You need to react instantly, so be prepared. I will send you spells, and you have to break them." Ceri instructs her. "Your reaction and senses need to be improved a lot. And I mean A LOT."

Bridget looks miserable, totally covered in dripping slime.

"You can use the bathroom down the hall. I will bring you some clothes. This is horrible to get off." Ceri can't hide her obvious delight with the situation. "We're going to have so much fun!" Bridget shoots her a look that says clearly otherwise.

"Here is an amulet; you need to wear it at all times. It will allow us to communicate. If you take it off, you can find yourself another teacher." Ceri hands her an amulet that looks like a wheel on a leather cord. "You better hurry, your flight leaves soon. You don't want to be late."

Bridget is cursing in the shower while trying to clean off the goo. It's horrendous! What was she thinking?! She thought Ceri would get a book or something. Her aunt is crazy. But there is no escape now.

BOSTON

In the meantime, Bridget's colleagues, Detective Hayes and Detective Connor, are walking down a street looking for Lucy's home. Detective Hayes is a weathered female cop—she isn't known for her patience. And Connor sure knows how to push her buttons. Connor is not a fan of Bridget after she rejected his advances. "Something is not right with Bridget. That story of how Tom got injured doesn't add up."

"You're only saying that because she didn't want you." Hayes tries to steer clear of gossip.

"That's a clear sign. Mark my words—"

"We're here," interrupts Hayes.

They look at the charming old Boston home. The little garden is full of cheerful flowers, the house is small, but cute and inviting. Soft classical music drifts through the open window, the laced curtains blow softly in the wind. They can't help but smile.

Lucy quietly watches the detectives, standing a little back, so they can't see her from the streets. She smiles when she sees that they're enamored with her house, the spells are working. Lucy checks her own appearance in the mirror—she looks like an adorable old lady. Everything you imagine about a loving grandma is coming through in her image. Her gray hair is pulled back in a loose knot at the back of her neck, some gray locks flow freely around her weathered face, softening her features. Her fashion choice is complimenting her disguise, something she usually wouldn't want to be seen in. Too many flowers and too frumpy, but it's perfect for the occasion. She grabs her witch staff and gives it a little shake; it morphs into a walking cane. She's ready when the detectives knock on the door.

Hayes gives another firm knock, and soon they hear the shuffling of feet.

"Who's there?" sounds a brittle voice.

"Police, ma'am. Can you let us in? We have some questions."

Lucy peeks through the curtains of the window next to the door. The detectives flash their badges. They hear her open multiple locks before slowly opening it.

Lucy gives them her sweetest smile. "Can I help you, officers?"

Hayes and Connor hide their surprise, not expecting this fragile looking old lady. "I'm Detective Hayes, and this is Detective Connor."

"Oh sorry, detectives, I mean." She puts some extra weight on her cane.

Hayes notices and says, "Sorry Mrs. Lockwood, we have some questions. Do you mind if we come in? Then you can sit down."

"That is so considerate of you, dear. I mean, Detective Hayes. Please do come in." Lucy shuffles down the hallway. Hayes and Connor slowly follow while they take in the house. It's dimly lit, and it smells slightly musky. The walls are filled with family pictures; old and newer ones, some hunting paintings, and a painting of what looks like a younger Lucy.

"Shall we sit in the parlor?" asks Lucy.

"Sounds good, Mrs. Lockwood." Hayes looks at Connor. It's hard to believe this elderly lady is a murderer. Let alone that she could be physically capable of it. Connor shrugs.

Lucy leads them into the sitting room. Like the hallway, it's everything you would expect from a charming old lady. Frilly and out of date, even a little dusty, as she's apparently not capable of keeping up with such a house. "Please sit." She motions to the couch and Hayes and Connor oblige. Hayes notices there is already a steaming pot of tea on the table with cups as if she was expecting them. She shakes it off—that's not possible. Mrs. Lockwood probably always has extra cups out; in case she gets any visitors.

"Can I offer you some delicious herb tea?"

"No, thank you," say Hayes and Connor at the same time.

"Are you sure? It's lovely herb tea, good for the soul." Lucy again throws them her best smile. Just to get the thing going, Hayes agrees, and Connor takes the lead in the questions. "Mrs. Lockwood, can you tell us where you were Sunday night?"

"I was here, dear. I don't go out at night, too dangerous. Why?" She hands Hayes her cup, Lucy's hands are slightly shaking. Hayes grabs the cup and smells it. Lucy smiles encouragingly.

"A local woman has been murdered, Alana Jannson, do you know her?"

"Oh my God." Shocked, Lucy claps her hands in front of her mouth and tears form in her eyes. "No. I can't believe it. I just saw her."

"I'm sorry, Mrs. Lockwood, you know her?" Connor wants her to elaborate.

"Yes. Such a dear sweet girl, she regularly stops in for a cup of tea. She doesn't forget the elderly like most people do these days." Tears now freely flow down Lucy's cheeks.

"When did you last see her?" Connor sits a little forward.

Hayes adds, "Are you okay? Can I get you anything? A glass of water?"

"No, no. I'll be fine," sniffles Lucy She's impressed with herself—what a performance! Giving herself a mental shake to make sure she doesn't fall out of her role. "Don't worry, drink your tea." Lucy manages a watery smile. "She was here, in that very spot." She points at the spot where Connor sits. "Sunday afternoon. We had a lovely discussion about herbal teas. She was very accomplished in herbal remedies. Did you know that?"

Connor shakes his head.

"Now, she's gone." Lucy stares out of the window, taking a moment to collect herself before she turns back to the detectives, just as Hayes takes a sip of her tea. Her eyes twinkle for a second, before quickly suppressing it. Looking shaken again, she leaves her own tea untouched. "If there is anything I can do?"

"Thank you, Mrs. Lockwood, You've answered all our questions," says Hayes, as she gets up. Connor doesn't understand; he has more questions. One look from Hayes and he snaps his mouth shut. "Thank you for your time. We're sorry to bring you this bad news." Lucy tries to get up, but Hayes puts a gentle hand on Lucy's fragile shoulder. "Don't worry, we'll find our own way out. Don't forget to lock up."

"Thank you, Detective," sniffles Lucy. She keeps her head down and waits till she hears the door shut behind them. Her old lady routine seems to melt away and her wicked self emerges. She throws her head back and laughs. Oh, that felt good. She has been operating in the shadows far too long. This is the most fun she has had in years.

NEW ORLEANS

Bridget rushes through the airport. Thankfully, it's small because she's running out of time. She already got a text from Luna asking her where the hell she was as boarding has started. TSA always takes longer than you expect; these people never seem to understand when you're in a hurry. And then there was Kiki, always ready to be difficult when it's most inconvenient. Chihuahuas are notorious nippers and Kiki is no exception. When the TSA officer tried to pet her, she bit her, and that set off a whole train of misery. It took all her charm and persuasive skills to get past that. Thanks, Kiki. Quickly she glances at the signs—Gate C5, which way? There it is! She run-walks over, and it looks like she's the last one to go in. Luckily, she couldn't get two seats together on the flight so she will have some time to relax before she has to deal with Luna. "I'm sorry I'm late," she says, while she hands the ground flight attendant her ticket.

"No problem, we're almost ready, so if you find your seat, we will still be able to leave on time." Bridget smiles and hurries toward the plane. She moves through the aisle looking for her seat 18D; Luna waves her over. Bridget glances back—no it's for her. She looks up, yes 18D. The seat is next to Luna's seat.

"That nice lady offered to change seats when she heard we were mother and daughter." Luna motions to a sweet old lady two rows behind.

Bridget gives her a wry smile. "Great," she says, putting the bag with Kiki at her feet and gently letting herself slide into the seat. "So generous of her." Gosh, this promises to be a long flight.

Meanwhile, Tara is airing and cleaning up her room. She feels much better today. Maybe it's her confession to her family, which is a weight off her heart, but it might also be that the house is livelier. Wes and the dogs brighten up the place. The pattering of the dogs' feet on the wooden floors, and the erratic energy of an artist. How she had missed that, she hadn't realized that until now. Of course, she appreciates Maeve living with her, but Maeve generally is pretty private and doesn't buzz up the place. Without realizing it, her family spends less and less time at the house. It used to be full of grandchildren, and this would be everybody's weekend hangout. When did that stop happening? Something to work on; they will need each other now that Lucy has one of the elemental objects. She highly doubts this will be the end of that.

"Luna and Bridget are on their way to Boston together. That has disaster written all over it. You might wonder why I suggested that," she says to Seamus, who startles awake in his portrait. "I know in my heart they need to heal. And what better way than to be forced to spend time together." Seamus gives a doubtful look. "Thanks for the support, honey." She rolls her eyes at him and walks over to her altar. She grabs the Seven of Pentacles and slides it back in her deck. Time to shuffle the cards and see what's up. She fans the cards and her left hand slides over them. This one. It feels right, slowly she takes it out and turns it around. Another seven, the Seven of Wands. A cat knocks over one of the wands on a checkerboard. He's in a losing position but determined not to give up. Time for action, fighting against all odds. Actually, a hopeful card, even though things look grim, there is a chance to come out on top. "See," she turns the card to show it to Seamus. "I'm right about sending the girls together to Boston." Seamus still looks pretty skeptical. "Things will work out. They have to."

BOSTON

Bridget parks her car in the hospital parking lot. They had made a quick stop at her house. Luna took in every detail, and it made Bridget very uncomfortable. Since the plane, she has been repeating in her head. *It's for Tom. It's for Tom.* Now it's time to see if Luna is as good as everybody seems to think. They get out.

Bridget grabs Kiki and puts her on the inside of her jacket with a firm, "Stay quiet." Kiki rolls up and is invisible. Luna follows it with interest. Bridget can't help herself, "What?!"

"I didn't know you could talk to animals." Luna is intrigued.

"I can't, I'm just good with dogs." Bridget dismisses it, not wanting to think about that.

"She really understands you." Of course, Luna doesn't take the hint.

"You can't talk with animals." Her gruff answer should shut her mother up this time.

"Keep denying it, honey, it will bite you in the ass, eventually." Luna swings her massive blond locks over her shoulders and walks toward the entrance as if she knows where she's going. Bridget grumbles, but she can't help but think about all the times she has calmed down dogs or asked something of them. They always respond, she never realized it was a gift. And not the least, a magical one. Damn, she has been such a fool to believe there was no magic in her life. It's all painfully clear now. No need to rub it in though. Irritated, she catches up with Luna. "It's this way."

Now Luna follows Bridget through the endless corridors of the hospital. Finally, they reach Tom's door, a nurse just steps out.

"How is he doing? Any changes?" Bridget is eager for some good news.

"No, I'm sorry, he's fine, but still in a coma. We're unable to find anything."

"Thank you." The nurse disappears down the hall. Bridget and Luna go into the room. Bridget tries to hide her feelings of overwhelming sadness when she sees Tom. He looks so small in the bed. And to think she could have prevented it. It makes her sick to her stomach. Luna doesn't say anything, but she stands close and lays a gentle arm over Bridget's shoulder. They stand there for a minute. Luna lowers her shield and takes in the atmosphere of the room. For a brief moment, they really feel like mother and daughter. Bridget clears her throat and straightens herself, walking away from Luna's reach.

"Luna, this is Tom. Tom, this is my mother, Luna." They always say that you can still hear when you're in a coma, so Bridget feels it is best to introduce her. "She has special gifts, and she will make you better." She turns to Luna. "I felt the spell, it seems to cling to his chest in the area of his heart." She motions above Tom's chest.

Luna takes a position opposite Bridget, she holds both of her hands above the area her daughter had indicated. The door opens, and she snaps her hands back to her side.

It's the nurse. "Sorry, it's time to change his urine bottle."

"Oh." Luna looks down. The bottle hangs close to her leg, almost full. "Please, go ahead."

The nurse is quick and efficient, nobody says anything. There's an awkward silence until a soft click signals the nurse is gone.

Luna snaps back into action, closing her eyes, and mumbling under her breath. Bridget could swear she could see Luna's hair move. She tries to concentrate on what Luna's doing. Time to learn something. Her mother uses her fingers to feel the strings and edge of the spell; to Bridget, it looks like a messed-up ball of wool.

Slowly Luna looks up. "This will take a while to unwind. There are many strings, and if I pull the wrong one, he very well could end up in a real coma."

"But you can do it?" Bridget can't hide her eagerness.

"I can, but I need time. I need to form a bond, so he feels grounded."

Bridget could hug her mother right now, but thankfully, she's on the other side of the bed, and manages to keep a blank face. She merely says, "Thank you."

"You're very welcome, but you can thank me when he wakes up. Now, do you have something else to do?" Luna picks up Tom's hand.

Bridget's hackles stand up in a reflex. Her mother touching Tom's hand triggers something in her. Not happy to leave her mother alone with Tom, she suggests, "I can help."

"Please, honey, you must give me room to do this. It's tedious, I can't have you breathing down my neck." Luna gently puts Tom's hand back down.

Reluctantly Bridget grumbles, "Fine. I'll be at the station. If you need anything, you can call me."

"Thanks." But Luna's attention is already on Tom. Bridget leaves her. Luna breathes a sigh of relief. This spell is a work of art and will take all her skills to unravel. She pulls up a chair and reaches for Tom's hand again. Step one is to get to know the victim and for him to get to know her. They might not be able to communicate through speech, but there are other ways. Gently she starts to massage his hand while she softly sings a lullaby.

Bridget manages to secure a parking spot close to the police station and the minute she gets out, rain pours down on her. Surprised, she looks around. It seems sunny. This makes no sense. Within seconds, she's drenched, and when she looks up, it's like a tiny cloud hanging above her head. Shit. This must be Ceri's doing! What is she thinking?! This will attract attention. When she looks around, people are already pointing at her. Great. She wants to rip off the amulet around her neck—this will all be over. The stone is warm, she lifts it up to give it a tug, hesitates, and let it fall out of her hand. *Stop being a pussy and do something.* She scolds herself. Otherwise, she will never learn. In the meantime, she's wet to the bone, so it doesn't matter anymore. Bridget closes her eyes and feels the spell. The rain goes faster and faster. Right . . . a smile forms on her face and she recites while she waves her finger. "Umbrella makes me happy and keeps me dry, *so et voilà.* " An invisible umbrella appears above her head. The rain stops falling on her. It doesn't stop the actual rain, it flows around her and sure doesn't help at all as it continues to attract people's attention. She steps forward and the cloud follows her. *Okay. Stop whining and do something! This is what you asked for, remember. Feel the spell.* Bridget is recalling what Luna did. As inconspicuously as possible she raises her hands and tries to feel the spell. It only seems to be two strands, so much easier than the one Luna's facing. She gives a good yank. Nothing happens, while the crowd around her is growing. Time to hurry up, no time for subtlety. She raises her arms, feels deep within and imagines herself pulling the spell apart. With her imagination, she sees it happening. When she opens her eyes, the sun shines on her once again. People around her cheer. She makes a mock bow and rushes into the police station.

Ping. She glances at her phone. "Too long!"

What is Ceri thinking?! "I attracted a crowd!"

"Better be quicker next time then. Use those senses." Gosh! Maybe she should have asked Freya instead. Stuffing her cell phone back in her pocket, she marches into the station.

"Gee Madigan! What happened to you?" shouts her friend Carla from behind the front desk.

"Don't mention it." Bridget's scowl would deter anybody.

Carla is not discouraged so easily. "Good to see you're back. How is Tom doing? Any news?"

This softens her a bit. "No. Nothing. I just came from the hospital. Anything up here?"

"I heard there was a lead . . . " Carla nods her head toward the stairs.

"Thanks. We'll talk soon okay." Her earlier irritation about Ceri is disappearing to the background.

"Time for some margaritas!"

Bridget blows her a kiss and walks up the stairs.

Cal sees a parking spot right in front of Lucy's home. This must be a good omen. Maybe his Grandma will go easy on him. The house is back to normal, stark and uninviting, no longer a cute cottage. He walks up to the door and is about to knock when the door is pulled open. Lucy quickly glances up and down the street and pulls Cal inside.

"For once you have perfect timing. The cops have been here; we have to leave."

"What do you mean?" Cal looks bewildered at the suitcases by the door.

Lucy pushes him toward the stairs down to her dungeon. "We need to pack the last things from my workspace, and then we head for Ti'tsa-pa house."

"We're going to Utah?" Cal is not a fan of that house. It's built on the crossing of ley lines, and its suffocating vibes give him nightmares. Lucy has taken extraordinary care in constructing that place.

"Hold this." Lucy hands him a box and immediately piles in skulls, candles, books, scrolls, feathers, whatever she can get her hands on. "Go get the Explorer and start loading up. We're leaving within the hour."

"What about this house?" Cal has a sinking feeling he will not come back.

"I'll take care of that. Hurry! I'm sure they'll be back. Probably sooner than we want." Lucy wants to add her small personal book of dark spells to the box, but it's already overflowing. Absentmindedly she lays it on a little ledge. She grabs the next box and starts to fill that up with witch paraphernalia from the table. Her hand caresses the table's scary looking legs made of twisted bodies, she's going to miss that. It has a lot of souls in it, and it was one of her first dabbles in dark magic. Ah well, it's a small price to pay if all her plans work out.

Luna takes her time studying the spell. The construction of a spell takes patience, and this one definitely had taken skill and precision to construct. Its weaving is complicated, and she is looking forward to taking it apart. Spells have always fascinated her—because of that and her natural talent, she became the family's spell weaver. You don't have to be a gifted witch to be good at making spells, but it certainly helps and gives the spell just that extra touch of magic, making it special, like her cocktails—never failing to lift up the mood of the crowd. Magical abilities run strong in the Madigan family; they all have powerful gifts, which is unusual in witch families these days. That it turns out that they are the keeper of a unique magical object doesn't surprise Luna. When she was young, other witches would already whisper around her about how exceptional she was, and talk about how it might be dangerous. And they would talk about how Tara and Seamus shouldn't have been allowed to marry since they're both from long lines of powerful witches. She never felt very different or powerful growing up. She always wondered how witches measured strength. Now she knew. If you see another witch, you can feel it. It's hard to describe. Maybe the closest is the amount of water that flows down a waterfall. It can be a gentle drip, or it can be a gushing stream. She's a gushing stream and so is Bridget, not as strong as her—not yet. If she would only embrace her powers. Tara is strong, but when you get older, it is as if the stream is widening, the force is diminished. And her sister Ceri is powerful, but she seems to want to hide it or not to take it seriously, it's hard to figure her out.

Anyway, she will need all her skills right now if she wants to save this man. The first step is forming a bond, so unconsciously, he will be drawn to her. She caresses his face and familiarizes herself with his features, his sharp nose, his full mouth. Her finger goes back and forth over his bottom lip. She can't help but smile—this man feels good. He seems like a good man. The spell is humming— very good, that means what's she's doing now is influencing the spell. Her hands travel down his chest, she plays with his chest hair on the spot where the spell is connected. It almost feels like angry needles pierce the skin of her hand if she lingers on that spot. Her hands travel down his legs, she grabs a chair and massages his feet. For a moment, she could swear she saw him smile. Not only perfect to make a connection but also good for the blood flow and possible blood clots. While she massages his feet, she thinks about some things she will need. Should she ask Bridget where she can find a good herbal shop? Probably not the best idea, better to Google it. She'll need some Siberian ginseng, some milk-vetch, lemon verbena, and rosemary for sure. Other things will come to her. Okay, time to get moving. Slowly she pulls the sheet back over Tom, and for a second, she glances around the room as if to make sure she's alone. Then she bends forward and very slowly gives him a tender kiss and whispers, "Come back to me." The room is shrinking and expanding a bit. And so it begins, the unraveling of the spell. Satisfied, Luna grabs her bag and throws it over her shoulder as she leaves the room.

Bridget is turning all sorts of green while she's still waiting outside the Captain's office. He was not pleased to see her! He's letting her wait. Not her strong point. At least, she's starting to dry up a bit. She doesn't know what she will say anyway. What can she do? The truth is not an option. She can only hope the evidence is clear and then, she needs to be there when they confront Lucy. The voices of Hayes and Connor startle her from her reverie.

She jumps up. "Did you go and see Mrs. Lockwood?"

Connor smiles when he takes in her disheveled state, and says, "We did."

"And?!" Bridget can't hide her anxiousness.

Connor checks to see if the Captain has seen them, but he has his back to them. "It wasn't her."

"WHAT?!" Bridget tries to control herself, and asks, "Why not? Her DNA . . . "

Hayes steps in, and says, "She was an old lady. I don't think she would be able to do it physically. Such a gentle soul."

"Everybody is capable if they want to," replies Bridget full of fire. This can't be happening.

"You didn't see her, old and walking with a cane, and she offered us tea." It is as if she slapped Bridget, who stumbles back. Damn it, why didn't she use her senses! She regains her composure and opens her witch senses. Shit. Lucy got to Hayes. Connor looks clean. Hayes seems to have some sort of weaving around her. Like a warm, fuzzy blanket. It doesn't look as complicated as Tom's spell, still . . . Bridget gently tugs it, but it tightens, and Hayes immediately turns restless.

"Come Connor." To Bridget, "don't tell the Captain we told you."

"Thanks. I won't, I appreciate you filling me in. Tom . . . You know, it's hard."

In a rare display of feeling, Connor gives her shoulder a comforting squeeze.

Bridget sags back into the chair. Her problems had just gotten bigger.

"Madigan!" Bridget jumps back up. "Come in."

Great, more misery to come, no doubt.

"I guess that Hayes and Connor filled you in." Bridget tries to come up with an excuse, but the Captain holds up his hand. "Forget it, I know they did. What are you doing back? I told you to stay away."

"I can help. I saw that woman too. Hayes and Connor must have spoken to somebody else or something. I'm positive it was her, Captain." Bridget tries to convince him.

"You're biased. It's an old picture, who knows what she looks like now. When Tom comes out of his coma, and he picks her picture out of a series, then we will know for sure."

"I know for sure!" Why won't he listen to her?

The captain rumbles, "Madigan."

That one word should have silenced her, but she knows precisely what Lucy looks like. Frustrated, she tries a different angle. "There is aging software."

"How did you think I became Captain? Of course, we're working on that. Go home. Go visit Tom. I don't want to see you here. Am I making myself clear?" He's done with her.

"Yes, Sir." Bridget gets up.

When she's at the door, the Captain adds, "I mean it."

Bridget gives him her sweetest smile. Which unfortunately is nothing like Maeve's. How she wishes she had some of her sister's charm right now. It would have come in handy.

Lucy stands in the hallway and takes one last look at her house. It has always been her preferred place to live. Boston's history makes it a city with lots of energy for witches to tap into. And her dungeon, as she likes to call it, was her favorite place to work in. These Madigans are messing things up for her. Ah well, they'll get what they deserve soon enough. It's not reasonable to expect that her plan would be without sacrifices. Unconsciously, she touches the Dagger, which is safely attached to her waist belt. Time to get this baby to work. Ti'tsa-pa house is unusual in a whole different way and very useful for the rest of her plan. The ley lines give that place a tremendous boost. A laugh escapes her—"Come on you Madigans, show me what you've got." With her wand, she touches the wall. A spiderweb of lines light up, and the house buzzes for a second. Cal walks in and wants to go upstairs. Lucy puts a hand on his chest and stops him, just in time before he steps on one of the activated lines. "Too late, you can't go into the house anymore."

"But I want to get a couple of more things." He tries to move past her.

"You should have thought of that sooner; the house is charged." She blocks him.

Cal's face falls.

"You can buy it. Let's go!" Lucy gently pushes him out the door and closes the door but doesn't bother locking it. *"Adieu, mon ami,"* she says and blows the house a kiss.

A little later, Bridget and Kiki stand in front of Lucy's home. The house is gray, dark, and uninviting. She can't believe that Hayes and Connor thought Lucy was sweet, even they should have picked up these vibes. Lucy must have disguised the house with a spell. Not anymore, Lucy is gone. No doubt about that, she actually used her witch sense to double-check.

Luna walks up and stands next to her facing the house. "She's gone."

Voicing out loud what Bridget just had been thinking, she says, "I know, we're too late."

"It's probably better, this way she can't hurt more normals. Do you want to go inside?" Luna asks, full of anticipation.

"I can't. I'll lose my job." Bridget doesn't look happy about that.

"Nobody needs to know," Luna tries.

"I said NO!" says Bridget, with maybe a bit too much force.

Luna holds up her hands and does a little step back.

"How did you find me?" She wants to know.

"I'm your mother, and I'm a witch."

Luna always knows how to make Bridget feel inadequate. If she hadn't denied her witch powers, she wouldn't have asked such a stupid question. Bridget easily fills in what is unsaid. Ignoring her feelings, she asks instead. "Is Tom awake?"

Luna holds up her bag full of herbs and other witch supplies. "Working on it."

"What now?"

"I need your kitchen. Let's go home." Luna tries to throw her arm over Bridget's shoulder, but she manages to step out of reach without it being too awkward.

NEW ORLEANS

Maeve, Tara, and Wes are drinking sparkling wine at the kitchen table. Soft music is playing, and sunlight filters through the plants, giving the feeling the light is dancing to the music. The delicious smell of a roast fills the room. Ron, his wife Selma, and their kids Mike and Lisa—the youngest grandchildren—waltz into the kitchen. Selma, not a witch, is invaluable as she's the one keeping the Hat working smoothly. Ron kisses his mother's cheek, while Selma peeks into the oven. Maeve introduces the kids to Wes and laughter fills the kitchen.

Wes' cell phone rings, making him smile—it's Bridget. "Hi, honey!" Wes tries to hear what she's saying, but the happy noises around him make it hard. Maeve pulls the roast out of the oven. "Can I call you back? We're just about to eat." Lisa pulls at his wild curls. He laughs. "Love you." And he hangs up.

BOSTON

Bridget stares at her phone, feeling a bit jealous. Wes has way too much fun with her family. It worries her; their relationship is still young. Will it stand up to the charms of Maeve?

"Maeve would never steal your boyfriend," Luna interrupts her thoughts.

"Are you reading my mind?!" Bridget's eyes shoot daggers.

They're in Bridget's kitchen. She's watching her mother prepare a spell and make herb bags to take to Tom. She was hoping she could learn something.

"I don't need to read minds for that; your face says it all." Luna dismisses her irritated reply.

This annoys Bridget even more. She opens her mouth but snaps it shut and instead starts to repeat her mantra in her head. *It's for Tom, it's for Tom.* No use arguing with her mother. Better let her make that potion. Once Tom is awake, she can go home. Luna shrugs and concentrates on her herb potion.

It's later in the evening, and it's quiet at the hospital. Bridget brings Luna in through the back door. Full of confidence they walk through the hallway and just when they want to enter Tom's room, a nurse walks over. "Visiting hour is over, ladies. I'm sorry."

Luna turns to her and says with a dark tone in her voice. "We need to see him for the next two hours, please leave us alone. We'll call you if we need anything."

The nurse's face looks confused and then she says, "Okay, I'll be down the hall."

"Thank you," says Luna with a friendly smile.

This is precisely why Bridget thinks her mother is scary. Goosebumps run up her arms. She could have stopped it if she only knew another way to get rid of the nurse. It's wrong. Apparently, she will do anything to wake up Tom. Even let go of her principles.

"Don't look at me that way. Do you want to stand guard? Now we know for sure we will not be disturbed." Bridget shakes it off and follows Luna into the room.

"I can't convince you to wait outside?"

"Why? Something to hide?" Bridget's hostility is prevalent.

Luna sighs. "Please stop being so childish. It's complicated. It will require all my attention."

"I was hoping to learn something. You know my skills are very rusty." That is the right button to push. "Okay then, but not a word." Bridget makes a motion as if she zips up her lips.

Luna places eleven candles in a circle around Tom. One by one, she lights them while she invokes the elements to guard her circle. Bridget sits quietly in a chair in a corner of the room. On the nightstand, Luna places an incense burner and lights a sandalwood one for purification. She fills a cup with water, and holds a small ancient-looking knife. A witches athame, this one is made by Inuit people, from seal bone and skin. Bridget is now leaning forward as she feels the energy building within the circle. She opens her witch sight. Luna is almost pulsating with power. The spell on top of Tom's chest buzzes like an angry insect. Slowly Luna places the little bags with herbs on Tom's chakra points. She had pulled the sheet back, and he's only in his underwear. Slowly, she rubs him with a potent herbal scented oil. This surprises Bridget, and she wants to say something, but Luna puts her hand up without looking at her and continues to rub the lotion. Once she's done, she places a gentle kiss on Tom's lips.

Bridget can't help it. "What the hell!"

Luna ignores her and takes out her wand—it's made from willow wood with a lapis lazuli stone on the tip. Very slowly and extremely carefully, Luna uses her wand to unravel the fiery ball of tangled spell lines. A constant Latin counter spell rolls fluently over her lips. Bridget can't help but be impressed; her mother is really good at this. To see the lines, stay focused, the power that rolls off her is pretty amazing. Transfixed, she follows Luna's hands and before she knows it, two hours are gone. The spell is now just a tiny ball with its line going straight into Tom's heart. He stirs but is still not awake. Bridget is fascinated and curious how her mother will dislodge that. Luna stops and takes her time to look at it from different angles. From her bag, she gets some balm of gilead and rosemary and rubs it together between her hands. Their fragrance fills the air, and slowly she brushes some on Tom's lips and on her own. Then her mother opens her mouth over what is left of the spell ball. It's like she's swallowing the spell. Slowly, like she's eating spaghetti, she follows the string to Tom's heart. Once her herb-infused lips cover his heart, his eyes fly open. Bridget jumps up and has to use all her restraint not to smudge the circle. Slowly Tom looks down at Luna's smiling face. Her head is resting on his bare chest. They smile at each other. Bridget scrapes her throat, and that seems to break the connection between Tom and Luna. Luna gets up. Tom looks around in confusion. "Who are you? What's this? Bridget?"

Luna grabs Tom's hand, "Calm down, we're here to help you. You've been sick. I'm Bridget's Mom. I'm an herbal healer, and she asked me to come, as conventional medicine wasn't able to help you. Welcome back." Luna quickly and efficiently deactivates the circle and starts to gather her materials.

Bridget now moves up to Tom's side. "Glad to have you back. You worried us."

"What happened? How long have I been out?" He feels his stubble.

"For several days. Let me get you a nurse." Bridget walks out to find a nurse.

Luna wants to leave quietly, but Tom reaches for her. She walks back and takes his hand. "I don't know what you did." He says, "You talked to me, while I was sleeping." Luna only smiles. "Thank you."

"You're very welcome." The nurse comes in. Reluctantly, he lets Luna's hand go. The nurse takes control. "You shouldn't be here. Please give us some room to work."

"Of course, sorry. See you tomorrow, Tom. So glad you're back!" Luna and Bridget leave, while the nurse checks his vitals.

In the parking lot, Bridget takes Luna by surprise when she envelops her in a hug. "Thank you. Thank you. This means a lot to me."

"You're welcome." Bridget lets Luna go and seems to snap back into her normal mode.

"What was that shit with all the kissing and stuff?!"

"Sexual attraction is a potent tool. I needed to make a connection with Tom to be able to pull him loose. As he apparently doesn't have somebody special in his life, I needed to be that someone to be able to break free," Luna patiently explains.

"You seemed happy enough to do it," Bridget sulks.

Luna laughs, "You're such a prude."

Bridget says something, but no sound seems to come out of her mouth. She tries again. And again. What the hell? Luna snaps her fingers.

"What the hell?!" shouts Bridget.

Ping. Luna's phone gets a text message. "Stop helping her."

"You asked Ceri's help?" Luna agrees but hides her approval because that would otherwise be the end of it. Out of all her sisters, Ceri is an interesting choice.

"That's none of your business," snaps Bridget.

Luna texts back, "Got it." With a smiley face.

Bridget walks to the car.

ON THE ROAD

Lucy wakes up in the Renaissance Hotel in Albany, NY. She had a wild dream and something is nagging at her. They didn't get far yesterday. After a three-hour drive, she was tired. It's not something she likes to admit, but she definitely feels her seventy-five years. One of the reasons she didn't wait any longer with her plans, otherwise she wouldn't have any time to enjoy her new powers. Time to wake up her idiotic grandson; she's ready to make some miles today. All dressed and ready to go, she wants to check something in her personal dark spellbook. If she remembers correctly, they'll pass an excellent supply shop today. There are not many around that live up to her standards, so when the opportunity arises to visit the shop in person instead of ordering online—it's a rare opportunity she doesn't want to miss. In her imagination, she already let her hands explore the rare magical items. Quickly she digs into her purse. The spellbook is not there! Where did she leave that damn book? Frantically, she searches in her suitcase. Not there either. Maybe in one of the boxes? Then it hits her—a flashback that she had put it on a little ledge in her dungeon. Oh no! So stupid! They must go back. There's years and years of research and knowledge in there. She closes her suitcase and is already on the phone to Cal. "We've got to go. NOW!"

BOSTON

In the meantime, Bridget is back with Tom at the hospital. It's so good to see his smile; he looks all back to normal. "They'll let me go later today. They don't understand it, but I'm tired of tests. I feel great. I'm ready to go after that wicked witch."

"The Captain put Hayes and Connor on the case." Her tone tells him what she thinks about that.

"I know, I know." He appeases her, "They were just here and showed me some pictures. I immediately picked that woman's—Lockwood is her name—picture out of the others. I'll never forget those eyes."

Bridget is concerned. "What are they going to do?"

"They said she was such a sweet old lady." He doesn't understand how they could think that.

"I told them they were probably played. There was nothing sweet about her when we met her." Bridget confirms this. "Are they getting a warrant?"

"I think they're going to pick her up on the way back to the station. I have to get out of here. I want to be there when they question her." He's eager to get to the bottom of this.

"You take it easy. I'm on it." Bridget is already at the door and waves at him. "I'll keep you posted."

Bridget looks at Hayes and Connor arguing in front of Lucy's house. Every now and then, she catches some words, but she can't follow their conversation. Finally, it dawns on Bridget. She can be so stupid. 'Use your senses.' She points her finger at them and recites, "Oh dear Goddess, I want to hear. Bring these voices near." She puts her intent in it and all of a sudden, it's like she's standing right next to them.

"This can't be it," says Hayes.

"It's the right address." Connor double-checks his phone.

Bridget smiles—why hadn't she done this before?!

"It looks totally different. Do you think we went to the wrong house yesterday?" Hayes says, doubting herself.

"No, I don't. This makes no sense. She also said her name was Lockwood." Even Connor sounds doubtful.

Hayes looks around, Bridget takes a step back into the shade of a tree.

"I don't like it. Let's hope she's home, this time we'll take her to the station." Connor is already on his way to the door. He rings the bell. Nothing happens.

"Please let her be home," mumbles Hayes.

Connor bangs on the door this time. "Mrs. Lockwood! Police—open up!"

The house is very quiet.

"Damn it. Let's get a warrant." Connor gives one last bang on the door. "The Captain will not be happy."

They head back to their car. Bridget makes another move with her hand and the spell snaps.

"So good to see you're finally using your talents."

Bridget gives a little jump. "Stop doing that."

Luna stands right next to her. "You shouldn't lose sight of your surroundings."

"Right." Bridget tries to squash her irritation. She needs Luna's help again. Pretty sad she will owe her mother big time. "I see you got the message."

"I'm always up for something fun." Luna is ready for some action.

"I'm not sure if fun is the right word." Bridget doesn't like the feeling of this. But she doesn't see any other choice. Once the police go in with their warrant, all the witch-related things will be ignored. It's their only hope. And they have to be quick, the others will be back soon enough.

ON THE ROAD

"Faster!" Lucy urges Cal on. She has a bad feeling about this. Hopefully, the police hasn't gone into the house yet. She would be so upset if she lost the book. Cal drives far over the speed limit. He knows that if Lucy wants something this bad, he'd better not mess it up. That will mean a week of punishment at least. He shudders at the thought of that and doubles his effort to stay focused. His witch senses are heightened, and he weaves through traffic with a formula one precision. "We'll be there soon, Grandma."

BOSTON

Bridget scans the surroundings. "Maybe we should try to get in through the back."

"Makes sense." Luna motions her to go first. They make their way to the little alleyway next to the house. A solid door blocks their entry into the yard. Bridget gets out her tools to break in, but Luna reaches past her, puts her hand on the lock and says simply "Open!" It clicks open.

Bridget can't hide her scowl.

"You should try it sometimes," winks Luna.

Bridget pushes the door open and is ready to step in, when Luna grabs her arm and pulls her back, "This is a witch's garden, not something to enter lightly."

Damn it, she can be so stupid, this time she motions for her mother to go first.

Luna throws her arms wide, and it's as a wave pulses from her. Sure enough, sparks light up the garden. It's protected. "Do you want to take care of this?" motions Luna.

"No. Go ahead. I don't want to mess it up." Bridget has no idea where to start.

"Try it. No pain, no gain. How do you expect to sharpen your skills?" Luna doesn't give up.

"We don't have time for me to fiddle around. The police could show up with a warrant anytime. Now hurry up."

"As you wish." Luna closes her eyes and it looks like she's drawing power from the earth. Bridget follows her movements closely. Now she sees her mother using the available energy around her. For a moment, she forgets to watch the alley and is fascinated by the grace of the weaving that Luna is making. Her mom is a formidable witch. She seems to use the plants in the garden to dismantle the security. Bridget would have never thought of that. Slowly the tension level in the garden subsides, and Luna nods that they can go in.

This garden is very different from Tara's garden. It feels as if the plants are reaching for you; it's not as tranquil as she would expect. They walk over a small path that seems to wind through the whole garden. Even Bridget recognizes some very toxic plants, and there are way more insects than usual. A colossal spider has made a web between two trees; centipedes, potato bugs, roaches, you name it, quickly scurry away. Finally, the path opens up and reveals the back door. Luna steps aside, Bridget feels the door—it's open. A musky smell comes from inside the house. For a moment, they get that fuzzy, sweet old lady feeling. Bridget shakes it off; this must be a remnant of a spell used on Hayes and Connor. Very carefully, she opens the door, and draws her wand from her back pocket. A small, satisfied smile plays over Luna's lips. Bridget doesn't step inside, but she touches the wall with her wand and asks with her inner voice, "Is it open? Is it safe? Can we pass in the Goddess' name?" As if she flipped a switch, the whole house lights up. Bright red angry lines travel all through the house.

Luna peeks over her shoulder. "Well, that will be a challenge."

"Can you deactivate that?" Bridget doesn't think they could maneuver in between the lines.

"No, it's too complex. It would take days."

"We don't have days. So, this is it?"

Luna rolls her eyes. "How did you ever become a detective? Don't give up so easily. There is always a way."

"I'm not giving up. But if we can't defuse it, what will happen when the police arrive and set it off." Bridget absentmindedly plays with the two amulets around her neck.

Luna touches the one Tara gave her. "That might work." She gives Bridget a little push into the path of the first angry red line.

"Hey! What the hell are you doing?" Frantically, she wants to step back, but the line seems to flow around the shield and stay connected. She freezes.

"Sometimes it's best not to overthink it," is Luna's deadpan reply.

Bridget gives her mother another killer look. "What about you?"

Luna smiles and pulls a similar amulet from her pocket. "What kind of witch would I be if I showed up unprepared?" Again, she knows to hit her daughter where it hurts. It takes everything Bridget has to let this slide and focus on why they are here. The earlier awe she felt for her mother is gone like a puff of smoke. She can't wait for Luna to go back to New Orleans.

"Let's get this over with," she says instead.

"Do you want to split up?" Luna is eager to explore the house.

Bridget shakes her head. "It feels too easy. Let us stick together."

The house is quiet; the musky smell hangs throughout the house, but now that they're aware of the effect, it doesn't touch them anymore. The interior is stark and modern, nothing cozy about it. The gray blinds are shut, and the little light that filters through makes the house feel spooky. Vampires are the first thing that comes to mind as they wander through the empty rooms with designer furniture. There's nothing personal on the wall and nothing witch-related. There must be something; this lady didn't cook up her spells on that twenty thousand-dollar couch. Luna motions Bridget over to the hallway—there is a door that Bridget hadn't seen earlier.

"It had a spell on it," whispers Luna.

Bridget grumbles, she has to use her senses. Right. They make their way down the stairs; it's pitch-black down here. Bridget gets her flashlight out and almost screams when she finds herself face to face with a goat skull. So much for being a tough detective. Luna suppresses a laugh behind her. It keeps getting worse and worse. All sorts of animal skulls are hanging from the ceiling. Rows of shelves are fitted along the walls and hold every dark witch necessity that you can think of and then some more. The place has been emptied in a hurry, but there's still plenty left behind. Intrigued, they walk along the shelves and stop and stare at various curious items. But nothing is as scary as the table that dominates the middle of the room. The legs of the table are wood carvings of humans in the most horrific poses. They look tortured and screaming. It's like she can actually hear their voices. The images are so life-like; Bridget could swear they are moving. When Luna touches the table, a yelp escapes her. Blisters form on her hand. "Oh my God, this is awful."

Bridget reaches for her mother. "Are you okay?"

For once, Luna seems lost for words. A tear escapes her. "I think . . . I think . . . there are souls in there."

"What?!" Horror shows on Bridget's face. "Are you sure?"

"We need to try to free them. These . . . these people have been tortured for a long time. We can't leave them like this." Luna looks around for something to help her do that.

Cal and Lucy stop in front of the house. "We're too late. Somebody is in the house."

Cal looks around but doesn't see anything. "I don't see anybody."

"I can feel it." Lucy throws the door open, right when Connor parks his car in front of the house.

"Shit! Grandma, get back in." Lucy shuts the car door, while Cal takes off at what he hopes is an inconspicuous speed. In his rear-view mirror, he sees Connor getting out. "What do we do now?"

Lucy glances back. "Loop around the block and park across the street, maybe we'll get a chance to slip in unnoticed. A pity it's not the female detective."

Connor stands in front of the house. This whole case makes his hair stand up in the back of his neck. Hayes is not herself. While she was busy getting a warrant, he thought he would do some more investigating himself. It all seems to start here, at the creepy house.

Bridget and Luna hear banging on the door.

"We're out of time, the police are here, we have to go." Bridget can't wait to get out of this depressing basement.

"I need to do this, you go." Luna rushes past the shelves and quickly grabs some herbs, candles, and feathers. "Go! I can do this." She starts to put the candles in the four corners, with a snap of her fingers, she activates a circle. It's not the way to do it, but it in a pinch it works. She rushes around the table while sprinkling salt around it and starts an incantation in a language Bridget hasn't heard before. It sounds ancient. The table responds. It bulges and swells. Luna is hyper-focused. Bridget feels useless and goes to the bottom of the stairs. It's quiet now. Maybe it was just the mailman or something. "Hurry up!"

But Luna is in a trance and doesn't hear her. She waves with the feathers and her incantation reaches a high. A loud boom. The whole house rocks on its foundations; the souls escape in a funnel of light. Searching for a way out; the whirlwind of souls rushes up the stairs, knocking Bridget over. Then it blows out the windows and the front door. It throws Connor off his feet. One soul hovers in front of Luna. It seems to say thank you while tears stream down her face. And then it evaporates into the air. Bridget and Luna scramble up. For a moment, it's eerily quiet. Then Bridget hears somebody shouting something. It's Connor calling for backup. He draws his gun and carefully approaches the house. Luna stares at the table—it exploded from the inside out. Wood splinters are stuck in everything; she even picks some out of her cheek. A small drop of blood starts to flow down. Bridget quickly looks around and notices a small dark booklet on a ledge. On impulse, she puts it in her pocket. There is no place to hide, so Bridget rushes up the stairs and drags Luna up behind her.

Lucy's anger rolls out of her in waves. Somebody set her souls free—all that hard work wasted. It also shorted her wards. This is infuriating. From her car, she sees the chaos. A police car comes charging around the corner, with the siren screaming. Connor slowly approaches the house with his gun drawn. She can't imagine it's the work of that ignorant girl, that granddaughter of Tara. It's clear she doesn't have the skills, so does that mean Tara is in the house? It would be typically something that she would do. Bleeding heart. Cal starts the car.

"Wait," says Lucy, "I want to see which witch did this."

Cal turns off the car again and stays quiet.

Connor looks around in the hallway when Bridget comes up the stairs followed by Luna. Reflexively, he points his gun out at Bridget. "Freeze!"

"Wow! Connor, it's me." Confusion washes over his face when he recognizes Bridget. "Madigan? What the hell did you do?"

Bridget minds races. She can't tell him they freed souls. "We must have triggered some device."

"What are you doing here?! And who's that? Is there anybody else in the house?" Connor frantically looks around and points his gun at Luna.

More police cars stop in front of the house and they hear them shouting outside.

"She's my Mom. You can put your gun down. There's nobody else here." Bridget calms him down.

"ALL CLEAR!" Connor shouts to the police outside.

One of them takes a peek through the broken window. "You're sure?"

"Let's do a sweep to double-check." To Bridget, he says, "You have a lot of explaining to do. Trespassing. Interfering with an investigation. What a mess! Did you at least find anything?" Bridget shrugs. "Take a look down below. This Granny was into some weird shit."

Connor looks at the stairs, and says, "Let's take a look."

Bridget follows him down, while she says to her mother, "Wait outside. Don't talk to anyone."

A police officer escorts her out. "Follow me, Ma'am. We need to have you checked out."

Luna only now realizes blood is still flowing down her face. "Don't worry, I'm fine." She fishes a handkerchief from her pocket and pushes it against her cheek.

Connor takes in the devastation in the basement. "What the hell happened here?"

Absentmindedly, Bridget fingers the little book she found inside. No need to mention that to Connor. "I don't know. The table exploded—it must have had some sort of explosive attached."

"You've been lucky." Connor's eyes glance over all the wooden pieces stuck in the walls.

Outside, Lucy looks at Luna and instantly recognizes another powerful witch. Next to her, Cal gasps "Wow, Grandma, she must be family." Luna resembles Tara, and of course, also Lucy.

"Yes, she is. Did you see her when you were in New Orleans?"

"No, I would have remembered." Cal is sure.

Lucy throws out a little probe with an almost careless flick of her wrist.

Instantly, Luna turns around and zones in on Lucy, walking to the car.

"Drive!" Lucy orders, Cal starts the car and speeds away.

Luna waves frantically to Bridget, who just steps outside. "It was her!"

When the car rushes around the corner, it gets hit by a spell. The car bounces and swirls but manages to make the turn and disappears. Bridget is ready to give her mother a tongue lash, but Luna is scanning around and zones in on a couple across the street. Bridget follows her gaze and recognizes Gwen. "Damn." Quickly, she crosses the street. Gwen and the unknown young man hesitate and decide to stay put. Luna is right behind her daughter as magic is involved, she better make sure to have her back.

"Gwen. What are you doing here?" demands Bridget.

"Do you think we would sit at home and let the police handle this? We're here to get our property back." Gwen's hostility is palpable.

"It's not here," says Luna. Gwen cocks her head and Luna feels a gentle caress over her aura. How rude. She doesn't hesitate to return the gesture. This witch is airy, like the Madigans are fire-y.

Bridget steps between the two women. "You shouldn't be here. We'll handle this. It's a police investigation and this is an active crime scene."

Dripping with sarcasm, the young man chimes in, "You and your Mom. Police investigation, my ass. You want it for yourself." Gwen puts her hand on his arm, and he falls quiet.

"We know how important it is to you. You have to trust us and let us handle this." Bridget tries to persuade her.

Gwen can't hide her skepticism "You promise to give it back?"

"Madigan!" Connor joins them not pleased with her. "What are you doing?"

Bridget answers smoothly, "We hoped they might have seen the license plate of the car."

"We did," says Gwen, "The number is NW7834."

"Thank you," Connor waves over a police officer. "Please give him your statement."

Bridget and Luna take the opportunity to quietly move away.

"Do you promise?" whispers Gwen's voice in her head while she walks away. Bridget pretends she didn't hear that.

This is apparently the day to get shouted at. The Captain is exploding, his face turning bright red, and the spray of saliva coming from his mouth fascinates Bridget. She has never seen him so angry. "What the hell do you think you were doing?! Interfering in an investigation. Losing a suspect."

Bridget opens her mouth—

"Don't! There is nothing you can say right now that I want to hear. This is such a mess. Taking your mother to a suspect's house?! I gave you the benefit of the doubt. Not anymore, you're suspended. Give me your badge."

"But Sir?!" She's shocked.

"GIVE ME YOUR BADGE!" he booms.

Slowly Bridget gets her badge and gun out. This hurts much more than she ever thought it could.

"What now?"

"Now you go home and cool off. First, we are going to get to the bottom of this case. Then we'll see what we will do with you."

Bridget sputters, but the Captain silences her. "Go! I don't want to see you." He turns his back on her. She's dismissed.

A million thoughts race through Bridget's head while she steps out of the captain's office. Time to find her mom. She scratches her leg; just what she needs—a stupid itch. Luna leans on the corner of Tom's desk, staring at a picture of Tom as if she's a million miles away. What is going on? Is it a by-product of the spell? Gosh, now the itch is on her back. She tries to reach the spot, but her arms are too short. Finally, a doorpost provides some relief. She scratches her back along the edge of the doorframe. Ahhhh, much better. She walks over to Luna. "Come, Luna, we need to go."

"Yes, we need to see Tom," her mother says.

"Why? He's healed, he will be out of the hospital soon enough." She doesn't want to waste any time on that.

"He's been through a trauma. Do you want to have him sort this out by himself? We used magic. We need to help him make sense of this all." Luna's lecturing tone is back.

The itch has moved to her arm. She scratches vigorously but all her attention is on her mom. Unconsciously, she mumbles a spell, "Itch go away, I don't need you today. Let me be, so mote it be." The itch vanishes.

Bridget weighs her options; her mother might be right. "Okay. Let's see how he's doing and we can give him an update. Or something. We need to get our story straight."

Ping. A text message from Ceri: "Much better! Keep it up."

Well, that's the only positive so far. For the first time, she reacted.

Lucy and Cal have changed cars and are restlessly waiting across the street until the police are finally gone from the house. It's dark, now is their best chance.

Lucy is already by the door, Cal rushes to keep up. Lucy feels the air, but only humans have been here recently. Impatiently she opens the door and without hesitation goes down the stairs. Her whole basement is empty. The police have taken everything. Those witches messed up her plan. Everything should have burned down. She needs her little book back. "We must go to the police station."

"We can't break in there." Cal senses that his grandmother is upset.

"We're witches." Lucy can no longer contain her anger and lashes out with her wand, and the now lifeless table catches fire. "Let's go." The fire starts to spread while they walk out. Even before they drive off, the first flames are visible behind the windows. Lucy doesn't look back.

Four of Pentacles

PART 4

FOUR OF PENTACLES "PROTECTION"

"Your silence will not protect you"

—AUDRE LORDE

NEW ORLEANS

The early morning sun washes over the Madigans' garden. Tara watches from her windowsill. The birds are awake; the bees are buzzing and gathering their nectar from the abundance of flowers in the yard. For a couple more minutes, she lets the sun rays warm her old bones. The last couple of days have been invigorating with the house coming back to life. Ever since Seamus has passed away, it seems that the heart of the family has been ripped out. He was the driving force, the glue that kept them all together. His energy, artistic visions, and colorful character were intoxicating. Now it appears that her granddaughter has brought home such a man. Wes's view of the world, his whirlwind personality lights up the house. Maeve is coming out of her shell, and the others are stopping by more often. Strange how one person can have such a positive impact. Bridget probably doesn't realize what a special person she has found. Like Tara never fully appreciated Seamus. Slowly she turns to his portrait. "Did

I take you for granted?" Seamus gives her a tender smile, which seems to tell her not to take it so hard. "Right. Let us see what the day will bring." She grabs the card from her altar, puts it back in the deck, shuffles, and fans the cards. Her left hand keeps moving back and forth. This one! She pulls the Four of Pentacles; her face falls. A possum fiercely protects his pentacles. The miser, what is she overprotecting? What is she holding onto too tight? With a sigh, she puts it on her altar. Again she glances at Seamus. "I know; it could be much worse. Not a great card, but definitely not a bad one either."

Anyway, she has been indulging herself long enough. Luna and Bridget had been to Lucy's home, and now Bridget has been suspended. Tara has no doubt they will show up soon, and that means peaceful times are going to be over. She playfully throws a bright colored shawl over her shoulders. "Time for breakfast." Seamus blows her a kiss.

BOSTON

Bridget's face feels wet, for a moment, she panics and scans around for a spell, but it's only Kiki waking her up with wet doggy kisses. Slowly she rolls over, grabs her watch. What?! Ten o' clock already, she can't remember ever sleeping this late in the last couple of years. The smell of fresh ground coffee urges her on, time to get her ass moving. Quickly, she put on some sweats and a T-shirt. This must be the only positive of having her mother here—a good breakfast. She freezes in the door opening when she sees Tom sitting at the kitchen table chatting with Luna as if they're old friends. "Hey, sleepy head. Glad you could join us." Luna gets up, fills a cup of coffee for her. Bridget plops down on a chair next to Tom. "They let you out?"

"Finally." Tom wastes no time and comes to business. "They're gone. They've changed cars. The Explorer was burned out under an overpass."

"What else could they find about her?" Bridget sips her coffee.

"Very little. Lucy must use a different identity or something. Really, she's a ghost." Tom is not happy.

Bridget puts her coffee down, ready for action. "What are we going to do?"

Tom gives Bridget a stern look. "You? Absolutely nothing. Don't make it any worse. Let me handle this, and you'll be back on the job in no time."

"I can't do nothing." Bridget looks a bit lost.

"Spend some time with your mom. I can't believe we've never met before."

Luna gives him a warm smile. Bridget is seriously creeped out by their obvious attraction.

"Mom," warns Bridget. She manages to put all her frustration in the one word.

Tom senses the tension. "I'm getting out of here. See what I can find out. At least I'm not yet *persona non grata*."

Before Luna can say anything, Bridget steps between them. "I'll walk you out. You be careful, all right? We've just got you back." She jabs him playfully.

"Don't worry about me. You be nice to your mother."

Bridget rolls her eyes at him, and says, "Get out of here."

She goes to her bedroom, before heading back to the kitchen. Somehow she had forgotten to take a look at the little book she had taken last night. Quickly she searches through the pockets of her coat that was thrown on the floor, and fishes out Lucy's dark spellbook. An unpleasant feeling emanates from it. Bridget hadn't noticed it in the dungeon, but now it feels almost dirty. Like she wants to wash her hands. Carefully she opens it. It's full of scribbles, drawings, and God knows what. That almost looks like a piece of human skin. Hesitant, she smells it. Oh dear, this book is evil, she just knows it. Firmly she closes it and takes it to the kitchen.

Luna is doing the dishes; her kitchen has never been so clean.

"Mom, you should take a look at this." Bridget holds out the little book.

Luna reaches for it.

"I took it from Lucy's house. It doesn't feel right. I think it's dark magic," Bridget adds.

This makes Luna cautious; she expands her senses. Bridget is absolutely right; this doesn't contain anything positive. Her hand hovers above it before opening it.

"I swear there is a piece of skin in it. And some other things I don't care to identify."

Luna goes through it. "Well done, honey. This looks like a spellbook. It's probably hers. Look." Luna points at a spell and says, "It says this is for some sort of rash."

"I don't think we should touch it. You should take it to grandma."

"Maybe we can use this against her."

Bridget looks skeptical. "You always say you shouldn't meddle with things that we don't understand."

"We could learn a lot." The unknown knowledge is tempting Luna.

"What about the threefold rule?" Bridget cautions her.

"We don't have to use it, to know what kind of spells she's capable of doing could help us prepare." Her mother brushes it off.

Bridget doesn't like it. "She's evil!"

Luna is impatient. "You should stop using the words 'good' and 'evil.' It's childish. Nothing is black and white. This is a great find. We should use it."

"Let's talk to grandma about it."

"Great. Like she tells us everything." Luna puts the booklet in her pocket.

"What are you doing?" Bridget is wary. She doesn't know a lot about magic, but doesn't black magic taint your soul? Better keep an eye on Luna. "You should go back to New Orleans. Nothing you can do here."

Luna sizes her up. "Are you coming too?"

"I think I'll stay and see what I can find out here."

"Fine. I'll give Wes a kiss from you." Luna smiles innocently. Bridget knows she's being manipulated, but she can't help imagining Maeve and Wes smiling at each other. Damn it. She sighs. "I'll come along."

Hayes stands in line at Starbucks. It's busy, and an old lady in front of her takes her sweet time ordering. She has the nagging feeling that she has seen the woman before but can't place her. Lucy has clouded herself in a disguising spell, which is a sort of deflection and far from perfect disguise. The tea that Lucy gave Hayes makes her susceptible to Lucy's wishes, but if Hayes would really recognize Lucy, she might still arrest her.

So far so good. Lucy gives her a sweet smile and moves over to the side to wait for her drink. Hayes is quick with ordering her skinny latte and stands next to Lucy. The barista is busy; nobody pays any attention to them. Lucy circles her walking stick and whispers in Hayes' ear. "Go find my spell book. A little black pocketbook, it looks very worn down. When you find it, bring it to me." Hayes shakes her head; it feels as if a fly buzzed in her ear. She glances to her side, but Lucy has distanced herself. Again Hayes feels that she looks familiar.

"Skinny latte," calls the barista. This snaps Hayes out of it. She grabs the coffee and heads to the station.

Tom sits behind his desk at the police headquarters, staring at his computer screen. The Captain told him to go home, but that doesn't appeal to him. There's nothing for him there except an empty house. He's been divorced now for so many years, but this is the first time he hates it that he's alone. If he only could remember what that old lady had thrown at his chest. Unconsciously, he puts his hand on the spot the spell was connected to.

"There's nothing wrong with you, sir," he hears the doctor tell him. Well, they're wrong. You don't end up in a coma for nothing. Quickly, he types Lockwood in the database, and the old picture of Lucy's arrest pops up. Those eyes, there's something about those eyes. When he closes his eyes, it's all he sees. That's maybe not entirely true, they sometimes morph into the eyes of that sassy mom of Bridget's. He can't believe she never talked about her. It's obvious there is a lot of tension between them. But he feels drawn to her. She's not only beautiful, but she seems to understand him like no other woman ever has. Bridget told him she's some sort of gifted herbal healer and that she managed to pull him out of his coma. The doctors were extremely skeptical about that, but he knows deep down there is truth in her words.

"Walsh?" Tom gets startled and almost knocks over a cup of coffee on his desk.

"Jesus, Tom. Are you okay?" Connor puts a hand on his shoulder.

He shrugs it off. Time to get a grip on himself—this is ridiculous. "What's up?"

"Have you seen Hayes?" Connor scans the room again.

"She came by maybe a half an hour ago, I think she was on her way to the evidence room."

"Okay, thanks. Good to have you back man."

Tom smiles. "Do you mind if I tag along? I'm getting a little stir crazy here."

"Ha! No kidding." Connor checks if he spots the Captain, when he's not in his office he shrugs, "Why not . . . "

Tom follows Connor down the hall, taking the elevator to the basement. Which is full of endless rows of shelves with boxes. The air feels oppressive, fluorescent lights and the dusty smell are no help with that. This is Sergeant Blake's home. He's rail-thin and reminds you of the Grim Reaper. His pasty complexion comes from spending days in the basement. A grated fence keeps anybody from entering without the Sergeant's approval. He sits behind his desk seemingly busy, but his face lights up with a big smile when Tom and Connor arrive. "Gentlemen, what can I help you with today?"

Connor steps forward, "is Hayes here?"

"She is! In the back. She's going through the stuff that came in yesterday from that house. Spooky things in there." He whispers, unlocking the gate. "Glad to see you out and about, Walsh."

"Thanks." Tom gives him a small smile and follows Connor. He always gets slightly depressed when he moves between the rows of evidence—so many boxes filled with things gathered from violent crime scenes. Connor freezes, and Tom bumps into him. "Hey! What—"

Connor holds up his hand stopping Tom in midsentence. He points at Hayes. She's in a frenzy. The evidence is scattered on the table and on the floor. This is far from ordinary. She's usually so neat.

"It's not here. It's not here." She rambles, slinging some bags aside.

"Hayes?" says Connor "What's going on?"

"I need to find it. It's important." She goes on without acknowledging him.

"What are you talking about? Stop. You're messing up the evidence." Connor is irritated.

"It is here somewhere." She still ignores him.

Tom passes Connor, who seems frozen, and doesn't know what to do with his partner. He grabs her arms and turns her towards him. "Hayes. Hayes!"

Her eyes are glazed over, and it looks like nobody is home. Hayes shakes him off and is back searching through the mess. She's getting more and more agitated when she can't find what she's looking for.

Connor is getting very worried. "What are you looking for?"

"A little book. About this big." She holds a space of six inches between her thumb and index finger.

"Why are you looking for it? What's in it?" Connor tries a different approach.

"I don't know; I need to find it." She turns her back on him and searches on.

Tom gets an uneasy feeling in his stomach. Too much weird shit going on with this case. Maybe Luna would know what this means. He shakes his head; why does he think of her? Fuck it, thinks Tom, and he reaches for his cell phone.

Bridget and Luna drive to the airport in total silence, each immersed in their own thoughts, probably because they don't feel like talking. Bridget is irritated, and Luna has no patience to deal with that. Hence the no talking—something they can both agree upon. Luna's cell phone rings. "Tom?"

Bridget's head snaps around to Luna.

"I don't know. What is she doing?" Luna replies in response to whatever he's saying.

Bridget tries to listen in, but the noise of the car prevents her from hearing anything.

"We're on our way," Luna promises.

"Yeah, to the airport," adds Bridget, but her mother has already ended the conversation.

"Somebody is acting erratically at the station, Tom wonders if we would be able to help," Luna explains.

"We? You. He didn't call me." In spite of her irritation, she swings the car around and speeds to the station.

When she pulls up, Tom is pacing up and down the sidewalk. The women jump out.

"What's going on?!" demands Bridget.

Tom hesitates, he feels a bit silly now for calling. "It's Hayes, she's not herself. And because . . . you know. Because your Mom helped me, I thought..." he lets his voice trail and mumbles something under his breath.

Luna steps in. "Start at the beginning."

"Did you say Hayes?" Bridget feels a lump forming in her stomach. Shit. She had felt something, and she didn't do anything about it.

Luna zones in on Bridget. "Tom, can you give Bridget and me a minute?"

He's confused. "I'll wait here," he says, motioning vaguely to the front of the police station. He gets so awkward around Luna.

She gives him a warm smile before she turns an angry look at Bridget. "You knew."

If Bridget could get any smaller, she would—she wishes she could disappear entirely. This is her fault. She's been so stupid—again. "I felt something. I think Lucy cast a spell on her. Hayes mentioned Lucy gave her tea."

"Damn it, Bridget. This is not the time to be sloppy or hold grudges. You should have told me." Her mother's disappointment is evident.

Of course, Luna is right. She should have told her. To be treated like a ten-year-old, however, always makes her angry. She will not give her mother the satisfaction of agreeing. "Yes, I should have done something about it!" she hisses. "But I didn't. Happy? Let's do something about it now." Before Luna can answer, Bridget pivots and walks towards Tom. It takes all of Luna's self-restraint to stop herself from throttling her daughter.

"Where is she?" asks Bridget.

"She's gone. That's why I was outside. After I called, she went crazy and rushed out. We tried to stop her." Tom sounds bewildered.

Bridget looks up and down the streets, but doesn't see her. "Do you know where she went?"

Tom shrugs. "Connor tried to follow her, but she punched him right in the face. When he got back up, she was gone."

"Shit," says Bridget, full of passion.

"Yep. That pretty much sums it up," he agrees.

"**What** was she doing?" asks Luna as she steps between Tom and Bridget.

"She said she was looking for a little black book. About this big." Luna and Bridget exchange glances. It's Lucy's spellbook. Luna touches her purse; it's still there.

"And when she couldn't find it, she went crazy. Hell, Connor will have a shiner."

"I want to do that all the time," Bridget adds. Tom shoots her an exasperated look.

"We'd better change our flight." Bridget fishes her cell phone out to call the airline.

Lucy meets Hayes in an alley just down the road from the station. Cal is in the car around the corner, keeping an eye out. "Do you have it?" Lucy can't hide her urgency.

Hayes is still distraught. "It's not there."

"What?!" Lucy is furious.

"I'm sorry. I looked and looked. It's not there." Hayes wrings her hands and is clearly scared.

"You're absolutely sure?"

Hayes nods. Lucy's anger bubbles up, and she lashes out. A beam of light scorches Hayes' eyes. She screams and covers her eyes with her hands. "What is happening?!!"

Lucy turns and walks out of the alley, into the car. Cal speeds away.

Hayes screams and screams and stumbles out of the alley. People come running. Somebody calls 911 while another tries to see what's wrong with her eyes. "Please, Ma'am, let me see what's wrong." Slowly, Hayes lowers her hands. There are two black holes where her eyes used to be. Now, she's not the only one who screams.

Bridget, Luna, and Tom are running down the street when they hear the screams.

"Police, make room please," says Bridget, and Tom is already on his knees next to Hayes.

He slowly pulls down her hands from her face. "It's Tom. You're safe. Let me take a look, Hayes." They all look in horror at the black holes. Bridget's eyes fill up with tears. Oh no. This is so horrible. It's all her fault. She should have done something when she felt the spell, and now—now Hayes is paying for it. She looks at Luna and sees the accusation written all over her face. Her mother is clearly disappointed at Bridget's inability to act upon her magic. "Don't say a word." Bridget turns and rushes around the corner before she bursts into tears. She's overwhelmed with guilt.

Luna snaps into action. "Did somebody call an ambulance?"

A red-headed woman replies, "They're on their way."

Luna takes over from Tom. "Detective Hayes, I'm Luna, Bridget's Mom. I'm here with you till the ambulance can take you to the hospital. Can you tell me what happened?"

Hayes hiccups and tries to say something through her panic. "I . . . I don't remember anything. What's wrong with my eyes. Where am I?"

"Try to breathe, in and out, in and out. We are outside close to the police station. You need to try to calm down."

"I can't see." Hayes scared words pierce Luna's heart. She feels for spells and recognizes a thin web of something clinging around Hayes' head. Not as complicated as Tom's, but not something she can get rid of with a snap of the fingers.

The ambulance arrives and they quickly hurry Hayes to the hospital.

Bridget is in desperate need of some kind words, so she calls Wes.

"Wes' phone." The melodious voice of Maeve echoes through the phone. Bridget can barely swallow a sob. "Bridget? Are you okay?"

Things are getting worse by the minute. Why is Maeve picking up his phone? "Is Wes there?" she manages to say.

"He's painting and left his phone in the kitchen. I saw it was you. I felt... anyway, how are things there? Is Mom still alive?" A gentle laugh follows her joke. It actually pulls Bridget back from her self-pity. That never helped anybody. She needs to get a grip. "Mom has a new admirer—my partner Tom. It's a bit weird."

"You know how she is. She always attracts men, that hasn't changed."

"Yeah, you didn't get that from a stranger." Bridget curses herself, why on earth did she let that slip. It must be the shock.

An awkward silence follows, then Maeve softly says, "Wes is totally dedicated to you. You know that right?"

"Yes. Yes, of course. Please tell him I called." Bridget brushes it off, realizing she needs to get back to the problem at hand.

"I will. Weren't you coming home?" Maeve wants to know.

"We had to postpone our flight. We'll let you know when we know more." Bridget disconnects. Talking to her sister has become so awkward. To think they used to finish each other's sentences. Something to think about some other time. More pressing things wait for her around the corner.

She slips her phone back in her pocket, turns, and bangs into an invisible wall. Agh! That hurt! Immediately, her head starts throbbing. That was the only thing missing. Careful she feels the wall, only now she noticed it's totally silent. A little voice inside her head snarls, *You have to use your senses! How many times do I need to tell you that?* Another growl escapes her, and she comes full circle feeling the wall all around. She's stuck in an invisible dome about three feet wide. Peachy. Slowly, she breathes in and out in an attempt to calm herself. When she's back in New Orleans, she needs to talk to Ceri about timing. A headache spreads, does it feel like it's hard to breathe? Panicked she looks around. Shit, it's a true dome, not only keeping things out but apparently, it's sealed or something. Quickly, she texts Ceri: "What the hell. You're trying to suffocate me."

An almost instant reply from her Auntie: "Don't waste your precious time texting me. DO SOMETHING!"

Bridget shouts in frustration, which doesn't help either. Finally, starting to use her brain, she breathes in, out, in, out. Spreading her arms, she touches the invisible wall on both sides, pouring her witch sense out through them. Much the same as a spider in a web, it feels the wall and quickly finds little inconsistencies in the structure. Like ivy roots, her witch sense wiggles itself into these tiny, vulnerable spots and pushes and pushes. At first, nothing happens. Bridget doubles her efforts. There's a soft noise as if glass is breaking, then cracks appear in the dome. She smiles. A bit more, she pushes even harder. A loud crack and the dome completely shatters. Ha! She did it!

Ping. A message from Ceri: "Took way too long." With a sad emoticon attached.

"I was a little busy," Bridget bounces back.

"Excuses. Excuses." With a rolling eye emoticon.

No need to respond to that. When Bridget walks back over, Luna and Tom are having a heated discussion, but despite that, they're whispering,

"I'm not calming down. Her eyes were burned out! For Christ's sake!"

"I know. I know." Luna lays a calming hand on Tom's arm. Bridget notices she doesn't use her powers; they have some sort of connection. What is going on between these two?

"Tom, do you mind giving me a moment with my daughter," says Luna.

"Of course, I'm going back to the station. See you there?" This apparently warrants a full wattage smile from Luna. Tom blushes and walks off.

"Seriously, Mom, what about Dad?" Bridget is happy to relieve some of her stress on her Mom.

"It's nothing." Luna ignores her. "I've been thinking. You should head to New Orleans."

"I don't think so; we need to take care of Hayes." The worry is back in Bridget's voice.

"I will take care of her. There's nothing else for you here. You need to go back. Work on Tara, she seems to trust you. Sort of. We need to know more about this Lucy."

Bridget looks at her in disbelief. "I can't leave; I need to fix this."

"It's too late for that." That's another slap in her face from her mother. As if she doesn't blame herself enough. Just once can't her mother make her feel better instead of rubbing it in?

"You go home," Bridget snaps.

"Stop being a brat. Think. It's the best way. I can take care of Hayes and her spell. There's nothing we can do for her eyes," Luna states matter-of-factly.

Unwillingly, tears well up in Bridget's eyes. She and Luna have a stare down. Bridget looks away. "Fine. Why don't you give me the little book? It's apparently precious, and we don't want it to end up in Lucy's hands again. We should give it to Tara, she'll know what to do with it."

Luna takes a step back and puts a protective hand on her pocket. "What if Lucy tries to get it back? You're no match for her."

"And you are?"

"Like it or not, I'm a very capable witch. How long did it take you this time to get out of Ceri's little assignment?" Bridget would have loved to wring her mother's neck right now. What a bitch! But instead, she just turns around and walks off.

Luna watches her daughter go until she disappears around the corner. They always had a hard time communicating, probably because Bridget is a lot like her. Two strong personalities butting heads. She's sure though that her daughter will grow into a formidable witch if she can finally accept who she really is. Till then . . . with a big sigh, she heads towards the station.

Lucy is fuming in the car. "Those arrogant witches stole my book. I'm sure of it now."

"Do you want me to get it back for you?" Cal eagerly offers.

Lucy flicks her hand against the back of his head. "Use your brain, for once. I'll do it when the time is right. They'll be on their guard now." It's time for her to focus on the Dagger and attune herself to it. Once she has that additional power, these women don't stand a chance. She'll be so strong. Ha! Then she'll teach them a lesson. "Drop me off at the airport. You can drive to Utah, and I will catch up with you there."

"Where are you going?" Cal expects to be slapped again, but in a rare moment of sharing, Lucy replies, "I'm going to London. I need to find a way to attune to the Dagger, and I can't seem to find anything here. I'm sure I will be able to find something useful in the old country."

"Is there anything else I can do?" He asks, wanting to please his grandmother.

"Contact your Dad and tell him to come to Utah." She orders him.

"Set?!" This is not going to happen; his father stays far away from his mother.

"Do you have another Dad? Make it happen. And tell Mara to prep the house for me."

Mara has always been Lucy's favorite and is free to roam where ever she wanted to go. He resents his sister for that; she never helped him with anything. "As you wish."

NEW ORLEANS

Wes' face lights up when he sees Bridget coming out of the airport. "Over here!" He waves, and the dogs start barking. Bridget rushes over and hugs him fiercely. "I've missed you."

"I thought you were having fun with your Mom," he whispers in her ear.

Bridget rolls her eyes. "Sure." Moon sticks his head through the open window and slobbers over her face. She takes her time to say a proper hello to all the dogs.

"They've missed you, too," says Wes while he snuggles up behind Bridget and nuzzles her neck. He kisses her cheek, she turns in his arms, and she takes her time to show him just how much she has missed him. When she comes up for air, a shaky laugh escapes her. "Let's go home."

"Home?" Wes' eyes twinkle with the thought of their new home.

"You know what I mean."

"Your family's house is an amazing place. I did so much in a couple of days, I can't wait to show you." Absentmindedly, he fidgets with something around his neck.

"It's filled with magic from many generations, it's a special place." As if that explains anything. In all honesty, she knows what he means, but can't really put it into words. It is an unique place. She zones in on the amulet around Wes' neck. Slowly, she takes it from him and feels the familiar medallion. It's gold, and it has a stag head on it. It used to be Seamus' favorite piece of magical jewelry.

"Tara gave it to me. She thought it would give me inspiration."

"Did she now?!" Bridget has a hard time keeping the envy out of her voice. She had a strong connection with Seamus, and after he passed, she had hoped Tara would give it to her.

Wes picks up on her tension. "Is that okay?"

"Of course. I'm glad you get along with my grandmother." To get the sting out of her words, she gives him another kiss. "Now, let's go."

Bridget wades through the lavender, bees are buzzing, and butterflies are everywhere. This is how a witch garden should feel, wholesome, full of life. Especially this time of the year when everything is blooming, it's invigorating. It replenishes the soul. For a moment, she takes the time to breathe in deeply, let the smells swirl around her, the sun in her face, the connection to the earth is strong. She swears she can feel the light seep in and make her stronger. This is the joy of being a witch. A smile touches her lips.

It vanishes in a flash when she recognizes the familiar piercing voice of Freya. "She's waiting for you." When she's opening her eyes, her aunt is there, sizing her up.

"Aunt Freya, what a surprise!" Bridget fakes enthusiasm.

Freya brushes her hand through the lavender and takes in the fragrance of the flowers. "Did you find anything out, detective?" The sarcasm is not lost on Bridget.

"Lucy's house burned down." She doesn't feel like sharing much information with her curt aunt.

"How convenient. Where is your lovely mother?"

"She's taking care of something in Boston and then, she'll be back."

"I bet she is," says Freya with the most insincere smile. "Tara has been asking for you. You're her new favorite now. Take care. It never lasts long." With those ominous parting words, Freya leaves. What the hell was that all about? Bridget has a feeling she missed the real message here. She's out of practice with all the family drama, that's clear. Ah well, one problem at a time.

Tara is harvesting the calendula. Her basket is full of the cheerful orange flower. Bridget always has a pot at home for scrapes and burns. Nothing, however, is as powerful as the *crème* Tara makes. It seems to amplify the already powerful healing qualities of the plant. She has to snag a pot. The last couple of days seem to have done Tara good. She looks rested and more like her old self. Bridget observes her grandmother for a while.

"Do I pass your scrutiny?" asks Tara with a smile. "Did you have a good flight back? I never understand the joys of traveling in a clunky piece of metal. I prefer my broom any day."

"I could argue that one, but it's good to see you're feeling better. Do you need a hand?"

Tara gets up, painfully slowly. It's clear her knees are bothering her. When Bridget tries to help her, she waves her off. "Let's take a walk." Tara motions her forward. They leave the herb garden, and once they're through the gate, Bridget playfully sticks her arm behind Tara's arm, so she gets the feeling Bridget just wants to be close, while she actually supports her a little while they walk. For the moment, they enjoy each other's company and the pleasures of a walk through the garden.

"Did you see her?" A hint of eagerness comes through Tara's question.

"Not really, she took off when we saw her. She's evil Grandma. I'm sorry. If you had seen her house. The souls that Luna freed. Hayes' eyes—" an involuntary shudder escapes Bridget.

Tara faces her. "Tell me what happened."

Bridget explains the horrible table, the dark things they saw in the house, the wicked garden, and the whole oppressive atmosphere "—and I took a little book. It seems to contain dark spells."

Tara looks alarmed. "Where is it? You didn't use it, did you?"

Bridget takes a step back and is a little bit thrown off by the force of Tara's reaction. "Luna has it. She wants to study it, to use it against Lucy."

A sigh escapes Tara. "Luna can handle it."

Bridget is not so convinced. "I'm worried Grandma, what if she gets tainted or something by dark magic. Or she gets over to the dark side. She seemed VERY interested."

"This is not a movie, Bridget. Your mother is the most capable witch I know. She'll keep it safe. And who knows, maybe she will find something in there that's of use to us." That seems to be the end of that discussion. But Bridget can't shake the uneasy feeling she's getting. Everybody thinks her mother is fantastic, but she has seen her dark side. It's there.

Bridget follows Tara through the wooded area, into the clearing with the tomb. It never ceases to amaze Bridget. How it can look so ordinary on the outside and have such vast space on the inside. Tara opens the door, motioning her to come in. The torches flare to life, and the light plays along the walls. Bridget follows the circle of the tombs, her hand touching them as she walks by. Whispers come from the caskets. She lets them flow over her, they recognize her, welcoming her back. When she's almost full circle, she comes to an empty spot. Tara walks up, and they both stare at the empty space. "I'll be there soon."

"Stop it! You're in excellent health." But when she turns to Tara, she sees that age and worry have taken their toll.

"I've never been one for fooling myself. Or at least that what I thought till now." A heavy sigh escapes her, and she tries to stand as straight up as her age allows her. "These are our ancestors, and this is our sacred place. They're here to guide you."

For a moment the whispers intensify, and it's almost like invisible hands caress her. What's going on? It's like something magical had happened and she missed the meaning of it.

"What just happened Grandma?"

"I've marked you. It's the first step." Tara is pleased.

"The first step of what?!" This is starting to freak her out.

"Somebody will need to guide the family when I'm gone."

This alarms Bridget. "What the hell are you talking about?"

"You're the chosen." Tara's simple words don't hold the weight of that statement.

"Hell, no." Bridget is so not buying this. She moves towards the exit, but the tomb door closes with a loud thud. "Let me go, Gran. Choose Maeve, she's always the sensible voice, or my mother, she's the most powerful witch in the family, after all."

Tara glides over until she stands in front of her. "Strength is not about who has the most power. It's about strength in here." Tara touches Bridget's heart. For a moment, the sun seems to shine from there.

"What the fuck?!" Startled, Bridget backs up.

"See," smiles Tara "I'm right. Or rather Seamus recognized it long ago and chose the Strength card for you."

"Nobody will ever listen to me, Gran, they hate me."

A small smile plays along Tara's lips. "They don't hate you, honey."

"Anyway, I'm not it. The chosen or whatever you call it. I don't even want this life." Her grandmother needs to stop with this nonsense.

"Right." Tara turns around and heads for the center with the altar. She knew Bridget would **resist**, but the first step is taken, she has planted the seed.

The family chronicles, their heritage, *The Book of Shadows* lies on the altar. Tara puts her hand on the cover. "I want you to study this. I think there is a lot here that can tell us about the elements and hopefully can give us an idea of what Lucy is after."

"I thought she was erased from there."

Tara's mischievous smile betrays there's much more to the story. "She is, but it contains a lot of knowledge, and with your police skills, I think you can have a different perspective on things. We need to use all the skills that we have. A storm is brewing, and we need to be prepared."

"I know; it feels like she's twenty steps ahead of us." The lights flare up for a second, Bridget immediately scans the surrounding.

"It's okay," says Tara. "It's the ancestors, they are letting you know they agree. Another thing that we need to do is to try to locate the other two families and warn them."

Bridget looks dubious "That could also expose them. Their anonymity keeps them safe."

"If Lucy could find the family that guarded the Dagger, she can find the others. They need to be warned."

Gran has a point there. "We need names if we want to track them."

Tara points to the book. "This can give you a good idea about where to start."

"Why don't you just tell me and save me the time?" Bridget starts to lose her patience.

Tara flashes her one of her mysterious smiles.

"Seriously, Gran. One of these days you'll realize your silence comes with a big price."

Tara's smile transforms into anger in a second. The voices in the coffins rise in volume. "I am still the head of the family." Bridget takes a step back and put her hands up in surrender. Her Granny can still look scary as fuck. It feels like an overreaction; she must have hit a sensitive point. She files that away for future consideration. The anger dissipates, and Tara looks like her sweet Granny once more. For a moment they just stare at each other. Again, Bridget has a feeling she's missing what Tara wants to say here. *"Open your senses,"* whispers her Aunt Ceri in her head. Bridget stands still and imagines herself opening up to sounds, smells, feelings, touch. Only then does she sense Tara's vulnerability, her fears, and desperation. "Oh Gran."

A door slams shut. Tara has left the tomb without another word.

The voices chatter away at her. "I know, but she needs to understand that she has to share information. We're at a disadvantage as it is, and Tara is telling us far from everything." A big smile forms on her face. "I can understand you!" The chatter answers. A big laugh fills the tomb, her senses are still open, and it is amazing. In her head, she thanks Ceri. Finally, some improvement. Now it's time to get to work. She opens the Grimoire and starts reading.

LONDON

In the meantime, Lucy arrived in London and sits deep inside the catacombs of the British library. The modern exterior can fool you, but in the archives, there are some ancient manuscripts. One of Lucy's many connections and a significant bribe landed her here at this hour in complete privacy, examining a pile of old papers, which you usually would not be able to consult without a clean room and a curator by your side. Somewhere in these books, she must be able to find a way to attune herself to a magical object. She wishes she wasn't in a hurry; there are so many exciting things in here. If she can ever find the time, she must come back and properly study them. The modern witch has lost so much knowledge. Time to focus. She wants to get the extra power that the Dagger offers and teach those Madigans a lesson.

BOSTON

Luna wanders through Bridget's house. What a treat to be able to see her daughter's life through her home. It's painfully obvious she's been trying to be normal. But once a witch, always a witch. Her connection with animals seems to have grown. The herbs in her kitchen windowsill garden are flourishing. The paintings on the wall all represent some form of nature or animal instinct. The wild and untamed feelings are bubbling beneath the surface. There is much more to Bridget than she wants to let on. It's sad, but Luna is almost sure that Bridget will never forgive her for what happened. Maybe she shouldn't have used her power on her. Teenagers just have a knack for getting under your skin and pushing you to your limits. Probably still not an excuse, but she had hoped that once Bridget grew up, she would see that her mother meant no harm. After three rounds through the house, she sits down on the couch and gets Lucy's spellbook out. You can almost see the virulence and anger drip from the cover. For a moment, she hesitates and contemplates whether she might need some gloves. Really, Luna, get a grip. It's magical; no glove can stop that. She fingers the amulet around her neck for comfort. She left it on after they went into Lucy's house. That should give her enough protection.

The first couple of pages are filled with doodles and drawings. Here the handwriting gives the impression of a younger person. No concrete spells, more explorations, and thoughts. Luna takes her time examining them with her witch sight from different angles. Making any real sense of it is hard. This younger

Lucy seemed to have been searching for who she is. Luna's phone pings. Without her noticing, several hours have passed. It's a text from Tom: "Want some company?"

She smiles, she should say no. Then again, he's cute, and they have a connection. He can also tell her more about her daughter and let's face it, it's been a long time since she felt wanted. Lusted after. "Would love to," she sends back a text.

NEW ORLEANS

It's dark by the time Bridget leaves the tomb. She made a lot of notes in her little book, and there is much to discuss. The family home beckons. It's strange how she still calls this home. Boston is where she lives now, although for the moment, her job hangs in the balance. She messed that up big-time. And Tom and Luna, she doesn't even want to think about that. When she passes the kitchen window, she can't help but feel a pang of jealousy. The table is set, and Wes is sitting at the table with Maeve and Tara, they're having a natural conversation. She knows she doesn't have any reason to suspect Maeve of snatching her boyfriend, but Maeve would make Angelina Jolie insecure. They're apparently waiting for her, so it's time to face them all.

An intoxicating smell overwhelms her like there's somebody with a huge amount of perfume around. Bridget's witch senses are still open after her long hours in the tomb. Immediately she recognizes Ceri's work. Without hesitation, she weaves a counter spell. The smell evaporates on the evening breezes. And of course, her cell phone pings: "Excellent job."

She smiles, it's been a revelation today, to have her witch senses in full swing. Can she always be this alert? Maybe, it's time for another chat with her aunt. But first food!

The warmth of the people in the kitchen opens up and draws her in. Tara gives her a smile, Wes gets up and gives her a gentle kiss, and even Maeve looks happy for her. Maybe she was too quick to judge or be paranoid. Bridget is glad she can finally sit down on one of the chairs while Maeve puts a big salad on the table. From the oven, she pulls something wrapped in aluminum foil. As she opens it up, the smell makes Bridget's stomach grumble. They all laugh. "Gosh, I must be ready for that!" Once they have all filled their plates and wine glasses, Tara turns to Bridget. "Did you find anything?" Bridget raises her eyebrow. She knows her grandmother must have known. Instead of arguing, she replies, "I did. I'm sure the four witches that took the elemental objects were sisters."

"Then they all should have the same name, right?" asks Maeve. "The woman that was murdered wasn't called Madigan."

"What if I tell you that we weren't called Madigan either." She smiles mysteriously.

"No. We always kept our mother's name. That's witch tradition," counters Maeve.

Bridget quickly shovels in a piece of salmon before she answers. "Our name is actually O'Seachnasaigh, or however, you pronounce that. I guess it's Gaelic." She looks pointedly at Tara.

"That's right," her grandmother confirms, not surprised at all.

"You knew?" Maeve is clearly shocked.

Welcome to the real-world, sister. This is only one of the many secrets Tara is hiding from us, Bridget thinks while she explains, "It's in the *Book of Shadows,* but you must read between the lines—piece it together. I think they decided it was safer if they all changed their names, taking the names of their husbands. So that's where we start if we want to find them."

"If they're family, can't we use our blood for a tracking spell?" Not a bad suggestion from Maeve.

"Don't ask me. I'm out of practice." They both look at Tara for an answer.

"I already tried; I think it's too many generations ago."

"Great Gran, when were you planning on sharing that tidbit of information?" Maeve can't hide her sarcasm. Tara just gives her one of her non-committal smiles.

Bridget shakes her head. "Anyway. Luna is still in Boston, she could search the town records and see if she can find four sisters around—" she checks her notes, "around 1780s. She can ask Tom to help her. I'm sure he will do that. He's besotted with her." Now she has a hard time hiding her irritation with her mother. Maeve picks up on it but decides to ignore it.

Bridget continues, "In the meantime, I think we should all brush up on our elemental magic, so we can know what to look for once Lucy starts to use the Dagger."

"Great idea! Why don't you include Diane in these studies? She has excellent resources and is the most Air in our family," adds Tara.

"I'll go and see her tomorrow about that." Maeve is happy to have a goal. Bridget shares her feeling. She's also much better at being pro-active.

Wes stays quiet throughout the discussion; the women seemed to forget he was there. He loves watching Bridget re-engaging with her relatives. She doesn't seem to realize how big a part she actually is of this family. The food was fabulous, and now he just watches them and sips his wine. His creative energy bubbles up—how fortunate to find himself surrounded by these exceptional women.

UTAH

Up from Indian Cove by the Salt Lakes in Utah is Lucy's house. The dry landscape of rocks and the occasional brush, feel alien and hostile. Upon an unnamed road, away from prying eyes, rises Lucy's home. In every way, it's a stark contrast to the Madigans' family home. This house is built with only one purpose in mind—power. Right here, the ley lines cross, the building's specific position and unique design has been chosen with a single goal—to focus and contain that power. It's made of steel and concrete, and there is nothing, absolutely nothing, cozy about it. At first glance, you would say it lacks anything personal at all, but on second inspection, it's obvious it reflects Lucy's personality accurately. From the ominous cellars with a power circle and dark witch rituals to the enormous open room with what could be interpreted as a throne dominating that space. Shackles line the wall and one can only imagine what happened here; there are drains in the floor, and reddish-black stains surround them.

Except for the throne, there is nowhere to sit. A skylight above it is the only light in here.

Mara wanders along the walls while she swings a large censer around, filled with their one-of-a-kind blend of herbs and incense to cleanse the house. She's Cal's older half-sister. Her father, Set, could never be faithful to one woman. Mara's mother is one of New Orleans' great voodoo priestesses. Her Creole heritage is clearly visible in her curves and her almost black eyes. It's obvious why she's Lucy's favorite—she's a powerful witch and voodoo priestess herself, and she likes to gobble up any knowledge Lucy is willing to share with her. Lucy only has to explain it once, and she'll know how to do it. Unlike her brother, who's a total oaf. What do you expect? His mother was one of those lovey-dovey new age dabblers. The devil only knows what her father saw in that woman. She completes her circle in the room when she's back at the entrance. The house sighs, and it feels like a door opens to let the power wash over the house. For a moment, she eyes the throne, why not?! Grandma isn't here anyway, she'll never know. Mara walks over and ever so gently takes a seat on the throne. It's positioned above the power circle in the basement and precisely above the crossing of the ley lines. She feels the warmth travel up her spine. Very quickly she shields herself—to take in too much of this power could burn her up. No need to be stupid. Wow, this is a power rush. She jolts upright and jumps out of the throne when her phone buzzes. It's a text from Lucy: "I found what I've been looking for. Are you ready?" She smiles, it is as if she knew Mara was in her seat. Granny doesn't tolerate insubordination. Quickly she glances at the shackles and shudders.

"I'm ready."

BOSTON

The next morning, Luna wakes up in Bridget's bed with a warm body snuggled up to her. Oh dear, her daughter will not be pleased. She smiles, as she truly couldn't care less. Tom's expert skills have left her sated and happy. It's been a long time since she felt this full. Sex is good for the soul and for your magic. She feels the magic humming through her veins. Oh, this feels so good! Tom notices she's awake. His hands slowly make their way down from her breast over her belly; she instantly reacts. The warmth grows between her legs, and a soft moan of anticipation escapes her. She feels Tom smiling against the swell of her breasts where he kisses her, and his hand explores further down. Her phone rings. For a moment, she wants to ignore it, but her sixth sense is on high alert. Better take it. She tries to wiggle free.

"Let it ring," says Tom, while he holds her firmly against him. She feels he's ready and in no way does he want to stop.

"It's Bridget."

"Shit." He lets her go. She manages to pick up before it goes to voicemail.

"Morning. Were you still sleeping?" Bridget's voice sounds as if she has been awake for hours. "Yes, you're actually waking me up. Must be the Boston air." Luna signals to Tom to be quiet. He is, but he snuggles back up to her and starts caressing her. Luna has a hard time sounding normal.

Bridget quickly explains what she found out.

"Good for you, to finally get a secret out of Tara. I'll ask Tom if he can help me and I'll get back to you as soon as I know more." Luna tries to get rid of Bridget.

"Great. Thanks." And Bridget hangs up. No bye Mom or love you. Ah well, at least she's talking to her—it's an improvement.

"What was that all about?" asks Tom while he pulls her close and his mouth hovers above hers. "We need to search some old records for some names," she says hoarsely.

"Right." And he covers her mouth and kisses her thoroughly. It seems they can spare some time for lovemaking first.

NEW ORLEANS

Bridget follows Maeve into Under the Witches Hat, the relaxed atmosphere washes over her. Even though it's not ten o'clock yet, some people are having cocktails at the bar. Their umbrellas twirl, fizzy bubbles make little twinkles above their drinks. They giggle, and Ron gives them a wink. Easy music flows, the light globes float around; the fresh scent of rain on a mountain meadow fills the air. Ron is pleased to see them, motioning them to follow him to the back.

The sun shines through the skylight in the back, and it makes for a stark contrast. Bridget blinks a couple of times to adjust to the light. Diane is floating around, humming while she works on some kind of spell. For now, she either ignores the others or is simply not aware they're there.

"Perfect timing, ladies!" says Ron. "The first customers will be here in ten minutes. Three tarot readings, one Lenormand, and if I'm not mistaken, a love potion. But it seems Diane is working on that." As if on cue, Diane plops back onto the floor. "Glad you're here," she adds.

"We're not staying; we were just here to ask you some things about elemental magic," Bridget tries.

"We can do that in between." Invisible hands seem to guide Bridget to Tara's workplace. "You can take Tara's table," smiles Diane innocently.

Ron has disappeared, and Maeve stands back and watches. There is no escaping the gentle nudges from Diane. "If you do a couple of readings, I will tell you all you need to know."

Bridget sputters, "We don't have much time."

"The Hat sustains the family. While you're here, you must pull your weight," her aunt dismisses her argument.

"Did you see something?!" Diane gives her only a smile, there is no doubt she learned that from Tara. Bridget opens her mouth to protest when the door opens, and Ron ushers the first customers in. Before Bridget knows it, she's sitting behind Tara's table shuffling a tarot deck. A young woman sits opposite her. With a heavy sigh, she falls back into her role as a tarot reader. It's like riding a bike!

"There's no need to be nervous. Do you have a question?" She tries to put the girl at ease.

"I . . . I don't know. Maybe if the man I've been dating will ask me to marry him?"

Some things never change. She starts a Celtic cross—when in doubt, always a good choice.

The time flies by and its afternoon before she realizes it. Four readings and she feels totally in control. She had forgotten how much she loves the cards. Enough of this, time to get what she came for. Somehow it's hard to shake the nagging feeling of urgency that's in the back of her mind. If she learned something from being a detective, it's to follow her instincts.

Diane sits behind the big table in the middle of the potion room. A large and very old looking manuscript lies in front of her. "Here," she points at the middle of the page. Bridget looks over her aunt's shoulder. "This is an essential part to understand the weaving of the elements. At first glance, it looks like they're very different. But in nature, it rarely is just one element. They flow together."

Bridget tries to make sense of the complicated drawing in front of her. She gets her cellphone out and snaps a picture of it. Diane shakes her head. "That's not the same. Here." She reaches for Bridget's hand and guides it towards the book. "Put your hand on it, feel it." Bridget gently puts her hand on the page. A rush of warmth, coolness, overwhelming smell, light, it's hard to describe rushes up to her arm and threatens to overwhelm her. She snatches her hand back. "That book is alive."

Maeve, in the meantime, shows her client out and joins the others.

"Yes and no. There's magic in this book and magic is always alive. You should have realized that by now." Diane explains, "It's as alive as the things around us. Almost like it's an own organism, living among us. Some call it the Universe, but it's only a name. Mother Earth, God, spirit, you name it, and the elements are part of that. We witches can tap into that energy and use it to weave spells, create protection, fly on a broom. Now do it again and this time, try not to fight it. Let it wash over you and learn."

"I don't know." Bridget doesn't feel confident, and it's hard for her to let her guard down. She likes to be in control.

"Move over, I will do it," says Maeve.

That's just the little push that Bridget needs. Before Maeve can move in, she centers herself and puts her hand on the drawing. The overwhelming sensation washes over her, but instead of trying to stop it, this time she lets it fill her up. For a moment she fights the panic of being overpowered by the elements. The impression that you're drowning in water, while at the same time, warmth rushes through her, and an intoxicating scent makes her gag. The different elements seem to swirl through her body. One hand is frigid, while the other feels as if it's on fire. Just when she thinks she can't stand it any longer, the elements seem to merge. For lack of better words, it feels like a swirl in the center of her body. The sensations dissipate, and knowledge fills her brain. Air, water, fire, and earth are one and four at the same time. Each has their own qualities and is powerful in its own right. When you merge the powers, it will be infinite; the person wielding that power will be extremely terrifying as the elements don't have the same moral conscience as people. Once you're a part of all the elements, you will be disconnected.

"Bridget. Bridget!" Diane gently shakes her out of the trance. Carefully, she pulls her hand from the page. Bridget blinks. "Oh my God."

"Yes, it's terrifying. Now you understand." Bridget slumps on a chair, unable to function.

"Can I see?!" asks Maeve eagerly. Bridget motions her to go ahead.

Maeve puts her hand on it, and it looks like she freezes. Diane keeps an eye on her but makes sure not to touch her.

"Is this normal?" Bridget asks as she thinks it looks like Maeve has had some sort of attack.

"I think so."

"You think so! Get her hand off that page!" Bridget is surprised to find she feels very protective of Maeve.

"Don't!!!" Diane swats Bridget hand away. "Once you start, you shouldn't stop. It's important she knows that as well." It's torture to wait. Finally, Maeve's head jerks back and forth and her eyes fly open. She lets go of the book. Bridget jumps up and turns Maeve towards her and looks into her eyes. For a moment, the twin bond feels as of old. Complete understanding of what the other is thinking. Then the connection is broken, and Maeve steps out of Bridget's reach.

"This is not good. I understand now why they tried to hide it," Maeve says a bit shaken.

"There is much we don't know," says Diane. "I'll search more archives and try to see if somebody has written more about this."

"Tara has been so irresponsible!" Maeve is agitated and, for the first time ever, is criticizing her grandmother.

"I never thought I would say this, but I think Luna is right. She holds too many secrets," sighs Bridget. "How can we get her to open up?" She hopes Diane could give them guidance in that. After all, she can see the future. "Don't look at me. I've never had a very close bond with my mother. It's up to you girls now."

"Great, thanks," Bridget and Maeve say in union. That makes them laugh, and the tension that has been hanging in the room disappears at last.

UTAH

Late that day, Lucy's plane touches down in Salt Lake City. Well rested from her first class flight, she breezes out of the airport and spots Mara. A warm smile forms on her face. Lucy walks over to the car, and they embrace. She loves Mara, such a gifted witch, wickedly beautiful, and the perfect student. One day, she will be able to wield the legacy. Lucy takes the front seat; it's time to catch up with her granddaughter. "You have to fill me in on what happened since the last time I saw you. And then, I need to deal with this." She holds up her big purse.

"The house is ready for you. Did you get a chance to sleep?" They fall into an easy conversation.

Soon, they reach the house. When Lucy approaches it, it's humming. Perfect, Mara did, of course, an excellent job of preparing it. This house contains a lot of power. It took her a long time to get permission to build it right on this spot. But oh, it was worth it. She can't wait, she mumbles a spell and the door swings open. Mara has to hurry to catch up before the door shuts behind Lucy.

Lucy descends the concrete steps to the ground level, with a pentagram in a circle and all the symbols etched into the floor. She drops her bag, walks to the wall and pushes a button. The walls slide apart, revealing endless shelves filled with witch supplies. With a snap of her finger, she activates all the lights in the basement, which create a soft ambiance. From her bag, she pulls an old manuscript. Gently she opens it and starts to search for the right page. Here it is! It's so hard not to try to rush, but she needs to make sure everything is done right.

"Can I help you with anything?" Lucy is startled, as for a moment she had totally forgotten Mara. "No dear, you've done enough. Leave me."

Mara is disappointed. "Do you mind if I look?"

For a moment, Lucy considers this. "It's better if I'm alone."

"Please, maybe I can learn something." Lucy doesn't look up but flicks her wrist, and Mara feels a slap in the face. Her cheek turns an angry red. "Sorry, grandma." Slowly she backs out of the room.

"And shut the door." Lucy doesn't even look up.

The door clicks shut behind Mara. Lucy quickly mumbles a small spell to make sure she stays alone. She doesn't blame her granddaughter for trying, but she can't have anybody involved in this. This power is not meant to be shared.

For a couple of hours, she's totally engrossed in reading the spell, again and again, so she can recite it without thinking. She has also gathered a long line of ingredients. It is time to get ready. In the far corner, there is a bathroom with a big bathtub in the middle. A dragon tap hangs above the middle of the bath. She turns it on and checks if the temperature is right. While the water flows into the tub, she generously adds sea salt. Time to do a cleanse before the ritual. When the tub is full, she undresses and slowly lowers herself in the water. It feels so good to soak her old bones. All that traveling takes its toll. Where have the days gone when she could do anything? She hates getting older and this sagging body. One of the reasons she didn't want her granddaughter around. This body doesn't radiate power anymore. It feels more like decay. The ritual needs to be performed naked. Being as pure as possible is important. Lucy closes her eyes and clears her mind of any thought. Easier said than done, it's always a challenge to empty the mind. One by one, she lets her thoughts soak into the water until she peacefully floats in the tub. She has no idea for how long, but the water is starting to cool when she opens her eyes. Quietly but with determination, she gets out, dries herself, and throws on a loose white gown. Barefooted, she walks into the ritual room. This time she opts for matches to light all the candles she has placed around her magical circle. She starts with the candle on the northern side of the circle, and moving clockwise lights thirteen candles. She lets her gown fall to the ground and stands stark naked, stepping into the center of her power circle. It hums in recognition. Empty, clean and quiet, she feels the ley lines collide under her and the power flow that makes this house so special. Time to put it to good use. Before the bath, she had carefully placed all the tools for her ritual in the designated spots. She kneels in the middle of the circle before the Dagger and raises her hands to the sky while she calls in old English on the elements to guard her circle. The circle snaps shut, and the power builds. No longer able to flow freely, it mounts up. Lucy lowers her arms and bows down till her forehead touches the stone. In the meantime, she recites the spell; it's an old text she found in one of the manuscripts, and Lucy's hoping she pronounces the old words right. It's not her style to bow down for anything, but she needs to be able to attune to the Dagger, whatever it takes. Quickly, she directs her wandering thoughts back to the rhythm and power of the words. It's getting hotter and hotter in the circle and sweat pours down her back and face. Her knees ache, and she's having a tough time staying in this pose. A wind swirls inside the boundaries and seems to go faster and faster. Slowly it becomes smaller and smaller and starts to close in on Lucy and the Dagger. The sound is overwhelming and soon drowns out the discomfort and pain. Lucy struggles to squash her natural instinct to react. She must submit to the power if she wants to receive it. Momentarily, she glances up, and an angry wind slaps her face drawing blood. Quickly, she bows her head again, but not before she sees the Dagger floating before her. The spell is in motion, and there's no stopping now. It's nerve-wracking not to know what comes next. She has always found it difficult to be passive and let things unfold. She feels a prick of the dagger at the top of her spine. It takes everything she's got, every ounce of self-control to let it happen. The Dagger makes a shallow cut from the top of her spine to the bottom of her back. Lucy screams! Pain shoots through her, and she feels drips of blood going down the sides of her back. Invisible hands pull her straight, still on her knees, but it seems as if she's being held up high. The Dagger hovers in front of her. The tip of the Dagger is pointing at her heart—she couldn't do anything, even if she tried. The wind blows so fiercely that she can't really see anything. The tip comes closer and closer. She can't help herself, and screams into the storm. The tip touches her skin, and she feels its pressure as it draws blood. The Dagger collects some of Lucy's blood while it withdraws. Relieved, Lucy leans into the power, she is held up by the power of air. Finally surrendering, the tip of the Dagger touches her mouth; she opens her mouth and feels a bit of her own blood touching her lips. As the Dagger withdraws, she swallows, and from the inside out, she feels a tornado forming inside her body, her insides are being torn to bits. It's like she is exploding into a million pieces and is twirling on the wind inside the circle. She has no idea how long she's in this state but all of a sudden, the wind stops, and it's like her body has been knit back together. Exhausted, she falls to the floor. She rolls over onto her back and laughs. It worked! The power of air hums in her veins. For a moment, she let herself enjoy the power rush. It seems to ebb to a feeling of content. It will take a while to get acquainted with her new friend.

Her body starts to ache in places she never knew could hurt. She's unable to get up. With a flick of her wrist, she opens the door to the basement and sends out a call to her granddaughter. Mara comes rushing down and finds Lucy in the middle of the circle on her side, the Dagger in her hand. Blood splattered around and the whole basement in disarray.

"Gran, are you okay?!"

Lucy turns on her back and laughs. "Yes. More than okay."

Mara learned early on not to ask questions. "Bring me to my room. I need to rest." Mara helps Lucy up. There are no visible wounds anymore on Lucy's body although she's smeared with blood.

NEW ORLEANS

Tara awakens with a start. The remnants of the power rush have touched her as well. Apparently, the power of the twin bond is not as forgotten as she thought it was. For a moment, she feels euphoric but quickly realizes it's not her own. She recognizes the feeling; she had that same feeling a long time ago. Lucy has attuned herself to the Dagger. For the first time, she wonders how much Lucy has felt from her power over the years. With a big sigh, Tara gets up. Not a chance of going back to sleep now. Better to put this energy to good use. Nothing good can come of Lucy handling one of the power objects. She's always been a very gifted witch, but now she's becoming seriously powerful. Hopefully, Luna can find the other families soon. She needs help, guidance; it would be so good to be able to discuss the experience with someone else. Sometimes, that's worth taking the risk of getting together. What is she going to do?

SALEM

Luna and Tom make their way through the streets of Salem. Even though it's all geared towards tourism, the roads radiate magic. Once, there were a lot of real witches in this town. Magic leaves a residue even if it's not practiced as often anymore. A shop window draws Luna's attention. It lacks any trinkets and has herbs, wands, candles and more for your witches needs. Clearly, there are still some witches here. She resists the temptation to check them out. Today is not a good day to socialize or draw attention to herself. Quickly, she pulls the protection spell she made this morning a little tighter around her. Tom doesn't notice a thing. He can't hide his cynicism about the witch town. For the first time, she feels the need to tell him who she really is, wondering if he would be able to accept it or if he will cut and run. When she remembers their lovemaking, an involuntarily pleasurable shudder goes through her. Tom knows all too well what that means. He gives her a quick kiss. Maybe she should wait a little longer before she opens up to him.

Here they are, Salem's town hall. The cheerful green doors are smiling at them. The two-story building is made of bricks, and their rounded windows make it an inviting place. Confident, they walk up the steps.

Luna had apparently forgotten the pleasures of bureaucracy, and she struggles not to use her gift. Better let Tom handle this. As it turns out, the police badge is pretty magical. After some back and forth, the lady agrees they can examine two old books themselves, which is highly irregular. Tom's badge and his charm have made it happen.

The smell of dust and a hint of mold fill the catacombs. This entirely lives up to the expectation. It's kept clean, but in a basement like this, it is hard to prevent mold and keep rodents out. They follow the lady, and she points at some old bundles safely stacked on a shelf, behind glass.

"These ones are it." She produces a couple of pairs of soft white gloves. "Please use these. In the middle is a clean room, it's best to open them there. You have an hour."

"Thank you. We really appreciate it," replies Tom. The lady has already marched away down the row of bookcases. He sighs, "Let's do it."

Carefully they open the glass door in front of the shelves. It gives a little sigh as it hasn't been opened in a while and the pressure inside is slightly different. Luna gently takes the two ancient volumes off the shelf. In the clean room, they sit down, and each take a volume and start searching for clues that could help them find the other families. They look for dates around 1780 and with Bridget's information of their true name, the odds of finding the names the families took are in their favor.

UTAH

Lucy finally wakes up. She has no idea what time it is; the blinds are drawn. The rush of power of last night returns and with great joy, she revels in the power of the element of air that runs now through her veins. Her mother never mentioned the instant growth of power. It doesn't matter if you wield the object or not. So, the whole "we should never use the objects" is a bunch of bullshit. It is simply a part of you. It makes her feel invigorated, and she can't wait to try out her new-found powers.

First, a shower, as she's still dirty and naked. The blood has clotted; her sheets look like she'd been murdered in her bed. Why didn't Mara bathe her? It seems she needs to have a word with her. This, however, can't possibly dampen her good mood.

The room is the total opposite of Tara's bedroom—it's stark and functional, nothing personal on the walls. A nun's quarters come to mind, except for the bed, which is a California King with soft cotton-linen sheets, and a frame made of steel. Like the table in her other house, it seems to be sculpted out of tortured souls.

Her bathroom is spacious and has a huge walk-in shower. Lucy lets the rain shower wash her clean. This grounds her, and she feels the power of air trying to lift her up. But it's not the time to act on impulse. The Madigans must have her book—that's the only logical possibility left if it's not in the police station. Time to lure them out. While she dries herself and gets dressed, a plan takes form in her mind. Surprised, she looks at herself. Blue? She had dressed in blue; she didn't even know her wardrobe had any color in it. She's more affected than she thought by her new powers.

NEW ORLEANS

Tara is hiding in her refuge—her herb garden. The sensation of the structure of the leaves and smell of flowers calms her. She's still reeling from the power rush that she got through her bond with Lucy and the concern she feels for what is to come. Apparently, she will not have the luxury of collecting herself, as her twin granddaughters are marching toward her. They don't seem happy with whatever Diane has told them. Clearly, they have finally worked up the courage to confront her. That extra power might come in handy. She loves her grand-daughters, but she's still the head of the family.

The dogs are trailing along. It's so good to see the girls together. There is still a lot to sort out between them. Quickly, she sends a little wish out into the universe—a desire that they will be able to sort out their differences and enjoy the pleasures of being twins, and not have to suffer the endless sense of loss, like an amputated limb. Tara never got over losing Lucy like she did. The little secret meetings they had over the years didn't come even close to being able to have a healthy relationship. She's always been convinced there is still good in Lucy, if she only got a chance to prove it. But now Lucy has one of the elemental powers attuned to her. Nobody knows what she will do. If only she could talk to her.

Hug her, be close to her, look into her soul. She's her sister—her twin—she knows she can reach the real Lucy. Not this power hungry, bitter old lady. The girls stopped just outside the gate and watch their grandmother, uncertain if they're welcome in the garden. They must have picked up on her doubts and discomfort. It can be so irritating to be a witch and be more attuned to feelings and moods. Quickly she rebuilds her shield around her—stupid to have let it slip. This is no time to be sloppy or to give in to her old woman's regrets. She needs to be there for her family. When she looks up, she's ready for what is to come.

A raven lands on the fence surrounding the garden. Tara, Bridget, and Maeve instantly know this is not an ordinary bird. The girls try to get a sense, but Tara knows who has sent this raven, and she raises her hand to cast a spell to throw a circle around her and the bird. She doesn't want her granddaughters to hear what it has to say. Before the incantation can leave her lips, it feels like a hand is clamped over her mouth and her hands are glued to her side. On the one hand, she admires the girls' spirit and is proud of Bridget's improved reflexes. On the other hand, she's pissed. Now there is no escape; the raven starts to speak, perfectly mimicking Lucy's voice. "Meet me tomorrow at noon at Tsé Bit'a í, Shiprock. We need to talk." Not wasting any time, the bird takes flight. When Tara faces her granddaughters, Bridget shows her, her impassive cop face but Maeve looks genuinely hurt.

"Care to elaborate on that?" Bridget can barely contain her fury. "How often have you met?"

"Not often enough," says Tara, resigned that a particular genie is out of the bottle.

"You lied," stammers Maeve.

"I didn't lie, I just never mentioned it. What would you do if someone forbade you from seeing your twin?"

Maeve's voice is full of anguish and pain when she replies. "Nothing. Mine did it voluntarily. For years." Ashamed, Bridget turns away. She's not able to face that pain. The silence stretches and is quickly becoming uncomfortable.

Finally, Tara glances around, "Let's go inside, I don't want to discuss this out in the open." Without another word, they make their way back to the house.

Tara has hardly closed the door to the kitchen when Bridget turns on her. "You better start talking! You've been holding back information on a suspect wanted by the police."

"I didn't lie when I told you I don't know where she lives. We never talked about such things."

"How often do you—" Maeve waves her hand as if she can't think of Lucy's name, "meet?"

"At first, we met almost every year, but we haven't been in touch for several years now." No need to mention she had tried to reach Lucy when all this started.

"We're going with you this time," says Bridget with a certainty that doesn't leave any options.

"We're not going. It's a trap." Tara dismisses that idea.

"She might want to touch base with you after all that has been going on. This is our chance to catch her." Bridget looks for her phone. "I need to call Tom."

"Lucy has attuned herself to the Dagger."

Bridget's finger freezes above the phone, "And how do you know that?" She searches for any clues on Tara's face.

Maeve's disappointment with her grandmother hangs like a heavy blanket in the air, while Tara says, "I felt it, through our bond. I only know what it meant as I felt that same power rush many years ago when the Wand became mine."

"Shit." Bridget starts pacing.

"Yes. That pretty much sums it up. Lucy just became a great deal more powerful." Tara sits down very carefully while Maeve makes tea—her solution for everything.

"What do we do now?" asks Bridget. "I can't get the police involved in this. It's only asking for casualties."

"We wait. I know she will act. Lucy is not known for her patience. But we will not go there unless absolutely necessary." Tara is sure that's the best way to deal with this.

Bridget is less convinced, "Where or what is Tsé Bit'a í?"

"It's in Navajo territory in New Mexico; the American name is 'Winged Rock'."

"Do you think she lives there?" Maeve wonders.

Tara shakes her head, "No. It will not be close to her home. This is a sacred place to the Navajo. It's ruled by Air; Lucy's powers will be even more amplified there."

"Like doubling up?" asks Maeve.

"Something like that. Even though I'm not going, something will happen. We need to inform the others." Tara sounds a bit less sure of herself now.

Several hours later, the house is buzzing with life. Tara requested everybody to come and stay at the family home. For safety, she claims, but Bridget is certain her Grandma feels insecure and dreads whatever is happening. To have her family around gives her comfort. Bridget has found a moment's peace in her and Wes's room. He's painting, and all the ruckus hasn't reached him yet. When he's painting, he is so focused the world around him disappears. She envies that; she wishes she could turn off the world for a couple of hours. Like now. She would give almost anything to be able to forget Maeve's pained face when she talked about Bridget abandoning her. What excuse does she have? That she was young? Angry? She has never been good at dealing with her feelings. If she could turn back time and do it differently, she would. Too late now. She has no idea how she can make amends; what would be the right thing to say? Sorry seems so inadequate.

UTAH

Lucy wanders through her supply room. Rows and rows of neatly organized herbs, bones, stones, books, candles—everything a witch could need. She lets her fingers trail over the shelves. It's a stark contrast to her dungeon-like cellar in Boston, but like everything in her designer home, it's thought through, very deliberate, and functional. The power of air still gives her goosebumps. Absentmindedly, she rubs her arms. What should she take to Shiprock? It's not like her to hesitate; she usually knows exactly what she wants. Maybe she doesn't need anything? Abruptly, she leaves the room and makes her way to the roof. In the middle of the roof is a tiny pentacle, marking the exact place where the ley lines cross. Out of habit, she stands on it. She touches the Dagger hanging at her side. A tingling sensation runs up her arm and makes her smile. Time for a little test run. She closes her eyes and imagines the air flowing through her and out of her hands, while her hands move around each other as if she's stirring a pot. A little tornado forms. Her eyes snap open, her hands stop moving and the tornado balances patiently above her hands. With her mind, she directs it to a couple of trees down the road, her hands give the tornado a push-up. It grows and whips toward the trees. The trees start to sway in the increasing wind. Once the tornado touches them for real, they bend back and forth violently, and the wind force rips them out of the ground. A victorious laugh escapes Lucy. She has never felt so alive. With a flick of her wrist, the tornado dies, and the trees fall back to the ground. A small wasteland with toppled trees is left. Well, this answers her question. She doesn't need to take anything except for the Dagger. Satisfied, she makes her way back inside.

BOSTON

Luna is back in Boston and sits on Bridget's bed while she FaceTimes with her mother. Tara is in her room, and Seamus is peeking over her shoulder, trying to follow the conversation. Luna looks at her notes. "Neumann and Giordano. Those are their last names. But now we can only begin searching."

"Things have become more complicated. Lucy has contacted me."

Luna has a hard time trying not to raise a quizzical brow. It's an interesting choice of words. She already heard what happened from Maeve, and there is definitely more to this story.

"I talked to Maeve." There's no reaction on Tara's face. No surprise there. "Do you want me to come home?"

"No, no. Everybody is here. Finding the other families is too important," Tara states. "I think it's time to reach out to the family who had the Dagger. It's a place to start."

Luna frowns. "What am I going to say . . . my Mom's evil twin stole the Dagger?"

"I thought you, at least, could be a little more subtle than that." Tara rolls her eyes at her.

"Didn't you say they were at Lucy's house? We must deal with them one way or the other. Better be on our own terms. As Bridget is here, this would be the perfect time."

Luna can't help but smile. Her mother hasn't lost her touch, it seems.

"Maybe you can take that man—what's his name—with you."

"Tom. His name is Tom."

The irritation in Luna's voice isn't lost on Tara. "Tom wants to help you?"

"No doubt, but I think if I involve him further, he needs to know who we are."

Tara leans forward, as if she wants to take a closer look at Luna's face. Luna does her utmost to give her a blank look. No need to tell her mother she's having an affair.

"Is that really necessary?"

Luna rationalizes her choice, "Lucy did bespell him. And that business with Hayes. He is getting suspicious of something."

Tara thinks for a couple of seconds and then merely nods in agreement. "Did you find anything in Lucy's spellbook?" Seamus eagerly leans forward in his frame.

"I didn't have much time, but it's fascinating, and there is much we can learn from it." Luna is not yet ready to share her thoughts on the book. She tried a small spell and felt the luring power of dark magic. It frightens and captivates her at the same time. No need to tell her mother that.

"Is it safe?" Is all Tara wants to know.

"Of course," replies Luna, while trying very hard not to touch it in reassurance.

"Great. Good luck with the search. Keep me posted." Tara is ending the conversation. The sound of children's voices is coming closer.

"Stay safe. And if you need me, I can be there soon. I can always take some road through Fairy."

"Don't do it. It's not worth it," stresses Tara. She looks distracted; the children have probably invaded her room.

"Only if there's no other way." Luna presses the end button. She'll need a couple of minutes to digest this conversation. It's always more about what isn't said than what is. She falls back on the bed and closes her eyes.

NEW ORLEANS

It's late, and with a big sigh, Bridget closes her bedroom door behind her. Nothing happened, and while everybody showed up and is settled in the house, Tara is back to her secretive ways. They made no plan, there wasn't even a discussion. Only quiet conversations in corners, as if allegiances need to be formed. Bridget feels very alone. Her family radar is rusty, and she's obviously an outsider. It will take time to rekindle her bonds. Luckily, she has Wes and her dogs. Nobody is aware they are her little spies. Freya aired her grievances to Ceri. Nothing new there. Actually, not much exciting to report. The general consensus is that Tara is overreacting, that they will indulge her for a day or so and then everybody will go back to normal. That had astonished her. They must also feel a tension building like something is looming on the horizon. Something bad. That this is only a moment of quiet before the storm.

"Are you coming to bed, or are you staying there the whole evening?" Wes asks, piercing her train of thought. A warm smile forms on her face. She rushes toward the bed, ditching her clothes on the way. Wes opens the sheets, and she slides in against him. She wiggles against his already happy body. "That's better."

UTAH

Cal is surprised to see Mara lounging next to a pile of suitcases when he finally pulls up to the house in Utah. He's tired, and in need of a shower. His sister is not his favorite person. No chance of a quiet entrance. Better get it over with, he stops the car right in front of her and gets out.

"Finally!" says Mara while she gets up. "Unload the car and load this up, we're leaving as soon as you're done."

"I just arrived. I drove hundreds of miles; I need a shower," Cal sputters, irritated with her.

"Stop whining. If you have a problem, complain to Lucy." She doesn't wait for his answer and trots inside. She knows Cal would never do that. With a big sigh, he gets to work.

BOSTON

It's the crack of dawn and Luna stands in front of the Jansson's family home. Even though it's in the middle of the city and the yard space is small, they have managed to make it magical. The scent of honeysuckle is overwhelming. Many different plants mingle; the colors of the flowers welcome you in. She had left Tom at home, as she didn't have the heart yet to come clean to him. For a moment, she closes her eyes and sends a little probe out to the house. No doubt, they have the house protected with wards, and this way, they will know when a witch stands at the gate.

Pretty soon, the front door opens and the young witch, Gwen—Bridget had called her—stalks toward her, none too pleased to see her. "What are you doing here. How did you find this house?"

Luna ignores her obvious hostility, and says, "We need to talk."

Gwen points out, "You were at that witch's house with the cop."

Luna swallows one of her snappy remarks and instead decides to use a friendly approach. "Please, I have important information to share."

Gwen uses her senses and sizes Luna up. Again, Luna reigns in her impatience. See, who says she can't be diplomatic. "Can we talk somewhere privately."

"We're witches," replies Gwen, "we can make it private wherever we want."

Luna gives her a 'don't get smart with me young lady' look.

Gwen smiles. "Follow me."

Five minutes later, they sit at a small table in the far corner of a funky coffee shop with a steaming mug of herb tea and a fresh backed pastry.

"Talk," is the only thing that Gwen says while she leans back in her chair.

"We, my family, know you lost the Dagger of Consciousness." Gwen shoots forward. Luna quickly puts her hand up to calm her and gestures to let her finish. "Our family also possesses one of the elemental objects. We felt a disturbance the night your sister got killed."

Gwen nods in acknowledgment as if this confirms her suspicion. "That's why that witch is on the case? Is she your daughter?"

Luna smiles. Always good if people jump to conclusions. Saves you from skirting the truth.

NEW ORLEANS

Ron cornered Tara in the sunroom. "What is going on, Ma? You can't lock us up in the house and have us all pretend we're one happy family. You either start explaining, or I take my family home. This has gone on long enough."

Tara's face stays totally blank. This was to be expected. It's a miracle they stayed quiet this long. She has heard them talking to each other quietly. Maybe she had overreacted. Ceri rushes in. "You have to see this!" Or perhaps she didn't overreact at all. Ron and Tara follow her into the TV room. Most of the family is already there watching the news.

A reporter stands outside Santa Fe. Behind her in the background some vast tornados touch down on the plains. The reporter is shouting over the wind, "This is an unprecedented sight, no indication in the weather pattern predicted these tornados. They're erratic and seem to form and dissolve in the blink of an eye. They come close to the town and then evaporate as if they're teasing us."

Bridget turns to Tara, and says, "This must be Lucy."

Tara turns white as a sheet. "Oh my God. I should have gone."

"We need to do something! What if she hits the town?" asks a distressed Maeve.

"We will be too late. By the time we drive or fly there, this will be over." Bridget tries to calm her down.

"But these people. How far do you think she will go?" Now they all look at Tara.

"She wants us to come." All her earlier confidence has gone. She had never thought Lucy would threaten ordinary people. This is not fair.

"Can't we do something?" adds Freya.

Ceri **mentions** quietly, "We could go through Fairy and be there within a couple of minutes."

"Go through Fairy! Are you crazy?!" shouts Ron, dismissing this idea.

Ceri looks at her mother. "It's the only way."

"We don't want to pay that price!" Ron turns red now.

"What price?" asks Bridget, she's clearly unaware of what it entails. "We need to try; innocent people might get hurt."

"This is what she wanted. I've been stupid, and there are no other choices than bad ones," Tara adds sounding resigned.

"OH MY GOD!" shouts the reporter in the background. "Look at the size of that tornado! It's coming for us." Just before the picture breaks up, a monstrous size tornado is seen making its way towards the camera.

Tara snaps out of it and takes control. No time to behave like a witless old woman. Her family needs her, and they need to do something about Lucy, right now. "Ron, Freya, Ceri, Maeve, and Bridget, get ready, we'll leave in two minutes. Take your wands and whatever other magical items you think can be useful. Hurry!"

"What about us?" Diane gets up.

"This fight is not for you. You and Alice need to protect the house. Are the boys at the Hat?" Tara looks around for Ron, but his wife Selma answers. "Dylan, Brian, and Fin are there."

"Warn them to be careful." Selma simply nods.

"Diane, you call Luna to fill her in. She needs to find these families as soon as possible. Tell her NOT to come home." stresses Tara

"Okay, Mom, are you up for this?" Ron sounds concerned.

"It's my fault, and I will take care of it." Tara turns around and leaves a stunned family behind in the sunroom.

Ron, Freya, Ceri, Maeve, and Bridget are ready in the hall. "Follow me," says Tara and she leads them outside. They rush past the herb garden and into the wooded area behind the house. A huge oak tree stands in the clearing next to the tomb. Tara goes straight for it, halting for a moment before she puts her hand on the tree. She turns to the witches that follow her. "Remember, be quiet and quick, we might be lucky and pass through undetected. If not, don't eat anything they offer, don't bargain. Let me do the talking." She takes a moment to center herself. Her hands follow the lines of the tree as if she is caressing a body. Under her breath, she mumbles in an ancient fairy language, and slowly a door becomes visible and opens up. "I'll go first, then Maeve, Ceri, Bridget, Freya, and Ron should bring up the rear." Without a word, they line up and follow Tara through the opening.

They step onto a balustrade. It's rusty and damp inside. The balustrade seems to stretch endlessly in both directions. The walls are made of white bricks. Moss and plants have wormed their way into the seams between the stones. It smells of lilac and rotted water. If they look down, it's like the building is flooded. The water resembles a mirror, and the whole building feels empty. Sun pierces through the filthy roof. It's made of glass, which apparently hasn't been cleaned in years. The entire place has a sense of an abandoned mental ward. Bridget looks up, and she sees a whale swimming through the air. She blinks.

They're not underwater. "Is that a whale?" Her voice echoes through the hallway. Freya immediately clamps a hand over her mouth and whispers: "Quiet. We can't make a sound." Bridget nods and Freya lets her hand fall away. Tara signals they have to go to their left. Bridget falls in line as they try to move quietly but quickly down the hall. Every now and then Tara puts her hand on a door and feels. It's fascinating; Bridget can't get enough. There's clearly a huge hole in her witch education. How does Tara know which door? A Fairy world you can travel through? What a place this would be to explore. It's beautiful in an eerie kind of way, and evidently normal laws of physics don't apply here. Why don't they use a spell to keep them from being heard? Does magic work the same here? She tries to squash her million questions and just take everything in.

Although they're quiet, their footsteps are bouncing around them, creating small ripples in the water below. The others seem tense and constantly look around. Flowers erupt from the wall and burp out butterflies. Bridget can barely suppress a laugh. So beautiful and cheerful. Freya pushes her forward and snaps her out of her trance. "Don't stare at anything. It will hypnotize you," she whispers angrily in her ear. Something disturbs the water. They look over the railing, and it seems like giant eels are making their way down the hall as well.

"Shit." Ron looks behind them, but the balustrade still looks empty. "Hurry."

They walk faster and make more noise, but they must take that chance. Tara feels another door when out of nowhere an old slender fairy, almost five feet tall, appears and balances himself on the railing. His clothing almost looks dull—it has browns and greens. Tight-fitted and made of a supple fabric. The smell of carnations suddenly surrounds them. He holds a long staff with a sickle at the end. On closer inspection, his dark cap is formed out of endless tiny bones.

"Well, well, the Madigans. Long time no see."

"Ferrymaster." Tara bows her head. "Always a pleasure."

Gracefully, he drapes himself on the railing like it's a comfy couch. "You weren't trying to sneak past me, were you?"

"I would not dream of it," Tara keeps her tone neutral.

"Where is the journey going?" he demands to know.

"Santa Fe, New Mexico." Short and to the point replies are best.

Ferrymaster looks from Tara to Maeve, Ceri, Bridget, Freya, and Ron. "So, who will pay the price?"

Tara's face doesn't show anything, "I was hoping for your good graces."

"Tut, tut, you know the rules." He smiles wickedly at her. His legs untangle, and he walks past everybody this time and takes them in. He stops in front of Bridget. "Hi, sweet lady. I don't think we've met before." He raises her hand and kisses the top of it.

"I'm—"

Tara cuts her off. "She's my granddaughter."

"Oh, I can see that." His eyes twinkle. He moves on and tries to touch Freya's cheek, but she steps back. Now, a wild laugh escapes him. "I've always liked you, Freya. Such a feisty name for a feisty lady." He only glances at Ron but leaves him alone. "One memory and the way is yours." He leans around the rest and looks at Tara.

"No payment. You promised me last time I could pass for free."

In an instant, he's right in front of Tara. "You already used that pass. Don't try to trick me, you won't like it."

"I would never trick you," Tara automatically replies.

"Ha! I know you and that nasty sister of yours." All friendliness has left his face.

"Give him a memory, and we can go on our way," says Freya impatiently.

"See, Feisty agrees with me. You're an old lady now. I'm sure you can spare me a juicy memory that you won't miss." His sassiness resurfaces.

"I will not give you any of my memories, and none of my children or grandchildren will either. I can promise you some herbs from my garden," Tara offers instead.

"Don't insult me! Pay or stay." With a snap, he disappears.

"Where did he go?" asks Bridget, while she looks around. Freya is frozen, Ferrymaster is now seven inches tall and stands on Freya's shoulder.

"For the last time, pay or stay." He might be smaller, but his voice remains the same.

"No memories, what else do you fancy?" Tara insists.

"You can take that door." He points his tiny finger at the door next to Tara. "I'll take her." Before anybody can say anything, the Ferrymaster and Freya disappear.

Ron frantically looks around. "No, no, no, no!"

"Come back, you little shit. I did not agree to that!" shouts Tara.

Laughter trails along the hallway, but the Ferrymaster doesn't return.

Tara looks from the door to the others. What an impossible choice, going after Freya or Lucy. Damn her sister for putting her in this position. The others watch Tara, waiting. She's clearly torn and doesn't know what to do.

"I'll **go after** Freya," says Ron, as he looks over the railing. Tara grabs his arm. "Ron . . . "

"We can't leave Freya, and we can't leave Lucy. I'll take care of Freya. You take care of the rest. Don't make this in vain." Tara looks at her only son and sees his determination. "You're not called Oberon for nothing. Be careful." She kisses him on the cheek.

Ceri slides next to Ron. "I'll go with Ron." Tara hesitates but before she can say something Ron jumps over the balustrade followed by Ceri. With a loud splash, they disappear under the surface.

Bridget is shocked. What just happened here?

Tara pulls on her arm and drags her two granddaughters to the door. "Come, we need to do our share." She opens the door, and they step out. The wind is blowing furiously, sand swirling all around them, which temporarily blinds them. When there is a lull in the wind, they finally see that they're on the top of a hill, north of Santa Fe.

NEW MEXICO

Lucy has felt Tara arrive. She is standing on top of 'Winged Rock' and has never felt so alive. All her nerve endings are alight with the power of Air. The power focusses her clear thinking; it has never been so easy to see the solutions to her problems. She knew Air ruled the mind, but never in her wildest dreams imagined it would amplify her thoughts. Her hands move and weave around forming one tornado after another. With her mind, she steers them towards Santa Fe. She had waited for Tara to arrive before she would do some actual damage. Let's test that moral mind of her sister. With one sweeping move, she sends three tornados down the plains.

Near Santa Fe, Tara struggles to focus. Bridget and Maeve have a lot of questions, but there's no time for that now. "Quiet! Maeve on my left, Bridget on my right. We need to focus. Put your hand on my shoulder and whatever happens, don't let go."

"What are you going to do?" Bridget asks, suspicious as always.

"Do what I say. Look!" Tara points towards the fast approaching storms.

"Right." Bridget and Maeve say while positioning themselves on Tara's side—putting each a hand on her shoulder. For a moment they look at each other, and no words are needed. They're worried. Tara centers herself and throws out her feeling. Ripples of her witch sense flow from her through the air to see if she can pinpoint Lucy's location. "Be ready, I'm going to combine our power. So, DON'T LET GO!"

"Do we need to do something?" asks Maeve.

"Relax and let me in." Before she can ask another question, she feels Tara's power knocking at her door. She can't find a better word for it. Tara's power glides around her aura. Maeve hears Bridget take in a sharp breath; it will be harder for her to surrender, she never liked that. Maeve drops her shield, and she's engulfed by Tara's power. Every witch has an affinity with an element. Tara's is Earth, but the power of the Wand gives her the rule of Fire. For both Maeve and Bridget, it has always been Fire. The power recognizes her. "Drop your shield, Bridget!" shouts Tara over the wind. "NOW!" Bridget closes her eyes and imagines her shield dissolving. She isn't ready for what follows. The warm power of Fire flares up in her. Tara seems to take charge of the flow of energy. Sharing, however, goes both ways and Bridget can't help but throw out a little probe herself to learn more about Tara's power. Tara shoots her a look, but there is nothing she can do. Tara needs all her attention if she wants to be able to divert this disaster. All three women focus on the coming storm.

Tara can't use fire as Air and Fire complement each other, and she doesn't want to get an out-of-control fire. Quickly she riffles through her options. The tornados are terribly close, and the roofs of some houses are getting caught up in the funnel. Without hesitation, she slams a gigantic dome around the storms. Bridget is in awe. She would never think something like this would be possible. But the enormous dome cuts off all air supply, and the tornados vanish.

"Wow! Gran."

"Don't get too excited. This will only work once."

She's right. Lucy fumes but is already making a new spell. This time, it's not as contained as a tornado but more like a storm, with no clear direction where it is coming from. Tara in the meantime feels along the land. As her affinity is naturally with the earth, she follows the pull of power through the soil and is drawn to the Winged Rock on which Lucy stands. With a snap of her finger, she breaks off three branches of a nearby tree. The makeshift brooms dangle in front of the three women. "We need to get close to Lucy, we can't stop everything she's going to throw at us. If we want to save these people, we need to take the fight to her."

"We will have to let you go if we want to fly," Maeve points out.

"Yes. Go low, go fast. Stay close to each other and as soon as we land, touch me and the bond will be back," Tara explains.

As if on cue, they let go, leap onto their brooms and follow Tara. Soon enough, the storm that Lucy sends hits them. It becomes near impossible to fly into the wind. The brooms swing and sway wildly. Maeve has the hardest time; her broom tips and she barely hangs on. She dangles twenty feet above the ground. A scream escapes her. Bridget tries to turn to help her—a mistake. She loses balance, and her broom is making a dive towards the ground. On her way down, she grazes Maeve and grabs her. Not sure if this improves the situation, but she pulls Maeve behind her on the broom, just like they did when they were young. But that doesn't stop the nosedive. The ground quickly comes closer and closer. Bridget pulls on the tip of the branch with all she's got. Just before they hit the ground the broom tips up and she manages to drag them across the dirt to a grinding halt. They have lost sight of their grandma. Shit. The storm howls, and it's hard not to fall over. Clinging to each other for support, they find shelter in a cave. "We need to find Grandma!" yells Bridget in Maeve's ear.

Unlike the girls, Tara does use her magic—she manages to cleave the air and move steadily towards Lucy. She will miss the extra power the girls provide, but she has to trust her skills and experience. After all, Lucy can only have her powers for about twenty-four hours. And what choice does she have? She partly created this mess.

The storm has reached Santa Fe and is tearing it apart. Roofs fly off buildings. Anything loose in the streets is airborne. Cars topple over, and powerlines break. People scream, sirens sound, the city is in turmoil.

Tara needs to hurry up, she might be seventy-five, but she can still fly a broom. Pretty soon she sees Tsé Bit'a'í. Its jagged top is sticking up all alone in the flat desert around it. It's been sacred ground to the Navajo, and they will not be pleased that two witches are going to battle on top of it. Another mishap that will add to her karma list. Lucy is standing on its highest point; she'll have the advantage here as the 'Winged Rock' is guarded by the element of air. Lucy chose her spot well. No surprise there; her sister has always been a formidable witch and very knowledgeable. If only she had half the patience for research. Ah well, she has other qualities, and hopefully, some that will be useful now. Time to focus, Lucy is waiting for her with open arms, literally. In her head, she searches for the protection spell that will let her land and be immediately protected. The rocks don't look too inviting, Tara slows down and chooses a place about a hundred feet away from Lucy. Tara drops her protection from the wind and immediately slams a shield in place. Just in time to deflect a fireball that Lucy slings at her.

"Lucy, please, stop! These poor people," shouts Tara.

Lucy only shakes her head and bombards Tara's shield with a series of icicles. Tara can't help but duck, her shield is veering inside where the icicles hit. A small tornado funnel picks Tara up. She's safe within her shield but helpless against the power of air. Lucy maneuvers Tara closer and unceremoniously drops her sister on the ground. Unfortunately, Tara's shield is not a bouncy ball, so she can't help it when a little cry of pain escapes her as her butt hits the rock.

"Sucks getting older, doesn't it?" Lucy gives her a compassionate smile.

Tara heaves herself up. "Please Lucy, I'm here. Kill the storm. There is no need for innocent people to get hurt."

Lucy shrugs. "You should have come when I asked."

Tara knows that no matter how she answers that question her sister will twist it the other way. Silence is generally a good choice in these situations.

"Finally, I have what I deserve. You've been holding out though on the amount of power you acquire." Lucy walks around her, while she absentmindedly fingers the Dagger. "I guess you didn't bring the Wand."

"I can't believe you killed a fellow witch. Karma will—"

Lucy lashes out, and Tara needs to reinforce her shield not to get squashed.

"Did you at least bring my book?"

"I don't have it," she says, which technically is true—she's never even seen the book.

"It is mine, and I will get it back. I saw your daughter and that other young pitiful witch. Give it to me, and I will let you go." Lucy's smile gives Tara the shivers, her sister is lying. Lucy seems consumed with the rational power of air; the ruler of the conscience mind.

Tara repeats, "I said, I don't have it."

Lucy turns around and holds her hands up to the sky. She mumbles a spell, and the storm in the distance lashes down on Santa Fe with renewed fury.

"I DON'T HAVE IT! STOP IT!" Tara feels the power of fire stir within her. Fire rules action and movement—it's time to put an end to this. Being forced to come through Fairy has now given Tara an idea. She pushes fire and earth beneath Lucy's feet. The rock beneath her turns into lava, which Tara separates into a doorway into Fairy. Before Lucy is aware of what's happening, Tara rushes forward and simply pushes her sister through the door. With a snap of her finger it closes, but not before Tara sees the surprise on Lucy's face. As Lucy disappears, the wind suddenly stops, and it's eerily quiet. Tara sinks to the ground. For a moment she lets the feelings of loss and despair wash over her. She always thought her sister still had some good in her, but no longer. It seems as if the power of air compliments her cunning side. She clearly has no conscience. Has she just been too naive to see it? Lucy has actually killed people. She needs to warn the others. Her feeling tells her that Lucy will not stop with the Dagger. Now her granddaughters land gracefully on the rocks and rush over. Maeve reaches her first while Bridget checks her surroundings. "Is it over?"

"She's gone, for now," Tara tiredly confirms.

"Then we need to go, there are some witches down below, she was not alone. Can you fly?" asks Bridget, while Maeve helps her up.

"Yes. At least far enough to get out of here." Without further delay, they help Tara onto a broom and fly off.

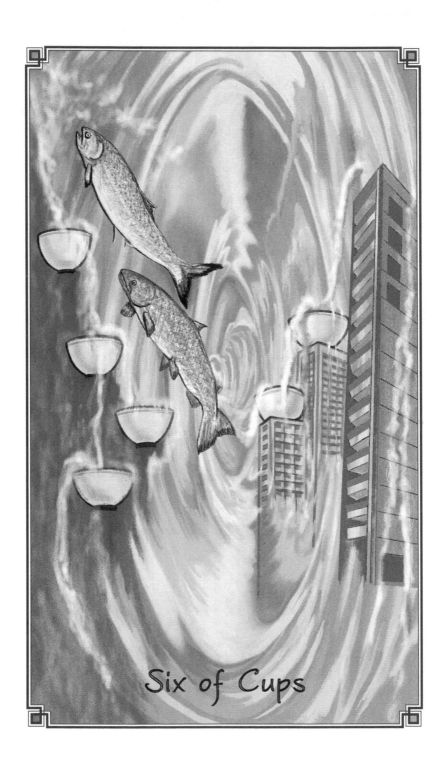

Six of Cups

PART 5

"All things truly wicked start from innocence."

—ERNEST HEMMINGWAY

FAIRY

Ceri is wondering why she volunteered for this mission. Fairy is lovely, tempting, and terrifying at the same time. She and Ron had plunged through the water surface on blind faith, knowing they will end up somewhere else, and that it would transport them to another part of this unpredictable land unharmed. It did . . . although this is not what they had in mind. Desert dunes as far as the eyes can see. The hot sun is beating down on them, and they immediately start to sweat. No shelter and no water, but huge wormlike creatures ridden by red skinned people wearing goggles and top hats and what looks like Victorian frock coats, which must be impossibly hot in this weather. They stand back to back, so they have their whole surroundings covered. You can use magic in Fairy, but you will attract attention, and it's frowned upon. On top of that, you're never sure if a particular spell is working or not. Always a gamble and you want to avoid attention at all costs. However, that seems to be too late now.

Ceri turns to Ron. "One of these worm things is coming our way. Do we run or stay?" Once again, they look around—running is useless. There is nowhere to go.

Warily they wait for the creature and its rider to come closer and closer. It's even bigger than they anticipated. The worm comes to a halt next to them. Its skin is leathery and smells like cow poo. Ron gags involuntarily. Ceri tries to breathe shallowly. The Red Rider bends forward—he looks tiny, but he must be at least fifty feet up.

"Strangers in a strange land. State your purpose and I will name my price." The voice is raspy and dry as the sand. At least they can understand him, and for now, he's friendly enough.

Ceri looks at Ron—here we go. Ceri takes in a deep breath and shouts, "We're looking for the Ferrymaster."

"He's not here."

Great, they had seen that for themselves. Being patient and very specific is vital in Fairy. "Can you tell us where we can find the Ferrymaster?"

"Yes." That is actually better than they could hope for. But it can't be this easy to find Freya.

"What are you going to offer me?" The Red Rider must be some kind of fairy. That is the most dangerous part—the bargain. In a flash, the Red Rider dismounts and stands before them. Without thinking, they take several steps back. This makes the red fairy smile. His teeth are pointed and razor sharp, and they look like they're in desperate need of a dentist. Ceri grimaces, and subtly puts her hand on Ron's arm. She hopes he'll get it that she wants to handle this. For once, he doesn't argue or try to be the man of the family. She understands it must be frustrating to be surrounded by so many headstrong women, that he needs to exert his manhood every now and then. She's grateful he keeps his mouth shut.

Without so much as a glance at Ron, she steps forward and curtsies to the fairy. "Dear fairy lord, we're humble humans in search of our sibling. They told us to look for the Ferrymaster."

"He has no power here. We don't care about your mission, but if you want to cross our land, you have to pay," he answers gruffly.

"We mean no disrespect. Please name your price." Her easy reply relaxes him just a little bit.

"You can leave your slave. A year's work and you can come and pick him up."

Ron is ready to open his mouth, but Ceri slides in front of him while smiling apologetically, "He's my brother, so that's too steep of a price."

"Why does he let you do the talking?" The Red Rider cocks his head. His neck bones make an uncomfortable cracking sound.

"He's a mute." Ceri looks at her feet as witches are the worst liars and the fairy can surely see that in her eyes. Ron chokes, he's surprised by his little sister. He has always felt very protective of her. She was wild and irresponsible, but now he realizes he never really treated her as an adult, although she now has children of her own. With renewed interest he lets her handle the situation.

The Red Rider bursts out laughing. "A month then?"

"No sorry, I need him. But I did bring this." From her pocket, Ceri produces a robust ring with a malachite stone in a beautiful setting. Its green waves stand strong like the desert they stand in. The rider bends forward with a twinkle in his alien eyes. Ceri tries to step back, but a claw-like hand snaps around her wrist. This time Ron steps forward, ready to attack.

"It's nothing." With a shove, he pushes Ceri backward into Ron.

"Don't lie to me, Rider. This stone is the Transformer. It will bring you riches. Not of money but the power of the mind and heart."

The rider cocks his head to the other side with another crackle of the bones.

"I like you. Maybe you want to stay?" Ceri holds the ring forward. For a moment they size each other up. Then the rider makes a bow to Ceri. "I'll take your offer. We can take you as far as the Green City. Our protection ends there."

"Agreed," says Ceri and awkwardly clasps his huge arm to seal the deal. Without further delay, they find themselves on a comfortable seat on top of a giant worm. They're committed now. She hopes Freya is okay, and that they will find her in time.

UTAH

Lucy finds herself back at her front door in Utah. Her grandkids are probably still searching for her at the Winged Rock. That damn sister of hers—Lucy hadn't seen it coming. If it weren't for the Dagger, she wouldn't have had the power to get out of Fairy so quickly. She couldn't afford to linger in Fairy. So annoying. Ah well, she'd made it. It's obvious she underestimated her sister and her family. That will not happen again. Time to regroup. Make a plan, and get that spellbook back and if she plays it right, maybe the Wand.

NEW ORLEANS

Tara has finally managed to escape the endless questions and concerns of her family. With a big sigh, she closes her bedroom door behind her. Seamus is startled out of his sleep in his portrait; he instantly sees something is wrong. With concern on his face, he tries to reach out to her. The portrait bulges and his fingers reach for Tara's face. She steps forward, and the fingers from the magical portrait caress her cheek. This ultimately does her in, and she bursts into tears. All her worries spill over. Seamus doesn't need words to express the sadness he feels for not being able to wrap her in his arms and comfort her. Tara manages to reach the bed and let her tears run freely. "Oh Seamus, things are spinning out of control. How could I be so naive to think I would be able to control anything? I let the Ferrymaster take Freya." Seamus' shocked face doesn't comfort her. "I needed to stop Lucy before she would hurt any normals. I had to," she defends herself. "I had no choice. But I knew Freya is no match for the Ferrymaster. Damn it. We can only hope Ron and Ceri find her soon." Seamus' face screams 'WHAT!' "Yes. I know." Another loud sob escapes her. "What if she runs into anybody from Mab's court?" For another couple of minutes, she gives in to her feeling of despair. Slowly, however, her inner voice starts to scold her for letting herself go. Nobody was ever helped by feeling sorry for themselves. Time to get it together. Old or not, she's still a capable witch. Her children arc accomplished witches, and she has to trust that they will be able to take care of themselves. When she looks up, she sees compassion on Seamus' face. A bit stiff, she gets up, and he smiles encouragingly. "I know, you never believed in letting your emotions overwhelm you. But you know, it also clears everything up." She waves her hand vaguely around her head. "Cobwebs are gone now. Let's see what I need to be aware of."

She walks over to her desk and snatches the Four of Pentacles off her altar. The bag with her deck is still on her desk. Quickly and with practiced hands, she puts the card back, shuffles the deck and thinks about her troubles. With her left hand, she chooses a card—the Six of Cups. Two salmons are making their way upstream; the old and new are reflected through a water mirror. Does this mean she's too nostalgic? Is she hiding away in her memories of happier times? Is something of her past coming back to haunt her? Or has she been too naïve? Funny, she mentioned that earlier. As she put the card on her altar, she lets her mind wander to a time when she and Lucy where happy. Not even ten years old, laughing and playing in the garden. Practicing silly spells as children do. It makes her smile and long for a time when things were different. With a shake of her head, she snaps back to the here and now. This is exactly what the card had warned her about. Focus on the future, not on the past.

BOSTON

Luna invited Tom out for a romantic dinner. Although Maeve had stressed Luna to come home immediately, this is too important for her. As much as she enjoyed their quiet time together, she can't afford to keep Tom in the dark any longer. He could be a great asset to the family, not to mention her spirit. Gosh, how she has missed sex and having someone who adores her. Grotto is a romantic Italian restaurant. They have a table in the back. Luna twirls her glass of Prosecco and observes Tom while he dips a piece of bread in the olive oil. She deliberately chose a public space to tell him, as it's less likely he will make a scene. Tom looks up, "Why don't you tell me what's on your mind? You've been simmering on something all afternoon."

"You noticed?" She thought she hid it well, but apparently not . . .

"I'm a detective, you know." He gives her a wink. He's so adorable. One more sip.

"I need to go home. Something happened, and I leave on the first flight tomorrow morning."

Tom's face falls—this was not what he had in mind.

"You could come with me." She waves her hand through the air, a habit when she's nervous. "If you can, with your work."

Without hesitation, he says, "Really?! I'm not allowed to work for at least another week or two. I would love to go, help you and finally see New Orleans."

Luna is touched. She melts even more, savoring this moment, as she's about to crush it. "Before you say yes, there is something you need to know about our family." Now she's got his attention. "I don't know if you ever noticed something strange about Bridget?"

"No. Not really. What should I have noticed?"

It's weird she has such a hard time saying it out loud to him. She never had that before, not even with Steve. "Well, eh, you know . . . " Tom raises his eyebrow, waiting.

"We are . . . Our family is different." What is wrong with her? Just say it!

"We're witches." For a moment nothing happens, he stares at her. "Tom?" Then he starts laughing. "You can tell me what's wrong? You don't have to make up something silly like this. I'm pretty open-minded."

She expected something like this. "It's true. Have you never thought Bridget had a powerful instinct?"

"She's a gifted detective. But witchcraft . . . " He makes a 'come on' face.

Okay, she needs something more to convince him. "Tom, the lady that injured you. Do you remember that? She hit you with a spell. Witchcraft. That's why the hospital couldn't heal you. I guess they still can't figure out what's wrong with you." He grows very quiet now. Luna labors on, "I'm the strongest witch in our family. That's why they sent me."

"I'm sorry, but this is just too farfetched." Here we go, he's leaning backward now. Time to land the final blow. "I feel very strongly for you. I even think I'm in love. I've never felt for anybody what I feel for you. It frightens me. I think it comes from the way I woke you up. I made a connection with you on such a deep level, it sparked . . . desire."

Another long awkward silence. Tom finally blinks. "So, you're saying what I feel is magic?"

"No. What you feel is real. It's because of magic. Magic is what I used to find you and bring you back."

"I appreciate that you brought me back, and I am very attracted to you. But come on, be real. This is crazy stuff."

Luna glances around; nobody is paying attention. She holds out her hand between them and turns it over. Above the palm of her hand hovers a little ball of energy. Tom looks at the ball and then at Luna. For a very long time, they stare into each other's eyes. Luna tries to keep a blank face, but she can't help showing him how much she admires him, wants him. It takes all her restraint not to say anything, to let the ball of energy hover there and let him work through it. After what feels like an eternity, Tom grabs her hand, and the ball of energy gets absorbed by their entwined fingers. A shudder runs through Tom. When he opens his eyes, the twinkle is back, Luna relaxes a little.

"I don't believe in witches and things like that, but I will go with 'different'. You do something for me that I've never felt before and I want more, I want to explore it. It feels good to be around you, so I'll play along." He gives her a big smile.

A feeling of gratitude floods through Luna. She might be a grown-up woman, but apparently, you can still be insecure about a man. If she only could understand why she cares so much about this one. Anyway, she's happy, very happy he is coming home with her.

NEW ORLEANS

Bridget got up early, sneaking out of bed without waking Wes and is running the uneven streets of the Garden District. Moon and Seeker, her other big dog, have no trouble keeping up. It's easy to get distracted by the beautiful mansions and gardens. The morning dew on the flowers and the chirping of the birds. She needed to get out of the house for a minute to clear her mind. It's been a long time since she had to stay in a house with so many people. The constant chatter and energy that sparks are too much at times. She needs to work on her protection, she needs to work on a lot. It looks like all her family does is talk about things. Bridget is someone who prefers action. So, this run will hopefully clear her mind and give her some ideas on what she wants to do.

On her return, she manages to evade everybody, hearing Maeve already in the kitchen. That girl needs to get a life instead of caring for the family. Go out, find her own boyfriend, laugh and love a little. This is not healthy. Maybe she should take her out one of these days. She shakes off the thought and decides instead to take a quick shower.

The water feels so good, as it cascades around her and she starts to relax. Soon she feels her mind wandering. On an impulse, she lets her witch sense open up and for the very first-time casts it out deliberately. Although water can negate some magic, it now stimulates her senses. It's like tendrils grow from her fingers and she can feel the world around her, sensing the other witches in the house—even her dogs. For a moment, she caresses them with her mind, and they respond, without words they can communicate. Her bond with dogs has always been exceptional—did she ever talk to them this way? Encouraged, she moves on and finds herself in front of Seamus' painting. Her grandmother is not there. Her imaginary finger pokes Seamus awake. His eyes grow large when he sees Bridget's airy form floating in front of the painting. A huge smile forms.

"Hello, granddaughter." Bridget is surprised she can hear Seamus; she thought this was only an image. An embodiment in the painting. Not really Seamus.

"It's me, alright." He answers as if he heard her thoughts.

"I don't understand. Why can I hear you while grandma . . . " She doesn't need to finish that sentence—a flash of pain crosses over Seamus' face.

"We've always had a special connection. Who knows how that works. The Goddess has a wicked sense of humor. And at last, you're starting to come into your power and connect to it. This portrait is a window to the afterlife. It's an experiment, and the Fates are not happy with it. I think that's why they don't let me talk to Tara." He quickly glances behind him. "We don't have much time. You can't tell anybody about this."

"But Grandpa, we have problems, big problems. We could use your advice."

"My time has passed. It's your time now, and that of the other kids." Seamus smiles encouragingly.

"What do you know about Lucy?" Bridget has trouble to keep herself out there, it's as if something is pulling her back to her body.

"Tara is not objective when it comes to Lucy," he reluctantly reveals.

"I'm starting to notice that."

"They were very close growing up, like yin and yang, black and white; it was hard to have one without the other. Although the last twenty years, they have hardly seen each other, some bonds never die—"

Bridget is jerked back in her body. She screams her frustration. Instantly, she feels someone is with her in the shower. She turns and pushes a naked Wes up against the wall. "Wow. It's me." Bridget blinks. Shit. This was why she had trouble focusing, Wes had joined her in the shower. A rush of anger comes over her, Wes' puppy eyes grow large. She manages to reign it in. "Sorry. I—" she has to come up with something. "I . . . I was meditating."

"In the shower?"

"Yes. It's hard to get away from everybody, the water calms me."

"If you want to be alone . . . " He opens the shower door. Bridget pulls him back against her. What better way to make him forget than some shower sex? Without another word, she slowly makes her way down his body with her mouth.

It's late afternoon when Bridget, Maeve, Diane, and Tara finally sit down at a table in the back of 'Under the Witches Hat' for a well-deserved cocktail. With Freya, Ceri, Ron, and Luna gone, they're low on personnel. Whatever happens, the show must go on. The boys can run the bar and do some readings, but they can't work twenty-four hours a day. It's been busy and even now around five in the afternoon, the bar is buzzing. Fin and Dylan are chatting up customers while they whip up cocktails.

"We need to talk." Bridget is so itchy from all this. Ceri, Freya, and Ron lost in Fairy; Lucy and the Dagger . . . It feels like they should be out there doing something. Not run the family business. Without a word, Tara pulls a spell around them for privacy.

"This—all back to normal—drives me crazy! Don't we need to go out there? Save them or find Lucy?!" Bridget blurts as soon as the spell falls into place.

Diane blows on her little umbrella; it starts to twirl again. Then she quietly says, "We have to trust Ron and Ceri to find Freya; we can't all run around in Fairy. It makes no sense."

Her aunt has a point, but she goes on, "Then we have to find Lucy. We must stop her."

"I agree, she's a scary witch. She doesn't care about anything but power," adds Maeve.

Tara turns to her and says, "You're right, we need to find her. Stop her. But how? She has become so powerful. We can't . . . can't kill her."

"GRANDMA!" shouts Bridget shocked. "Of course not. Why would you think that?"

"What options do we have?" Tara's fatalistic attitude makes the others wary.

"We could capture her and contain her," offers Maeve.

"Lock her up?" The tone in Tara's voice makes it clear what she thinks about that idea.

"Yes, we can make a power circle in the tomb and keep her there. We can't turn her over to the police. A normal cell won't hold her." Bridget supports her twin's suggestion.

Tara looks depressed. "Then we might as well kill her."

"Jesus, Gran! Don't be so dramatic. We need to diminish her powers," suggests Bridget.

"How?" wonders Maeve.

"We need to steal the Dagger." All heads whip to Diane, she rarely offers advice, and this probably means she has seen something.

"It will not take away her powers over the element of air. Once you're attuned, it lives in you."

This raises some eyebrows. It's something Tara had neglected to mention earlier.

"I think it will weaken her enough, we should try before we decide to do anything more drastic." Diane seems certain.

"Great, how do we do that?" Bridget is happy they have some sort of goal.

Right then, the door opens, and Luna and Tom walk in. Bridget's face darkens. What is Tom doing here? It doesn't escape her attention that he has his hand on Luna's lower back as they walk to their table. Tom takes in the Hat with amusement. Clearly he thinks this is all fake. Bridget stands up and steps in front of Luna. "What is he doing here?"

"Hey! Watch your language," says Tom immediately in Luna's defense. Luna quietly puts a hand on Tom's arm to show him she will handle this. He grumbles but steps back. The others at the table watch in silence. "Tom is here to help and we . . . hit it off."

"You hit it off?" Bridget's anger is building. "With my partner from work?"

"He's special." Luna tries to stay calm.

"I bet. What about Dad?'"

"Yes, what about Steve?"

"You show up with a . . . boyfriend, and you ridicule Dad?" Now Bridget is off, like all her frustration with her mother is back in full force. "It's always all about you. You're so wise and smart. We should all listen and bow to you. It's a miracle he stayed with you. Nothing has changed. They all seem to worship you. But I've seen the real you, and it isn't pretty."

Luna doesn't say anything, but tears start to flow down her face.

"Yeah, start crying." Bridget has no patience for that. She quickly glances at the others. Diane is engrossed in her drink. Tara looks shocked, Maeve and Tom are angry. Without another word, she storms out of the bar.

Maeve catches up with her a little down the street. "Wait!"

Bridget turns around. "Don't start."

"You're so full of it. At least as bad as Mom." Bridget is about to bite her head off; Maeve raises her hand to stop her. "When is the last time you spoke with Dad?"

"I didn't stay in touch with him either," she admits.

"Right. And I know you asked Fin about him, but you didn't attempt to go and see him."

"He said he was teaching out of town."

Maeve doesn't say anything, and she doesn't need to. Bridget knows she ignored this on purpose. Like the others, she had cut off all communication. She didn't look forward to seeing the pain in her Dad's eyes. She could only handle so much guilt at the time.

"That's what I figured. Here, this is his address. Go see him. Then we'll talk." Maeve turns around and heads back to the bar.

Bridget looks at the address, which is in walking distance. She can clear her head on the way.

Bridget finds herself in front of a cute, pink shotgun home in the Bywater. She glances at the address Maeve gave her. Yes, this is it. For a moment, she hesitates. It's been a long time. How will he react? She never had a problem with her father, unlike her problems with Luna. Steve was the voice of reason at home, quiet and a mediator. No use delaying any further, she rings the doorbell. A bubbly young woman opens the door. She can't be much older than Bridget. Her gentle curves and ready smile explain the pink home.

"Maeve? No, you're not Maeve. Are you Bridget?" Bridget focusses on the wrinkles that form in the woman's forehead—anything as long as she doesn't have to think about what this could mean. She gathers her cop training, breathes out, and replies: "Yes, I'm looking for Steve. Does he live here?"

"Oh my God!" The woman jumps up and down and hugs Bridget. "He will be so happy to see you!" She steps back and blushes. "Where are my manners?! It's just that he told me so much about you. I have a feeling we've been friends forever." She thrusts her hand forward. "Lillian Neumann, I'm your father's new wife."

Bridget feels the color drain from her face. Her father had married someone her age?! What the hell had happened? Why didn't anybody call her? Scratch that stupid question. Damn it, poor Luna. Bridget feels so ashamed.

Lillian is unaware of Bridget's reserved response. Nothing seems to penetrate her eternal happiness; she shouts into the house. "Steve! Come here, you won't believe who's here to see you." She turns to Bridget, "Come in, come in." She ushers her inside. Bridget makes her way through the living room, she's taking it all in—the supernormal room. Everything that Bridget had wanted to accomplish—well. . . maybe with a little less pink. Her Dad pops his head around the kitchen, and they both freeze. He has aged and turned gray at his temples but other than that, he's still the same. A smile breaks his shocked stare. He rushes over and hugs her tight. Bridget can't help but smile. It's good to see her father—she didn't know how much she had missed this hug. She wants it to last forever, but eventually, they let each other go. Lillian has disappeared, and Steve holds Bridget at arm's length.

"Look at you. Wow, a grown woman." He gives her another quick hug. "I've missed you."

Bridget gives him a bright smile. "I've missed you too!"

"Come, do you want a coffee, tea? I want to hear all about you."

Bridget follows Steve into a cozy kitchen. Lilian has left a fresh pot of tea and some biscuits. Somehow this irritates Bridget—the apparent play to try to win her over. Strangely enough, this brings her back to earth. Although she's not a fan of Luna, her mother did not deserve to be left behind for a younger woman. And she's angry with herself, for judging her mother before she had all the facts. This lesson in humility angers her. The warm and fuzzy feeling she felt earlier melts away. She slides on a barstool and bites into one of the cookies before she looks at her father again.

"What happened, Dad? You left Mom?" She goes straight for the jugular.

Steve glances away, still a bit embarrassed. "It's complicated."

"It always is. Trust me, I understand complicated." Bridget has a hard time keeping her tone neutral.

"Lillian and I fell in love, and you know how your mother is. Nothing you do is good enough. The constant critique. Of all people, I thought you would understand."

"Gosh, that I understand. But Dad, Lillian must be my age. Did you meet her at one of your classes?" Bridget is doing the math in her head. Lilian must have barely been eighteen when they met. That's . . . disgusting.

Now Steve becomes defensive. "We love each other, that's what counts. After you left, I wanted to leave, but I didn't have the courage. Luna is overwhelming, I didn't want to drown." Bridget has a hard time with this. She curses Maeve for not giving her a heads-up. Now she understands. It's hard to swallow that your father has left to be with someone your age. Somehow, it doesn't feel right. She can't stay here; she needs to think about it. She jumps up. "I have to go."

"You didn't tell me anything about you? What do you do? Why are you in New Orleans?"

He wants to touch her arm but Bridget moves out of reach. Pain crosses his face before it turns into resignation. "Sorry Dad, I . . . I need some time." She waves her arm in the general direction of where she thinks Lilian went. "I . . . I . . . " and then she just turns and gets out of the house as quickly as possible.

Outside, she takes in big gulps of air and calms herself down. She brushes away tears she didn't even realize she had shed. Who would ever think she would feel sorry for her Mom? She has so many mixed feelings and curses out loud.

When Bridget finally arrives back at the house, it's dark. Quietly she enters and hears conversations in the kitchen and living room. Moon is waiting for her in the hallway. She crouches down and pets him, while she whispers in his ear. He stares at her intently for a minute and tells her Luna is upstairs in the fall room. She gives him a quick kiss before gathering her courage and walking up the stairs. The fall room is facing west at the end of the hallway. Without further delay, she knocks on the door. Nothing happens. She knocks again, this time she hears noises coming from the room and Tom opens the door in his robe. She swallows a snappy comment. He's not happy to see her at all. "What do you want?"

"I came to apologize," she quickly explains.

He raises an eyebrow. "It's about fucking time. You're a brat, Madigan."

"I'm sorry. There's no excuse, I should have—you know . . . " Tom lets Bridget sweat, the bastard.

"Have all the facts?" Tom fills in with a wry smile.

"Something like that."

"Luna is sleeping." Now it's Bridget's turn to raise her eyebrow, as she can hear Luna walking through the room. She and Tom have a stare down; he eventually steps back. "Behave."

Luna stands in the doorway, back to her arrogant self. For a moment all things unsaid hang between them.

"I'm sorry, Mom. I didn't know." Luna doesn't respond. "What Dad did sucks, and I shouldn't have talked to you that way." Bridget is no longer able to look in her mother's pain-filled eyes, she stares at her feet. "I'm so sorry." She feels her mother's tension fading and dares to look up again. When she meets Luna's eyes, she sees relief. Luna steps forward and hugs her daughter for the first time since she came back. Bridget tenses but then lets herself be enveloped by her mother's hug. For now, it's enough—maybe the first small step towards healing their relationship.

FAIRY

If they hadn't been so worried, Ceri and Ron might have enjoyed their time in Fairy. It feels like they've been traveling for four days and they can't imagine what Freya is going through in the meantime. It feels like they are making such slow progress. What happened to the rest? They can only guess how the show-down with Lucy went. Then there are their families to worry about—kids, wife, and husband. Wondering what they're making of this. Time doesn't work the same in Fairy. It could be an hour in the real world or a month. There are stories of people who spend a day here, which turned out to be tens of years in the real world, and on their return, they found their families all grown up and old. They can only hope that's not the case—that would be unimaginable. Ron convinced Ceri they shouldn't worry too much about that. There's nothing they can do about it and worrying will only cause stress—something fairies will home in on and abuse to no end. So, every morning they spend an hour meditating, centering themselves, and stay focused on their magic, so that it's ready to be used at a moment's notice.

Today the landscape is finally changing. The worms glide forward at a steady pace. Their host is amiable and chatty. Ready to point out something that he finds noteworthy. This part of Fairy seems to be desert-like, in that the sand dunes go on and on, and there is little or no vegetation. At night their wasp-like creatures are as intent on getting your blood as our mosquitos. The Red Rider has a little pill that keeps them at bay. They gave up on the 'not eating' rule in Fairy, as they're going to be there for some time. At certain times, day or night, there would be groups of what looked like steampunk-like scooters zipping through the air at considerable speed. There must be some sort of air travel going on in Fairy. Ron would love to get his hands on one of those, but they never came close to a settlement or something. Maybe in the Green City.

Ron and Ceri spend their days talking about everything and nothing, they haven't spent much time together once they moved out of the house. Ron is consumed by the Hat and his family. And as Ceri rarely works at the Hat and has young children of her own, they only run into each other if something is going on with the family. Not a time for serious discussions. It's the only good thing right now. To be able to get to know each other as adults. Ron is pleasantly surprised. He only knew Ceri as a party girl, but that is long behind her now. She's a sensible witch, with quite a lot of power. As the youngest she manages to stay unnoticed most of the time. Apparently, she does that on purpose. The advantage of being the youngest is you can learn from your siblings' mistakes.

Ceri is equally impressed by her only brother's insights and humor. Funny how this forced time together has made them reconnect and develop a renewed appreciation for each other.

They're deep into the family analyses when the Red Rider makes a growling noise. They've learned this means that something is up. When they look up, there is green on the horizon. Excited, they jump up. Ron holds his hand above his eyes to keep the sun out as to have a better view. He can't make out much yet, but it feels good that after days of inaction, they can finally try to find the Ferrymaster.

It takes at least another couple of hours before they reach this imposing city. A massive wall of impenetrable plant life surrounds the city and gives it its green color. Strange-looking flowers pop open when they get closer, and the Red Rider shouts a warning not to come too close. They shoot poison arrows if they don't like you. The city itself is made out of a giant tree, an unimaginably big tree, with what looks like branches spread out and morphed into natural beehives. Fairies are buzzing around them like busy bees. Every pod looks like a home. Between the hives are enormous open elevators. Big platforms that go up and down, operated by giant gears. The sound of buzzing, clicking gears, and fairies talking is almost too overwhelming after the peaceful desert. And the sweet smells make their mouths water.

The worms come to a halt about two hundred feet away from the gate. The Red Rider turns to them. "We don't go any closer than this. You need to get off."

After a couple of days, they had the hang of sliding off the scruffy beasts. Ron and Ceri now turn to their host. Ceri smiles at him, and says, "Thank you so much for your hospitality and kindness. Any advice you can give us?"

The Rider shows them what looks like a sad smile. Is that compassion they see in his face? "We wish you good luck. The city is . . . " He pauses to think for a second before he continues, "unpredictable. Don't linger longer than necessary." Ron and Ceri glance at the city. It feels like an ominous warning. When they turn back, they find the Rider is on top of the worm and already moving. He never turns around.

Ceri frowns, "Well, that doesn't sound very encouraging."

Ron shrugs, "What choice do we have? Let's get it over with."

They make their way over to what resembles a gate. It looks like two giant Hawaiian lei in the form of a curtain, with bright colors and exotic flowers slowly billowing in the wind. When they come closer, the leis reach for them. Ron holds Ceri back. "Don't forget about the poison arrows."

"I know. But otherwise, how are we going to get in?"

Ron scans his surroundings again. "Right. Carefully." He lets her arm go, and they inch forward. The closer they get, the more curiously the leis seem to move. They're like a living creature wanting to examine them. Like being frisked at TSA. It feels very overwhelming, but so far, they don't appear hostile. There's not a regular fairy in sight, but this 'gate' might be a fairy or some other creature as far as they know. The leis envelop them, Ron stands rigid, while Ceri relaxes and enjoys the experience. Ron has never been good at going with the flow. He likes to be in control of everything. Ceri, on the other hand, enjoys the difference and finds it easy to adjust. The leis caress them, the flowers sniff them, for the lack of a better word. After several minutes, they are satisfied and move back like a curtain to welcome Ceri and Ron inside. Ron lets out a long breath, Ceri laughs. "That was fun!"

"Yeah, it was great," replies Ron, his voice dripping with sarcasm. Nobody pays any attention to them. Fairies fly through the air. It all looks very chaotic, but there must be a method to the madness. On the large elevators are supplies or things being moved up and down.

Once they step inside, the loud buzzing noise completely overwhelms them. The wall must be doing something else, as the noise is horrible, too much for human ears. Before Ron even begins to think, he mumbles a spell and the noise is reduced to a gentle sound. But the noise stops altogether, and all the fairies turn to them. Angry faces look down on them. They try to move back to the gate, but they're cut off. It's obvious they don't take kindly to the use of magic. One of the fairies starts chirping in a language they don't understand.

Ceri bows, and says, "We're very sorry. The noise—it was too much for us." The leader narrows its eyes at her. With one flick of the hand, all fairies start to buzz around them again, until they're entirely surrounded by angry fairies—like a ball. They get lifted off the ground and transported up into the tree.

NEW ORLEANS

Bridget leaves the tomb. At the moment, she feels more comfortable talking to the dead instead of the living—a first. Her magic is growing. There is so much to learn. Moon trots up to her; Bridget opens her mouth and snaps it back closed when she hears a warning in her head. Moon wants her to be quiet. He doesn't use words, but she knows exactly what he means. With his nose, he touches her hand and looks in the direction to the right—the wildest part of the garden. The scrubs and trees are thick here. As quietly as possible, she follows him, which is a challenge. The branches whip against her, scratching her arms. Then she remembers, she's a witch! A spell flows from her lips, and sure enough, the trees and bushes are parting for her—happy to let her pass in peace. Soon enough, she hears hushed voices. She strains to see if she recognizes who is out there.

"What are you doing? Be careful. Give it back." That's Luna—she recognizes that voice anywhere.

"Don't be ridiculous, it's totally safe. I know my sister." And of course—Tara. They pretend they don't get along, but when it comes to magic, they're thick as thieves. Bridget and Moon inch closer and closer till she can see them tucked away between some hazel trees. It's a cozy spot with a bench and a small wooden altar. It must be one of Tara's hideaways. Bridget can almost taste the magic that's swirling around the women. It's not the usual flavor of sunlight or flowers—this taste is bitter and resentful. Shit. They're meddling with Lucy's spellbook. She wants to step out, but Moon catches her pant leg. "Wait!" The word pops in her head. She looks from Moon to the women and back. "Okay," she communicates. He lets her go. They settle in their hideout, Bridget puts her arm around Moon, and he leans into her.

Tara and Luna are way too busy to notice Bridget. When Luna suggested they go out and try a spell out of the book, Tara jumped on it. It was hard to believe only a couple of days ago, she was so happy to have the house full of family. And now . . . she longs for quieter days. Tara is no fool, and she's well aware that this thing with Lucy is far from over. Soon, very soon, they will need to decide how they're going to take the Dagger away from Lucy. If only she had any clue how to do that. What would happen to the connection? Will Lucy be able to sense the Dagger's location even if she doesn't have it? If that's the case, where could they hide it? After all, Tara can feel the Wand lying with her grandmother in the tomb right now. Too many variables.

"Mom!" snaps Luna.

Tara shakes her head and tries to focus on what Luna is doing. She stands in the middle of a small pentacle that Tara had made in the stonework in this little clearing. They have closed the circle; whatever Luna is doing should be contained. The spell they want to try suggests they could communicate with the dead. So they think they could try to reach Seamus. A dark cloud is forming in front of Luna. It's growing and pushes against the boundaries of the protective circle.

"I can't see anything," says Tara while she tries to figure out what's in the dark cloud.

"I didn't even call Seamus yet." Luna sounds slightly panicked.

The cloud starts to swirl around Luna and bounces against the circle. But there is no way out.

"Let me go!" booms a deep voice.

Luna and Tara frantically scan the cloud; they can't make out a form.

"Send it back! Stop the spell!" urges Tara.

Luna tries to focus on the spell in the book, but the cloud knocks it out of her hand. A scream escapes her, and the cloud bursts out laughing. This pisses Luna off, and she turns around, weaving her hands and shouts, "Reverse the spell, go back to where you came from!" With her hands, she makes a movement as though she is pushing the cloud away. Nothing happens. Tara looks more and more concerned. There's nothing she can do as she's outside the circle.

The cloud seems to be sucked up by one specific spot in the circle.

"HA! That will teach you," says Luna, as she comes closer to see where the cloud is sucked into. Faster and faster the cloud disappears in a little hole in the ground. With a loud PLOP, the last swirls disappear. Luna peers at the spot.

"Is it gone?" asks Tara in anticipation.

Luna shrugs. "I think so."

"Maybe we should call it a day."

"Yeah. We should research more before we try anything," Luna agrees. With one last look at the hole, she walks the protective circle anti-clock to open it up. Once she's done, she picks up the black book and pockets it.

"Wow, that was weird. Do you know what you called?" Tara still feels a bit uneasy about it.

"It didn't seem to come from the spirit world."

A rumble comes from the spot where the cloud disappeared. Both women whip their heads back in the direction, just to see a tiny girl in cute, frilly dress climb out of the hole.

Moon growls, Bridget quickly puts her hand on his snout.

Luna and Tara are fascinated by the little creature. Slowly they move closer.

"Help." The thinnest little shrieky voice comes out of the little girl. Luna wants to bend forward, but Tara puts her hand on her arm to caution her. Something is off here.

The little girl waves her tiny hands in the air for help.

"We need to help her." Luna shakes off Tara's hand and steps forward. She crouches down and sticks out her hand.

"DON'T!" shouts Tara, but it's too late. The little girl jumps onto Luna's hand and Luna lifts her up in front of her face. The little girl touches it. "Oh, I like your soul." Her eyes shine like little diamonds. Luna frowns; the little girl's face transforms into something ugly with a gaping mouth that holds rows and rows of razor-sharp little teeth. Luna screams and throws the little girl in the air. A booming laugh fills the clearing. The little girl zigzags away between the trees.

"Shit. Give me the book," orders Tara. Luna is about to object. "NOW." Quietly Luna hands over the book. Bridget follows everything—this is interesting. Tara just made Luna feel like a five-year-old. Her Grandma can be scary—something she files away for later.

Tara quickly leaves through the book and finds the spell Luna chose.

"Damn it. We released a creature of the underworld." Tara's face falls.

"No!" Luna snatches the book away. "Here." Luna points at some words in the book. "It says: other world."

"Under World. It says Under World." Tara says resigned.

Luna squints. Oops.

"Who knows what we just set free in this world. Dear Goddess, please don't let this come back to haunt us," Tara appeals to the universe.

"She looked so innocent," says Luna wistfully.

"Those are generally the worst," replies Tara with a voice full of doom. "No wonder Lucy wants this book back."

Bridget and Moon quietly recede, giving Tara and Luna some time before they follow them to the house.

When Bridget comes into the hallway, there is the sound of someone shouting coming from the kitchen. Quickly she pushes through the door and sees that Bert, Ceri's husband, has cornered Tara. He's shouting at her. "I want my wife back! Why aren't you helping her? Wherever she is. You're all milling around drinking cocktails in that ridiculous bar of yours while Ron and Ceri have disappeared!" His face turned bright red; normally he's such a chill dude.

Bridget decides to take a chair next to Maeve, who's also staying out of this. Tara's stoic face doesn't help the situation. "Say something!" he yells in her face.

"They're in Fairy. We don't know where, so we can't help them. They're capable witches and will be back as soon as they can." Tara states calmly as if that will be the end of this conversation.

"FAIRY! Do you think I'm a child?!" Steam is coming out of his ears now.

Luna picks this moment to add some fuel to the fire. "Time is different in Fairy, it may feel like only a couple of minutes to them, or maybe the other way around, it can feel like years."

Now Bert looks genuinely horrified. "You're all crazy!"

Tara finally decides to turn on her motherly charms; she puts a calming hand on Bert's arm. "You married a witch, you must understand that strange things can happen. Ceri must have told you." By the look she's getting, it's clear there is a whole lot that Ceri didn't tell him.

"I told Tom. That way, he knew what he was getting involved with," adds Luna.

Tom holds up his hands in defense as Bert turns on him. "For the record, I didn't believe you."

"Right." Bert is happy to have someone on his side. "Who believes all that."

"Well, it's true." Tara finally shows some compassion. The poor guy, he didn't sign up for this. "They will be back as soon as they can. In the meantime, we're all here to help you with the kids." Slowly she ushers him to the door. Luna motions Tom to take him outside. Tom winks at Luna and throws an arm around Bert. "Come on buddy, let's get some fresh air."

Tara slides down on a chair, while Luna starts to make some tea. Diane flows into the kitchen, conveniently missing the ruckus.

"We need to do something, Grandma," says Bridget. "Diane suggested we steal the Dagger. It's time to make a plan."

"Yes. Yes." Tara doesn't try to show it, but the confrontation with Bert has gotten to her. She has never needed to defend her actions before. Ceri has not been truthful with him. She had let that slide, and now they must deal with the consequences. Her youngest daughter has always been able to make her do whatever she wants, Tara had gone soft.

"Grandma!" Maeve calls her back to the present.

Luna puts fennel with chamomile herb tea on the table, to calm the nerves. The sweet scent already has a relaxing effect on them.

"There is a binding spell in Lucy's spellbook. If we can lure her out, we will be able to catch her," offers Luna.

"What do we do with her?" wonders Diane.

"I don't think we should use her spells. Who knows what kind of effect they have!" Bridget looks straight at Luna, but she doesn't even blink. When she glances at Tara, her grandmother blankly stares ahead.

"Why not? It's a good spell. We only need time to steal the Dagger. I don't think we want to keep her. We're not a prison," Luna sounds convincing. They all nod. This makes Bridget instantly suspicious. Is her mother using her gift to convince them? The others seem to approve, and what other options do they have? She has no ideas herself. She feels a sense of urgency.

"Luna needs to lure her out of hiding with that spellbook. We snatch the Dagger and keep it safe," states Tara, as if it's as simple as that.

Bridget sits back, letting her family hash out a plan. Observation is an important skill she learned at the police academy. She leans back and follows the back and forth between the women.

FAIRY

Ron and Ceri are in trouble. The mob of angry fairies have dropped them in some sort of blank space. A round white bubble, no sound or smell coming through. They can't even see a door. And worst of all, it's a magic-dead zone. They huddle together on the bottom of the orb. It's so scary to be deprived of your senses. Thank goodness, there is a soft light. For the first time since they entered Fairy, Ceri is really freaked out. She's so used to feeling her magic, never before has she been cut off. It's hard to describe, as it's always there and as it turns out, she constantly uses and depends on it. Maybe not consciously, but now she realizes how much magic is intertwined with her life. Ron is awfully quiet.

"Ron." No reaction. She turns to him and shakes him lightly. "Ron!" The sound is swallowed by the room. Even though she speaks very loudly, it appears muffled. "Are you okay?!"

Ron turns toward her and shakes his head. "I'm sorry." And he bursts into tears. Great, just what she needs. An emotional brother. He's always so strong and sure of himself, it's a shock to see him this way. Why does he have to break down now? She gives herself a mental shake—it won't help to lose her temper. Stay focused. First Ron needs to snap out of this mood. "It's a reflex, that's how magic works. You didn't know they would react this way. I'm sure they will let us out soon so we can explain." He keeps sobbing. Hmmm, the understanding touch is not working. "Ron?" He looks up, and she slaps him in the face. Shock and anger snap him out of it. "What the hell?!"

"Ah, you're back. We have no time to feel sorry for ourselves."

As if on cue, a panel slides open, and a tall, slender fairy stands in the door opening. His golden hair almost touches the ground. In his hand, he carries a stick. On his back, hangs a curious looking machine gun. Not sure what it shoots, but it will probably be lethal nonetheless. "The Queen will see you now." His melodious voice has no trouble sounding normal in the orb. Awkwardly Ron and Ceri get up. The floor is hollow, but they manage to get to the door. With a sweeping motion, the fairy urges them to walk in front of him. They enter a hallway, which looks like the inside of a tree branch. The walls are like bark texture and the earthy brown, green colors resemble tree leaves, Soon the hallway splits into several hallways. He steers them effectively to the right. They pass several fairies, but they avert their eyes. The hallway moves up and down in gentle slopes, and it feels like they're walking for half an hour. Going left, right, left—it's hard to keep track. All those turns really affect their sense of direction. Suddenly they're standing in front of two enormous doors. The guard touches the door with his wand, and it opens without a sound. It reveals a gigantic room full of wonders. It is as if nature has met modern technology, but not like human technology, which often looks hard and clunky. Here it flows and whirls. A true merger of magic and science. For a moment they forget their troubles and just stare at the room in wonder. The space is used in a three-dimensional way. Wherever they look something is happening, from left to right, top to bottom. Little islands are floating around, and colorful fairies are gathered in different spots arguing about something. In between the islands are flexible roads that move as if they're alive. You could look for hours and still not see it all. Their guard has no patience and shoves them forward toward the back of the hall. The wall is alive with real bees; they part as soon as they come close. The next room is a lot smaller but no less elaborate. The walls are decorated with natural art, made out of living things that form different images. The four seasons are clearly represented. In the middle of the room stands a huge tree-like chair. Artificial light graces the branches and emanates a gentle light on the most beautiful creature you have ever seen. Once your eye falls on her, the rest of the room falls away. It's Queen Mab—they're in serious trouble if they're in the private rooms of the Queen of Fairy. Their mother would fill them with terrible stories about her when they were young. Tara was always worried they would travel to Fairy to explore.

"Well, well, well." The most soothing and lovely voice of Mab reaches them. "Welcome."

Unsure about what is expected, they both make a graceless bow. They're quite aware they will not live up to the expectation.

Mab turns her full attention on Ron. "You used magic in my city. That's forbidden."

Ron blushes. "I . . . I . . . didn't know. I'm so sorry." He again bows in the hope that it will help.

"You know I could use a witch in my entourage."

Ron looks scared. "My Lady, we have families. Please. I want to go home."

Her beautiful face changes very briefly into something terrifying and dark. Ron takes a step back. Mab's voice booms through the hall. "I'm the law here, not you, Witch. You need to pay for your crimes."

"But . . . but . . . it was just a little spell," Ron stammers.

Ceri takes a step forward. She knows that they won't get away unless they do something Mab wants. This is bad. How did they end up here? Mab usually doesn't bother the humans.

"What can we offer you?"

Mab's attention swings to Ceri. She snaps her fingers, and all of a sudden, Ron and Ceri can see all the others in the room. The Red Rider, the Ferrymaster and—

"Freya!" cries Ceri, and she feels the trap snap shut. This must have been a setup. The wheel of fortune is on its way down. Her heart sinks.

"You know . . . " Mab's voice is back to her charming self. "Tara and her sister used to travel across Fairy together when they were young. Such gifted witches. They came and visited with me regularly. It was always fun to see them. One day that stopped. It might have had something to do with them luring one of my trusted consorts away. After he finally came back, I had no use for him anymore." With a careless gesture, she waves towards a fairy in the far corner. He looks aged, which is unthinkable for a fairy as they're immortal, and his wings are clipped. His emerald eyes seem to bore into Ceri's—it's unnerving. "As you can see, his fate is sealed, but your mother and aunt never paid their price. I know they have used the ways through Fairy every now and then, but this time I got word that you were coming, and I was prepared." Ceri glances at Freya, who looks very pale and evades her eyes.

"We are not our mother, and I apologize for her behavior. But you cannot expect us to carry her burden." Mab is right in front of Ceri. Startled, she wants to take a step back, but Mab has grabbed her chin and studies her face. None of the humans had seen Mab move.

"Please, let my sister go." Ron says, as he finds some courage.

Mab casually shuts him up with a flick of the wrist. He stands frozen. "I'm not interested in you. I think you're boring. But this one." She lets Ceri's face go. "I like you. Did we meet before?"

"No Ma'am, I would have remembered." Ceri refuses to cower.

Mab laughs, "Maybe I should keep you."

Ceri starts sweating. She doesn't want to stay here—she worries about her children. Her mind races. She needs a solution. "I offer you a favor. I'm not my mother, but I'm willing to take some responsibility."

"Ceri, NO!" shouts Freya before the Ferrymaster shuts her up with a hand over her mouth.

Mab cocks her head. "A favor." She lets that roll off her tongue. "How generous of you. One, however, is not going to cut it. Five favors."

"Two," counters Ceri.

"Three," smiles Mab.

"You have to let Ron and Freya go. And I want to be able to go home and see my family if I'm not needed." Ceri tries to be as precise as possible.

"Have you ever made a bargain with a fairy before?" Mab narrows her eyes on her.

Ceri shakes her head.

"You're pretty good at it. Please remember though, that I'm the Queen." Mab drapes herself back on the throne.

"I'll accept your bargain. You stay here for the first favor. Then you can go home until I need you again. You will do them without question and drop whatever you're doing when I summon you. Agreed?" Mab sums up their deal.

"Agreed," says Ceri.

Mab snaps her fingers and Ron and Freya are gone. Ceri is scared—she's terrified.

"Come, sit my child. Let us talk business." Ceri slowly makes her way to the chair that has grown out of the ground next to Mab. While the aged fairy in the corner looks on with dread.

Eight of Wands

PART 6

EIGHT OF WANDS "RESULTS"

"You may never know what results come from your action.
But if you do nothing, there will be no result."

—MOHANDAS KARAMCHAND GANDHI

NEW ORLEANS

Tara feels her body relax as Freya and Ron come back through the tree. Until she learns Ceri has made a deal with Mab, the fairy queen. Things are quickly going from bad to worse. Bert isn't taking it very well that Ceri isn't coming back anytime soon. It feels like *déja vu,* back in the kitchen with Bert shouting in her face. She can't blame him, and she isn't able to comfort him either. Her history with Mab doesn't bode well for Ceri. Bert's words wash over her, while her mind wanders. Whatever possessed Ceri to do that? Ron said she did it to save them. That clearly didn't sit well with him. He's always so in control and then to be protected by your little sister. Luckily, his wife Selma is smart and caring; she'll get him through this. Freya just pretended nothing was wrong, but behind her eyes, panic was bubbling up, and she couldn't wait to go home. What did she have to give up? They will only find out if they ever need that memory. That's what's so scary about it—you have no idea what has gone missing.

"I'll go to the police!" Bert shouts.

This snaps Tara back to the present. "Please Bert, that won't help anyone." Tara finally tries to calm him down, and quickly she glances at Luna, no words are needed. Luna moves next to Tara, while Maeve, Bridget, Tom, and Wes still sit at the table having their breakfast.

"You have to calm down, Bert," stresses Luna. The timbre of her voice has a calming effect on everybody in the room. Immediately, Bridget's hair stands up on the back of her neck. She turns towards the conversation.

"All will be well." Luna puts a comforting arm around him while he starts to calm down.

"Luna, NO!" Bridget jumps up. But Luna doesn't hesitate.

"Go home, take care of the kids. It's perfectly normal that Ceri will be away for a while."

The others at the table nod their heads in agreement, also affected by the words.

Bridget is too late. "Bert, wait." He ignores her and leaves the kitchen.

She turns on Luna and shouts, "How could you?" And then turning to Tara, she says, "You made her do this! There are rules! We shouldn't cross this line."

Tara only sighs and sits down on the first available chair. "What would you have done? You know very well we can't let him go to the police or stir things up. This way at least he's content. It's all so stressful for him. It's for the best."

"It's wrong. You know it's wrong. It's not for you to decide for him."

Wes gets up and throws his arm around Bridget. "Let it go, honey. Come have some breakfast." Bridget shakes off his arm. "You're siding with them?"

"Oh, come on, these muffins are to die for." Disappointment shows all over Bridget's face. She turns around and storms out of the kitchen. Wes is torn between going after her and joining the rest.

"She'll be back. Here, have a muffin." Maeve holds up a blueberry muffin—his favorite. With a last glance towards the door, he sits down.

Bridget calls her dogs and takes them outside. Happy to have her to themselves, the dogs run around her and give her comfort. It's always been the best way to calm down and clear her head. There's nothing like the unconditional love of the dogs. Moon licks her hand. She crouches down to give him some love and the others join in. Before she knows it, she's laughing. The dirty feeling of Luna's magical voice leaves her. The sun and the dogs touch her heart, washing it away. This is what magic should be about. Love and positivity. What is happening to her family? The biggest shock is the ease of Tara's use of Luna's 'gift'. Although she has started to heal the bond with her mother, this is a stark reminder that she needs to keep her objectivity, and turn on her cop mind. Her mother is still using her dark gift and Tara might be a sweet grandmother, but it's important not to forget she's a powerful witch with lots of secrets. Slowly she makes her way through the wooded area as she mulls over the events.

Tara is standing at her bedroom window when Bridget makes her way back to the house. Bridget's confident stride makes her smile. She'll be perfect as the next guardian. Tara is pleased that Bridget was the one able to resist Luna's voice—it says a lot about the witch she's growing into. Also, it's good she has such a strong moral compass. Tara isn't proud of herself for asking Luna to take care of Bert this way. It's just that she's tired—so tired. To be young again and to have endless energy. Pleased with her choice of successor, she turns away from Bridget and glances at Seamus. He doesn't look pleased at all. "Please don't judge me. What choice did I have?" Seamus' face shows very clearly what he thinks about that nonsense. "Ceri is a strong witch. We have to trust her." Seamus is very upset about this and turns away from her. That really hurts, and Tara can't stop the tears from forming in her eyes. Slowly one after the other, teardrops fall but Seamus doesn't turn back. The tarot card on her altar calls her. Carefully she makes her way over, feeling her aging bones. Seamus has always supported her through thick and thin. All those years he never made her feel she did anything wrong. Never questioned her about the choices she made for their children. That he turns away from her now is like a dagger through her heart. Pensively she picks up the Six of Cups. Nostalgia. Time to move on. Seamus is not here anymore, and the magical portrait is great, but it's not the same as having him physically present. She's here, and she needs to make the decisions, and sometimes they're hard and have unpleasant consequences. So be it. She'll do anything to keep her family safe. With a practiced move, she puts back the Six of Cups, fans out the cards and lets her left hand move back and forth over the cards until one card draws her attention. She pulls it from the deck, and with anticipation, she turns it around. A sigh escapes her lips, finally something positive. The Eight of Wands—a bird of prey dives down in between eight wands. Things are going to move quickly. Any which way, it will lead to some results—good or bad. But it's better than waiting, any decision is better than no choice. Feeling slightly more optimistic, she puts the card on her altar and when she turns around, Seamus is smiling at her again.

Several rooms down the hall, Luna is basking in the afterglow of having sex with Tom. That man seems insatiable, and that is fine with her. This was just what she needed after seeing the disappointment on Bridget's face. That damn conscience of hers! Even she should understand that this was what was best for everybody. Poor Bert was so distraught, at least now he will be able to bear it.

"Does your brain ever stop working?" whispers Tom in her ear while he snuggles even closer.

"I was thinking how good you make me feel." She turns around, and she senses he's ready for another round. His mouth finds her, and for another half hour, she is distracted.

While Tom is having a snooze, Luna turns toward the bedstand where she left Lucy's spellbook. It has been quietly trying to lure her for the last hour. It's like the book has been growing closer to her. Every time she opens it, it feels more familiar, and the book seems at ease with her now. They're forming a bond. Lucy did an amazing job creating this *Book of Shadows,* it's different from their family book—more alive and more tempting in many ways. So much knowledge and old magic are poured into it. After their little experiment, Tara warned her not to use it, but it caresses her in places that even Tom can't reach. What the heck. She grabs it from the nightstand and gently opens it. She pores through it to the very end. Here Lucy mentions the search for the Dagger as the book is a combination of spells, magical drawings, and a diary. Luna skips over the page. Stops. And rereads it. Shit, Lucy explored the spell she used on Alana and even mentions her by name. Would this be proof? Her head snaps to Tom, who's still snoring. She relaxes, quietly scoots out of bed, and slips into something comfortable. Before she even thinks about it, a little spell falls from her lips to ensure he will sleep for a while longer.

Luna knocks on Tara's door. It takes a while before the door finally opens. For a moment, Luna is struck by Tara's age. Although she already lost her father, it's hard to imagine life without Tara. "I found something in Lucy's spellbook. Proof, I think, that she wanted to kill Alana."

"What did Tom say?"

"I didn't tell him, I thought . . . you know. We could talk about it first."

Tara looks at her daughter; she has surprised her. "Come in." Tara opens the door, and Luna quickly steps inside.

Tom stretches and opens his eyes; he can't remember having felt this rested. His hand reaches for Luna, but she's not there. Slowly he looks around the room. His eyes rest on Luna, fully dressed, looking nervous in a chair at the opposite end of the room. A small feeling of panic rushes to the surface. Something must be wrong. "Are you breaking up with me?"

"No, but maybe you'll want to break up with me after this." Tom looks at her hands nervously fingering that little black book that she has been carrying with her. He has seen it. He's a cop—he notices things. These women seem to think men are idiots. They're so secretive, it only sparks the curiosity. Tom waits and doesn't say anything. For a moment, a pregnant silence hangs between them. Luna sighs and gets up. "Do you mind?" She motions to the bed. Tom scoots over and makes room for her to sit by him.

"When Bridget and I were in Lucy's home, and something exploded . . . we were in the basement, Lucy's workroom as you would call it." Tom smiles encouragingly.

"We took something that we didn't share with the police." She holds up the little black book. Tom reaches for it, but she draws it closer to her. "Wait, there are some things you need to know about it."

"You should give it to me." Tom moves and sits straight up. He puts his hand out. Gently Luna pushes it down. "I will. Hear me out." He leans back and doesn't look pleased anymore.

"It's her spellbook. And as she's a dark witch, a lot of spells in here are extremely dangerous. Most won't work for a normal, but some do. If you would utter them out loud, it could create serious problems."

Tom stifles a laugh. "Come on, you know I don't really believe that."

"Tom! After all that you've seen in this house, you must have some idea. That we're . . . different."

He reluctantly nods.

"So, I need you to be very careful with this book. Don't read out loud from it. Promise."

For the longest time, they stare at each other. All sorts of thoughts race through Tom's head. His cop mind and the things he has seen since he arrived here are battling over what is real. Finally, he nods in agreement. Slowly Luna hands him the little black book. He feels she's reluctant to let it go. "The book is a mix of spells, thoughts, and a diary. If you go to the very end, you can see she mentioned Alana, the witch that got killed." Tom snaps into cop mode and quickly checks the end and his eyes race over the page.

"And you're telling me this now?! How long have you known?" He can't hide the anger in his voice.

"I swear, I only just read that part. When you were sleeping." The room shudders in reaction to the witch's promise.

"Sure." His voice is full of disappointment.

"It's true. I swear. And a witch doesn't swear lightly; it can have big consequences for us."

His heart leaps, he wants to believe her, but he manages to keep his face blank.

"Please. Tom. I don't want to lose you over this," Luna pleads with him.

It's so hard not to hug her, but she kept evidence from him. "I need to think about this."

She stiffens next to him.

"I'm sorry, it's a lot."

"I understand." Luna gets up and leaves the room shutting the door quietly behind her. Tom can't believe it. He re-reads the part. This is the proof they need. He jumps out of bed, gets dressed in record time, and rushes out of the room.

He finds **Bridget** in a quiet spot in the garden, watching the dogs. When she looks up, and they smile at each other, it's for a second as if they're still partners, and nothing happened. He misses that but he also realizes that things will never go back to normal. Not now that he knows she's a witch. Although he does not fully understand what that means.

"Have you seen this?" he holds up Lucy's spellbook and shakes it.

Bridget answers without hesitation, "It's Lucy spellbook."

"So, you know." Tom can't hide his irritation with her. "How can you? You're a cop."

"It contains spells. At least that's what Luna tells me. She has had it ever since we took it from Lucy's home."

"You haven't read it?"

"No. And believe me; you have to be careful with it. Don't read anything out loud from that book. You never know which spells work for normal people as well." Bridget blushes.

"Explain. You're blushing." Tom figures there's a lot more to this statement.

"I'm not." Now she positively looks embarrassed.

"Spill or I will read this spell." He opens the book. "Abrevia—"

"STOP!" Bridget jumps up and tries to grab the book from him. He darts back and tries to read the next word. Shit, why can't spells be in a normal language?

"Stop. Please. I'll tell you." Tom stops but stays out of reach. He raises his eyebrow, encouraging her to start talking. Quickly, the story of Wes and her spellbook spills out. As if she wants to get it over with as quickly as possible. Tom starts laughing, he can't help it. The image of Wes calling for help while the tree is engulfing him is too much. This makes Bridget smile. She's happy they at least have this part of their relationship still. As Tom recovers, he gets back to business.

"You didn't read the book?" he asks her one more time.

"No, I didn't."

Tom looks her in the eye and believes her. "Luna founds Alana's name in it."

"WHAT?! And she tells you this now?!"

"That's what I said." He lets Bridget snatch the book from his hands. "It's on the last pages."

She quickly reads through it. A bright smile forms on her face. "We've got her. We need to go back to Boston."

Tom can't hide his relief. "You're coming."

"Of course. But first, I have to talk to Luna." Bridget is ready to give her mother another piece of her mind.

"She did swear she hadn't read it before. That she came straight to me," Tom adds.

Bridget turns to Tom. "She swore?"

"Yes."

"Okay then. Let's get packing." She whistles for the dogs.

"Just like that?" Tom is puzzled.

"If a witch swears something and it turned out she lied, she will get it returned on her three-fold. That's generally not something you want. So, if she swore, I believe her."

Tara stands in front of her bathroom mirror. There's an itching sensation between her shoulder blades—a feeling of being watched. Seamus' portrait can't see in the bathroom, and she made sure she was alone. A little spell on the door makes certain it stays that way. Anyway, she still glances around, takes a deep breath, and stares at herself in the mirror. Old, she looks old. Old as dirt, her mother used to say. Now she finally knows what she meant as if you can turn into dust in an instant. "You're pathetic," she scolds herself. Without further hesitation, she pulls her athame, her ritual knife, from its sheath. Again, she looks in the mirror and reaches deep within herself with her feeling, her heart, and thinks of Lucy. Something stirs, like an old clock that starts to tick again. First one hesitant click, then another and another. Something old and unbreakable unfolds within her, and it reaches out for her other half. Tara relishes the feeling—it has been too long. How she has missed this. Will Lucy feel her reaching out? She shivers and throws out her feelings. Slowly her knife moves to her finger and swiftly makes a shallow cut. First, she doesn't feel anything, but the sting soon follows. Her hand reaches for the mirror.

"Remember this spell, remember it well. Sisters forever, hear me now."

Then, Tara starts to write on the mirror.

UTAH

Lucy is in her workroom in her house in Utah. She has fully recovered from her loss at the Winged Rock. It's been a busy couple of days. Making plans, practicing new spells with the Dagger and whipping her grandchildren into shape. She shivers, it's like a finger tingles up her spine. Something is trying to find a way in. Irritated she gets up and goes to her bathroom. Again, a shiver, this time it feels like a caress over her heart. Not on her chest, but literally over her heart. A laugh escapes her. Well, well, her sister is getting inventive. Calling on a spell they made when they were fifteen. Lucy faces the mirror and letters written in blood start to appear. MM MN AP, Meet Me Midnight Astral Plane. What does she want? Is it a trap? Will she bring some of her nasty children?

1S. Alone Swear. Hmmm, now she's intrigued. If Tara swears . . . Lucy reaches out her hand, and the Dagger comes flying to it. Quickly she pricks in her finger and writes on the mirror. K. Okay, she'll bite.

NEW ORLEANS

Luna, Tom, and Bridget are hanging out on the doorstep waiting for their Uber to take them to the airport. Tara has a hard time hiding her impatience. She can't wait to get rid of them, she will need the time to prepare for her meeting with Lucy tonight. The Astral Plane is dangerous enough without adding a crazy variable like her sister. Luna and Bridget are way too perceptive, it's fortunate they chose to leave straightaway for Boston. Bridget is glued to Wes, who never wants to leave the house anymore. That boy reminds her of Seamus, once they're painting, you might as well not exist. Well, he does no harm and Maeve seems to like some company. Maybe she'll finally come out of her shell. Thank the Goddess, here comes the car. Luna walks over to her mom. "Take care. We'll let you know when we get there and when we will go after Lucy."

"Good luck. Please be careful, don't underestimate her! Tom. Make sure to take Bridget and Luna if you find her. It will not be safe to let normal people arrest her," she stresses.

"Of course," Tom clearly indulges her.

"I'm serious. Look at me."

This makes Tom a little nervous, it's hard to look at Tara and not think of Lucy.

"Luna is the only one who can keep you safe. Don't forget." And she touches his heart where the spell had hit.

"I haven't forgotten," he grudgingly admits.

"Good. It will make you careful."

Wes and Bridget throw the suitcase in, and with a last lingering kiss, Bridget says goodbye to him. Luna and Tom get in and off they go.

Wes walks over to Tara and throws his arm around her. "Don't worry, they'll be fine."

"You're a sweet boy." She plants a motherly kiss on his cheek and walks into the house.

It's 11 pm—and it's quiet in the house. Some very soft footsteps shuffle through the hallway, Tara is as quiet as she can be. It's harder being stealthy at her age. Moon lies next to the front door and raises his head when Tara approaches. Gently she pets his head. "I guess you'll be coming. Clever girl, your Mommy." When she opens the door, he follows her out. It has been raining—it's still warm, and the humidity hits you in the chest. The overpowering smell of fresh rain and flowers flows around Tara and Moon while they make their way to the tomb. She should have worn her boots. When they arrive at the tomb, her feet and the bottom of her gown are soaked. The door opens just enough to let Tara through, hoping to keep Moon out, but he manages to slip in. Ah well, he might as well watch over her. Who knows what Bridget asked him to do. She's a little jealous of her talent of conversing with animals. Not to mention frustrated, because Tara is well aware that the dogs might be spying on them. The others don't seem to notice, but she has seen that there is always a dog around when things get discussed. Something she can appreciate, only not when she's the one being spied on.

Moon walks around the room and sniffs. Tara doesn't hesitate further and gets her supplies out, to cast the protective circle and put on her talisman to go on the Astral Plane. She hadn't forgotten her last close call with the demon-like creature. One by one, she lights the candles on each of the wind directions and calls for protection. She walks the circle clockwise, and she feels it snap shut. Like a quiet hush—a bubble around her. Only then, she realizes she's not alone. Moon looks at her from under the altar. Tara glances at her watch. It's close to midnight, and she doesn't have the time to open and close the circle again. With a big sigh, she sits down and crosses her legs. It's hard to stay in one position for a long time, and her body won't be thankful if she chooses a position which will give her pain. She won't feel it when she leaves her body, but when she returns . . . it won't be fun. Moon stirs and lies down behind Tara, as support for her back. Wow, she has to reconsider the dog thing. This one seems to be very attuned to her needs. Maybe Bridget will let her keep him. Enough, she needs to hurry. Breathing in and out deeply, she calms down and she lets her feelings for her sister come out and let her spirit be drawn out of her body onto the Astral Plane.

The wind hits her in the face, her hair swirls all around her; she should have braided her hair. A squeal escapes her as she feels something rubs against her leg. She jumps to the side and recognizes Moon. How the hell?! This is a first. He nudges her hand. She pets him while she takes in her surroundings. It has been a long time since she visited this particular spot. The spot she and Lucy picked many, many years ago to meet in secret. It has changed, probably together with their relationship. It's how these places work—they represent your moods and darkest thoughts, your intuition and feelings. Evidently, their relationship is on the rocks. It's dry. The dust swirls around her and only one lone yucca, the Lord's Candle, graces the earth. It's in bloom too, which means it will die soon. Great.

A growl escapes Moon. Tara turns around and is face to face with her sister. For a moment she catches her breath. Lucy has grown old too. Still, it's like looking in the mirror. Strangely enough, she didn't register that on the Winged Rock. She was too busy with other things. She remembers Lucy as a strong woman in her forties. Although she looks as old as she does, a strong presence of power emanates from her. Like the power of fire recognizes the power of air. An extra attraction to their relationship.

"You're picking up stray dogs now." Typical Lucy, to go for the jugular.

"Lucy, I'm so happy you came!" Tara awkwardly tries to hug Lucy, who stays rigid.

"You threw me into Fairy."

"You didn't leave me any choice."

"'There's that." Lucy's face breaks into a smile. "I've missed you." She hugs Tara back. For a moment, the sisters reconnect. The feeling of having the other twin close by. They both have missed that. Even Lucy, who prides herself on being able to remove herself from such feelings. More flowers sprout from the ground around them, and the wind seems to die down. Tara sees it as a good sign. There must still be some good left in Lucy. "You killed a woman, Lucy. How could you?"

Lucy doesn't miss a beat; her face turns full of anguish. "It was an accident. I didn't want to do that. It happened. I wanted to grab the Dagger, I never intended for her to die."

Tara feels sorry for her, but she squashes that feeling resolutely. Accident or not, that's a serious crime. "That is serious, Lucy. I don't understand."

"I wanted to feel how you feel. The power you wield. You know I've always been tempted. I know it's not the best quality to have, but I could feel it. Through you, how you have become so much more than I am." This touches something in Tara. Only recently, since Lucy had attuned herself to the Dagger, did she fully understand how much her sister must have felt of her power. It must have been agonizing for someone who wanted to have that. She feels guilty, although she never chose this path. Lucy goes on. "Please Tara, you have to believe me. You can feel me. I didn't want to kill her." Lucy projects her horror and doubt onto Tara. For a moment, Tara can only blink. So much pain washes over her. Her sister must have been through a lot. Tears start to roll down her face. Lucy touches her arm. "Please, don't cry for me." Tara is torn between her feelings for her sister and the things she has done. She wants to be able to reach Lucy, maybe pull her back from the brink. To believe that's still possible. There must still be good in her. She knows it, she can feel it.

"Tara please, help me." This is it. How can she refuse? She can't let her sister go down. She probably wouldn't survive it. Lucy sees Tara's struggle and waits. "Why did you contact me?"

Tara had wanted to know, to feel, if there was even the slightest chance of saving Lucy—something her children would not understand. And there is this little shimmer of hope. She knows Lucy is probably lying, but she can feel, really feel her heart. Lucy can't hide that. There is hope. So, she can't let her sister be captured by the police. "I came because I wanted to convince you to stop whatever you're doing. Let us work together. Let me help you."

Lucy takes her sister in a fierce hug, letting her feel close. But Tara can't see the wicked smile on Lucy's face. Somehow, she has mastered how to disguise her true feelings. Tara has always been a softy. When Tara breaks free, she looks deep in Lucy's desperate face.

"We can work this out," agrees Lucy.

Moon growls. Tara puts a hand on his head. "I need to get back. Let's meet again soon. Where can I find you?" Suddenly the lights go out. Moon growls really loudly now. It's pitch-black. "Lucy?!"

Lucy's voice seems to be coming from farther away. "Something is coming. We need to go."

"Wait!" Tara is disoriented.

"Go, Tara, we will talk soon." Lucy sounds from afar.

"The police. They have proof! They're coming for you!" She shouts into the void.

Tara feels a brush of a kiss on her cheek. A thank you from Lucy.

A howl pierces the dark. Tara doesn't hesitate and reaches out to her body and plops back into safety. For a moment, her body doesn't seem to work. Too long in the same position. Comfortable or not, it simply doesn't work at her age.

On the Astral Plane, Lucy is laughing as the light returns. Her sister is, and always will be, a sucker.

BOSTON

Bridget is ready to climb the walls in her apartment. It's so quiet without the dogs and Wes. Tom took Lucy's spellbook to the station, and they're looking for Lucy in full force. However, she's still not allowed to join them. There's only so much you can clean while waiting. Her mother's scent was still lingering in the house when she arrived, and she couldn't stand it. To be rid of that is at least something. Her mother gave her a lecture after they visited Hayes, who's finally home. It was painful to see her that way, of course, but it's much more painful for Hayes. She lost her eyes. Hayes lost everything. There's no escaping the mountain of guilt that rests on her conscience. But Luna being Luna had to rub it in. Angrily, Bridget had driven off. Luna could make her own way back to Tom. Thankfully, they're staying at his house.

Lucy and Mara wasted no time making their way to Boston. They left Cal at home, this is a mission requiring subtlety and power, neither of which he possesses. Casually, they stroll past the police station while they scope the place. The ladies' arms are full of shopping bags from Neiman Marcus, Alan Bilzerian, and Barneys New York. No reason not to combine business with pleasure and it makes them blend in with the crowd. Or at least that's what they think. Lucy's and also Mara's presence is hard to miss. Their auras take up too much space to go by unnoticed. Mara throws out her witch sense and feels out the building. This shouldn't be too hard. Ordinary people are so pliable; she's surprised her grandmother brought her along. It's something that she could do with her eyes closed. There's a tingle across her spine—Mara spins around, but nobody is there. Not for the eye to see. This must be a talented witch, if she can hide from them so easily.

"Yes, we're being watched," smiles Lucy, "ever since we left the airport. I expected that. It's probably Tara's daughter, the one I've seen here before."

"Do you—" Mara wants to stop and investigate, but Lucy swiftly holds all her bags in one hand and hooks her arm around Mara's arm. "Don't worry. Give an old lady some support."

Cheerfully, Lucy leads Mara down the street.

Luna breathes out heavily. She was sure that Lucy's granddaughter spotted her. The disguise spell she made is topnotch. That the young woman could sense her means Lucy made some powerful offspring. Who else did Lucy bring? Or is she arrogant enough to just bring her granddaughter? They were the only ones at the airport. Luna was excited when Bridget left her. That way she didn't have to convince Bridget to let Luna stand watch at the airport. And she wanted to reconnect with Gwen. After all, Luna had promised to stay in touch.

It made the most sense for the Lockwoods to show up at the airport. Luna picked up their trail when they came out and had been following them ever since. From the airport to the Four Seasons, to fancy shops—only the best for Lucy. This was the first interesting thing they did. It was time to talk to Tom and Bridget.

Bridget is fighting the urge to start pacing. Her disguise spell requires her to stay as still as possible. She can feel the dawn pushing away the night on this early Sunday morning. After endless conversations last night, they agreed that Lucy and her granddaughter would probably try to get into the station this morning, as it would be relatively quiet and there would be minimum staff around. It took them the better part of the night to set protective spells around the precinct and to secure the book. Tom is inside, wearing one of Luna's amulets, hopefully it will keep him safe this time. There's that nagging feeling in the back of her mind that they forgot something. What if they missed someone in Lucy's party? What if they turned out to be too strong for them? It isn't right to take a risk with all these normal people around. Luna seems confident in her powers, but she has seen Lucy at work, it's scary. Even though she's not the fondest of her mother, she doesn't want to see her hurt. Their plan is shaky. Too many things can go wrong. A little tingle draws her back to reality. A witch crossed one of their wards. Nervous anticipation takes over—the adrenalin rush of what's to come. Sure enough, when she peeks from her hideout, she sees two vague figures making their way towards the steps of the precinct. Bridget is surprised that she's thrilled to take on other witches. The challenge is giving her a boost. She didn't know that this was missing in her life.

Time to focus. Her witch sight is opening up, and the world is instantly extra vibrant. The witches, although still veiled are more pronounced, and Bridget can make out the difference between Lucy and Mara. Luna steps from behind the building and slings a spell toward the witches. Lucy lifts a hand but is a second too slow, and their disguise vanishes. Luna rushes down the road, and Lucy follows. However, Mara stays put and scans the area. Bridget freezes; she was ready to rush after them. Shit. Does she stay and take care of this witch or does she follow Lucy and Luna? Mara doesn't hesitate and enters the police station. Damn it! This was one of the holes in their plan. Bridget looks down the street, and Luna already disappeared around the corner to Congress Street. Lucy is the most dangerous witch, so she decides to stay with the plan. She must trust Tom to take care of this. They set so many security spells on the book. It should be fine. Without further delay, she rushes after Luna and Lucy.

Mara smiles while she pulls a charming spell around her. Lucy was right, the witches were there, and they followed her. She wishes she had the sight of her mother, the voodoo priestess. To see glimpses of the future could be handy in cases like this. Confident, she strides into the police station, her already stunning features take on a lovely, seductive edge and it would be near impossible for a normal person to resist her now. Time to make her grandma proud.

The moment she sets foot on the top of the stairs, an agonizing scream escapes her. Her spell is stripped, and it's like she's naked in the lobby. All heads turn toward her, and the first police officer's hand goes for his gun. Those witches! She'll get them for this. Her instinct kicks in, and the first spell flows from her lips. *"Frigus maneat manere tranquillitas. Hic non sum. Remitte mihi, et obliviscator. Remitte mihi, et obliviscator."* Stay calm stay cool. I'm not here. Look away and forget me. A powerful wave of magic leaves her, and when it hits the police officers, it confuses them for a second. She immediately put her disguise back in place. A little bewildered, but everybody is back to normal and back to what they were doing before she came in.

Pfffft, better pay attention. It's apparently not as easy as she thought, but she can manage. With a megawatt smile, she approaches the desk. The officer behind the desk can't help but smile back.

"Can I help you, Miss?" he chirps politely.

"Where can I find the evidence room?" Her melodious voice caresses his thoughts and even before he says it, she knows.

"Down the hall. Take the stairs down, it's on your right."

"Thank you, officer." Quickly, she makes her way down.

Tom quietly follows her, pleased that he wasn't affected by her spell; Luna's amulet must be working. He's shocked to see what happened to his colleagues. The last week or so in New Orleans have made him aware there might be more in this world, but this really brings it home. Dangerous women.

Luna quickens her pace, but Lucy doesn't have any problems keeping up. That point between her shoulder blades is itching like crazy. If Lucy is as powerful as everybody says she is, this will be dangerous for her. She's relieved when she finally spots the Old State House. A seven-minute walk can seem endless when somebody is following you. The red bricks and yellow windows are a welcoming sight between the modern high-rises. Despite everything, it makes her smile. So much history, she can feel it. Quickly, she rounds the building and is pleased to see it's still empty down here. The wards to keep away ordinary people must be working. Although it's still quiet at this time of day, they couldn't take any chances. Luna slows down and casually strolls toward the memorial of the Boston Massacre. It's a powerful seal over the spot where five people were shot by the British, put there to commemorate the first to die in the fight for American freedom. Lucy is catching up, and Luna feels her weaving a spell. She spins around and activates her ring. A dome-like shield hums to life. Not a second too soon as Lucy's spell makes her stagger.

"Well, well, well. I see Tara raised you properly." It's unnerving to see her mother reflected in this evil woman.

"Let's talk, we don't need to fight." Luna tries for some diplomacy.

Heartfelt laughter escapes Lucy. "Seriously, you think I will fall for that?" Lucy is closing in on Luna. Bridget is visible right behind her. Luna steps back while Lucy steps forward. They're both now in the enclosure of the seal on the ground. Lucy freezes and scans her surroundings. Luna doesn't hesitate and slings a binding spell at Lucy. For a moment, Lucy is bound tight, but it only takes her a split-second to get out of that one. Boldly she steps towards Luna who takes one more step back. Out of the circle of the seal. With a snap of her finger a pentacle snaps to life. Its center is the seal of the Boston Massacre. Lucy's face darkens, and a snarl escapes her. Right then the veils fall, and she's surrounded by five witches. Disbelief shows on her face. The points of the pentacle represent the four elemental powers, and the fifth is for Spirit. Luna guards the point of Spirit. Tara guards the point of Fire. Bridget guards the point of Air. Maeve guards the point of Water, and Gwen guards the point of Earth.

"You betrayed me!" shouts Lucy.

"You've betrayed me long ago, sister," Tara sounds awfully calm. This whole thing has definitely taken its toll on Tara. To convince her children that this was the right way, to deceive and lure Lucy, and to even take Gwen along. It took quite some convincing to have Gwen on board with this plan. Who can blame her? Lucy killed her sister. Tara didn't have much choice in whom to take. They needed five witches to contain Lucy. So here they are.

Lucy sends an electrifying spell towards Tara, but the barrier of her prison doesn't let it through. It's like a light show bouncing around the circle. When it finally dies down, Lucy looks slightly frazzled.

"I wouldn't do that if I were you," adds Luna totally unnecessary. Bridget feels for Lucy; her mother can make things even more irritating than it already is, and by the look on Lucy's face, she's ready to strangle Luna. Lucy swallows her anger and starts to feel the boundaries of the circle. "What do you want?"

"Give me the Dagger!" demands Gwen. Tara shoots her a look. This is not what they had agreed upon. "You're a danger to people, we can't let you use the Dagger," states Tara.

"I want my book back."

"You can't have that either."

Lucy looks around the square. "You can't keep me here forever you know. People will notice that they can't get to the square. What on earth possessed you to catch me here?"

"There is blood spilled here."

"There's that," smiles Lucy wryly. "I can wait you out, you know." Slowly she lowers herself to the ground, making herself comfortable.

Gwen shoots angry looks at Tara. She had pointed that out to her when they discussed the plan.

"You were right, honey," Tara smiles at her. It looks like they will be here for a while.

In the meantime, Mara has made her way down the stairs and talked her way past Sergeant Blake at the evidence room. There are rows and rows of tagged bags with God knows what in it—if she had to search in there, it would take days. However, that's not necessary. The book shines like a beacon. There are so many protective spells on it. Her hand glides along the shelves while she slowly approaches the spellbook. For a moment, she feels something behind her and snaps around. Tom hides behind the shelves. Mara smiles, she has felt him before, he has some protection spell on him. For now, she'll let him watch. Her finger twirls around and she mumbles an incantation. It will set a protective circle around her, just in case he decides to try something. With the circle in place, the hum coming from the book is more pronounced. She cocks her head and lets it speak to her for a minute. The book pulls her, draws her in; it probably recognizes her. Slowly, very slowly, she walks around the book while she lets her witch senses examine the protective spells. Hmmm, a pretty potent memory loss spell, a burn spell, and an iron casket weave. Well, these ladies know what they're doing. The memory loss and iron casket will be a piece of cake for her. That burn spell might present a challenge. With a quick glance towards Tom, she cracks her fingers and gets to work. She places both her hands on each side of the book, just out of reach of the spells. The first one is the iron casket. It reminds her of her youth. Her mother would lock her in one when she didn't want to be disturbed, but Mara was a curious child and eager for knowledge. Soon enough she managed to escape and spy on her mother doing her voodoo work. The trick with the iron is to find one minuscule weakness and work that. Her witch sense follows the iron bars, up and down, up and down. Patience is key here. After what looks like an eternity, she finds the tiniest dent. Quickly she mumbles a weaving and a drop of cold liquid forms on her fingertip. Ever so gently, she touches the soft spot, and the cold liquid finds its way into the iron. With a loud crack, the casket spell falls apart. One down two more to go.

Tom is startled by the loud noise and inches forward. Mara is already busy with the second protection. What a remarkable woman—getting this close to her makes him in awe of her. He shakes his head. Even with his safeguard, he feels the influence of her charm. Absentmindedly, he fingers his gun. The cold of the steel pulls him back to the presence. No time to lose his head. A cascade of laughter makes him think she probably made progress with getting rid of the spells. Maybe he should have caved and let one of the witches stay with him. But he's a detective for crying out loud, he can take care of himself.

Mara is indeed down to the burning spell. Pondering on how to remove it before it is able to burn the book. That would be bad—really bad. Grandma doesn't tolerate these kinds of mistakes. And as she has still only the one police-man down here, she knows she still has time.

Lucy has made herself as comfortable as possible on the cold floor in the seal of the circle. She will not show signs of weakness. Let them think that she's waiting, this will give her time to examine the binding. It feels awfully familiar.

Tara studies her sister; she's well aware that Lucy's working on her escape right now. Let her, they made their own plan. Time to go to the next phase. With a caress of her witch mind, she lets Luna know it's time to move on. Luna is the Guardian of the Spirit in this circle, and when they cast this prison for Lucy, they left open a tiny crack. Luna starts a weaving of spirit. Deep within the earth, the blood that was spilled answers and the souls of the five killed are sparking to life. Lucy senses a slight vibration and gets up. The spirits fight Luna, obviously not happy to be disturbed and used by witches. Drops of sweat pour down Luna's face. Lucy whips around and looks at each of the witches, while she pushes on each one of the pentacle arms, to find a weakness. Every one of them is focused. Too bad, something is coming up and she would rather not fight that. Bridget looks at her struggling mother, with her witch sense open, she sees behind her mother a tranquil pond with crystal clear water. From the sky falls one very black drop; with a plop, it lands in the water and creates a ripple effect. It colors the water ever so lightly gray. As if it's now contaminated. Bridget feels her barrier bulge—shit, she let herself be distracted. With all her will, she strengthens her part of the pentacle. Unfortunately, that isn't as easy as she hoped. Lucy's wicked smile comes into focus and Gwen and Tara are yelling at her. That vision had shaken her. Without hesitation, she reaches deep in the core of her power—Strength. With pure willpower, she slams the wall back in place. In the meantime, Luna has finally mastered the spirits and one by one, they emerge from the ground. Their ghostlike features flood through the seal until all five surround Lucy. Not happy but compliant, they await instructions from Luna. Lucy, not one to panic, measures them up. After all, death is one of her specialties, and she has trapped her share of souls. Luna commands unceremoniously. "GRAB HER." As one, the ghosts grab Lucy. A frustrated scream escapes her, and she thrashes around wildly, but the ghost hands seem to be everywhere. Tara lets no time go to waste. A flash of fire pierces through the circle while she recites, "Elements together, elements as one. Air come. Air come to me." Tara points the Wand at Lucy. The Dagger quivers by her side. "Come to me. Unite!" She pours all her command in it.

Lucy shouts "No!" One of the ghost hands tries to cover her mouth.

Tara repeats. "Come to me!" The ghosts manage to keep a fighting Lucy under control, and even cover her mouth and eyes. The Dagger at her belt edges loose. Slowly, it floats toward Tara. Lucy struggles partly free. "No, you're mine!" The Dagger goes back to Lucy.

Luna throws her intent at the ghosts, and they go for Lucy with renewed energy.

Tara doesn't hesitate and uses all her gifts combined to lure the Dagger. "Unite. Air and Fire!" With Lucy occupied, the Dagger moves through the hole in the circle and touches the Wand. A violent, fiery funnel of fire starts to whirl around the pentacle. The witches look worried; they didn't plan this. It's mesmerizing. For a moment, the world only seems to exist in a mix of Fire and Air. It's a potent combination. Finally, Tara snaps out of it and pulls the elemental objects apart. The Wand disappears in its usual spot, and she wraps the Dagger in a magical cloth to try to shield it from Lucy's pull. The ghosts have taken their chance to drag Lucy into the ground while the witches were distracted. Only her head and arms are visible. Desperately, she tries to struggle free. Luna tries to regain control over the ghosts, but it's not working.

Bridget scans the surroundings. "We have to go." The wards are crumbling. The force of the elements messed everything up.

"We can't leave her like that," says Maeve in horror.

"Of course, we can," replies Gwen. "This is our chance to escape. Come on."

They all look at Tara. Tara mouths "I'm sorry" to Lucy before she urges everybody to get moving. "Let's go!"

Lucy looks frightened when she finally disappears underground. Tara doesn't move despite her words—it's still her sister. She can break free, right?! Bridget grabs her grandmother's arm and pulls her towards the other end of the square. Tara was supposed to take a broom with Gwen, and the others would scatter, to make it more difficult for Lucy to follow. They weren't sure whether that was still necessary. This was not how they had planned it . . .

A ripple goes through the square. This is not good. "Go. Go. Go."

Tara hops on her broom and takes off, followed by Gwen. The others run to Bridget's car.

Lucy finally manages to shake off the spirits. Once Luna is gone, they've lost their purpose and Lucy swiftly pushes them back to the other side. It has cost her quite a bit of energy to dig herself out of the ground.

Tara knows she doesn't have much time and stops on top of one of the high-rises. The Dagger needs to be safe as soon as possible. Gwen stops next to her. "Something wrong?"

"We don't have much time. We need to hide the Dagger." Tara looks around.

"Up here? We need to stick to the plan. Or better, give it to me. Our family will take care of it. It's ours." Gwen is becoming suspicious.

"It won't take Lucy long to escape. We messed up." Tara knows her sister is coming.

"More reason to give it to me and keep moving," Gwen insists.

Tara takes her face between both hands. "Please don't argue and listen." Gwen opens her mouth. "Please." Her mouth snaps shut.

"Lucy will be coming. I need to hide the Dagger in another realm. I need you to guard my back. Can you do that?" For a moment, Tara drops her guard and Gwen sees Tara's desperate plea.

"Of course, I can. Anything to keep it safe."

"Thank you," says Tara simply and before she lets go of her face, she plants a quick kiss on her cheek.

Resolutely, Gwen scouts the roof while Tara frantically feels through her pockets. Shit, she had taken it, didn't she? Damnit, her brain is mush these days. Where did she put it? Relieved she feels the familiar bump of the Tarot Deck. "Whatever you hear, don't mind me. Just make sure to keep us hidden."

Gwen is already busy with perimeter spells. Tara moves in between the air conditioning out of Gwen's immediate view. Quickly, she flips through the Deck. Whom should she give the Dagger to? Ceri? No, that won't work if she's in Fairy—too much power close to Mab. Ron? He's too strait-laced. Maeve? She would love to, but she's too compassionate. Again, she holds Bridget's card. It seems to always come back to her. Tara concentrates intently on the card.

Bridget drives the car through a light Sunday morning traffic as quickly and responsibly as possible. It's quiet in the car. Luna sits in the back, staring straight ahead, looking white as a sheet and Maeve stares out of the window. They're all shaken from the encounter with Lucy. It didn't go as planned at all. The spirits that dragged Lucy down were harrowing. They were to take public transportation in different directions, but without further discussion, they had all jumped in the car, not willing to stay another second close to the site. Bridget feels queasy—who wouldn't after what they had done? She looks at her hands, and it seems like they stretch. Shit. This has happened before. Quickly she moves to the side of the road, nearly grazing a blue Beetle.

"Hey!" snaps Maeve. When she looks at Bridget, she dissolves.

"No, no, no, NO!"

"Grandma! I was driving!" is the first thing that comes out of Bridget's mouth when she appears in her hunter's tunic on the rooftop. The lion by her side roars.

"Everything okay there?" inquires Gwen.

"Yes. Yes. Stay focused," Tara shouts back.

In the meantime, Lucy struggles out through the seal. She looks horrible. It sucks getting old. That devious sister of hers! Furious and without hesitation, she throws out her will to find the Dagger.

The Dagger resonates in Tara's hands. It's hard for her to keep a hold on it. Tara and Bridget stare at it. "Lucy is back." Bridget looks around.

"Take it!" Tara orders her.

"What am I going to do with it? I'm not strong enough." Bridget steps back.

"It will go back in the card with you, and it will be out of this world."

A scream travels up the building. The lion answers with another roar.

"She's almost here. We have no choice," urges Tara.

Gwen is chanting a cover spell.

Bridget takes a long look at the Dagger. There doesn't seem to be another option. She grabs the Dagger and snaps it on her belt. As if it has always belonged there. The power of the Dagger feels like a comforting blanket, even though it's not attuned to her. Once it's on her belt, she immediately starts to dissolve.

Before she completely disappears, she sees a frazzled Lucy fly up to the top of the building.

Tara deftly puts the card back, and the Deck is in her pocket before Lucy lands.

Lucy screams as if she's in agonizing pain. She can feel the Dagger's power being cut off from her. Something in the air shimmers and disappears. Tara must have sent it into a magical realm. Away from her. She still has some of the power of Air, but her connection is weakened.

"Where is it?" she demands. Gwen comes running, but a flick of Lucy's wrist throws a stun spell at her and Gwen falls backward.

"It's out of your reach," states Tara, calmly.

"You'll pay for this! Where is it? The Astral Plane?" Lucy is fuming.

Tara looks at her stoically, even though she's a total mess inside.

"That would be too easy." Lucy thinks, and slowly something dawns on her. "You didn't?!"

Tara looks down as if she's guilty. Best to let her draw her own conclusion. She doesn't know the cards exist.

"FAIRY?!" Lucy's face is turning purple.

"You left me no choice." Tara even manages to show a tear.

"You will be sorry." Lucy says while she makes a whirlwind and opens a gate into Fairy in the air next to her. Without looking, she steps through it. "Once I have the Dagger back—" The gate snaps shut.

Tara lets out a big breath and rushes over to Gwen, who's slowly regaining feeling in her limbs.

Bridget is back in the car, and Luna and Maeve are bombarding her with questions. Bridget doesn't say anything, but just rests her head on her arms on the steering wheel. Damn Tara, this is all becoming too much.

Mara is busy disabling the burning spell. Tom has been debating if he should pull his gun on her. He has a feeling she's aware of him. Now that she's preoccupied, he grabs his chance to secure her. Slowly he inches closer. Her eyes look like burning coals—very scary this lady is. From his pocket, he fishes his tie wraps, the quickest and easiest way to tie her hands. Her chanting intensifies—it's now or never. He grabs her arm and screams! It's like he's grabbing hot coals. The pain takes over everything. He's unable to let her go. Mara is pulling the burning spell into herself, and unintentionally, he has given her an outlet. The burning spell runs through him and grounds itself in the floor. The only thing that keeps him alive is the protection spell. Otherwise, it would have literally burned him up. Tom is paralyzed, and Mara quickly grabs the book, turns to Tom and blows him a kiss. "Thank you." And she runs up the stairs with her grandma's book safely in her pocket.

Bridget finally looks at Maeve. "I'm sorry, Tara pulled me out through the Magical Tarot Deck."

"The what?!" Maeve shouts confused.

"Let's go to the station and see how it went over there. Then we'll go home and Tara can explain it all to all of you at the same time."

"No, Bridget. You need to tell us." Maeve is fed up.

Luna seems to have snapped out of her trance. "Please, we need to go to the station. Something went wrong. I can feel it."

"Shit." Bridget has the car going and doesn't waste any more time.

Luna and her daughters run into the police station, but it all appears totally normal.

"Tom!" shouts Luna, heads are turning their way.

Bridget rushes to the police officer behind the desk. He recognizes her. "Detective Madigan. What's wrong?"

"We're looking for Detective Walsh. Have you seen him?" The urgency in her voice spurs him on.

"I think he went down to Evidence." He waves in the general direction.

"Thanks." Bridget signal Luna and Maeve to follow her, and they run down the hall.

"Wait! You can't take them down there!" They're already out of view.

The door to the Evidence Room is open, and Sergeant Blake looks dazed. Bridget points at him, says, "Maeve?" and moves on. Maeve stops and runs her witch sense over the officer. He has been enchanted. She goes to work.

Bridget sees Tom curled up on the floor. She rushes over when Luna pushes past her and is on her knees next to Tom in record time. Luna holds Tom's head between her hands. His face is in agony. Her witch sense is already homing in on the problem. In his core, there is a heat radiating. A spell flows from her lips and Tom is visibly relaxing. A water spell subtracts heat from Tom. His muscles spasm, and he makes unnatural noises. His color returns to normal, and he finally registers Luna presence. Completely exhausted, he collapses in her arms.

"She got the book," he rasps and passes out.

It's late in the day when Luna walks into Bridget's kitchen. There is a tense silence hanging in the air. Gwen tries to contain her impatience. Maeve has taken over the kitchen and pulls something from the oven. The smell of baked goods always seems to have a positive effect on everybody. It's one of Maeve's gifts, to influence moods with her cooking. The kettle is boiling. Bridget jumps up. "How's Tom?"

"He'll recover, without the protection spell, I don't know if he would have made it." Luna sounds shaken.

"Does he remember what happened?" asks Gwen.

"Lucy's granddaughter charmed the precinct. Tom followed her, and he wanted to grab her while she was distracted. Which turned out to be a big mistake. The burning spell we put on it unloaded itself through him, and a human body is not made to withstand that," she explains.

Tara winces. "I'm sorry. I'm glad he's going to be fine."

"What happened to the Dagger?" demands Gwen. She needs to know.

Luna points at Tara and asks, "Yes. Where is it? You have some explaining to do. What happened to Bridget? Hell, what happened with Lucy?"

Tara scoots back and forth in her chair. She had hoped to avoid any need to explain anything. But things had gotten out of hand, and now she has to share at least something with the women in the room. "I will explain, but you all must promise to keep it between us. Lucy will come back for it, and we need to keep it a secret. What the others don't know, they can't give away."

"Okay," agrees Maeve, always wanting to please Tara.

"I don't agree to anything until I know what it is," rejects Gwen.

"I agree with Gwen. You can't expect them to agree to something they don't know. I think we all earned the right to have a say in this." Tara doesn't look happy at all, especially with this coming from Bridget, and she gives her a hostile look. "As you leave me no choice . . . " Tara is pouring herself a cup of tea and looks pointedly at each of the witches. Luna has a hard time not rolling her eyes.

"The last few years before his death, Seamus worked on a Magical Tarot Deck. Every family member is on it."

"Who's Seamus?" asks Gwen.

"Seamus is my late husband, and he was a gifted witch and an artist," explains Tara.

"Even the children are on it?" Luna steers the conversation back to the Deck.

"Yes. Seamus and I, our children and spouses, and grandchildren. We made it to give you all a tool to use to ask advice for generations to come."

"Even when we're dead?" wonders Maeve.

Tara shrugs. "We didn't really get a chance to try it out before Seamus died."

"You don't know how it works?!" Luna can't believe the stupidity.

Gwen agrees with her, as she follows this family's exchange with wonder. Her family is small and they're very open. This family, however . . .

"Well, I recently found out. As I played around with it," continues Tara.

255

This is taking too long. Bridget explains, "If you ask the card a question, the cards come to life. Show them the Deck, Grandma."

"Bridget!" She pointedly looks at Gwen.

"Gwen's family is in this already. Show it! They need to know. It was probably a great idea. However, it's freaky and even dangerous. But they all should know." Bridget's stern look allows no opposition. Again, Tara weighs her options. Grumbling she gets the Deck out, she fans it, images up, on the table. Gwen, Maeve, Luna, and Bridget bend over it and study the images. Luna spreads them out further, so everybody is visible.

"They look so lifelike," muses Maeve while she looks at her own image. "I'm Temperance?" The Maeve on the card stands by a fountain and has two cups in her hands, water falling from one in the other. It's as if you can see her hair flowing in the wind. "Is it moving? How does it work?"

"Yes, it's moving," replies Bridget. "Actually, the image in the card changes to life-size, and you will be pulled from wherever you are. That's what happened to me in the car."

"That was you on the roof?" asks Gwen. It's hard to believe.

"Yes and no. It's weird, it's me, and it's the card me. A sort of blend. You'll look exactly like the image on the card."

"Did Tara give you the Dagger?" Luna, as always, focuses back on the heart of the matter. Tara closes her eyes. Luna has always been smart as a whip, and she quickly put two and two together. Bridget looks at Tara. Now she lets her grandmother handle it. "Not really to Bridget, but it's hidden in her card. That way it's in a magical realm. It somehow cuts Lucy off from part of her power."

"Do you have access to the Dagger's powers now?" Gwen wants to know.

Bridget shakes her head. "I don't feel any different." Bridget turns towards Tara. "What happened to Lucy?"

"She felt the Dagger's power disappear into a magical realm and she concluded I dropped it into Fairy. So, she followed it."

"We're safe now?" says Maeve hopeful.

This makes Tara smile. "At least for a while. I might have tipped off Mab that she would show up."

"The Dagger is our responsibility. I want it back." Gwen gets up.

"As soon as it's back on earth, it will draw Lucy's attention," says Tara. "Better leave it where it is for now. Your family is no match for Lucy, we need to work together."

"I will not leave it." Gwen tries to stare down Tara.

"Why don't you come and stay with us?" suggests Maeve. "That way you'll be in the loop."

Gwen looks at the witches. Tara is right. Her family is small and with Alana gone . . . She takes a deep breath and nods. This makes the women relax. They might have lost the spellbook. For now, Lucy is gone, and they have secured the Dagger. It might not have gone according to their plan, but they got the job done.

The women raise their teas and toast. "Let's keep it safe."

Cling. It's like a bell resonates in history. They all feel the weight of that promise as they echo a promise made many years ago by their family.

FAIRY

Lucy takes a minute to orient herself. This whole affair has taken its toll on her usually impeccable appearance and her energy. Her age weighs heavily on her. Not the smartest move to drop herself in a random spot in Fairy. She can't feel the Dagger. That doesn't necessarily mean anything. It would have been too easy. That damn sister of hers. Never in a million years had she expected this sort of calculative thinking from Tara. Maybe she did learn something also during all those years apart. Someone behind her clears their throat. Lucy spins around and faces a vaguely familiar face.

"Hello, Auntie."

"Thank you for reading. If you enjoyed this book, please consider leaving an honest review on your favorite store." —Marieke.

LIST OF CHARACTERS:

Alana Jansson; The guardian of the Dagger of Consciousness.

Alice; Diane Madigan's wife.

Bert; Ceri Madigan's husband.

Bouncer; Bridget's black Labrador.

Brian Madigan; Freya and Jason's oldest son.

Bridget Madigan; Maeve's twin sister, daughter of Luna.

Cal Lockwood; Lucy's grandson. Son of Set and Helen.

Ceri(dwen); youngest daughter of Tara Madigan.

Diane Madigan; Tara and Seamus' third child.

Dylan Madigan; Freya and Jason's youngest son.

Emily; Ceri and Bert's daughter.

Felaern Finvarra; A fairy, the Keeper of the Land of Fairy.

Ferrymaster; a fairy that guards the realm of Fairy. He will let you pass in exchange for a memory.

Fin Madigan; Luna and Steve's son.

Freya Madigan; Tara and Seamus' oldest daughter.

Giordano Family; one of four families that guard an elemental power object. They protect the Cup of Plenty.

Gwen Jansson; Alana's sister.

Jansson Family; one of four families that guard an elemental power object. They protect the Dagger of Consciousness.

Jason; Freya Madigan's husband.

Jax; Steve and Lilian's son.

Kiki; Bridget's Chihuahua.

Liam; Ceri and Bert's son.

Lilian Neumann; Steve's new wife.

Lisa; Ron and Selma's daughter.

Lucy Lockwood; Tara Madigan's twin. Banned from the family and forced to take another name.

Luna Madigan; Tara and Seamus' second child. She's the mother of Bridget, Maeve, and Fin.

Mab; the Queen of Fairy.

Madigan Family; one of four families that guard an elemental power object. They protect the Wand of Wisdom.

Maeve Madigan; Bridget's twin, daughter of Luna.

Mara Lockwood; Lucy's granddaughter. Daughter of Set and a Voodoo priestess from New Orleans and Cal's half-sister.

Mary Madigan; the first Madigan to guard the Wand of Wisdom.

Mike; Ron and Selma's son.

Moon; Bridget's Rottweiler.

Neumann Family; one of four families that guard an elemental power object. They protect the Pentacle of Growth.

O'Seachnasaigh; the family name of the four sisters who originally took the elemental objects and pledged to never use them.

Ron Madigan; Tara and Seamus' only son and fourth child. His full name is Oberon. He runs the family business Under the Witches Hat.

Sarah Madigan; Tara and Lucy's mother.

Seamus; Tara's husband, a powerful witch and artist. The creator of the Magical Tarot Deck.

Selma; Ron Madigan's wife.

Set Lockwood; Lucy's son, her only child.

Steve; Luna Madigan's ex-husband.

Tara Madigan; the matriarch of the Madigan family and Lucy's twin.

Tom Walsh; Bridget's police partner.

Wes; Bridget's boyfriend. Artist.

GLOSSARY:

Astral Plane; A parallel dimension that witches can visit. It has similarities with earth but is inhabited by dangerous creatures. Only your spirit travels there, but any injuries you receive while there are reflected on your body on earth.

Book of Shadows; a witch's book full of spells and occult wisdom, passed down in the family. Constantly updated with new knowledge, it also chronicles the family's history.

Cup of Plenty; one of the four elemental power objects denoting the element of Water.

Dagger of Consciousness; one of the four elemental power objects denoting the element of Air.

Elements; Air, Fire, Water, and Earth.

Fairy; a magical world where fairies and other creatures live. You can enter the Fairy world through portals.

Fates; Maiden, Mother and Crone, three mythological goddesses, who decide the destinies of humans.

Magical Tarot Deck; a tarot deck of 22 major arcana cards that depict the three generations of the Madigan Family, grandparents, children, spouses, and grandchildren. When used the images on the cards come to life and the person comes out of the card. That person will disappear from their current life until the querent's question is answered.

Pentacle of Growth; one of the four elemental power objects denoting the element of Earth.

Portal; a doorway into another world.

Querent; term for a person asking a question during a tarot reading.

Ti'tsa-pa; native American name for the Great Salt Lake, it means 'Bad Water.'

Tsé Bit'a í; Navajo territory in New Mexico, the American name is 'Winged Rock.'

Under the Witches Hat; the Madigan family business. Cocktail bar and witch store.

Wand of Wisdom; one of the four elemental power objects denoting the element of Fire.

ILLUSTRATOR

Nicole Ruijgrok has been drawing ever since she could hold a pencil. Her inquisitive mind likes to explore any kind of creative outlet. Not one for the conventional routes, after her communication and multimedia design study, she took over her father's body shop.

She loves art, music, reading, museums, and motorcycle riding. There are just not enough hours in a day! Her current favorite pastime is designing jewelry. She has a goldsmith degree from the only school in the Netherlands, where you can get such a degree, in the historic "silver" town of Schoonhoven.

Nicole and Marieke have been besties since they were six years old. Growing up, you would rarely see one without the other. They always made-up fantasy worlds and built fairytale castles of hay on the Lexmond family farm.

Even though they have pursued many different things in life, they've always remained close. The Madigan Chronicles was the perfect project to collaborate on!